Fairway Tales and Rough Lies

By

Duncan Smith

Pen Press Publishers Ltd

First published in Great Britain by
Pen Press Publishers Ltd
The Old School Road
39 Chesham Road
Brighton BN2 1NB

ISBN 1-905621-17-5
ISBN13: 978-1-905621-17-0

Printed and bound in the UK

A catalogue record of this book is available from
the British Library

Cover design by Jacqueline Abromeit

To Charlie Rankovic

Acknowledgements

I would particularly like to thank Terry and Carole Allsop, David and Linda Mackie and Graham and Pauline Smith for their encouragement during the writing of this book, though not for some of the dismal golfing experiences we've shared over the years, the memories of which were always quickly erased at the 19th hole. I am grateful to Patrick McAteer, head green keeper at Nefyn golf club, for the information he provided for parts of Ch 5. I would like also to thank my wife, Gwyneth for her support during the months this book was in preparation. Thanks are also due to Paul Crampton, the editor and all the staff at Pen Press.

About the Author

Duncan Smith was born and educated in Wales and taught in schools in London and Wiltshire and at Worcester university. As a reserarch fellow at Warwick university and later the director of a management centre and education software publishing company, he wrote and contributed to a number of publications for both education and industry. 'Fairway Tales and Rough Lies' is his first novel. Duncan Smith and his wife live near Abersoch in North Wales and both are members of the Nefyn golf club.

CHAPTER 1

THE PROFESSIONAL'S TALE or 'That your normal swing, sir, or is it the haemorrhoids, again?'

Mark Richardson had always wanted to be an internationally acclaimed top golf professional. From the moment he had started playing the game at the age of ten, with clubs he'd begged, borrowed or even 'acquired' by various nefarious means from careless or absent-minded members of the nearby club whose fairways happened to be adjacent to his parents house, his dream had been to travel the world playing exotic golf locations competing with the likes of Ballesteros, Faldo and Montgomerie. In his later teens, that dream had somewhat naturally expanded to owning a personal executive jet, staying in luxury hotels, dining in expensive restaurants and leisure clubs and owning that sleekly designed, high velocity sports car into which he firmly believed, given half a chance, he could entice some of those equally aerodynamically proportioned, 'high octane' females that now regularly seemed to frequent every international golf tournament.

Now in his late 30s, Richardson's dream had, sadly, remained exactly that, though there had been one or two occasions on the Tour, during the short time he played on it, when success had been within his grasp. His failure to fulfil the golfing dream had largely been attributed by most of those people who knew him well, to what they described as a persistent flying right elbow. Not an affliction linked to any inherent technical failure in his golf swing, more of an inability to prise himself off a bar stool ahead of the barman's desperate calls for last orders. Richardson came to regard the bar in the same way as golfers view 'ground under repair': somewhere you were entitled to find relief as often and as regularly as required.

All too often, therefore, the evening prior to the final round of a tournament, with a real chance the following day of earning some badly-needed and much overdue bucks, would be spent in lavish and lengthy, but equally premature, celebrations. The morning of the final day would arrive with Richardson usually staring down at the necks of a large number of empty wine bottles and frequently up at the scantily-clad, reclining figure of some young woman who had been assured that she was spending the night with next Jack Nicklaus. Unfortunately, as a result of the alcohol-induced haze and the young woman's total ignorance of the world of golf, she'd mistaken Nicklaus for Nicholson and firmly believed she was on the famous casting couch for the next Hollywood blockbuster.

So, after a year or two of near misses, both on and, it has to be said, off the golf course, what he actually found himself doing was running a golf shop in an obscure, singularly unattractive part of the Midlands, at a club which had seen four other professionals come and go in nine years. His dream of luxury living had also stalled as he took in the view of block after block of high-rise flats, offices and smoking chimneys from his one bedroom flat and, more immediately below him, his six-year-old Ford Mondeo. All of this had singularly failed, with a few exceptions which, as he put it, 'never got very far down the fairway', to attract the hoped-for queue of females, anxious to sample his talents away from the golf course. There had been that brief encounter at the back of the 17th green with the lady handicap secretary whose unexpected invitation to help her line up her putt from a prone position could also have seen his own early departure from the club.

Swancliffe and Ankerdine Golf and Country Club was a bit of a mouthful, even when sober, so locally it had acquired the inevitable and, in many people's opinion, well-deserved tag of 'Swankers,' comprising, as it did, the usual collection of 'swingers', 'shankers' and naturally, of course, 'the other sort'. 'Spankers' was a label that had also recently found its way into clubhouse gossip among certain 'in the know' members, following the well-reported antics of some of the club's senior officials on their recent golfing trip to Spain

Richardson's aspirations of golfing stardom had been reduced, therefore, to re-studding members' often extremely odious golf shoes, re-gripping clubs which should have long been donated to the Royal and Ancient's golfing museum and selling course planners to some of those equally odious golfers who couldn't tell you from one day to the next how far they could hit a five-iron!

Richardson's one hope of reducing the tedium of the job of club professional was that he would at least inherit a bright, young assistant who would be prepared to be in the shop from when the octogenarian hackers arrived at 7.00 am on a Monday morning to when the last of the young golfing 'guns' left the practice green at 8.00 pm on a Friday evening in search of their weekly supply of liquid and female sustenance.

Alas for Richardson, even that dream was not to be, for he had inherited 'Shanks', who had contributed about as much to the smooth operation of the pro shop as the Pope had to liberal guidelines on family planning. Actually, his assistant's name was Franks, but a mixture of bad handwriting and Richardson's overwhelming desire to wind up the useless sod on every possible occasion, had resulted in 'Shanks' sticking. Hardly the best name for a teaching professional, thought Richardson, but there again what 'Shanks' could teach the club's members was hardly going to put them in the running for Walker Cup selection!

Richardson's arrival at the pro shop, therefore, was the prelude to his daily outburst of sarcasm, criticism and down-right humiliation of his long suffering member of staff whose only error was holding on to the sadly mistaken belief that he would one day become a highly successful golf professional by hanging on the every word of his wise and talented mentor.

'Morning, 'Shanks', had any eager customers through the door this morning anxious to donate their life savings to our worthy cause?' inquired Richardson in his usual sarcastic tone.

It was the kind of question Richardson asked every morning and he would have been rushed into intensive care had the reply been any different.

'Nah, guv, no-one's been in, everybody just went straight out to play.'

'Speak to any of them on their way to the tee then, did you?'

'Shanks' ability to communicate with anyone on any subject in any form that was publicly recognisable was still unproven.

'Nah, can never fink of anyfink to say to them.'

Richardson wondered just how long it would take for his assistant to be able to link the words, 'game', 'golf' and 'good' together.

'Tell me 'Shanks', what precisely is this place that you and I work in?' asked Richardson.

'Ah, you mean a golf club, guv.'

'No, 'Shanks', I don't mean a golf club. I know it's very early for you to be playing these intellectual mind games, but try. I'm talking about this building we're standing in.'

'Ah, you mean a golf shop,' offered 'Shanks', believing he'd got his boss's drift.

'No, 'Shanks', wrong again.'

Richardson knew that he was now attempting to scale uncharted cognitive heights with his assistant, but decided to press on.

'Shanks', what exactly do you think shops do?' asked Richardson.

'Well...er...they...er...sell things, don't they,' replied 'Shanks' wondering where this early morning 'grilling' he was getting was leading.

'Well done 'Shanks', one out of three and without even having to phone a friend.'

'Well, we're a shop ain't we?' suggested 'Shanks' defensively.

How, thought Richardson, do I break the sad news to this prat?

'No, 'Shanks', that we're very clearly not. What we are in, is a depository... and by the way, before you ask, that's not something you get on prescription from the chemist to stick up your backside for an embarrassing personal condition... for golfing memorabilia. Some of this stuff's been here since Peter Alliss was in short trousers and Anika Sorenstam still thought an eagle was just a bird of prey.

'What did you sell yesterday, 'Shanks'? I'll tell you; a packet of tee pegs, three cross out Slazengers and a pencil. Hardly the basis for my application to the executive committee for an increased retainer, more like the basis for making you part-time at the local chip shop.'

Richardson had always wondered just how much of the PGA's training course for assistants was getting through to 'Shanks'. He'd been half expecting to hear for some time that his so-called protégé was receiving the Association's counselling for another career, ideally as far away from golf as he himself was from getting an entry into the Masters.

'Well nobody seems to want to buy what we've got,' complained 'Shanks' in his defence, 'and when they do want something, they're off to American Discount or Nevada Bob's. I've heard them talking.'

The sound of those two organisations was enough to get Richardson reaching for his lob wedge and applying its 60-degree loft to 'Shanks' skull.

'Oh, so you do listen to what the members say sometimes, then, do you?' barked Richardson. 'Well, listen up right now. If I hear any mention of Nevada Bob's or any other bloody discount golf store around here, your fish frying days will just have moved that bit closer, sunshine. And anyway, which part of your highly expensive training programme informed you that you only sell golfers what they want. Most of these prats have no idea what they want when it comes to golf equipment, some of them couldn't even tell you their inside leg measurement. And as for knowing what would actually improve their game, forget it. So, all the more reason for taking every opportunity to off-load some of this stuff on some of the more gullible and preferably well-oiled club members.'

'Shanks' was beginning to think that he should, perhaps, have paid more attention to the PGA's marketing module, but remembered that his attention span had been slightly blown off course at the time by the thoughts of the impending first weekend away with his new girlfriend and the sneaky glimpse he'd had at certain of the more mouth watering contents of her suitcase when she wasn't looking.

'Yeh', he pleaded, 'but I've never been very good at pushing stuff at people who don't want it. I feel guilty.'

'Believe me 'Shanks', you'll feel a whole lot more guilty when you tell that blonde popsy of yours that instead of working your way to the top of the golfing ranks, you're working your way through cod, chips and mushy peas at the local chip shop for half your week.'

The problem for 'Shanks' was that, like his mentor or more aptly as he was beginning to realise, his tormentor, he didn't want to spend his time running a shop either. While he liked admiring and sometimes trying all the new golfing equipment and accessories from the top manufacturers, he hadn't really got the first clue about two key skills, namely, how you actually got the item from the display stand into the hands of a prospective customer and their money into the till.

'So, guv, how can we get shut of...er, I mean...' – desperately trying to remember something of the jargon in that marketing module as well as the recollection of the embarrassing bulge that had developed in his trousers during most of the presentation – 'market, promote and sell this stuff to our potential customers'?'

'Christ, 'Shanks' where the hell did you get all that from?' asked an amazed Richardson, 'you must've accidentally tuned into the late night Open University channel instead of your usual lascivious destination, Men and Motors. The secret, 'Shanks' is to think 'people' when you're trying to sell. Let me give you an example.'

Richardson was aware that 'Shanks' ability to think, let alone think of people as customers linked to products, was probably akin to asking David Beckham to write the foreword for a book on nuclear physics.

'Take someone like Barker in the club, what exactly would you say was his problem? And I'm talking, by the way, about his golf, not anything else you may have recently heard about in the clubhouse.'

'Well, he can't chip, putt, has that enormous slice and is no good out of bunkers or the rough. Basically, he couldn't hit a cows arse with a banjo.'

'Very perceptive and whimsical, 'Shanks', but if you listen to the daft sod talking, it's only his putting that's stopping him from playing off single figures instead of the 22 he actually plays off. So, what should we be doing 'Shanks'?

Richardson waited with bated breath for even the slightest hint that 'Shanks' might have managed to mentally disentangle the clues he'd been offered.

'Encourage him to buy a new putter, guv?' offered 'Shanks' tentatively.

Richardson gripped the edge of the counter, firmly believing that instead of 'Shanks' standing in front of him, he'd suddenly acquired one of Mark McCormacks' top IMG consultants.

'Shanks', I do believe you've cracked this selling lark.'

'Yes, but what sort of putter should we try to flog him?' inquired the slightly puzzled assistant.

'Oh Christ, 'Shanks', I knew I'd spoken too soon,' complained Richardson. "Shanks', it doesn't matter what sort of putter we flog him – he'll never be a good putter while his arse faces the ground. The trick is to get him believing that a new putter, preferably one which has the highest mark up for us, will cure his four putting problems.'

While light was beginning to dawn on 'Shanks', he wasn't quite out of what you might term the 'marketing and selling woods' yet.

'But guv, he doesn't come into the shop other than to complain about someone's slow play or, like last week, when we sent a society of 24 taxi drivers out in front of his friendly three ball.'

'Ah now, that's where your ingenuity and skill comes in, 'Shanks' - bugger me, I can't believe I've just said that - but never mind; the next time he's on the putting green, you're out like a flash with the very latest putting technology, preferably holing putts from everywhere. Get the damn thing into his hands and give him the spiel – like everybody will be after one of these soon, particularly after the article in Golf World and did he just happen to notice that Ernie Els had one on the putting green at The Open?'

'Right,' said 'Shanks', 'I think I'm beginning to get your drift, guv, I'll give it a go.'

'Hang on 'Shanks.' Remember how that very expensive training programme of yours works? You now have to demonstrate to me that you have understood the principles of selling by giving me an example. You've heard the old joke about the trainee salesman who, when asked by a male customer for a packet of sanitary towels for his wife, asked him if he would like to buy a lawnmower on special offer. When asked by his manager what the hell he was thinking about by trying to sell the guy a lawnmower he said, 'well I could see that his weekend was knackered so I thought he might like to cut the lawn!' Go for it 'Shanks'.'

There was a moment of panic on 'Shanks' face as he desperately tried to recall any member of the club with whom he'd had any more than a 30 second conversation, let alone been astute enough to identify them as a target for marketing some unusable piece of golfing technology.

'Ah well now, let me think.'

'Do stop if it starts to hurt, 'Shanks', I wouldn't want you off sick on grounds of mental cruelty,' said Richardson.

'Now what about Mrs Crowther-Phillips? – I saw her coming off the course the other day absolutely soaking wet; I think I could persuade her that she could do with a nice new golfing brolly.'

'Shanks', you really are off scratch when it comes to talking absolute crap. We're discussing strategies for selling highly expensive, state-of-the-art golfing equipment here, not bloody fashion brollies. You'll be wanting us selling matching bras and knickers with the club logo on next.'

'Shanks' momentarily went off into a not-too-unfamiliar world of his own, imagining the shop as some sort of promotional outlet for a new range of Ann Summers-like golfing products for ladies.

'Do you really think that idea could catch on 'guv'; it might improve our turnover dramatically?' inquired 'Shanks' excitedly.

'Shanks', you are a complete barm pot. The only turnover that those kinds of items would hasten is your move to the pie and chips menu down the chippy. I was merely trying to illustrate the irrefutable fact that when it comes to ideas for marketing golf products, you're about as much use a rubber lob wedge.'

'Shanks' was beginning to get the feeling that his guvnor's continued references to the local 'Easy Greasy' as it was known locally, were, if he was not careful, going to result in the pursuit of a very different kind of chipping than the one he was currently trying to perfect.

'Wake up 'Shanks', just a couple of key points; we're running a golf equipment shop here, not a branch of Versace and, just in case you hadn't noticed, we haven't got any sodding brollies. Now, get selling or you'll be swapping those golf instructional books for Delia Smith's suggestions on how to do lightly battered fish. I'm off to see how Patsy Smythe's shaping up after my last golf lesson with her,' said Richardson.

'She's shaping up very nicely, judging by the last time I saw her, but her golf's still crap,' said 'Shanks'.

"Shanks', just leave the humour to the experts and get on with the job of exercising your limited grey matter to ways of shifting this dust-covered merchandise,' replied Richardson.

'What shall I tell your latest girlfriend if she rings asking to speak to you, guv?'

'Tell her I'm in an urgent meeting with the secretary arranging your secondment to a Hull trawler.'

Richardson hated giving golf lessons to club members with almost the same intensity as hearing news of the latest special offer from an American Discount Golf store or being regaled with the latest savings made by some flash bastard who'd just come back from the States with a TaylorMade driver, 'for less than half what you're selling the old model, mate.' Trying to teach even the most rudimentary parts of the golf swing to the majority of the prize incompetents which this club seemed to have acquired was about as appealing as having to sit through a three-hour sales pitch for a timeshare in Spain.

Most of the members fell into three categories of learners. Firstly, there was his group of 'no hopers' who knew they were and seemed to take a perverse delight in constantly pointing this out to Richardson – 'I'll never get the hang of this take away' - as they slogged ball after ball 15 yards across the driving range, taking large chunks out of the practice mats. His suggestion that they might try to find another sport at which they could excel, or his more magnanimous offer of recommending a fellow teaching professional, 'who had more experience of teaching people with your problem,' had so far singularly failed to dislodge these golfing limpets from clinging on to his every piece of badly directed advice – most of which they found unintelligible anyway – 'I don't know what you mean by, 'I'm shut at the top' – should I see a doctor about this?'

His second group of 'no hopers' consisted of those who believed that success, 'was just around the corner' because they'd picked up all the golfing jargon from the television, read all the books and magazines and, more annoyingly for Richardson, seemed to have re-mortgaged their house to buy the very latest equipment. It was the sort of equipment which, he guessed, had come from 'Bob's Bargain Golf Basement' or some other set of 'flash gits' in a prime 'high street' location who knew absolutely bugger all about golf club design, but had the requisite black BMW with tinted windows outside their showroom and sported the matching shirt and tie. This 'never-to-be-repeated offer' into which they'd been so easily conned also seemed to have included a bag which would have put Frank Bruno in hospital had he had to carry it for more than two holes.

His strategy with this group, of finding them increasingly more and more technical features of the golf swing, would have required these 'hapless hackers' to have had a doctorate in physiology and a figure like Lara Croft. Sadly, for Richardson, it had not worked and, week after week, they'd continued to unearth yet another obscure piece of advice about the golf swing - 'it says that to get sensitivity into my swing, I've got to imagine myself sitting on a barbed wire fence, gripping a rattle snake – do you think this will help?'

His final group of 'no hopers' consisted of those who started off defiantly by saying things like, 'I'm happy with my swing, I don't want you to change it dramatically, just give me a few ideas on how to improve it,' then proceeded to hit four drives over the practice ground boundary fence onto the adjoining by-pass. Among this group, there were also a small number who, when given even the smallest piece of corrective advice, drove Richardson into a life-threatening rage by saying things like, 'oh well, when I had a lesson off that nice pro at the driving range down the road, he said my swing was sound.' It took all his self-control to resist telling them that perhaps it would be better if they buggered off back to that cretinous prat down at the golf range who, unbeknown to them said the same thing to all his groups of 'happy hookers' but, by so doing, managed to keep his bloody appointments book fuller than Lynford Christie's shorts.

In truth, Richardson had no time for any of these tiresome groups of 'golfing inadequates' that pitched up week after week expecting him to give them the golfing panacea that would help them achieve an experience, which one lady member famously described as a 'golfing orgasm', by finally getting their names on the club's honours board. The only slight consolation was that his inflated teaching rates contributed to his seemingly ever-dwindling bank account.

There were, however, two notable exceptions to Richardson's dislike of this group of golfing 'untouchables'. Lady golfers were one, particularly the younger ones, who, equipped with some of golf's latest fashion wear, could excite Richardson much more than any six-under par round. Sadly, he reflected on the very few female members of the club in this category who he would happily have draped over his golf shop counter, like the scantily-clad models at the Turin Motor Show, employing their own smooth lines to cover up those of the latest Ferrari.

Regrettably, the lady golfers he seemed to encounter dressed as though they were planning a weekend away in the Alps with Chris Bonnington and could probably still have legitimately featured in a reprint of Victorian golfing fashions. All his attempts at stocking the shop with the latest stylish offerings from Pringle or Glenmuir, seemed to fail with this group in favour of what could have passed for 'Oxfam's golfing range of mediocre, colourless, ill-fitting specials for the less discerning lashers.'

One event, however, which currently brightened up Richardson's mind-deadening week, was his regular teaching session with Patsy Smythe. She fulfilled all of Richardson's criteria for his own annual award for the 'Most Up and Coming' lady golfer. Predictably, his criteria did not relate to any particular golfing prowess and, so far, this category had not featured in the club's annual presentation evening. Richardson was working on plans for his own personal award ceremony.

'Morning Patsy, how's the golf? I hope those changes to your swing shape we worked on are paying off.'

Patsy was aware of Richardson's reputation with the ladies and had, since starting these lessons, been desperately trying to avoid joining, what was rumoured to be, a long set of notches on his putter.

'Thank you, Mark, clearly your close attention to my swing shape was giving you cause for concern.'

'Let's just say I was... er mildly disturbed when I first saw some of the... your... er swing features.'

In truth, the word 'mildly' rather understated his condition on their first encounter, as he recalled, and he'd been rather hard pressed - a somewhat unfortunate turn of phrase when he thought about it - to concentrate on the main purpose of the lesson.

'Now, would you like to hit a few balls to warm up? Well, that's looking a lot better; but I think we need to work a little more on your posture. So, let me explain; if you concentrate on rotating around your waist in the backswing like so, keeping your bottom more like that and think of your left leg more as a pivot through the swing, OK? Then you'll get both length and direction.'

'I see,' said Patsy, 'well you've successfully managed to cover my waist with... er your one hand, familiarised yourself with my bottom with the other and finally traced the main outlines of my left thigh as an encore – is this a groping or a golfing lesson?'

'I assure you, I'm simply trying to get the main parts of your posture in the correct position,' claimed Richardson innocently.

'If you carry on like that for very much longer, you'll have to go off somewhere to re-adjust parts of your own posture into a more correct position,' replied Patsy, 'now, can we concentrate on the golf or would you like to take a break for a cold shower?'

Never one to be deterred by these little outbursts of female resistance and confident that he was only with Patsy, what he'd once described to his closest friend, in golfing terms, as a 'short chip away from a birdie', he thought he'd suggest a few holes of golf.

'I think we'll go out in the buggy now and play a few holes to put some of these routines into practise on the course,' suggested Richardson.

Patsy had heard from fellow lady members of such trips out in a buggy with the pro. Alleged engine failures at the furthest point from the clubhouse were reported, regular solicitous enquiries were recounted, reputedly at the request of the manufacturers, as to whether the plastic seats on the buggy were the cause of any discomfort, particularly to shoulders and bottoms. And the apparent necessity for every entry and exit from the buggy to be accompanied by the ever attentive helping hand to areas where such help was of little use in ensuring either safety or speed in those two processes. Patsy herself had recently been the recipient of these so-called 'customer relations' tactics, as Richardson had once rather suggestively described them.

'OK, but based on last week's experience, I think I'd like to play the holes within sight of the clubhouse,' agreed Patsy, determinedly.

'Look, I'm sorry about that business last week, but I was simply trying to show you that you were open at the top.'

'Yes, I know and had two lady members not appeared at that precise moment, I probably would not have had a top at all, open or closed,' replied Patsy.

These so-far failed attempts by Richardson to entice Patsy Smythe to donate her unwilling body to the ignoble cause of what one or two of his fellow professionals and friends had mischievously dubbed the 'Richardson Grip it and Grope it Golfing Academy', had been slightly marred by the news that she had been seen with this 18 stone rugby-playing gorilla of a guy called Roy, who also just happened to be a member of the golf club. Richardson had no real desire to have his facial features treated to the same pressure as was applied to this guy's latest TaylorMade driver on the first tee on Sunday morning. He was all too well aware of the fate of one or two other club professionals who had either fallen victim to the advances of a lady member behind the buggy shed on the pretext of a flat battery, or who themselves had got overly zealous about demonstrating the virtues of the cross handed putting grip. Being pursued by angry, one-iron-wielding spouses threatening to give his private parts the same treatment as his over-priced Titleists was not his idea of a fun day at the office.

It was these thoughts that were going through his mind as

he considered what other ploys he might use to prise Patsy out of the hands of 'Roy the Gorilla' without having to call on the professional golfer's health insurance scheme.

'Right, now let's see you play a chip shot over that bunker on to the green. Remember, rotate around the waist, out with the bottom and firm up on the left thigh".

'Mark, why does every golf lesson with you sound like an extract from a coaching manual for directors of porno movies?' inquired Patsy.

'Patsy, I'm just trying to give you a simple phrase to help you remember the form and shape to your golf swing.'

'Yes, I'm sure you are. I can see that by the way you're beginning to dribble around the corners of your mouth.'

'We'll just practice one or two bunker shots before we head for the putting green. OK, so you've landed in the middle of this steep-sided bunker, but the ball is sitting up quite well. Tell me what thoughts are going through your mind about getting out.'

'I'm thinking mainly of keeping you firmly, if you'll pardon the expression, in my sights and well out of reach as I swing, so as to reduce the chances of you pouncing on some swing-offending part of my body which you feel passionately about trying to correct.'

Patsy had been wondering whether she should mention Richardson's amorous overtures made in the name of improving her golf technique to Roy, who would probably have gone ballistic and threatened to introduce Richardson to a whole new concept of a 'handicap system' very far removed from the one associated with one's golfing ability. So far, she had decided that she could handle this 'golfing octopus', though she was beginning to wonder whether her golfing skills were improving at the same rate as her abilities at diverting badly directed advances from someone who was obviously a 36 handicap, over-active sexual 'lunger.'

'Well, Patsy, let's finish the lesson here on the 18th green with some putting practise. You've got this 20ft putt across the green. Bend right down behind the ball and the line of the putt and tell me what you see. I'll stand alongside you and tell you what I can see.'

'From where I'm standing, I can see a 20ft slightly downhill putt which is going to break from left to right from about 3ft outside the hole. From where you're standing, you can probably see right down the front of this very low neck golf top I happen to be wearing, which you so magnanimously and uncharacteristically claimed you had reduced in price on the very day I happened to book my first golf lesson with you.'

'OK, Patsy, that's it for this week, same time next week. We'll concentrate on techniques for getting out of the rough next week.'

'Fine, but can we agree on my criteria of rough as grass just over my shoes rather than what I hear from other lady golfers is yours, where the waistline appears to be the yardstick?' demanded Patsy.

'Can I tempt you into spending some of your hard-earned cash in the shop on any of my special offers?' inquired Richardson.

'No thanks, Mark, when you put the words 'tempt' and 'offers' together in the same sentence, I hear that most of the lady golfers here either race to find the club's health and safety guidelines or the section in the Royal and Ancient's Rules Book on extracting one's self from difficult lies. See you next week. Oh and by the way, Roy sends his regards and said something about hoping your visit to the rugby club's physio helped with your little problem.'

Richardson's other exception to his unswerving rule to strenuously avoid anyone who even hinted at their desire to use his services to improve their game, was that select group of male members of the club whose wallets could regularly be relied on to release frequent and generous amounts of the folding stuff to supplement Richardson's paltry retainer from the club.

His success at persuading these particular 'golfaholics' that their game would improve out of all recognition with a combination of regular golf lessons and the very latest, top-of-the-range golfing technology, was in sharp contrast to his achievements in trying to convince most of the other members that his shop was not the equivalent of the famous 'road' bunker at St. Andrews' 17th hole – somewhere you rarely visited without incurring the loss of one's dignity, self control and possibly worse, one's weekly salary.

Richardson fully recognised that the combined coaching skills of Butch Harmon and David Leadbetter would never be able to improve on the manic flailing techniques some of them currently employed in their desperate attempts to get the golf ball past the ladies tee and away from areas of the golf course where a strimmer would have been preferable to the three-wood they often used to extricate themselves.

Standing on the practice ground in the freezing cold, watching these guys employing a swing which resembled an octopus having a heart attack and claiming that they'd, 'never been hitting the ball so well,' as yet another missile set off in the direction of the nearby cemetery, was only mollified by the thought that another injection of cash was winging its way into his account and postponing yet another embarrassing encounter with his bank manager.

The most notable member of this group of golfing 'banshees' was Dickson who, as one might have imagined, when it came to golf, had earned some well-targeted and in most peoples' opinion, very accurate nicknames from his partners. He fitted Richardson's criteria to the letter – large wallet, even larger ego, usually to be found in the company of some other influential group of 'wheelers and dealers' planning their latest scam to extricate money from some unsuspecting investors, little or no golfing skills to speak of, but with a level of unwavering self-belief and confidence to put even the most thrusting, self-opinionated politician to shame.

It was these thoughts that fuelled Richardson's relentless attempts during those tedious and brain-numbing sessions on the practice ground to keep Dickson hungry for more golfing achievements with which he could entertain or bore his companions, depending on one's point of view. Top of Dickson's list of golfing priorities, he had confessed to Richardson, was his wish to be the club's vice captain. Richardson happened to know that Dickson hadn't a 'cat in hell's chance' of getting this appointment – there were too many members of the executive committee who had experienced at first hand 'Slicky Dicky's' greasy pole activities in other contexts to let that happen.

Richardson, therefore, found himself in the difficult position of wanting to keep this lucrative source of his yearly revenue on side and hungry for more fame and success while, at the same time, distancing himself from any those 'Dodgy Dickson' tactics which might result in him personally receiving the 'bums rush' from the executive committee.

'Morning, Derek, how's your golf?' inquired Richardson, adopting a slightly more concerned and conciliatory tone with Dickson than he would have with anyone else.

'Brilliant, mate, cracked the game at long last, got the driving going straight as an arrow, flushing it miles off the fairway and putting like god.'

Richardson suspected that the truth was that Dickson's drives were behaving more like a badly designed boomerang, his fairway woods were barely getting above ankle height and that his putting style bore all the resemblance of someone fanning a wasp with a toilet brush.

'Let's see you actually hit some balls then Derek,' suggested Richardson with what seemed to Dickson like a bloody annoyingly pointed emphasis on the word, 'hit'.

Dickson proceeded to unleash the usual motley collection of slices, hooks, pulls and outright tops that Richardson had been witnessing for the previous six weeks. There was no evidence that even the most rudimentary coaching tips that Richardson had painstakingly tried to communicate to Dickson had managed to lodge themselves in the darker recesses of that area that passed itself off as Dickson's golfing brain. As for the evidence of Dickson's earlier claims to Richardson regarding his deity-like golfing progress, the 'golfing judges' would have had Dickson for serious contempt of court based on what he'd observed in the last three minutes.

'Christ, Derek, watching you swing a golf club is rather like watching the final movements of one of those rubber pump-up dolls after they've suffered a puncture,' said Richardson, back in his usual 'wind-up' mode of coaching.

'Piss off you sarky bastard; I came here looking for help with my golf swing not to listen to your stand-up comedy routine. I'm not paying your exorbitant teaching fees just to help you hone your ever-increasing array of sarcastic and demoralising verbal assaults on my efforts.'

Golf club members had, in a very short space of time, got used to Richardson's style of teaching, which had more in common with a medieval public flogging than a golf lesson, containing as it did liberal amounts of humiliating and downright insulting comments and taunts on the increasingly unsuccessful attempts being made to launch the golf ball over the early morning wormcasts, 'Ralph, you're swinging that club like a ruptured rubber duck.' Most had got used to extremely vivid descriptions of their golf swing which might have come straight out of a Tolkien golf guide, had he bothered to write one, though it must be said that the language used by Richardson was not for the ears of the more sensitive and easily-offended group of his 'tortured tutees'.

Richardson's other source of pleasure at the expense of these 'long-suffering lashers' was frequently to announce their abject golfing failures to everyone else in the form of a 'golfing naming and shaming ritual'. So, it came as no surprise to some members to overhear in the bar, their own personal golfing affliction being graphically discussed by their fellow 'gougers' as reliably reported by Richardson from the practise ground.

'Derek, your timing is all to cock, mate, slow it down to a blur for god's sake or you'll do yourself a mischief apart from anything else. You've only hit ten balls and the catering staff could do a fried egg on your old 'boatrace'.'

'Well last week, you were telling me that I'd got to attack the ball more. I recall the phrase you used to describe my swing as, 'fanning the ball with my hat'. I never bloody know where I am with your never-ending pearls of bullshit.'

'Look,' explained Richardson, 'you've got the very best that money can buy in terms of golfing equipment, but you've got to let the clubs do the work. You're attacking the ball as if it represents the last remaining photograph of your mother-in-law and your footwork resembles a Spanish flamenco dancer with piles. Now, let's see you swing it slower and smoother.'

'You're a right sarcastic sod sometimes, Mark. I don't know why the hell I put up with some of your flowery outbursts. I'm surprised that someone hasn't stuck one on you as a result of some of the things you're supposed to have said about their golf.'

In fact, Richardson was also wondering the same thing about Dickson and his willingness to put up with the weekly verbal pounding that passed for a golf lesson. He suspected that it was something to do with the fact that Dickson liked to give the impression that he was part of the club's inner circle of influence, though where he got the idea that Richardson was a part of that, he'd never understood. Dickson had certainly enjoyed the occasions that Richardson had schemed to get him invited as a member of his team in local tournaments, thus ensuring unlimited amounts of free booze and food at Dickson's expense.

It was almost worth the embarrassment of the one occasion when Dickson had managed, by dint of his manic swing manoeuvres, to put a ball clean over the clubhouse roof and into the garden of the club's steward, which just so happened to contain a washing line full of his wife's undies. Undeterred by this small setback, Dickson went off in pursuit of the offending ball, untangled himself from the somewhat voluminous garments and then, to the great consternation of his playing partner, threatened to try to get the ball back in play over the aforementioned roof of the clubhouse.

Dickson's patronage of Richardson, therefore, continued to flourish in spite of the weekly tongue-lashing he received, though another motive for this clawing support was soon to reveal itself.

'OK, Derek, on to the putting green. I seem to recall in the past that your style with the putter rather resembled the actions of someone trying to dislodge a swam of ants from up their arse.'

'You'll be trying to dislodge the head of my putter from up yours if you carry on with your brand of whimsy for much longer,' complained Dickson.

'Take the putter back slower, you're snatching at the ball like a drowning man being thrown a lifebelt.' Keep your head still and just rock the shoulders backwards and forwards. At the moment, there's more moving parts in your putting swing than a Swiss watch.'

'Richardson, I hate you, you supercilious twerp. Now, I want a word in your shell-like about this club vice captaincy business. You know I'm after getting some support and a nomination from the executive committee, so I need some sound advice from you with none of your usual blend of caustic cynicism and below-the-waist phraseology you usually use to describe its members.'

Richardson had been hoping that he could have avoided another round of this 'cat and mouse' game that he was slowly being sucked into. He had no real wish to get embroiled in Dickson's nefarious attempts to ingratiate himself with some of the executive committee members. Regardless of his own predilection for a good few 'tinctures' at the bar at the end of the day, he had been trying desperately to distance himself from Dickson's sudden, but entirely predictable, outburst of hospitality towards certain members of the club's hierarchy now that the race was on for next year's nomination for vice captain. These were the very same committee members who, 12 months previously, Dickson would not have loaned a tee peg to, let alone bought them a drink.

Free drinks, invitations to dinner parties, tickets to local night clubs and theatres, even a day's hospitality at the local horse racing meeting for one member, had all suddenly begun to descend from Dickson's wallet, like ticker tape on the 4th July, into the waiting hands of some of those members of the committee who Dickson thought would be the most susceptible to such approaches and the most likely to get in behind his application.

Unbeknown to Dickson, however, with one or two notable exceptions, these blatant attempts to ingratiate himself with the executive committee members would be about as successful as an attempt by Saddam Hussain to get a nomination for the Nobel Peace Prize. Most were happily accepting his largesse while it lasted, knowing full well that once the failed attempt at gaining the vice captaincy had emerged, they would be dropped from Dickson's circle of cronies faster than it took to hole a six inch putt. Richardson was all-too-aware of this situation from his conversations with some of the members who had confided to him that Dickson's application form would be a paper aeroplane within seconds of the appointing committee meeting getting underway.

'Derek, I can't stay late tonight, I've got a long journey tomorrow to a pro-am tournament, I've got an early start.'

'When did you ever let golf get in the way of a drink, Mark?' said Dickson, trying vainly to return some of Richardson's own brand of sarcasm with interest, 'OK then, just a quick one, as the actress said to the bishop, eh.'

Richardson had heard that tiresome attempt on Dickson's part to be funny, a thousand times and it really was wearing a bit thin. Richardson recalled that a 'quick one' with Dickson had, in the past, had a habit of finishing with the arrival of the milkman.

'Mark, as I see it, I've got about four of the exec committee in the bag so far, they've as good as said that they'll be supporting my application. That's old Finchy, Jenkins, Crowther and 'Spotty' Porter. That leaves another half-dozen who I'm not sure about, but I'm working on.'

'Derek, a little word of advice my old mate, you want to go easy on these tactics of trying to buy the pants off all the committee, they're going to suss out what you're about soon, that is if they haven't already done so, and it's going to backfire,' suggested Richardson.

'Crap, Mark. They wouldn't tell me one thing and then go and do another.'

That's exactly what at least one of them is definitely going to do, thought Richardson and one other was seriously considering doing, after being told that Dickson's promise of continued gratitude for his support would very likely survive just about as long as a tent in a nuclear war.

'What about the other candidates for vice captaincy, Derek, there are two others who are in the running?'

'Ah, you mean Robertson and Johnson. Christ, what a couple of no-hopers, they are. They wouldn't know how to captain a golf club properly if they were locked up for a year with the entire Royal and Ancient and PGA Committees. God help the club if ever either of them get the job.'

I've heard a fair number of members saying the same thing about you, Derek, thought Richardson. Visions and descriptions of the club under Dickson's captaincy had varied from 'Return of the Wild West' to 'The Windmill Theatre meets the Folies Bergeres'. Most members greeted the possibility of Dickson's captaincy with about as much enthusiasm as Alcoholics Anonymous would have once welcomed a talk by George Best.

'Mark, do me a favour, I need you to keep your ear to the ground to find out what the rest of this bunch of incompetent half wits are thinking in terms of the man for the job. I need to know if I'm up against all the rest of them or just one or two.'

'Derek, I'm not running a bloody confessional here. No-one's going to come clean to me of all people about whom they're supporting. You know what it's like here, it's easier to find out who the next Pope will be than find out who's going to be next year's vice captain.'

'Mark, don't give me that bullshit. You hear things from the 'holy of holies' upstairs, particularly old 'Barnacle', the club secretary. All I'm asking is for you to spill the beans if you hear a whisper from any of those 'movers and shakers' on the exec.'

'Barnacle' Barnes, the club secretary, had earned his nickname because of his reputation for sticking rigidly and immovably to his own, often ludicrously out-dated and outmoded ideas on all sorts of matters to do with running the club, regardless of what others said or what commonsense should have dictated.

Richardson wouldn't have described any of the executive committee in those terms, unless suddenly and without his knowledge, someone had contracted symptoms of a serious and life-threatening medical condition.

'Derek, I'll do what I can, but remember, I'm just a paid employee here and as such I have about as much influence or access to the 'movers and shakers', as you describe them, as our new part-time barmaid. In fact, from what I've heard, you're more likely to get the real SP on the vice captaincy stakes from her than from me, judging by the amount of time some of the exec members have recently been spending leaning and leering over the bar at her, 'assessing the lie' as one lecherous old sod described it.'

'Thanks, Mark. We must talk about a replacement for that old banger of yours sometime. It's not good for you to be seen trundling around in something that should be in Lord Montague's motor museum.'

'Don't let's get into that old chestnut, Derek and anyway from what I understand, even you couldn't afford what the famous Lord has in stock.'

From choice, Richardson very rarely played golf with the members of the club if he could avoid it. Those he did play with were usually selected on the basis of their alcohol consumption, willingness to 'cough up' for a variety of golf wagers and their skill at playing a mean game of poker. He had little desire to spend his precious Saturday afternoons and Sunday mornings wandering about those parts of the course which resembled the more uninhabited areas of a safari park than a golf course with a group of 'slammers' who thought that five hours for 18 holes was, to quote one member, 'pushing it a bit.'

Apart from the misery of spending those endless hours accompanying a group of 'golfing point-to-pointers' make their circuitous route around the course negotiating their own personal hurdles and obstacles, looking, after five hours, like some long lost and forgotten tribe in search of civilization, he also resented their frequent attempts to use these opportunities as a buckshee golf lesson.

'Can you just tell me how I can stop the ball slicing 50 yards off to the right all the time?'

Yeh, with a swing like that, it's simple, give up the game and take up morris dancing, was what he'd felt like saying.

'How can I get backspin on the ball when it hits the green like the pros do?'

In your case you don't hit the bloody ball far enough to need backspin, you prat, was what he almost said on one occasion to one of these golfing 'nomads'.

'Can you help me to read putts better, I never seem to be able to read the correct line on the greens?'

'Yeh, Specsavers are doing a special offer this month on glasses designed by Ping for golfers who have problems putting; they've got a bubble in them like a spirit level to help you see the line.'

'Bloody hell, have they? I must get hold of a pair of those, they could solve all my putting problems.'

Yes, and make an appointment for a brain transplant while you're about it, thought Richardson as another 'gullible golfer' went off in search of golfing nirvana.

The other tiresome aspect of having to play with some members was that they thought that it was a golden opportunity to show off in front of the pro and try to outdo him in every aspect of the game.

'What did you use there, Mark, a five-iron? Well, I made it with a seven.'

No, you didn't make it with a seven-iron, you stupid sod,

you hit a seven-iron 30 yards short and left and it bounced the rest of the way off the bank,' thought Richardson.

'I noticed you hit an eight-iron there, Mark, I just hit a gentle wedge.'

Gentle wedge my arse, thought Richardson, you hooded the club and lunged at the ball so hard, you nearly fell over, you lying twerp.

The only thing that made these experiences remotely more bearable than a vasectomy, without an anaesthetic, was the chance to relieve the opposition of substantial amounts of cash. The occasional 'high roller' who stood on the first tee suggesting, 'let's make it interesting shall we and play for a quid' was firmly offered a quite painful destination for the week's pocket money he'd obviously been allocated by "er indoors.'

Fortunately for Richardson, most of them, while not exactly deliriously happy with the idea of 'a tenner a corner' with the usual 'bits', did not want to be seen to lose face and object. What this income-generating strategy of Richardson's did guarantee, of course, was that for all but a very few of the members who could comfortably have afforded to treble Richardson's bet, for the rest, their game went to pot from the very first tee shot, as a series of what could best be described as 'uncontrollable catatonic twitches' sent the ball into undergrowth where bag spotters rather than ball spotters were required.

A subtle variation of this strategy sometimes involved the opposition being 'allowed' a head start over the first nine with the suggestion that the stakes be increased for the second nine. Eagerly seeing this as a possible chance to recoup some of their previous losses, they would often accept Richardson's offer, only to find themselves being soundly thrashed over the remaining holes and required to part with a sum of money that would easily have paid for renting a villa on the Costa del Sol for a week.

The combination, therefore, of a golf swing which defied description, a short memory and an unfailing belief that, 'one of these days I'm going to beat the arse of this sod,' meant that on those rare occasions when Richardson did venture out with these inveterate optimists, his somewhat meagre weekly earnings from other sources were guaranteed a substantial boost.

Richardson's only real obligation as a pro to play with the members each year was in the ten match challenge accompanying the captain to raise money for his designated charity. Consequently, no money ever found its way into Richardson's pocket, so the best he could hope for was a few rounds of free drinks at the bar for the pleasure of toiling around with the current club captain, popularly known as 'Denis the Dredger' on account of his well renowned efforts to haul out and liberally spray around great swathes of the course's finest turf as he made his very slow and ponderous way around the 18 holes.

On one very famous occasion, a bogus letter had appeared on the club's notice board, reputedly from a distinguished university's archaeological department offering the captain an honorary doctorate for, 'his long and distinguished services to notable excavations in the area.' No-one ever discovered the perpetrator of this joke, but it was well known that Richardson had been quite friendly for short time with a secretary from one of the university's departments.

Captaincy of the club, on the basis of one's ability to consistently get the ball past the ladies tee and begin the second hole with the same ball, had long since lapsed. Currently, what got the election committee's salivating attention was such criteria as the size of one's bank balance, one's level of influence among the political 'movers and shakers' in the local corridors of power and one's skill at enticing local businessmen to regard the club as their second home and pour large quantities of their money into the various hair-brained schemes dreamt up by the committee. In return, these hardly great and definitely not-so-good pillars of the local community would be treated to a mouth watering invitation to the captain's dinner, an experience which any self-respecting chef would have gone to the most extreme lengths imaginable to avoid.

A round of golf with 'Denis the Dredger', therefore, was not only a hazardous experience in terms avoiding being in the line of fire from divots the size of dinner plates and drives which threatened the long term health of one's ankles, but also for the dreary and mind-deadening conversation to which one was subjected for the best part of four and a half hours.

The tedium would begin for Richardson barely before they reached the fairway of the first hole.

'Had lunch with Parkinson the other day, Mark, got talking about the committee's idea to erect a plaque on each tee with the name and profile of a past captain. Thinks it's a great idea and will support it wholeheartedly.'

Another ego trip for the current captain, thought Richardson and a way of Parkinson ingratiating himself even more with the current set of 'apple polishers' that masqueraded under the name of the executive committee for the moment when another vacancy occurred in their ranks.

Richardson would initially try the minimalist response strategy, 'oh well done, I think this is your ball, Denis.' No effect.

'We're going to cost out the project and put the sponsorship idea to his board of directors. Doesn't think there'll be a problem.'

I bet he doesn't, thought Richardson. Parkinson had a reputation for getting what he wanted and any directors who had the nerve to disagree with him needed to quickly start searching the job vacancy columns of the local paper.

Richardson would then try his closure tactic. 'I'm sure the members will be delighted with the idea of doing this for past captains. Oh, bad luck, Denis,' as about 12 inches of turf hurtled over Richardson's head and the ball sped off towards the open doors of the green keeper's shed.

This statement, in fact, could not have been further from

the truth. Almost every member who had heard of the idea thought that this was yet further evidence of the need to get the entire executive committee certified. Most of the members who had any recollection of the past captains would more happily have subscribed to a plaque bearing their name, attached to the toilet cistern in the gent's changing room.

'We're planning a special dinner to unveil all the plaques. I've had a word with the house committee to put on a special evening,' explained Denis.

With the standard of catering provided by the current cretin occupying the post of chef, you'd better alert the local hospital to be ready to accept a load of outpatients on that night then, thought Richardson. He wondered what kind of extravaganza the house committee were currently dreaming up. Knowing some of the 'geriatric giants' that currently held that post, as Richardson in fact did, he had visions of a night of unbridled boredom that would rival a synchronized knitting marathon. In a previous year, the committee had scaled the dizzy heights of social entertainment with a quiz night featuring among other things, what seemed like an interminable number of questions on the life and songs of Daniel O'Donnell. Rumour had it that the wife of one committee member had met the famous Irish warbler and become a knicker-lobbing fanatic.

Denis droned on over the next five holes with equally nausea-inducing trivia about these bloody plaques of past captains, such as shape, size, colour, texture and suitable points of location, to the point where Richardson was seriously tempted to reach for his driver and dispatch Denis prematurely into the category of past captains.

Richardson suspected that this conversation with Denis was leading to a conclusion that involved him. He wasn't wrong and didn't have to wait long for Denis's other request.

'I've told Parkinson that you'll take him and a couple of his directors for a round next week sometime – OK Mark? – so they can use the opportunity to discuss where to site the plaques.'

Bloody great, thought Mark, not only do I have to entertain

Parkinson, whose self-opinionated outpourings were not just limited to his business practices, the world economy and every form of political and religious bigotry, but freely ranged over virtually every other subject including the state of European golf and the inability of most golf club committees to 'organize a piss up in a brewery', but to put the tin hat on it, I have to put up with two of his sycophantic sidekicks.

'Fine, Denis, be delighted to entertain them', lied Richardson, trying to hide his distorted facial features, which would have betrayed an altogether different sentiment.

He wondered how quickly he could contract some life-threatening illness, with the help of a young nurse he'd just met, and get 'Shanks' to do the honours. Then he reflected on the potential havoc that 'Shanks' might create, with his monosyllabic mutterings and comic book outbursts, not to mention the slightly dubious jokes and immediately thought better of the planned incarceration in hospital.

Richardson's thoughts turned to how he could maximize the event to his own benefit. Thoughts which centred not only around money, free meals and drinks, but also the potential for a yearly sponsorship from Parkinson's company. Richardson would find no difficulty in displaying promotional details of a company specializing in drain cleaning and sewage disposal if those details were being carried on the latest model from Porsche or Lotus.

If that plonker 'Barnacle Barnes', the club secretary, could extract a BMW from the local agency for doing nothing more than making a complete bollocks of managing the club's affairs and doing incomprehensible promotional interviews with the local paparazzi, then he reckoned he should be in with a shout with Parkinson's 'shit and shovel' brigade.

At the conclusion of this brain-splittingly tedious game of golf, therefore, Richardson saw some possible light at the end of the 'golfing tunnel' in the shape of an improved bank balance and the possible departure of the six-year-old Mondeo, possibly by flogging it to that unsuspecting prat, 'Shanks' for whom it would be like a step up to the latest Maserati.

Denis was his usual up-beat self at the end of the game in spite of having lost eight balls, been out of bounds three times, only come in on three holes and, on Richardson's calculation, finished at least 14 over his 20 handicap.

'Great game there between us, Mark. I reckon we 'ham and egged' it well, never thought the win was ever in doubt.'

Where the hell have you been for the last four hours, Denis, thought Richardson. We actually scraped home by one hole and I shot seven under, but restricted his comment to what he hoped would not be detected as too sarcastic a reply.

'Yeh, thanks Denis, I always enjoy the challenge of playing with you.'

Denis, however, was not the sort of person who understood when he was being the butt of someone like Richardson's acerbic sarcasm or caustic wit and so usually ended up saying something equally ridiculous in reply.

'Yeh, I feel the same, these challenge matches always seem to bring the best out in my game. Let's get a drink off the losers.'

No game of golf with the male members of the club, however, could come even close to that never-to-be-forgotten, excruciating excursion with the lady captain in the mixed foursomes' club competition. If someone had even suggested to Richardson that he would one day actually volunteer to play in a mixed 'gruesomes' golf match and furthermore, agree to play it with the lady captain, he personally would have put out a call on their behalf for an immediate delivery of the white coats.

In all fairness, the term 'volunteer' was not quite accurate. Richardson had had the misfortune to be propping up the clubhouse bar one weekend when the lady captain 'torpedoed' her way through the usual Saturday crowd of 'thirsty thrashers' requesting the presence of some poor unsuspecting male golfer in the following day's mixed tournament. The reason for the sudden departure of her original partner was not clear, but rumours of sudden, but up to that point, unheard-of tendencies to self-mutilation, once news of the pairings had been announced, had spread through the club like wildfire.

The 'volunteering' had certainly not come from Richardson, but rather from some vindictive sod who had recently lost a 'shed load' of money to him in a four-ball.

'Yeh, ask Mark, I'm sure he'd be delighted to make up the four with you, lady captain, if you're really stuck for a partner.'

Richardson was into his sixth large gin and tonic and had not heard, as everyone else had, the lady captain's request. The immediate effect on 98 per cent of the male population of the bar on hearing the request, was an overwhelming and urgent desire to empty the contents of their bladder in as lengthy a stay in the Gents as was deemed necessary for the recruitment of some other victim. The remainder of the bar's occupants had reached an alcoholic state that rendered them beyond the point of caring what fate was in store for them from this golfing vision of Wagner's operatic heroine, Brunhilde.

The mention of his name, he had at first, associated with an invitation to have another drink and so found himself readily accepting, with some misdirected comment as, 'sure, be a pleasure, got absolutely nothing pressing.' It was only when the lady captain thanked him for such a 'charming and somewhat unexpectedly generous response' and told him that he and she were teeing of at 8.00 on the Sunday morning that he realized that he'd rather drunkenly accepted to take part in golf's equivalent of an Islamic 'fatwah'.

His initial thoughts were to fake a sudden onslaught of the first-known public appearance of the combined symptoms of Parkinson's and Alzheimer's disease, but even he realized that such extreme measures would find little sympathy with the lady who was known to have reduced certain members of the club's executive committee to a quivering mass, when they had dared to contradict her on a rules decision.

'Are you sure it's in order for me to play in your competition, I wouldn't want to cause you any embarrassment by breaking the rules and getting you disqualified?' he desperately inquired, hoping against hope that he might uncover some obscure local ruling which prevented a professional from taking part in this act of public humiliation.

'Oh no, it's quite in order within the club's rules for you to play off a plus four handicap,' replied the lady captain.

Having to play with you, you old bat, is enough of a handicap without having to play off plus four, thought Richardson.

His other thought had been to find the sod that had dropped him in it and assist him in an early departure to the accident and emergency dept of the local hospital. With no obvious candidate for this award left in the bar, he headed off to the Gents in the hope of extracting a confession, either from the doomed culprit or a duplicitous witness. His entry was, however, barred by the sanctuary-craving drunken occupants until he gave them an assurance that the lady captain was not in close proximity in pursuit of an alternative victim.

'Richardson, if you've got 'Brunhilde' with you waiting to pounce on us the minute we come out, you're dead meat, mate.'

'If it's a choice between having to play with her or going to early morning mass, tell the priest I'll be there at 7.30 am.'

The dishevelled occupants of the Gents looked for all the world like a group of hostages cowering from the inevitable arrival of a life-threatening terrorist hit squad.

Thus it was, that with no success at finding either the perpetrator of the joke who, in spite of his extensive injuries, would certainly have found himself taking Richardson's place, or an alternative lamb to the slaughter, Richardson found himself on the first tee at the ungodly hour of 7.50 on Sunday morning.

The hours between eight and ten on a Sunday morning were usually reserved for 'rest and recuperation' from the ravages and excesses of the previous night. Hence the reason for the regular presence of the unsuspecting, ever faithful 'Shanks' at this so-called 'red eye' slot. Richardson would have readily admitted, therefore to not being quite the finely tuned, perfectly honed athlete that the lady captain was expecting to accompany her that day.

He'd half suspected that the previous night's particularly strong curry in close association with the liberal quantities of various alcoholic beverages, might serve to impede what was grudgingly admitted by most of his regular playing partners, to be his usual highly professional playing performance.

'Morning Mark,' bellowed the lady captain, thus adding further pain to that which was already residing in just about every corner of Richardson's head, caused by what felt like the band of the Coldstream Guards marching about inside, 'this is Albert and Vera, they're getting 28 shots. Of course, we're only getting 12 shots because of your handicap.'

Oh god, thought Richardson, they'll have called last orders by the time we get in.

'Albert and I have never played with a real professional golfer before, we're ever so excited,' said Vera.

He wondered whether the term 'real' was an accurate description of him in his present state.

You're also going to be very shocked and distressed in a minute if the messages I'm getting from my stomach are transmitted to my bowels in the next two minutes, thought Richardson.

Luck seemed to be on his side from the start, however, as, what seemed like an eardrum-splitting fart he emitted while waiting his turn on the first tee, was drowned out by the shouts of 'fore' from his fellow golfers as their opponents drive headed for the clubhouse car park and the bonnet of a spotless new Audi.

His subsequent progress around the first few holes had to be accompanied by a non-technical, at least in the golfing sense, clenching of the buttocks on every swing in order to avoid a repetition of the disastrous first tee cacophony.

'Are you all right Mark?' inquired the lady captain, 'you seem a little tense and nervous, you don't have to worry about playing with us, you know.'

You'd be tense and nervous, thought Richardson, if you

were dragging around the lethal concoction from the Indian subcontinent that I consumed last night.

'Oh, I'm alright, I'm just working on a new set up to try to hold everything together through the take away,' he replied, fighting off yet another desperate attack of the 'lamb jalfrezis' with extra chilli's' that was coursing its way through his tormented digestive system.

As he had predicted, the total golfing experience was on a par with every epic disaster movie ever made. It wasn't long before the inadequacies of the lady captain's golf game became apparent. Her failure to be able to move the ball more than a matter of a few yards from even the shortest areas of rough, her look of sheer panic when his approach shot landed in a green side bunker followed by her orbital attack on the ball to match the speed of an Exocet missile did not bode well for their progress over the next three hours.

'These bunkers are not at all well maintained, you know, Mark, they need raking more thoroughly, they don't make it very easy to play a good shot out of them,' complained the lady captain.

I'm waiting to see you play the first good shot from any location, thought Richardson and we've played eight holes.

Her ability to judge the pace and direction of putts was on a par with a young baby's first attempts to find its mouth with a knife and fork, and the frequency and regularity with which her attempts sped backwards and forwards across the green, had Richardson feeling that he was watching tennis on Wimbledon's Centre Court rather than playing in a golf match.

'They've cut these damn greens far too close again, Mark, I told the green keeper again, only the other day, that they'd damage them if they weren't careful, it's ridiculous how fast they are.'

My god, thought Richardson, it's just typical of your type; you've no bloody idea how to play the game. Your window-boxed size garden is a wilderness, but you're a sodding expert on every aspect of golf course management and have the 'brass neck' to tell those who actually do know what they're doing that they're doing it wrong.

The most amazing part of this whole experience for Richardson was the manner in which his partner reacted to these disasters. Most golfers he knew, and played with, would have been utterly devastated had they performed so badly and their apologies would have equalled the penitent confession of life-long serial killer. Not, however, the lady captain. Most of her golfing 'sins' were followed by a defiant growl and some irritating comment such as, 'oh never mind it's only a game' or 'oh well, you get us back on the green, then, you're the pro' or the all too-frequently heard comment destined to drive Richardson to even greater levels of insanity, 'I played a much better shot than that here, yesterday.' The age of miracles wasn't only confined to first century Palestine, then, thought Richardson.

As for their opponents, they were suffering from those acute first time nerves of playing with a professional and behaved as though their failure to play well would be reported to the Royal and Ancient and result in them having their handicap certificate endorsed with three penalty points for incompetence.

'You'll have to tell us where we're going wrong, Mr. Richardson, we've only just joined this golf club on the recommendation of that nice man down at the driving range.'

Richardson made a mental note to drop the latest copy of Golf Monthly's situations vacant through his fellow professional's letterbox, hoping the vacancy in Stornoway might catch his eye.

'You just relax and pretend you're just playing a social game with a couple of good friends,' replied Richardson, hoping that some kind words might reduce the frequency with which he was required to venture into areas of the rough which threatened to reduce his latest Ashworth's to the role of dish cloths.

Richardson found himself feeling genuinely sorry for them as they struggled to throw off the impression that this was their first acquaintance with anything approximating to a golf course other than beach-side crazy golf as well as having to deal with the far from exemplary behaviour of the lady captain. He would have suggested that she might have taken a few tips from their partners on the art of delivering a grovelling apology, but realized that she would probably have had trouble recognizing the term 'sorry'.

At the conclusion of this golfing odyssey, which by some amazing stroke of good fortune on the part of the golfing gods, they won three and two, the lady captain delivered the ultimate golfing tactless 'whopper' with the comment, 'I do love it so much when one plays well and so thoroughly deserves one's win.'

Yet further proof, thought Richardson, if more was actually needed that honesty, tact, diplomacy and a sensitivity towards other peoples' feelings were notable absentees from the list of criteria for selection to high office in this golf club. Richardson's personally compiled, but as yet unpublished, list of criteria included, 'propensities towards self-opinionated, egotistically minded, self- delusory acts of self-aggrandisement on a par with the combined monarchies of Western civilization.'

Making his apologies, he shook hands and headed for the relative sanity of the bar and the nerve and mind restoring properties of several gin and tonics.

'Morning, Mark, we saw you the other day, trying to help Patsy Smythe sort out those dangerous curves of hers and, of course, that slice she's got as well,' said Bellingham with his usual brand of mediocre humour.

Bellingham and his mate, Watson practically lived on the course from Saturday morning to Sunday afternoon and when not playing golf, were regulars on the snooker table or in the club's resident card school.

'Oh, morning you two, it's not like you two to be here at this time,' said Richardson.

'Ah well, we've been summoned to meet his highness, 'Barnacle Barnes', said Bellingham.

'You two been naughty boys again, then? You'll be getting the heave ho, if you're not careful; how many times is that now you've been up in front of the 'judge'?'

‘Ah, he’s got some bee up his arse about something that happened at the captain’s dinner and he’s decided that we’re ‘in the frame’, so we’re in line for his usual brand of authoritarian bullshit with perhaps a bit of that old style ‘police cell’ brutality tactics thrown in for good measure,’ explained Watson.

‘Oh, by the way,’ said Richardson to Bellingham, ‘I’ve got that new rescue wood you ordered in the shop.’

‘Christ, it’s finally arrived, has it, Mark?’ adopting Richardson’s own brand of sarcasm, ‘you’re still using that courier service from Outer Mongolia, then. Anyway, thanks, I think I’ll come and get it now and take it with me to meet ‘Barnesy’, it might come in handy if things get rough.’

Richardson eventually made his way back to the shop in the unlikely event that ‘Shanks’ had run out of stock of a particular item and was, at that precise moment, offering to give the customer the telephone number of the nearest American Discount Golf store rather than be bothered to get the ‘top off his pen’ and capture a valuable order. Worse still, he might be phoning that prat down at the driving range to ask him if he has any of those particular items in stock and if so, would it be in order for him to send a couple of customers down.

What was more likely was that he was tucked up in the store cupboard clutching some grubby ‘girlie’ magazine, trying to pick up a few tips for keeping up with the sexual gymnastic demands of his latest conquest. Given that ‘Shanks’ had problems understanding the instructions, let alone the assembling of a display stand in the shop, even when pictures were provided, Richardson imagined that the ‘girlie’ magazine would simply have already reduced ‘Shanks’ to a confused and frustrated ‘twitcher’.

‘Hi ‘Shanks’, how’s business been going in my absence, been a run on the Cobra drivers has there, mate?’ said Richardson sarcastically.

'Shanks' looked a little puzzled, but Richardson put this down to the strain his eyes had been under trying to read that mag in the semi-darkness of the store cupboard.

'Nah, guv, haven't managed to shift any of those today, but I did sell a bag stand,' said 'Shanks' proudly.

'Oh well done, 'Shanks', that should improve our trading figures this month by at least 0.1 per cent. Oh and by the way, just in case you were trying to sell the Cobra drivers I mentioned, I ought to perhaps point out that we don't actually stock those,' remarked Richardson icily.

'Ah well, that explains it then, why no-one asked for one, guv,' said 'Shanks', looking justifiably relieved that he hadn't apparently committed any major gaff.

Richardson wondered to what combined level of sarcasm and unpleasantness he'd have to descend before 'Shanks' finally got the message that, as a salesman, he was a complete and utter waste of space.

'There was a phone call for you while you were out, guv,' said 'Shanks', 'funny sounding sort of bloke; I think I got most of what he was on about, but it weren't easy with him being foreign and all that.'

Richardson could only think of his local curry house and the launderette as the two possible sources of the call, based on 'Shanks' very lucid description of the caller, and neither of the two owners had given him any inclination of their desire to play golf. There had been that brief problem with the owner of the local Chinese restaurant when he'd caught Richardson with his daughter in the back of the Mondeo in the restaurant car park, but he was sure that was all forgotten, particularly as he'd agreed to pay for the damage to the girl's dress.

So, he was on his way out, when it occurred to him that he should quiz 'Shanks' in a bit more detail about this mysterious caller.

'Can you give me the gist of the message, 'Shanks', just in case I need to contact Interpol?' inquired Richardson.

'Nah, guv, it wasn't Interflora or whatever you said; he said his name was Mr. Tomori,' explained 'Shanks'.

'And what exactly did Mr Tomori want, 'Shanks', is this the golden opportunity I've been waiting for to ship you out as a teaching pro to Tokyo?'

'Don't think so, guv, he just wanted to play golf, I think,' said 'Shanks'.

'So, what's the problem, did you book a starting time for him?' enquired Richardson.

'Ah well, no, not exactly, that's when I told him it was probably not possible for him to play.'

'Oh, and why was that?' asked Richardson, wondering just how long it was going to take to screw the final details out of this prat.

'Well, he wanted to bring 24 other Japanese golfers with him, didn't he? From what I could make out, they're touring around and wanted two rounds of golf here. I told him it probably wasn't possible, but I did keep his number just in case.'

Thank god for that, thought Richardson, the guy isn't a complete twat after all.

'Let me get this straight, 'Shanks'; this guy rings up wanting to bring 24 Japanese golfers here to play two rounds of golf, presumably over two days, knowing how long it takes those buggers to play 18 holes and film every moving moment from first tee to 18th green; and you told him it probably wouldn't be possible.'

'Yeh, guv, something like that,' said 'Shanks', not a problem is there?'

'Right 'Shanks', get your coat on, we're going to buy you an apron,' said Richardson.

'What do I want an apron for, guv?' inquired a slightly puzzled 'Shanks'.

'Because you're starting in the chippy as from tomorrow. 'Shanks', what few brain cells you possess must reside permanently in and around your groin; didn't it occur to you that 24 Japanese golfers here for two days probably means a 'shed' load of money going through the till in purchases as well as lessons probably? Here was a wonderful opportunity to get shut of some of the crap we've been hoarding and you've passed it up, you wazok.'

'But there's quite a few people already booked in for that day, there's not much room left,' argued 'Shanks' in his defence.

'Cancel them; tell them the greens have developed a dangerous fungi and they can't play; tell them there's been a minor earth tremor and we've got a team of seismologists crawling all over the course; tell them anything 'Shanks', but get those starting times free; I'm going to try to get Mr. Tomboli or whatever his name is back on the phone; just keep your fingers, your legs and, for that matter, any other part of your anatomy that can withstand that strain, crossed.'

'Why's that guv?' asked 'Shanks'.

'Because, if in the meantime he's managed to get tee times elsewhere, you're for the deep fat fryer. Now get your arse into gear and make those phone calls.'

Richardson wondered as he headed off to make the call, somewhere where he wouldn't be disturbed either by the sight or sound of 'Shanks', just how early the Voluntary Euthanasia Society accepted applications; might it just stretch the rules a little and accept a 24-year-old assistant golf professional?

CHAPTER 2

THE SECRETARY'S TALE or 'I don't care if it's Ballesteros, no visitors before 2pm at weekends.'

To many golfers, at least that is, those male members of the species, golf club secretaries have come to closely resemble what the prospective mother-in-law does to the erstwhile suitor; namely, someone who stands irresolutely between them and their single-minded, passionate pursuit of the object of their desire and the tantalisingly elusive source of their immediate emotional satisfaction. That is to say, a damn good game of golf with their mates, followed by a good few 'tinctures' in the bar, all spiced up with a heady cocktail of abuse of their fellow golfers' game, unrepeatable jokes and scandalous gossip featuring the club's executive committee.

Many among this strange breed of humanity frequently seem to see it as their bounden duty, almost one sometimes might think, part of their unwritten job contract, to frustrate and divert every attempt by the luckless golfer to engage in what is meant to be a relaxing and restorative pastime, designed to recharge either the 'batteries' that sustain them through the tedium of their working week or maintain their sanity in the face of an encyclopaedic list of household chores that suddenly appear, as if by magic, every time the word 'golf' is mentioned.

The role of the golf club secretary has undergone substantial changes in the last 20 years, changes that probably rival those of a map depicting the rapid decline of the British Empire. Gone are the charming and polite old gentlemen who saw their major raison d'etre as providing the golfer with every possible assistance and piece of information to ease their passage through the minefield of golf club procedures and competition regulations.

In their place, the average club golfer now finds a human obstacle who, in terms of their ability to release the essential ebb and flow of club information, is as about as effective as the Thames flood barrier at a high tide. What most golfers would regard as fairly vital and harmless pieces of public information appertaining to the organisation and smooth running of their own golf club, appear to be viewed by these 'guardians of the force' as top secret files and subject to the Official Secrets Act.

Significantly, many have shed that rather harmless and inoffensive 'secretary' label for the more grandiose title of 'manager' or the even more frightening nomenclature, 'director'. The effect of this has been to change the formerly respectful and relatively subservient employee of the club, who would greet members politely and enquire after the state of their game and the well being of their partner, with someone in possession of the combined powers and self-developed ego of a UN Secretary of State and a NATO general.

A visit to the occupant of the club's 'inner sanctum', therefore, is not the occasion for an exchange of social pleasantries and polite solicitous inquiries on matters ranging from golf to grandchildren. Rather, it takes the form of a verbal 'barbecuing' on the scale of the Grand Inquisition demanding to know whether one's visit was actually necessary, whether one could not come back at a more convenient time and would it not, in fact, have been much more sensible to have put one's inquiry in a letter so that it could have been dealt with through the 'proper channels'. Hardly the kind of treatment and procedures one expects to have to endure when simply reporting the on-going malfunction of the Gents' loo.

For some well-intentioned, but misguided golfers anxious to be as helpful and supportive as possible to the club's management, even a face-to-face exchange at the 'high priestly altar' of golfing administration is barred. Greeting them – though in truth, the term 'greet' is a serious misnomer – is a formidable figure, usually female, whose sole job it is to repel all attempts by a club member to be allowed an audience with her senior and very reclusive partner. This, in spite of the fact that the latter can be clearly seen through the glass panelled, but golfer-proof window with his feet up on the desk, a cup of coffee lovingly provided by his overworked secretary at his side, studying the racing page of the Daily Express. The enquirer is reliably informed that his 'eminence' is far too busy to be interrupted by a matter so trivial that it barely deserves her breath being expended in relaying it.

Her promise, however, that the message will be passed on, at some 'convenient moment' and that, 'in due course', a reply will be forwarded has all the sincerity and credibility of an answer phone message at the Samaritans.

Those more shrewd and forward-thinking members, of which clubs would claim there are a few, who mistakenly thought that a prior telephone call to the office might unblock the communication blackout that frequently seems to strike that area of the clubhouse, are met with a set of monosyllabic and incomprehensible replies that would rival the best efforts of the government's press officer replying to journalists' inquiries about alleged sexual misdemeanours by some senior Cabinet minister.

Some frustrated golfers who have been subjected to this 'border control-like' treatment have, however, on regular occasions also witnessed the early departure of these two club employees for an extended lunch hour taking in some of the more remote beauty spots of the local countryside.

Golf club secretaries vary as widely in personality and behaviour as the headmaster of Rugby school in 'Tom Brown's School Days' does from Groucho Marx. Their level of competency at the job also spans similar extremes. Occupying this role at any given time, one might find retired army personnel, headmasters, accountants, second-hand car salesmen, insurance salesmen, policemen, bank managers, solicitors and even ex-clergymen.

Club members' treatment at the hands of this motley collection of has-beens, very much depends, therefore, on the post they previously occupied. With headmasters, club members have frequently been addressed and treated like a miscreant male who has just been caught behind the bike sheds having a quick drag or a quick fumble inside the blouse of a classmate or a teacher who has inadvertently parked her car in the headmaster's unofficial parking spot. The golfer's misdemeanour: no worse than playing outside of their start time on the first tee.

With the ex-army types, members have been subjected to close inspection of dress and length of hair in the bar, the wearing of inappropriate or mud-spattered footwear in the restaurant and the most heinous of all crimes, the changing of shoes in the car park. One member told to 'stand to attention' about the latter crime, was then justifiably pissed off to find a lout of a youth dressed in combat trousers, denim top and 'sneakers' occupying the lounge bar. On inquiring why this was allowed, he was informed that the 'lout' in question was the son of the current captain.

Ex-bank managers administer their role towards members with the same relish and in the same vein as they would foreclosing on an over-draft facility for a long-time loyal customer. Ex-policemen and solicitors regard most golf club members as bordering on the edge of the criminal fraternity, to be treated with the utmost caution and suspicion and certainly guilty until proof-positive is produced of their innocence.

Ex-car or insurance salesmen seem to regard members as gullible, intellectually impaired patsies, capable of being duped into believing any old rubbish about the club's finances, the state of the course or the competence of the executive committee, providing it's all delivered with an ingratiating smile and a handshake.

Even ex-clergy men have been known to treat the golf club office as some kind of confessional in which the crimes of unreplaced divots, un-repaired pitch marks and particularly that of taking the name of the lady captain in vain at the bar, had to be repented with ten readings of Rule 24-2 relating to dealing with 'immovable obstructions.'

As for the competence of these self-styled 'ex-perts', a term commonly used to describe someone who is past it being put under even greater pressure, the 'golfing jurors' are generally unanimous in their verdict – 'guilty of gross incompetence'.

Year after year, members look in vain in the report to the club's annual general meeting by the committee and directors for this well-deserved announcement of the verdict, along with the ritual delivery of 'boot to backside', only to discover that yet again the 'overwhelming thanks and gratitude of all club members' have been warmly extended to the secretary for his untiring and self-less efforts on their behalf.

As all golfers know, of course, the fault for the catalogue of administrative disasters, lies not in the skill-set, or lack of them, of the poorly paid, over-worked incumbent, but on the advent of technology into the running of golf club affairs. Had secretaries been left to carry on using pencil, rubber, notepad, ten year-old Casio calculator and 'golf ball' typewriter, none of these problems would have occurred. Instead of which, some golf club secretaries now appear to be sitting at what looks like the helm of the 'Starship Enterprise' equipped, as they are, with their slim line monitors, PC, palm top organiser, multi-channel telephone exchange and mobile phone, naturally with its 'bluetooth' headset for parading around the clubhouse or for that rare foray on to the course itself. The word 'appear' is used quite deliberately because in truth, these 'captains of catastrophe' are probably only capable of using about two per cent of this equipment's multi-functional facilities. High levels of absenteeism have been reported, together with the obligatory attendance at a significantly large number of funerals by some golf club managers to coincide with the arrival of the long-dreaded 'Japanese piano' and its related software.

Terms such as, 'megabytes', 'browsers', 'search engines' and 'e-banking' were all part of a language which these 'intellectual skateboards' had escaped from in their previous 'incarnation' only to find to their dismay that the evil 'gods' of computer jingoism, with their hernia-inducing manuals, had caught up with them and were about to find their 36 'megabyte' handicap rather wanting in the highly competitive 'info-techno club Stableford.'

'Barnacle' Barnes, now only answering to the term, 'manager' at 'Swankers', was the archetypal golf club secretary in almost every respect. An ex-police sergeant, whose views on practically every subject imaginable, including the running of golf clubs and the management of its members, were very squarely to the right of Genghis Khan. Most members were viewed as potential troublemakers, hell bent on disrupting the smooth running of the club and making his life a confounded misery. Had he been able to have his way, many of them would have been strenuously helped to find alternative pastimes as far a way from 'his' golf club as possible.

A discussion that took place in the club bar on one occasion and in which Barnes had reluctantly got involved, centred on the general view that most golf clubs these days were run in ways that would be considered archaic 30 years ago and that the majority of those who held office in them were about as receptive to change as the average American motorist would be faced with legislation requiring the compulsory purchase of a Nissan Micra as their standard form of transport.

It had taken all of the somewhat limited supply of self-control that Barnes possessed to stop himself from instantly throwing the entire group out and banning them from future use of the clubhouse facilities. To Barnes, the very idea of change in any matters pertaining to his way of life and now, more importantly, his ideas for how this club should be managed was anathema. The very thought that these 'jumped up' apologies for business men should consider that this was the place for their new 'fangled' management practices, demanding more open and democratic decision-making processes, was enough to send Barnes' blood pressure reading into seismic Richter-scale proportions.

His authoritarian, 'I know best', 'don't you try telling me how to run things' approach, as might be imagined, did not go down well with many of the members, particularly the more misguided ones who desperately hung on to the mistaken belief that the club was run for their benefit.

His proud and consistently well-broadcasted boast, that as a station sergeant, he had run a very 'tight ship', where everyone knew their place and where 'lines were clearly drawn' as to 'what was and was not acceptable behaviour', was either greeted with gales of laughter or cries of disbelief based on what the members themselves had heard, witnessed or experienced at first hand in their previous dealings with him.

Had Barnes been a half-decent golfer, his entrenched views, which not only encompassed the club's administrative matters, but also everything from overall course design and green keeping to pin placements and the length of the rough, might have found some sympathetic ears. He was, however, ranked very firmly in the bottom quartile of the club's group of 'golfing grislies', as one member had christened certain of its very high handicapped hackers, and with no foreseeable prospect of his promotion to any higher ranking.

His well-reported meeting with two members, following the captain's annual dinner, was a classic example of his style of management. This event was an all-male affair that, in the past, had earned a reputation for developing, over the evening, into a very boisterous and over-exuberant free-for-all following the consumption of liberal quantities of alcohol. On one occasion, before Barnes' arrival as secretary, the unexpected appearance of a well-endowed young lady as the captain's special 'strip-o-gram', complete with leather golf gloves and other similarly manufactured items of exotic underwear, had culminated in a number of the members, equally scantily clad, joining her in a version of the 'conga' through the golf club car park and down the first fairway.

In spite of these reports of alleged unseemly and disorderly behaviour, no one had ever seen fit to complain or take action against the perpetrators of these pranks. No one, that is until 'Barnacle Barnes' arrived as the new club secretary, as his job was then called. His tolerance levels for this sort of 'buffoonery', as he described it, was of miniscule proportions and he was determined to see an end to it, regardless of what it did to his already barely measurable popularity ratings.

Watson and Bellingham, two of the members who had occupied the table from where most of the hilarity and raucous behaviour had allegedly emanated, had been summoned to Barnes' office to account for their behaviour. Barnes had informed the chairman, Neil Tomlinson, that he proposed to see these two and in his words, 'give them a right bollocking for turning the evening into a farce.' The chairman was not entirely convinced of the wisdom of Barnes' strategy on two counts. Firstly, because the chairman himself had been very much involved in that previous year's episode with the 'strip-o-gram' down the first fairway and didn't want to risk the possibility of these two 'miscreants' reviving memories of that incident with Barnes. Secondly, Barnes hadn't even been at the dinner, so wouldn't exactly know what took place. On the other hand, the chairman had to concede that a lack of evidence had never been a problem in getting a result in Barnes' previous occupation, so these two shouldn't pose a problem.

'You two buggers are in deep trouble', said Barnes in his usual 'no-messing', straight-to-the-point bluntness. 'Everyone's just about had enough of your prating about and your latest stunt has just about put the tin hat on it.'

'Us two buggers, as you've so charmingly chosen to address us, are Ian and Paul; we have no objection to you using our first names, we won't be offended, Basil,' said Ian, first off.

Barnes hated people using his first name in that sarcastic tone of over-familiarity and had gone ballistic on one occasion when he heard it used in conjunction with the long-standing nickname, 'Barnacle'.

'Right couple of smart arses, you think you are, don't you?

Well, the chairman doesn't think your stupid pranks are that smart, I'm telling you. You two are for the bleeding chop from this club if my guess is anything to go by.'

'Odd that,' said Paul, 'he never mentioned anything when we gave him a lift home the other night 'cos he was a bit the worse for wear and you're 'old lot' were apparently cruising about.'

'Basil, we know that we're not very high up on your Christmas card list, but would you mind getting to the point and telling us what this is all about,' said Bellingham, 'instead of engaging in this childish name-calling game of 'what's the worst words I can find to describe these two.''

On hearing the word 'childish' used to describe his behaviour, Barnes went almost apoplectic with rage, but vaguely remembered the words he used to the chairman promising, 'to get to the bottom of this latest piece of lunatic behaviour and get an apology, not engage in some slanging match.'

'Right, well the two of you know what I'm talking about don't you? It's the other night at the dinner and what happened,' blustered Barnes, trying to regain control of himself and the situation.

Watson and Bellingham both knew where this was leading but decided to squeeze the maximum amount of irritation as possible out of the secretary.

'Basil, with respect, we don't know what you're talking about because you haven't said anything that's made any sense yet and as for what happened at the dinner, we could be here until tomorrow trying to guess which particular things that happened you'd like us to recount to you.'

'You know damn well what I'm talking about; you lot were paralytic for most of the night, shouting across to people on other tables, laughing loudly at the speakers, swearing and generally making a complete nuisance of yourselves. And, if that wasn't enough, some prat then went and threw that bread roll which hit the captain's guest of honour on the head, causing him to spill an entire glass of wine all over himself.'

The wine glass incident had admittedly brought the

evening's proceedings to a bit of a temporary embarrassing halt, particularly as the guest of honour was a distinguished member of the area PGA, who the club was earnestly trying to win support from for a prestigious pro-celebrity tournament.

Both Watson and Bellingham had been on that particular table, but neither was disposed to take the rap for everyone there. They were also not prepared to give this prat Barnes the satisfaction of proudly boasting to the chairman that he'd given this pair a 'telling off they'd never forget and had got them to offer their sincerest apologies and assurances that it would never happen again.'

They also had the advantage of knowing that Barnes' knowledge of what happened was only from a third person because he'd not actually been there. Rumour had it that the captain and chairman had deliberately organised the evening when they knew Barnes was away on holiday, knowing full well that the relatively harmless 'goings-on' that usually developed at these 'do's' would have probably prompted Barnes to call for police backup to calm things down. Watson and Bellingham decided to turn the heat up on Barnes and go on the attack, not in any hope of getting an apology out of him, but just for the sheer pleasure of seeing him sweat when actually confronted with trying to establish what had happened.

'How many people were on our table that night, and who else besides us Basil?' enquired Bellingham.

'I'm not sure, about eight, I think; I can't be expected to remember all the seating arrangements. Anyway, what's that got to do with it.'

'Ah, so you're not actually sure who was there or, in fact, how many,' said Bellingham, 'we'll happily tell you, you twerp, what this has got to do with it. If you're so damn sure where all the trouble was coming from, why haven't you got everyone else here who was on that table? Well, we'll save you the embarrassment of not being able to answer that as well, Basil; it's because you haven't really got the faintest idea of what went on and neither have you got the bottle to face every one of us, you whinging old sod.'

Barnes began to sweat profusely, not only because he strongly resented being called a 'whinging old sod' by anyone, least of all these two hooligans, but also because he was aware of the fact that he had, unaccountably, only got a very sketchy account of what had actually happened. Furthermore, he had no intention of putting his head in the lion's den by demanding that all those 'bun throwing' buffoons pitch up and make his life even more of a hell than these two were already managing to achieve.

'I asked the chairman and he said he thought that the bread roll might have come from the direction of your table. That's good enough for me.'

'Bloody hell, Barnesy, did you carry out your policing enquiries with this amount of rigour and attention to detail? If so, it's no bloody wonder that there were so many unsolved crimes and suspect verdicts on your patch.'

Barnes was not prepared to have his reputation as a sergeant tarnished and brought into question by these two ne-er-do-wells.

'You two should watch what you're saying to an ex-police officer, I can still make life difficult for you, you know.'

He knew instantly that he should not have gone down this route and that these two would seize on this gaff.

'Ah, threats and intimidation; now you're in much more familiar territory Barnesy, aren't you; when do you get the thumb screws and the rubber truncheon out?'

'Look you two, why don't you just admit what you did and apologize and then we can all go to the bar?'

'We'll tell you why not Barnesy; because firstly you've no sodding proof that we were actually on that table and two, you certainly can't prove that it was one of us who threw the bread roll and finally if you propose to give us a bollocking for shouting and joking with the other tables, you'll have to get all the other buggers who were there that night to give them the same treatment. And, if laughing at the speaker's jokes has suddenly become a flogging offence, you'd better give us time to pack our pants with paper.'

Barnes secretly knew he'd lost it with these two and that an apology was about as far away as his chances had once been of becoming chief constable. He couldn't understand what had gone wrong; he'd assumed that they'd come in and freely own up to their wrongdoings, like guilty little boys, apologize and promise never to do it again. What was it with this generation; had they no respect for the truth or for other peoples' feelings?

Unfortunately, instead of trying to fill the hole he'd just dug himself in, he carried on digging in the vain hope that he would have something to tell the chairman, not that he suspected that even he was, by this time, remotely interested in getting to the bottom of the affair.

'OK, lads, I know that perhaps it wasn't all to do with you and that you were simply unfortunate enough to be on the same table as those other fruitcakes, so tell me who really threw the bread roll and was sick in the Club Championship Bowl?'

'Barnesy, you are a complete 36 handicap bastard. Not satisfied with trying to pin a completely unsubstantiated accusation on us in the hope of getting our grovelling apology, you've just compounded your absolute stupidity by now trying to get us to grass on our mates. No bloody wonder with your aptitude for 'gaffs', you never progressed past a desk sergeant. Have you any idea how this will sound when we relay it back to the chaps waiting in the bar for our return from this charade?'

Barnes now felt as though he'd just played himself into quite the largest 'administrative bunker' it was ever possible to be in. With nothing to report to the chairman, after all his promises to unearth the truth, at least nothing that accurately represented the contents of the last 30 minutes discussion and the threat that he would now be branded as someone who would set out happily to 'get someone at any cost', he felt it was time to close this painful encounter.

'Well I'm not sure the chairman's going to let the matter rest here. You know we might have lost the chance of the pro-celebrity tournament here next year as a result of the incident with the bread roll.'

Watson and Bellingham's parting shot as they left his office partly answered Barnes' question as to why the chairman had seemed reluctant to pursue this matter from the first and certainly not offered to support him at the meeting.

'Barnesy, the loss of the pro-celebrity tournament next year was probably more to do with the chairman's loss of his trousers, somewhere between the dining room and his eventual acceptance of a lift home with your lady assistant, who just so happened to be waiting outside the clubhouse at the very moment our honourable chairman made his departure. Maybe, we'll see you in the bar for a drink later, Mr. Secretary.'

Barnes optimistically thought that his day could only improve after the verbal battering he received from those two, but then remembered with dismay that he was expecting a delegation from the ladies' section, headed by the redoubtable, lady captain, 'Brunhilde' Maddox.

Gazing out of his window earlier, he'd seen Patsy Smythe leaving the practice green, her 30 minute golf lesson having unsurprisingly managed to absorb well over 55 minutes of 'Randy Richardson's' ever-so precious time. He'd often thought about asking Richardson for a few useful tips on how to deal with those more 'in your face' members of the ladies' section, but couldn't bring himself to admitting his failings in that direction with that 'sex-on-legs machine'.

As a police sergeant, he'd successfully managed to divert almost all of those female members of the local community that occasionally cluttered up his station, to one of his female colleagues, irrespective of the reason for their visit. Owners of lost cats, purses or husbands, through to drunks and 'druggies', were all firmly dispatched to a member of the 'knickers and knockers team', as they had been christened by some of the chauvinistic members of the station.

He'd quickly discovered that his professional and even his social skills for dealing with the range of females that passed through the station were almost nonexistent. He couldn't deal with either the 'weepers and wailers' who burst into floods of tears at the first sight of a uniform or, at the other extreme, those hard-faced, foul-mouthed types who threatened to take him and the station apart if they didn't get a fag and a cup of tea while they were waiting to see their 'nice solicitor.'

Now, of course, he found himself fairly regularly having to deal with the ladies' section of the golf club, particularly after the arrival of 'Brunhilde' Maddox as lady captain. He couldn't, as he had once found to his cost, delegate that job to his part-time assistant secretary, Denise Ratcliffe.

At first, he'd not been quite sure why this appointment of Denise had been necessary, particularly someone whose typing skills were limited to the use of two fingers, her computer skills to little more than playing patience and her telephone manner, which left callers wondering whether they'd contacted the speaking clock. He had, however, been reassured by the chairman, who had personally overseen her appointment after an uncharacteristically long interview and a lengthy lunch at a local restaurant, that her, 'hidden pool of talents', would soon be producing substantial benefits for the club.

Denise's not-so-hidden talents had, in fact, soon become the object of the chairman's undivided attention, as evidenced by various coincidental arrivals and departures from the club by the two on an ever increasingly regular basis. The most public of these had been the evening of the captain's dinner. As a result of the alleged unavailability of the entire fleet of the areas taxis and his wife's absence on one of her regular business trips abroad, the chairman had, in his words, 'very reluctantly had to call on the services of the club's assistant secretary.' The nature of the 'services' provided had certainly been the subject of some lengthy discussions in the bar for some days after, particularly as prior to leaving, he'd had to raid the lost property basket in the changing room for a pair of ill fighting shorts to replace his lost trousers.

Barnes had decided, on one particular occasion, to see if Denise's skills and attributes that were clearly working so successfully on the chairman, could be employed to pacify an enraged group of lady members. They had reported being harassed for a good part of their round by a group of visiting male golfers who had regularly driven golf balls over their heads and treated them to some flowery descriptions of their golf swings and some extremely unflattering phrases aimed at certain of their physical attributes.

Whatever skills Denise was employing to reduce the chairman to the level of a sex-crazed delinquent teenager, singularly failed to have any impact on this group of irate lady golfers. They dismissed her patronising attempts at pacifying their damaged feelings and egos with the speed to rival Schumacher's departure from the start line of a grand prix.

His own failure to appear from behind a strategically placed filing cabinet and retrieve the situation immediately was greeted by the ladies with a quite extraordinary outburst that virtually reduced the other clubhouse occupants to nervous wrecks. Emerging some time later in the car park, when he thought the coast was clear, he was confronted by a Greenham Common-type encampment, comprising of a few of the more determined members of the group, who made it very clear that if he wasn't capable of doing the job to which he was appointed, then they would personally 'move heaven and hell' to see that the club got someone who could.

Having to deal with the ladies' section of the club was, in itself, not exactly what one might term 'a stroll in the park', but, of course, what made matters worse was that he was regularly confronted by the more senior, power-wielding members of their committee, who seemed hell-bent on making his life a complete misery at every opportunity.

Facing a deputation from the ladies' committee, or even worse, the entire bunch of those 'handbag hooligans', was probably, he thought, a similar experience to that endured by the Roman soldiers when first faced by Boudicca's chariot-driving antics and attendant hordes or by the British constabulary trying to prise the Pankhurst sisters off Parliament's railings.

Based on his previous confrontations, he was now trying to first-guess what the agenda for this latest visitation might consist of: probably the lack of soap in the ladies' changing rooms, the state of the on-course toilets or the length of grass on their tees, he suspected.

He was somewhat relieved to find that only three of the committee had showed up this morning; the others were probably still at home putting the final touches to the manacling of their better halves to the domestic 'cell' to ensure that all chores were completed on time and to the required standard and to forestall any sloping off to the local for a few lunchtime bevvies. On the down side, the three did include Brenda Maddox, the lady captain and Jeanette Tyler, the lady vice captain, who had led the earlier 'ambush' in the clubhouse car park.

'Good morning, ladies, what a lovely day for a game of golf, pity we have to be stuck inside on a day like this, isn't it?' opened Barnes in the best conciliatory tone he could manage.

'Morning, Mr Secretary, when there are important matters needing to be dealt with, golf sometimes has to take second place,' replied the lady captain.

Barnes didn't like the sound of this at all, so thought he might try the 'another urgent meeting' tactic, but then wished he hadn't.

'Mr Secretary, we ladies regard this meeting as both urgent and important; we would not be here otherwise. So, we suggest you get your secretary, that is if she has now mastered the operation of the telephone system, to make your usual polite apologies to whoever it is you've 'set up' to ring you in a moment on the pretext of an emergency meeting about course drainage.'

The bloody cheek of the woman, thought Barnes, he pitied the poor bugger who was daily on the receiving end of this sort of mental and psychological cruelty.

'We've just had our copies of next year's golf club diary, Mr Secretary which, of course, has our ladies' section in it and we are, yet again as last year, faced with some quite disgraceful and this time embarrassing errors, which we attribute entirely to your total incompetence at the job of checking the proofs before the printers are instructed to run it off,' said the lady captain.

Barnes was beginning to wish the agenda had been about the absence of soap in the ladies' toilet, because this unexpected item had all the early indications of delivering a 'shed load of egg on face'. With the mood these ladies appeared to be in, he would count himself lucky if it was only the proverbial eggs that were broken and scrambled at the end of this meeting, rather than some other more sensitive parts of his anatomy.

The lady captain proceeded to toss the offending diary across the desk at him with the uncompromising threat, 'the ladies suggest you get this back out of circulation in the next 24 hours, make whatever grovelling apology you need to and set about getting a reprint done, this time, one without your schoolboy howlers.'

Barnes could not believe what he was hearing; how dare this woman come in here threatening him and demanding immediate action to retrieve all the club's diaries? He couldn't begin to guess what offending items in the diary had managed to fuel this outburst; it had looked fine to him when he gave it a cursory read the other night while he'd been watching Match of the Day on the box.

'What exactly is the matter with the diary, lady captain?' he tentatively enquired, 'I haven't received any complaints from any other quarter yet'.

'Probably not, Mr Secretary, because very few of the members of this club, we suspect, particularly the male members, appear to be in possession of the necessary literacy skills to be able to spot the kinds of errors that an average eight-year-old would have identified immediately. As regular readers of 'The Sun', they couldn't be expected to concern themselves with such trivial matters as spelling and punctuation.'

If Barnes could have tape recorded this conversation, he thought, he could have produced a back-lash in the club to rival that of the public's response to Thatcher's introduction of the poll tax.

'It is also significant, Mr Secretary, that this catalogue of errors is confined solely to the ladies' section of the diary, confirming our long-held belief that as far as you're concerned the ladies' section of this club ranks no higher in your priorities than the correct siting of a golfers' shoe-cleaning machine.'

Barnes was now beginning to look in desperation for some early resolution of this verbal personal assault, before he had recourse to clean the first aid kit out of aspirins.

'Perhaps you'd care to point out the offending items in the diary that seem to have been overlooked,' he offered, by way of getting a swift conclusion to his growing discomfort.

'Mr Secretary, our President this next year is Lady Penelope Schuster, not as it appears in the Club diary, 'Lady Penelope Schyster', remarked the lady vice captain tersely.

Oh my god, thought Barnes, how could he have missed that one? He could imagine the reaction that this gaff would cause in the bar when it finally got out. He'd never actually met the old bat, but he knew she had a reputation as a right 'ball breaker', judging by what others had said who had met her.

He knew her husband, of course, the poor old sod. He had been a frequent member of the bench when some of Barnes' cases had appeared before the local magistrates. As he recalled, on most of the occasions that Schuster appeared on the bench, he seemed to require the close assistance of his colleagues to help him keep track of the current time, day and month, let alone the precise nature of the case on which he was required to make a judgement. His magisterial comments and observations bore all the clarity and definition of a badly preserved sound track from a Donald Duck movie.

Barnes knew that there was more to come from this terrifying golfing 'triad' and half suspected that it might even be worse news.

'Mr Secretary, we'd like you to take a look at the competition for July 20th and reassure us that this was not a deliberate ploy on your part and your fellow jokers to extract the maximum embarrassment from the ladies' section,' demanded the lady captain.

Barnes hardly dared look at the offending date. What he saw did, at first, produce a sense of embarrassment, which after a moment, was replaced by an uncontrollable urge to burst out laughing.

The competition details should have read '4 Ball Better Ball Stableford; ladies to each bring their lucky draw prizes for the raffle.' What it actually read was, '4 Ball Better Ball Stableford; ladies to each bring their lucky drawers as prizes for the raffle.' He was damned sure that this was not what he had read in the proofed copy and began to wonder whether the selection of the printers recommended to him by one of the club's self-styled comedians was proving to be a grave error on his part.

A conspiratorial plot was, he felt, emerging as a distinct possibility here, one designed to inflict the maximum amount of embarrassment and discomfort on his rapidly sagging shoulders. The problem, as he fully realised, was that responsibility for sign-off lay with him and his failure to give the proofs 100 per cent of his attention had brought this verbal onslaught down on him with all the ferocity of a Florida hurricane.

He did not now dare look into the faces of the delegation, but sensed by their even more exaggerated movements that they were about to deliver their final 'nuclear administrative missile.'

'Mr Secretary, this club and the ladies' section in particular, are very proud of the fact that it has been chosen to host the most prestigious event of this county's golfing calendar. Unfortunately, your sheer incompetence and lack of professionalism in your job has irreparably damaged our reputation as a club worthy of such an honour.'

Barnes wondered whether things could get any worse other than to find himself being held solely responsible for two Iraqi wars, the astronomic rise in crude oil prices and the combined catastrophic fall of the DOW and FTSE indicators on the world money markets.

'Take a look at August 15th, Mr Secretary and tell us if you see anything amiss with the entry you've submitted for that championship competition.'

Barnes went pale as he spotted the typing error that should have been picked up when the proofs had been first sent to him. How could he not have spotted the embarrassing misspelling of the word 'County'; that single missing letter that was now going to require on his part, the biggest single grovelling apology that it had ever been his misfortune to have to deliver. The expression on the faces of the ladies' delegation intimated that a mere 'sorry' would fall very well short of the forelock-touching, outright self-denunciation statement that they were here to demand.

'Ladies, I can't think how I came to miss this error; what can I say or write by way of an apology to the ladies' section?'

'That's easy, Mr Secretary,' said the lady captain, 'we don't want an apology, spoken or written, you'd probably spell it wrong anyway; we just want the whole thing corrected and you've got one week. Our letter to the chairman, with the detailed minutes of this meeting will be on his desk tomorrow.'

At this, the delegation were up and out of his office before he had a chance to explain the cost involved in a complete reprint of the diary, even if he'd had the nerve to introduce such a grubby detail as money.

How the hell, thought Barnes, am I going to break this news to Brown, the chairman of finance? He could well see a large contribution being asked for from him, knowing his well-earned reputation for not spending a penny more of the club's money than he had to and certainly not on bailing out other peoples' incompetence. He suspected that this week's meeting of the executive committee that he was required to attend and report to, could well be a re-enactment of the 'Good Friday' crucifixion.

Barnes' arrival at the monthly meeting of the executive committee had all the semblance of the early Christians' entry into the Roman Coliseum, facing the prospect of complete mutilation by a group of bloody-thirsty carnivores. The sudden lull in the social chit chat, the ensuing silence as he took his seat and the absence of a welcome greeting from any committee member, suggested that he was about to experience a very hostile, threatening and potentially humiliating 'mauling' at the hands of these latter-day golfing gladiators.

Having gone through the usual opening business of apologies for absence and previous minutes, Tomlinson, the chairman launched into the main agenda items.

'Right, ladies and gentlemen, to the main business matters of the meeting. To start with, we have this bloody farce over the errors in the club diary to sort out; this matter is making us look like a right load of prats and if we re-print, it's going to cost the club a packet.'

'Mr Chairman, we all know who the prat is that's responsible for this cock-up. I want to know what he has to say for himself,' said Brown, the club's chairman of finance, staring straight at Barnes.

'Mr Secretary, do you have anything you'd like to say at this point?' offered the chairman.

'I have apologized to the ladies' section in my weekly meeting with them and accepted full responsibility for the error. I did not discuss their demand that it be reprinted,' grovelled Barnes rather sotto voce, by comparison with his usual high decibel delivery.

'Barnes, the truth is, you're absolutely bloody hopeless when it comes to managing the affairs of this club; I don't know how you came to get the sodding job in the first place,' argued Brown.

'I know how he got it,' said the lady captain, 'he inveigled his way into the good books of our past captain who railroaded his appointment through committee.'

'That's absolute bollocks,' said Anderson, the past captain, who was now chairman of the house committee, 'I resent that accusation from the lady captain who, if we're trading accusations here, has just managed to get her friend and next door neighbour appointed as handicap secretary who, I understand from my sources, had to have the term 'Standard Scratch' explained to her in a recent ladies' committee meeting.'

'I would appreciate it Mr Chairman, if you could ask the chairman of house to modify his language, which might be appropriate among the more loutish members of his golfing partners, but is deeply offensive to other more sensitive members of this committee.'

'I'd be most interested to learn what the lady captain knows about sensitive members,' said the chairman of house, which brought an uncontrollable fit of the giggles from various male and even some of the female members present.

'Mr Chairman, if the gentleman, and I use that term loosely, continues to speak to me in those terms, I will request that he be asked to leave the meeting.'

'Gentlemen, ladies, this is not helping us reach a decision on what to do about the diary,' interjected the chairman.

'Well it's damned obvious isn't it, it's got to be done again,' said Dickson, 'it's deeply offensive to the ladies; I'm not at all surprised by their anger and frustration at what's happened.'

Everyone was deeply suspicious about the sudden support for the ladies' section of the club that Dickson was now demonstrating, given that in the past he was well known as one of the leaders of a gang of 'retards', campaigning to actually reduce ladies' rights and playing times on the grounds that they paid less than the men in annual subscriptions. Most now suspected that this generosity of spirit related directly to his need for support for his nomination to the selection committee for the club's vice captaincy.

'We shouldn't let that prat off the hook,' said Rowlands, the handicap secretary, 'these mistakes are happening all too often. Take what happened at that presentation evening the other month, when the secretary was left to announce the winners and award the prizes.'

Barnes was wondering how long it would take for some

sod to resurrect that gaff he'd made over the business of the prizes.

'Fancy starting with 20th prize and allowing the person in last place to help themselves to the best of the prizes,' said Rowlands, 'if it hadn't been spotted so soon, there'd have only been the box of three golf balls, the flowers and the tablecloth left for the winners to choose from. Everyone had to bring what they'd taken, back and we had to start afresh, the visitors thought they'd pitched up at the local mental hospital's annual prize giving.'

'That statement is deeply offensive, Mr Chairman, the handicap secretary should not make disparaging remarks about people with such impairments.'

'The only person displaying mental impairment is our damn secretary,' said Rowlands.

'Mr Chairman, while I am aware of that unfortunate incident over the prizes, I don't see why I should have to sit here and have to listen to such personal abuse,' said Barnes

'The secretary was not so quick to react when the ladies were the subject of such abuse on the course the other week,' said the lady captain, 'he chose to hide behind the filing cabinet and his secretary's skirts when we attempted to confront him with what we'd had to endure from that group of louts.'

'At least he wasn't hiding inside his secretary's skirts,' muttered someone.

'Mr Chairman, this really is not acceptable, will you please take more control of the meeting to remove the objectionable contributions made by some members of the committee?' interjected the lady handicap secretary.

'I do not require prompting from members on how to run a meeting,' added the chairman tersely, 'but I would appreciate it if we could get back to where we started and a decision about the diary.'

'Oh for god's sake, I propose we get the thing done again and get on to the next business, we're going to be here all night at this rate; the bar shuts in two hours,' said Dickson agitatedly

'Oh and I suppose you'll foot the bill for the reprint will you, or explain to the members why their subs had to be used twice to print the diary,' said Brown.

Dickson had no intention of facing an angry AGM if he got the vice captaincy, with the news that the club had paid twice for the diary.

'I suggest we try to get the printers to do it free in return for our business next year or at least ask them to do it at cost.'

'Are you kidding, you idiot?' said Thompson who'd, unbeknown to most of the committee, surreptitiously got this print job for a friend of his, 'they're not running a bloody charity you know and anyway, it's not their fault, they just print what they're sent.'

Barnes was not at all sure about the truth of this statement and was deeply suspicious about whether some tampering with the proofs had gone on, but he knew he'd never be able to prove it. He wished now that he'd made a copy of what he'd sent them.

'How about Barnesy coughing up for the cock-up?' said Rowlands. 'Maybe next time he'd be more careful and not proof read it at the same time as planning his summer holiday.'

'I think the golf club has, at the end of the day, to take the responsibility and cover the cost,' said the chairman, 'we can't ask the secretary to pay.'

'Well I propose that this job of producing the club diary in future is done by someone who can read and write to a standard that bears an accurate resemblance to the Queen's English,' proposed Rowlands, 'otherwise we'll be here again next year discussing the same problem.'

'Oh and I suppose you'll put yourself and one of your cronies forward for that job as well,' said the lady captain to Rowlands, 'someone with all the experience and skill of a devoted 'Sun' reader.'

'The lady captain seems to know an awful lot about the vital requirements for employment at that particular newspaper, Mr Chairman, I must have missed her entry on page three somewhere,' remarked Rowlands in return.

'That is a deeply offensive remark, Mr Chairman and I would like you to ask for an unqualified apology from the gentleman.'

'Mr Rowlands, I think you're gradually reducing this meeting to the level of the contents of a University Rag magazine and I would ask you to apologize to the lady captain,' demanded the chairman.

'Mr Chairman, it appears to me,' said Rowlands, 'that our honourable secretary has already, unaided, done my job for me by reducing the club diary to the level of a Rag magazine, but I apologize for any inaccuracy relating to the lady captain's previous employment.'

Barnes was, at long last, beginning to enjoy this because he was witnessing a rapid and quite satisfactory end to this agenda item. He was also enjoying the verbal gymnastics that was going on between the members, particularly those trying to out-do one another on the personal abuse stakes.

'Right ladies and gentlemen, do I have a proposer and seconder for the proposal that the diary is reprinted, that the old copies are recalled and that we ask the printers to do it free or at worst, at cost, with the promise of the job next year,' said the chairman.

'Hang on, Mr Chairman, you can't bundle all that bloody lot together and railroad it through as one proposal,' said Rowlands.

Here we go again, thought Barnes, now we've got another skirmish on our hands.

'Rowlands,' interjected Dickson, forgetting for one moment that he was canvassing him for support for his vice captaincy, 'will you just shut up and vote on the proposal as requested, I'd like to get one drink in before the bar closes.'

'Right, ladies and gentlemen, the majority seem in favour of that proposal, so can we now move on to the next item on the agenda.'

'Would that be the appointment of a new secretary, Mr Chairman?' muttered Rowlands, just loud enough for everyone to hear.

Barnes thought that if he ever got the opportunity to set up that irritating, self-opinionated little sod for some public misdemeanour, he would see to it that the maximum amount of local publicity, naturally from sources unknown, was lavished on his case.

At that particular moment, the thought of attracting media attention and press publicity acted as a stark reminder to Barnes that the following day, he'd regrettably agreed to meet a journalist from one of the national golf magazines that was proposing to include a feature in a forthcoming edition on golf clubs in the area.

Although he'd eventually agreed to the meeting, he was secretly not particularly looking forward to it as his previous encounters with the paparazzi, when in uniform, particularly the local bunch of 'hackers', had usually ended in a monumental distortion and misrepresentation of what he'd said or, at least tried to say under the pressure of their 'Gestapo-like' questioning techniques, to the point where it was almost unrecognisable. As a consequence of what they had done to his photograph on one occasion, a mischievous poster had appeared at the station, claiming that the figure represented was now the subject of an Interpol investigation for suspected terrorist activities.

He had, however, been reassured by the latest recipient of 'Swankers'' ever-increasing catalogue of money-wasting appointments, namely, the self-styled marketing manager, that this was an essential strategy in keeping the club, 'in the golf marketing and promotional loop,' as he had expressed it. Barnes failed to see why there was the necessity for the club to be in any form of sodding 'loop', whatever the hell that meant; everybody knew it was here, they knew what it did and if they wanted to know more they could damn well pitch up and find out for themselves.

Barnes had never quite understood why the executive

committee had suddenly, in its misplaced wisdom, decided that it needed a marketing manager. As far as he was aware, he was quite capable of drafting the odd notice or two for members, though his recent exploits with the club diary had provided a bit of a 'wake up call' on the old checking skills. He'd even managed to produce one or two worthwhile pieces for the local papers, not to mention a short 'sound bite', or whatever the hell these media wallahs called it, for local radio, though this had been slightly marred by an unexpected fit of hiccups that had somewhat reduced his contribution to a series of bullet-like utterances made by someone who had just completed the London Marathon in six hours.

Now, he was being asked to cooperate with this jargon-generating, theory-crazed twerp who would never use five words if 15 were thought to be more impressive. The first time he'd met him to speak to, he reckoned that he'd only understood about 10 per cent of what he'd actually said, the rest sounded like a series of management and marketing jargon phrases culled from a 'Bluffers Guide to Sounding a Complete Prat.'

To Barnes, the name 'Julian' reminded him of one of that famous pair of 'poncey' characters created by the actor Kenneth Williams in a radio series with Kenneth Horne. He had come with what Brown the chairman of finance had assured him was an impeccable CV, listing a second class honours degree in media studies from a university that Barnes never even knew existed, a six month spell after graduating, working in McDonalds, 'awaiting the right opening for my talents' and a spell with the local 'rag', covering all the thrills and spills of garden fetes, local council meetings, school sports and WI open days. Barnes noted however, that he'd also come with cast iron assurances from Brown that, 'his nephew was bristling with new ideas about how to put the golf club on the map.' Barnes was not yet sure that even given this so-called map, that this latest addition to the nepotistic ranks of golf club employees could have actually found his way to the golf club entrance.

Barnes suspected that this latest visit from the 'journos' was more about keeping the face of the new marketing manager in 'the public eye' and ingratiating himself with his uncle and his co-conspirators on the committee than anything to do with benefiting the golf club.

'Morning Barnes, 'are we go' for this morning's strategic face-to-face with the golf 'journo' on the subject of the club's strategic corporate communication and marketing policy for improving both customer and organisational rapport?'

Here we go again, thought Barnes, another delivery of incomprehensible bullshit guaranteed to drive one's senses into meltdown.

'Of course, Julian. I've made a few notes on the plans for the extension to the car park and the new lighting planned for the ladies' trolley shed,' said Barnes, wondering whether 'Jules' could recognise a piss-take when it hit him.

'Yes, well, er fine, but I think we should extend the parameters of the discussion a little to encompass some other more product-orientated developments for this vital segment of the local leisure industry with a little more specificity. Don't you agree?'

I might, thought Barnes, if I could understand what the bloody hell you're on about. The arrival of the 'journo' with his photographer precluded any further damage to Barnes' mental processes from this barrage of academic drivel.

'Gentlemen, perhaps you could start by telling me about how the club has developed over the last two or three years, important changes, significant additions, you know what I mean?' said the 'journo'.

'Well Geoff,' said Julian, 'until very recently, the club had no clear strategic plan or mission statement vis-à-vis potential organisational or operational developments. There had been very little market research carried out into customer needs or, for that matter, the segmentation of customer expectations and aspirations in the golf sector. No real thought had been given to positioning the organisation in relation to its competitors and no SWOT had been done.'

The expression on the face of the 'journo' said it all, thought Barnes, as the poor sod struggled to try to take notes from the tirade of tripe to which he'd just been subjected. The photographer had clearly given up after five words and was already staring out of the window at a particularly attractively attired ladies' four-ball going down the first fairway.

'Yes, I see,' lied the 'journo' in a desperate attempt to give the impression that this was the type of critical information which his editor had sent him on a 400-mile round trip to gather and for which their monthly readers were waiting with uncontrollable excitement.

'So, can you tell me what our readers can look forward to if they decide to spend a day here?'

Barnes thought it was about time to give him something he could actually spell and the readers could understand without having to use a management thesaurus, so was about to give him details of the course, the food, the bar and the other facilities like the full size snooker table and the swimming pool and squash courts, along with the plans for another nine hole golf course, when the marketing maestro struck again.

'I've spent a considerable amount of time developing a USP for the organisation, coupled with a more customer orientated approach towards offering a more market-led product that will fit with the identifiable niche in which we see ourselves competing.'

Barnes couldn't believe his ears, this 'walking management encyclopaedia' had only been here three weeks, but made it sound as though he'd been running the place for months. He could tell that the 'journo' was desperately searching around for anything intelligible that he could take back to his boss, otherwise the excessively high expense claim he would be putting in for the trip was already dead in the water.

'Tell me about some of the outstanding features of your course, in particular which you would regard as the 'signature hole' that we might use for a photograph.'

Barnes was wondering what jargon-ridden response 'Jules'

was going to use to grace this simple question, given that he'd never actually set foot on the course and would be hard pressed to actually identify one hole from another.

'Essentially, we have a uniquely designed golfing environment, ideally suited to a cross sectional mix of our own customers and those others we have identified as our potential target market. In its design you will find a blend of innovative features that provide a challenging and rewarding experience, but you will also observe certain imitative features that resemble the highest quality standards in this particular field of recreational activities.'

At this point, the 'journo' metaphorically hoisted the 'surrender flag' with the suggestion that the photographer be shown around in order to gather some shots of the course. The panic in the eyes of the 'snapper' was clearly visible at the prospect of being escorted around by this 'incontinent talking dictionary' and in a clearly directed plea to Barnes said, 'Mr Secretary, perhaps you'd be good enough to drive me around in one of the club's buggies to point out the main features of the course,' hoping against hope that the 'patron saint of snappers' was looking after him and provide only a two-seater buggy.

Barnes was only too happy to escape from any further incomprehensible utterances from the 'nutty nephew' and left the 'journo' searching for his own excuses for having to make a sudden and unforeseen exit.

After the trials and tribulations of the day so far, it was positively sybaritic driving around in the buggy in the relative peace and quiet of the course and away from the aggravation and irritation that seemed to have been hitting him like a tidal wave of late.

Then he spotted the head green keeper heading his way at a fair rate of knots, with a demeanour that resembled an ancient Crusader preparing for battle, and knew that he was about to be the unwilling recipient of yet another verbal onslaught that would threaten to ensure that his blood pressure would probably remain at the stratospherically dangerous level it had reached since he'd taken over this damn job.

'Hi there, Bert, you look as though you're about to allow me to qualify for an entry into the Guinness Book of Records for the most amount of aggravation suffered by a golf club secretary in one week,' said Barnes, attempting some cheerful way of defusing the inevitable onslaught.

'Bloody, Watson, chairman of greens' committee, I hate his guts,' shouted Bert. 'What that guy knows about looking after a golf course wouldn't cover a torn stamp.'

Barnes suggested to the 'snapper' that he take the buggy and head for the 14th green with its unbroken views of the remaining holes, that is, providing he carefully angled the lens away from the nearby breakers yard, the local cemetery and some open cast mining activity and, more importantly, out of earshot of any more of Bert's choice metaphors of his so-called line manager.

Bert's run-ins with Watson and his committee were legendary and on a par with any Lord of the Rings feature-length movie. On the one hand, you had someone whose whole life had been devoted to the highly skilled business of cultivating fine quality turf for tees and fairways, coupled with unrivalled seasonal knowledge of what to do and when, in terms of producing superb greens. On the other hand, you had a second-hand car salesman appointed as chairman of greens whose knowledge of cultivating and maintaining greens barely extended beyond the basic rule of 'green side up'. To add insult to injury, Bert had been saddled with a committee whose combined skills in this area would hardly have qualified them to look after a hanging basket, let alone a 120-acre golf course.

'Now what's got you gunning for that sod again, Bert?' enquired Barnes. 'This must be the sixth time this year you've been threatening to reduce him to compost.'

'Well he's sent me this note hasn't he, telling me that the

greens' committee want me to hollow-tine all the greens in the next week. The daft sod doesn't understand anything about it. You can't do it now, it could ruin the greens for the rest of the year and then the shit would hit the fan,' explained Bert.

Barnes was partly relieved that he was not, as he first suspected, the object of Bert's explosive anger, but that somebody else would soon be getting the full decibel count. The problem for Bert, of course, was that he had no regular direct access to the committee. All communication was via these curt notes that, almost daily, he found pinned to the door of his shed. The chairman of greens had never even considered the idea of inviting Bert to a meeting or at least talking to him immediately before a meeting to discuss the latest plans for maintenance of the course. Barnes suspected that Watson was secretly terrified of Bert's forthright style, as well as his knowledge, hence the minimal contact approach.

The committee took the arrogant view that, not only did they 'know best' about what was needed, but were of the collective opinion that the head green keeper and his staff were simply there to implement their well-informed instructions. It had never even occurred to these 'golfing ostriches' that the course and the club might actually benefit from listening to what someone with over 30 years of course management experience could offer a motley collection of estate agents, accountants, shop keepers, insurance salesmen and travel agents.

'Bert, what do you want me to do? You know that that shower never listen to a word I say and my personal star is not exactly in the ascendancy at the moment. I simply turn up to the greens' committee meetings as a paid employee to listen and record the confounded drivel that regularly gets referred to as, 'the wishes of the meeting'. Very rarely does the chairman ask for a vote on any item because everyone knows that the whole bloody issue has been decided by two or three people before the meeting ever gets started.'

'Barnesy, I've had enough of these plonkers who think they know best,' complained Bert. 'Between you and me, I've had an offer of a job as head green keeper, with a club who've offered me a car, a house, more staff, a bigger budget and half as much salary again as I'm getting here. I'm seriously considering giving this lot the elbow.'

Sadly, thought Barnes, this was, of course, exactly what the committee had been working towards for sometime, in the belief that they could then appoint someone who would be prepared to dance to their every tune instead of that 'cantankerous bastard we've got now,' as one member, almost, but not quite, out of earshot of Barnes, had so callously put it.

'Bert, you're never going to get your own way with this lot, as you well know, but there again, you and I know that golf clubs, like many other clubs, are not renowned for being places where one's hard-earned, professional knowledge and skills are ever going to be truly recognised or appreciated. They're places where money, influence, a loud voice and, generally, all the appeal and charm of a Rottweiler carry much more weight than anyone with a legitimate claim to actually knowing what they're talking about.'

Barnes left Bert pondering on his and, for that matter, his own future at the club and went in search of 'Harry the Snapper', hoping that he hadn't encountered the local resident whose garden acted as a boundary to the golf course and for whom the regular and persistent arrival of golf balls in his garden, or worse still on the roof of his conservatory, was the subject of an extremely large file of letters in Barnes' office.

Please god, thought Barnes, if you're listening, spare me for the rest of the week from yet another 'close encounter' with a set of irate golfers, male or female, an enraged or deranged set of club officials or a homicidal house owner, all seemingly hell bent on making the life of a golf club's secretary feel like on a par with an inmate of an American-style 'death row' penitentiary.

CHAPTER 3

THE CAPTAIN'S TALE or 'I believe this club deserves the very best, I'm pleased to accept your nomination.'

Taking on the job of captain of a golf club is rather like agreeing to be strapped into one of those nerve-jangling roller coaster rides that have become so popular at some of the more well-known British theme parks and holiday resorts. As you're slammed and buffeted from side to side, frequently subjected to unpleasant levels of pressure on various parts of one's anatomy, uncertain as to whether you're on your head, your feet or your back-side or, for that matter, which way you're facing, the only consolation is that the bowel-loosening ride only lasts for three minutes, whereas the yearly captaincy of a golf club can seem to last for what feels like an eternity.

Watching you during both these experiences, of course, will be many of the gleeful faces of those who you considered to be your friends and who encouraged your participation in this piece of jollity, now standing well back observing your pain and discomfort from a very safe distance. If, as you hurtle through the air at ever-changing speeds and in ever-changing directions on one of these rides, you are lucky enough to be accompanied by these friends, you do at least have the satisfaction of witnessing their own particular levels of discomfort. As golf club captain, you frequently feel that you're the only person on this 'ride' and that the maniac at the controls is going to keep you on it until your sanity is history.

Both experiences begin with a mixture of eager anticipation and even excitement at the prospect of the pleasurable moments that lie ahead. At the same time, both are tinged with a degree of anxiety, uncertainty and foreboding as to whether one should be embarking on such a crazy venture. As you literally or metaphorically 'strap' yourself into both of these tortuously designed sets of experiences, you wonder why the hell you volunteered to put yourself in this position or why you allowed the masochistic sod, whose idea it was to get you 'aboard', to get within a day's march of you.

Admittedly, it is fair to say that both experiences do take the hapless individual to some dizzying heights of quite pleasurable experiences, but can equally catapult them down, at a most alarming speed, to unexpected depths of discomfort and pain. Both experiences are, in their own particular way, quite capable at any moment of removing any sense of balance, dignity and clarity of the senses the 'traveller' might claim to possess, as their familiarly discernible world is suddenly turned upside down at some unexpected turn of events.

The overriding feeling that you are hurtling along both these dangerous 'journeys' without, in any real sense, being in control or command of the 'vehicle' to which you've been assigned can be quite alarming. Changing direction, reducing or increasing the pace at which things are happening to you, or even stopping altogether, are not freely available options to either of these 'joy riders'.

So, why then does someone actually choose to become the captain of a golf club? The fact is that, in spite of sound advice and incontrovertible evidence from their predecessors that accepting this role could do more damage to their health than smoking 60 cigarettes or consuming a couple of bottles of gin a day, there is never any shortage of volunteers willing to put their heads in this 'lion's den of golfing administration'.

Threats of divorce proceedings from their spouse, immediate departure from home by their children, rejection by their beloved pets and the loss of their much-prized company parking spot by their business partner do not seem sufficient deprivations to deter these 'golfing devotees' from embarking on this perilous pilgrimage.

There are very few known instances of the offer of captaincy being rejected, though clearly the appeal of the job did, in one case, very rapidly evaporate. At the AGM of one particular golf club, the point was reached in the agenda at which the key positions for the following year, including the captaincy, were to be ratified. Having sat through more than three hours of heated argument, complaints, votes of no confidence, calls for the resignation of existing post holders and levels of personal abuse of quite alarming proportions from some of the more bullish members, the captain elect stood up, asked that his nomination be withdrawn and walked out of the meeting. There followed a hastily convened meeting of the selection committee in the Gents' toilet to try to fill the vacancy with another 'sacrificial lamb'.

Motives for taking on the captaincy vary enormously. They range from the loyal and thoroughly altruistic desire to give something back to one's club and long-time supportive colleagues, to an out and out desire to wield imperious levels of power and gain control of what such candidates regard as a bunch of incompetent no-hopers who could not be trusted to run a Christmas raffle properly, let alone the administrative and managerial affairs of a golf club.

Those nominees, for whom status and self-aggrandisement are the driving forces, regularly seek out this opportunity with all the determination and ferocity of schoolboys in search of their sporting hero's autographed photograph. Neither must it be said are they above using the same aggressive, no-holes-barred tactics as their younger counterparts to achieve their ends.

It is not uncommon, of course, for the acquisition of this prestigious position to produce chameleon-like changes in the holder. Previously friendly, unassuming, self-effacing, mild mannered individuals, on discovering they've inherited this 'poisoned golfing chalice,' have been known to metamorphose into raging, uncontrollable, intolerant tyrants for whom the slightest hint of dissent or opposition is a cue for acts of wholesale 'golfing genocide'.

Very occasionally, of course, captains 'disappear' in their year of office, some literally, others metaphorically. Some have been known to disappear, according to many members, because their sudden rise to fame has also been accompanied by entirely predictable, 'risings' and 'failings' in the club's notorious 'Sexual Scramble' as opposed to golf's more traditional version, the 'Texas Scramble'. Often these entanglements involve fellow members of the club, with the resulting division of loyalties between the two sets of followers and the club's rumour and gossip machine working in overdrive. For such highly-tuned sexual athletes, thus forced to 'fall on their sword', it may have brought a premature end to their membership of the golf club, but is often merely a stepping stone to 'postures new' in the local rowing, tennis or squash club.

Other captains have been known to disappear in the sense that their presence at the club and their contribution during their year of office has hardly broken the surface of members' consciousness. Predicted, prior to their appointment, to be among the greatest of the 'movers and shakers' in the club, they completed their year with all the impact and punch of a box of damp fire works. New members were left asking if the club actually had a captain and the existing members behaving as a group of courtiers in waiting, longing for the return of an exiled and often ridiculed predecessor.

If some peoples' motives for accepting the captaincy are shrouded in mystery, the same can certainly be said for some clubs' methods of electing one of their members to this esteemed position. As one captain aptly described the process, 'it felt more as though I was being anointed rather than appointed.'

In some clubs, the appointment appears to adopt a set of

complex processes not too dissimilar from those used in the election of a new Pope to the Vatican, with its own form of closed nominations for preferred candidates, secret balloting, bizarre short listing criteria and voting procedures which would baffle the most knowledgeable of general election pundits.

At the conclusion of such convoluted processes, both the successful candidate and the unsuccessful candidates are left wondering whether the real object of the exercise, far from being to ensure the appointment of the right person to the job, was more about fulfilling the overwhelming ambition of those power-wielding control freaks in the executive committee to scale even greater heights of self-importance.

At least, in these cases, it could be claimed that some form of due process for making the appointment had been discussed and established and, in the very broadest sense of the term, adhered to. The process may not have appeared fair, but at least the candidates were aware of these idiosyncratic procedures when they allowed their name to be put forward.

By contrast, in some clubs, the appointment of club captain is more akin to an ecclesiastical 'laying on of hands' by some notable and ancient worthy of the club, whose dust-gathering administrative skills could rival some of the ancient golfing equipment hanging on the clubhouse wall in terms of their effectiveness for contemporary use. The style and approach is characterized by the whispered hint, the knowing nod and, in some cases, even the telltale handshake.

The formal 'trigger' to this charade begins with the all-important telephone call late into the night at the conclusion of some clandestine gathering of the local 'coven' of committee members, pulled together to ratify a decision that had, in fact, been made many weeks earlier. The recipient of the call is honour-bound to continue the role play by exhibiting an exaggerated sense of complete surprise and astonishment that he was even being considered for such a high office and was truly of the opinion that there were more worthy candidates for the post. Additional melodrama is provided by the recipient's protestations of inadequacy and a sense of utter humility at having such an honour bestowed on him, coupled even with a plea for a short time to consider the invitation, naturally in consultation with his long-suffering partner.

This elaborate charade, of course, is being played out against the backdrop of the fact that he has already made it known to the 'coven' that he would unequivocally accept the invitation in order to avoid any embarrassment to the 'worthies' of having their ever-so magnanimous gesture rejected. Coupled with this is the fact that his name already appears under the title 'Captain' on the proof copies of the club diary currently sitting on the printer's desk and that an appointment has already been made for him for a fitting at the local gents' outfitters for his captain's blazer.

All demands or pleas by the more enlightened and emancipated members of the club for a more democratic process of election are rapidly dismissed with the assertion that this is the 'established way of doing things in this club and it has always worked well for us in the past'. One mutinous-minded member of a certain prestigious golf club, faced with this asinine logic, was heard to reply, 'the same justification was used for the methods employed to identify witches in the middle ages.'

In yet other clubs, the principle of employing the 'old friends' network as a means of appointing a captain from one year to the next can still be found alive and flourishing. The practice is for the in-coming captain to approach a long-term friend with an invitation to act as his vice captain on the understanding that the job of captaincy will naturally follow.

The more astute people watchers in these clubs will witness the hastily formed friendship circles surrounding the incoming captain when the appointment of vice is imminent. The jockeying for such ignoble positions at the captain's side as chief drinks provider, table clearer, chauffeur, foursomes partner, bridge partner, dinner guest and all round dogsbody and shoe cleaner could not be more transparent if the individuals concerned were to go around wearing a label with the words, 'Me, Me' on their shirt fronts.

With the wide scale variation in the ways in which golf club captains are selected, it is no surprise to find that the criteria used for this task are equally diverse.

In what is now the very dim and distant past, there was a tradition that the captain had, at least, to have a reasonable level of competence at the game, frequently playing off a single figure handicap and ranked among the top two-dozen golfers in the club. The captain was expected to be knowledgeable about every aspect of the rules of the game and would, in the absence of the professional, be frequently asked to arbitrate in disputes on members' golfing misdemeanours.

Captains in the past were expected to be able to speak coherently, confidently and with authority on its behalf at special private and public events, both inside and outside the club, occasionally with the close attention of various forms of the media. Their knowledge of the etiquette involved in playing the game and of the appropriate codes of behaviour and dress, both on and off the course, was taken for granted.

Times have changed. Ability to play the game well is now no longer an essential requirement for the captaincy, as witnessed by the antics of some holders of the post at their inaugural 'drive in', when their opening drive either leaves the tee at ankle height, barely getting past the ladies' tee or balloons into the air and sets off in the direction of the members' car park. Their subsequent progress around the course is accompanied by shouts of 'fore', frequent visits to relatively un-charted areas of the more wooded parts of the course, regular and predictable visits to the golf bag for yet another new missile and the equally essential evasive action from their playing partners as life-threatening swings, and their highly predictable results, head unerringly for the more vulnerable parts of their person.

Rather predictably, their knowledge of the rules of the game is extremely scant, as witnessed on those occasions when their ball, or that of their partners or opponents, is in the rough, a hazard, out of bounds or lost. All kinds of weird and wonderful interpretations of even the simplest rules are produced, largely in order for the honourable gentleman and captain to be allowed to continue playing the hole and not require a calculator at its conclusion to work out his score.

At one golf club's monthly quiz night, specifically organised to help members acquire a better understanding of the rules of the game, the captain's team, comprised of some of the club's golfing notables, was reputed to have had the lowest total of any team, including a team made up of the very best junior golfers. Their failure to be able to distinguish between different types of water hazards, their ignorance of the rules on getting relief from various objects and the penalties for playing the incorrect ball in the various forms of the game, was highlighted with some well-delivered sarcastic humour by the handicap secretary and quizmaster in his announcement of the results.

Copies of the Royal and Ancient's Rules of Golf were subsequently to be found in the captain's pigeon-hole, sellotaped to the windscreen of his car, his golf buggy and the captain's chair in the clubhouse, as well as to the captain's bell hanging at the bar! There was even a copy found hanging in the Gents' toilet with the tag, 'Not for any use by the captain other than reading'.

Occasions for listening to the oratorical skills of these 'doyens of drivel' should, if at all possible, be avoided like an on-course lake filled with man-eating crocodiles. Many so-called performances are punctuated with so many incoherent mutterings, stutterings, hesitations, repetitions and mispronunciations that one might easily be forgiven for thinking that you'd inadvertently been connected to a very bad telephone line in Azerbijan. Attempts at delivering anything faintly humorous are usually followed by a prolonged period of embarrassed silence from the audience, but thoroughly unjustified gales of laughter from this would-be Billy Connolly. Everyone present is desperately praying that this excruciatingly, bum-aching performance is not going to conclude with a hole-by-hole account of the round to which his fellow partners and opponents have been subjected.

Visions of sartorial elegance, either on the course or in the clubhouse, are now also a rarity, as some of these newly appointed golfing 'moguls' turn out in apparel that they appeared to have donned in the dark, while still under the influence of the previous nights drinking excesses. Some of the items, for that matter, frequently look for all the world as though they had, in fact, spent the night in very close proximity to the wearer.

Creased and crumpled trousers that have long parted company with the top of the shoes, sweaters that have more holes than a Gruyere cheese and the entire ensemble all topped off with a hat that appears to have been recently recovered from beneath the wheels of a steam roller. Those more daring members of this fraternity can occasionally be seen in those ill-fitting, baggy khaki shorts, the condition of which would make Baden Powell turn in his grave. Matters are made worse by the fact that they are usually accompanied by a pair of badly matching coloured socks which over the course of 18 holes make their inevitable descent in a series of uncoordinated wrinkles to somewhere just above the ankle, leaving the wearer looking like a candidate for the lead in a re-make of Wurzel Gummidge.

There are, of course, exceptions to this vision of the golfing world's fashion equivalent of Steptoe and Son. Some captains step on to that first tee on their opening day in the role, resplendent in the very latest offerings from the combined talents of such designers as Lyle and Scott, Pringle, Ashworth and Cutter and Buck. Sadly, for many however, their performance around the more verdant and deeply overgrown parts of the golf course, coupled with the vagaries of the British climate, rapidly reduce the visual impact of these expensive fashion accessories to the status of car boot sale bargains.

Clearly, golf club selection committees do have criteria for selecting their captains, though very few people would claim that it's an exact science. Time and money appear to be high on the list of requirements, since most captains, rather like doctors, are expected to be on-call 18 hours a day for golf club business, as well as holding down their actual day job.

The expectation of the captain in some clubs is that they will play in every competition, attend every function and meeting, travel to other clubs' competitions as its representative and generally be around and be seen by the members seven days a week.

Money, rather like oxygen, is also a major requirement, not only to be able to cover the amount of time required, but also to fund, at least in part, some of the expensive shenanigans which adorn every captain's year. Top of the pile, naturally, is captain's day itself, but there are many others that require the presence of the captain's wallet as well as his person.

A liberal portion of clout and influence in the local and even wider community does not go amiss with those in charge of getting the proverbial 'white smoke up the chimney.' Golf clubs are often in need of friends in high places when things like planning permission, favourably priced contracts or a source of cheap or even free goods and services are sought. If the captain can ease the club into and through the tortuous corridors of local power politics, then he's already got one arm up the sleeve of the cherished blazer.

There are, of course, some other essential, but not so easily measurable criteria for the job of captain, including skin the texture of a rhino to be able to take the knocks and bumps that come with the territory. A slight hearing impairment can also be of value in minimising the impact of the continuous complaining that will be directed at him from every quarter of the membership. It's also useful in closing out the more unpleasant insults, accusations and downright libellous statements that will find their way to the surface of many clubhouse conversations, just at the moment that he puts his head around the door.

Stir into this heady mix of knowledge, skills and characteristics, qualities such as the patience of Job, the wisdom of Solomon and the determination of an Olympic gold medallist combined with a degree of cunning and deviousness that would be the envy of a front bench parliamentary spokesman on crime and law and order and one has the ideal recipe for a first rate golf club captain.

Denis Scott, more popularly known as 'the Dredger', the current captain at 'Swankers', had most of the aforementioned skills and qualities in spades, particularly those that might be defined as rather to the 'left of the tracks' when it came to matters requiring an economic use of the truth and sleight of hand.

Denis was catapulted into the role on the 'old pals' ticket by his mate and fellow golfing hacker, Roger Dempsey who had taken the role of club captain in the previous year to new and unrealised heights of incompetence. Among the best-remembered disasters of Dempsey's year was the erection of an elaborate and ultimately extremely expensive starter's hut by his own building company. Opened with a great fanfare by his wife on captain's day, the building lasted all of two weeks before being totally destroyed in an evening of moderately high winds, with debris from the building being discovered, in some cases over a mile away.

Denis Scott had been Dempsey's vice captain and their combined performance in the two roles was generally acclaimed by the members as an act to rival the very best comedy performances of Laurel and Hardy.

Undeterred by the criticism and, in some cases, the outright hostility of some of the more vociferous members of the club to his appointment as captain, Denis swept into office with all the panache of a new president taking over at the Royal and Ancient. He had vowed that his overriding aim was to be a captain that every single member of the club knew and would remember for the pace and scale of the initiatives he had been dreaming up for over a year. When he voiced this intention at his inaugural dinner at the club, members were seen to visibly shake, either with mirth or anger at the prospect for the coming year.

'As many of you know, I have been looking forward to this evening and my new role in the club for many months now. They haven't, however, been wasted months, spent just dreaming about the job, that's not my style, as most of you know well. No, I've been scheming and planning, putting together a set of initiatives that will change the running of the club out of all recognition and your experiences of it.'

Members began to grip the sides of their seats and stare at one another in disbelief at what they were hearing. They didn't fancy someone like Scott tampering with their experiences, thank you all the same. Various individuals were heard muttering things like, 'we've already had a taste of your scheming and we didn't like it,' or 'who the bloody hell does he think he is, the arrogant prat' and 'he's only the sodding captain, he hasn't bought the place, has he?' asked someone in desperation.

'I'm going to lead this club, over the next 12 months through the most exciting times it's ever witnessed. I'm going to get everyone, including myself, who work for this club, giving a 120 per cent effort in a drive to be more efficient and streamlined in the way we work. I'll be meeting with all the committees, the chairman, the secretary and the newly appointed marketing manager over the next few days to forge this new action plan for the immediate and long term future of the club.'

Barnes, the club secretary, made a mental note to fill his desk diary up with some urgent meetings next week, preferably ones which were being held at least 30 miles from the club. The chairman wondered how quickly he could arrange a last minute holiday to some deserted location without the benefits of modern telecommunication systems. Various other members of the executive were desperately trying to recall long forgotten relatives they might visit or deathbed commiserations they felt they should deliver in person. The only person with a smile on his face was the new marketing manager, Julian, who had some plans of his own he thought he'd like to share with this new management 'dynamo'. Barnes, seeing his expression, momentarily pondered on the nature of the discussion that would take place between these two 'verbal incontinents'; what percentage of it the two would actually understand and who would be the first to flee the room.

'I see this club at the very heart of the leisure and recreational activities of the area and our golf course as the jewel in the crown to which people from far and wide will want to travel to experience the challenge of this great course. I will be here to drive these plans through and I will personally guarantee that no-one will fail to be impressed by what is about to touch each and every one of you.'

'Bloody hell,' said one old lag in the back of the room, 'he has bought the flaming place by the way he's talking, he'll be suggesting an increase in our fees next.'

Some more desperate members of the club were reputed to have spent days, following this meeting, on the telephone trying to locate other golf clubs that would have them as members with immediate effect. Every one viewed the prospect of hoards of visiting golf societies clogging up the tee times and then monopolising the bar and dining room with their raucous presentation ceremonies with absolute horror. Many were quite content to be members of a golfing 'backwater' that very few people knew about and even less actually wanted to play. Neither did they want any more of the local 'low life' clogging up the place on the pretext of using the available leisure facilities, 'this is a golf club, not a bloody community centre,' said one irate member.

Of course, the anger, rage and white-hot hostility that was running at an all time high at the meeting, was, ten days later, nowhere to be seen. So, the meeting room used by the captain, chairman, secretary and marketing manager to discuss his plans, was not the scene of unruly picketing by banner-waving members with eggs and flour to dispense over these pompous up-starts. Nor were the proceedings interrupted at any point by protesting hordes, hell-bent on de-railing the grandiose plans that, as yet, hadn't even been presented.

Neither Barnes nor Tomlinson, the chairman had had any success in putting their emergency plans to get out of the meeting into operation. Barnes was particularly pissed off with his assistant who had dropped him right in it by revealing to the captain that his diary was, in fact, completely blank for that week and so would be available at any time to meet him.

Both men turned up at the meeting to find that 'Jules' had already arrived armed with a file the size of the chancellor of the exchequer's budget dispatch box, in which he had placed all manner of reports, articles and personal jottings related to what he called his 'Corporate and Strategic Marketing Plan'. Barnes and Tomlinson looked across at one another, feeling rather like two hostages about to be subjected to solitary confinement with two maniacal terrorists plotting the total destruction of their very comfortable, sane and stable world.

What they were actually treated to, of course, was something very far removed from the global golfing holocaust that had been promised by the captain in his inaugural speech.

'Well, ladies and gentlemen,' he started, before realising, of course, that naturally no ladies had actually been invited, 'let's make a start, there's a great deal of work to be done. In front of you are my four priorities for the first three months, I'd like us to get started on them immediately.'

I like the use of the word 'us' thought Barnes, I wonder just how much 'Dredger' will get his hands dirty in this lot, despite his elaborate promises to the members; he'll be too busy with sherry parties and 'brown nosing' it with the great and the good.

'I want the past captains' plaques up on the tees by the end of next month, I want all 18 holes to have names, I want a flag pole for a club flag built outside the clubhouse and new signposting erected so visitors know where to go to find different people in the building.'

Christ Almighty, thought the chairman, I gave up the chance of five days in Tunisia to come and discuss this crap; right now he thought he'd happily settle for two nights in Weston-super-Mare if it would get him away from this tiresome bullshit.

'I think those are splendid ideas to start with,' piped up Julian, 'Swankers' alternative cheapskate answer to Saatchi and Saatchi. 'Perhaps we could also put up a 'Welcome' board in the reception area with the names of anyone visiting the club on particular days.'

'Splendid idea, Julian; now that's what I want to see at this club, people with fresh, exciting, new ideas. We'll have the words 'Welcome from the Captain and the Committee'. Make a note of that Mr Secretary.'

Yes, thought Barnes and we'll have 'his majesty's voice' on a tannoy in the toilets giving instructions on the correct use of the flush system. Where is this all going to end? He could just see the expression on the faces of the notorious practical joke brigade of the club when this lot hit the gossip fan. God knows what they would do to this barm pot of a marketing manager when their fertile imaginations starting to roll.

'Now, gentlemen, beyond that I want all the club's headed note paper redesigned, a totally new web site and I want a video made of the club and all its facilities. I shall also be instigating a captain's newsletter, a captain's notice board and what I believe is a particularly interesting development, something I shall be calling a 'captain's clinic', an opportunity for members who want to come to talk to me about any matters to do with the golf club that are bothering them. I'm also thinking about having something called the 'captain's call' which will take place every Sunday lunchtime to announce items of interest and importance to the members.

Barnes and the chairman looked at each other across the table in utter dismay. The prospect of this package of megalomaniac measures festooning the clubhouse did not bear thinking about and the possible damaging repercussions of implementing some of these crackpot schemes was a cause for some considerable concern.

Barnes felt he ought perhaps to sound a word of caution and suggest a slightly lengthier timescale for these sweeping new ideas. He wished he hadn't opened his mouth.

'Mr. Secretary, I'm going to take this club into the 21st century right away, not in six months time or nine months time, but right now and I propose to do it with those who are prepared to give me their 100 per cent support. Those who don't want to give me that commitment should consider their position.'

'Quite so, Mr. Captain,' said the sycophantic Julian who could see his own star in the ascendancy with the arrival of the new captain. 'Perhaps Mr. Captain, you'd like to hear one or two ideas that I've put into my Corporate and Strategic Marketing Plan for the club.'

'Thank you Julian, but perhaps some other time, I think we've got enough to be going on with from what's already been tabled; I've got a reception with the mayor to attend in the next hour.'

Thank goodness for that, thought Barnes, the idea of having to sit through another load of unintelligible garbage, on top of what they'd already been subjected to, didn't bear thinking about. He couldn't help smiling as he saw 'Jules', rather despondently sliding his report back into the brand new leather briefcase that had coincidentally arrived with that of the captain's own flamboyant document holder, complete with initials and title, 'Captain, Swancliffe and Ankerdine G.C'

'Right, gentlemen, that'll be all for today. Same day, same time, two weeks from today to discuss your report on the progress you've made so far on what we've decided today.'

I don't remember deciding any bloody thing, thought the chairman. I distinctly remember being told a lot of things, but as for actually being involved in making a decision, I must have missed that bit.

'When we meet next time, I'll have my plans for captain's day ready for you,' said the captain as he swept out on his way to anaesthetising the major with his latest compilation of social dross.

Over the next few days, various missives from the captain arrived on Barnes' desk, rather like persistent demands for the payment of bad debts. Artist impressions of the past captains' plaques, plans for the siting of these monstrosities, drawings of the captain's noticeboard and recommendations for its location, suggestions for naming the holes, ideas for sign-posting and so on; all to be circulated to committee members, not for anything remotely democratic as their consideration and further discussion, but purely for information and immediate implementation. All these accompanied by the curt concluding remark to get on and see them carried out.

At the same time, the chairman was being inundated with irate letters from members of the executive committee demanding to know what the hell he thought he was playing at, allowing this self-styled dictator to treat them like disenfranchised victims of a military coup. He was also made aware of some serious mutterings from certain quarters of the membership, threatening him with an extra-ordinary general meeting and the introduction of a vote of no confidence in the committee. It was noticeable, however, in all the pieces of correspondence he received, that the expectation was that the chairman 'should jolly well do something about it.' The idea that, as members of the executive, they should all put their collective heads 'above the parapet' and register their dissent was never even mentioned.

Brown, the chairman of finance wrote him a long and quite abusive letter. In it he demanded to know on whose authority the captain had been allowed to authorise the spending of substantial amounts of the club's funds on what he described as a 'set of such infantile initiatives that he had, at first sight, thought he was the recipient of another prank'. Once before, Brown had been the victim of a hoax letter from the club's resident jokers, purporting to be from a middle-eastern potentate offering a huge sponsorship deal in return for life membership of the club for his entire family. It was only when he'd rather over-enthusiastically presented this at the AGM and seen the smirks on the faces of those 'in the know', that he realised that he'd been set up for another embarrassing 'piss take'.

Barnes and Tomlinson decided that they would try to ride out both these potential storms by waiting to see what actually transpired. They proposed to gamble on the fact that the chances of any of these schemes actually coming to fruition was about as likely as 'Swankers' getting into the much-prized list of the Golf World magazine's top one hundred courses in the United Kingdom.

For Denis, the next most pressing engagement in his captain's calendar was his 'drive-in,' followed by the traditional match between captain, vice captain and the lady captain and her vice captain. He was very much looking forward to the 'drive-in', as it officially got his year off and running. As to the match, he would have been quite content to have been diagnosed as having suddenly contracted a very rare and contagious disease, requiring total isolation for a week, rather than have to go through the misery of that experience.

Throughout his golfing career, he'd strenuously and quite successfully avoided getting involved in any form of golf with ladies, in spite of attempts by colleagues and friends to inveigle him into what he regarded as the nearest thing that golf could offer to sadomasochistic practices. He had made it very clear that while he had no objection to ladies having all the same golfing rights and privileges as the men - a pronouncement that had certainly startled some of the more misogynistic members of the club - he personally did not want to be a part of that particular form of 'ritual blood-letting'.

He'd frequently had described to him, or witnessed from a distance, some of the more brutal manifestations and outcomes of a typical mixed foursomes or greensomes match and decided that since he'd never been partial to hospital food, he'd stay well clear of any golfing experience that might end with him requiring his food prepared and delivered by the local infirmary's 'meals on wheels' service.

Now, of course, he'd voluntarily put himself in a position where he had no choice other than to pitch up and shut up. The whole affair was made worse by the fact that he and the lady captain were, to put it mildly, not on the best of terms. In fact, to put it bluntly, they hated each others' guts. Denis prided himself on being able to get on with most women and, in fact, enjoyed the company of almost all the female members of the golf club, frankly preferring to be in their company than some of the more tediously boring male members of the club who, quite suddenly, seemed to have latched on to him as the new captain.

The exception was this year's lady captain, Brenda 'Brunhilde' Maddox, a quite obnoxious, self-opinionated and thoroughly pompous individual with, in Denis' opinion, all the charm, poise and appeal of a dangerous Rottweiler. The problem was, of course, that the lady captain, whether explicitly asked or not about her opinion of Denis, and she had been, had no hesitation in describing Denis in exactly the same terms.

Denis' arrival on the tee for his inaugural 'drive-in' was greeted, like every one of his predecessors, with the inevitable mixture of best wishes, ribald comments and acerbic humour from those surrounding the practice green and first tee.

'Good luck, mate, we've got the white coats and your reservation at the 'funny farm' for when you get back.'

'I've got 20-1, that you don't get your drive past the ladies tee, Denis,' shouted one idiot.

'Should we get the traffic on the by-pass to park up for safety for a few minutes?' suggested another comedian.

'We tried to get Golf Monthly to show up, but they said their picture gallery of 'Spectacular Golfing Disasters of the Year' was full.'

Denis well knew from past experience that the 'premier league' of the club's practical jokers, ably led and encouraged in their efforts by that ageing hooligan, Richardson, the club professional, would be out in force, but could not predict precisely what forms of public humiliation they had in store for him. He had specifically requested, without much hope of having it complied with, that the practice of the members standing at the point where they considered his opening drive would land, be discontinued.

'I do not want to see members running about the fairway rugby-tackling one another, scrummaging about in a maul of bodies trying to retrieve my drives', said Denis.

In fact, very few of these particular members felt there was much point populating the fairway directly in front of the tee, as it was unlikely that Denis' opening drive would pass within 100 yards of such a location.

'Nor do I want to see those less generous-minded members standing in the adjoining cemetery waving fishing nets or brollies in the hope of capturing one of my more stray deliveries.'

There was, of course, no hope that either of these requests would be heeded, as was evident when Denis arrived on the tee to witness the usual collection of white flag-waving, crash-helmeted, telescope-carrying members.

The practice at 'Swankers' had been for the out-going captain to 'putt out' his year on the final hole of the 18th green, hand his ball over to the in-coming captain who then drove it off the first tee. Somewhere between these two locations and unbeknown to Denis, who was being diverted with best wishes and handshakes by one or two members who'd been delegated to the task, a switch was made and the first ball he hit exploded on impact with his club, covering him and those nearby, in a white powdery substance. Some wag standing nearby was overheard to remark, 'oh that's the way he gets the stuff into the country.' He was handed another ball, little knowing that this possessed all the internal consistency of a jelly, causing it when struck, to roll all of about five yards off the tee.

Finally, deciding to use one from his own collection, he teed up the ball, took a few anxious looks down the fairway and swung. For Denis, the result wasn't half bad. The ball covered about 150 yards in roughly a straight line before predictably turning right in a gentle arc towards the boundary with the cemetery, but thankfully falling short. What was totally unexpected, however, was the accompanying noise as he made contact with the ball. Someone had concealed the club's tannoy system close to the first tee and at the precise moment of club impacting on ball, what sounded like the most rip-roaring, trouser-splitting fart was heard across the tee and surrounding area.

Embarrassed giggles and whispered asides about Denis being the only golfer capable of simultaneously imparting backspin and back-draft on a golf ball accompanied his angry departure from the tee, in preparation for the next episode of golfing humiliation: the match.

The four contestants arrived on the first tee and waited to be announced by the starter. Quite why it had been necessary for the starter to be there was a mystery, since only a few close friends of the lady captain had turned up, and support for Denis and his partner was limited to three or four of the veterans who hadn't even realised there was a match being played and a few of the junior members who were there only because their parents hadn't turned up to collect them. Denis and his partner had decided that they would use a buggy, partly because they suspected that they might be out there for some time, wandering the outer reaches of the course and partly because it would reduce the actual amount of face-to-face contact with their opponents.

In truth, Denis wouldn't have minded a bit of face-to-face contact with Jeanette, the lady vice captain who, since her arrival at the club, had become a fairly regular topic of discussion in the men's bar. With a figure that would not have been out of place on a Paris fashion house 'cat walk' and outfits that left very little to the imagination, her arrival in the clubhouse had undoubtedly been the single greatest cause of spilt drinks, collisions with the furniture and missed-footings amongst the club's male population.

While such accidents were readily appreciated and accepted by fellow males as perfectly understandable occurrences, faced as they regularly were, with this Lara Croft-like vision, those unfortunates who demonstrated their human frailties in front of their 'other halves' were promptly informed of the immediate withdrawal of all sexual favours and services, 'until they could learn to behave themselves'.

For this event, this reliably reported, 'high maintenance' lady had chosen to turn up in an outfit that stretched over her figure with an intensity that would severely restrict even the slightest body movement, with or without a golf club. It comprised essentially of a pair of extremely tight white trousers clearly revealing the line of a pair of knickers barely able to cope with their contents and a golfing top that was being subjected to a similar kind of strain from two perfectly proportioned orbs.

Both Denis and his partner seriously wondered whether they had sufficient self-control and restraint to stop themselves continuously gawping and drooling over this blatantly distracting piece of eroticism in order to concentrate on winning the game.

'Christ, she's got a cheek, coming out like that,' said his partner.

'Yes, I think from where I'm standing, you'd be more accurate with the plural form of the noun,' said Denis.

Snide remarks were also heard from fellow male golfers on an adjacent tee about 'beating the pants of that pair'.

Their fantasy world was quickly disturbed by the arrival of the lady captain, who, judging by her ensemble, looked to have just arrived from two weeks in an area of the Himalayas experiencing one of its worst winters on record.

'We're getting 18 shots, we're giving no putts over a foot,

it's our honour to drive off first and we don't expect you to go charging on in front of us in that contraption,' was her idea of an opening greeting.

'We'll keep well out of your way, believe me,' was Denis' pointed rejoinder and casting another glance at the lady vice, added, 'we'll just follow at a discrete distance behind the pair of... er both of you.'

The match progressed with its fair share of minor disasters, ill-tempered sarcasm and frequent unpleasant and sometimes, downright rude remarks from both pairings in an effort on both their parts not to be out-faced by the other.

Denis ran over the lady captain's ball with his buggy and incurred the comment, 'you drive that thing with the same level of skill as you use to drive the golf ball – very little.'

His reply, 'yes, but I hadn't bargained on needing the driving skills of a rally champion to get me out of the places you've hit the ball.'

The lady captain shanked a drive that cannoned off the side of Denis' buggy, for which he was promptly castigated for, 'parking it in such a ridiculous position.' Denis' partner, as a consequence of this outburst, refused her a free drop from beside the ladies' toilets, where yet another of her errant drives had finished.

Accusations followed accusations from both sides on the number of shots taken at certain holes and the comment from the lady captain that, 'had I known we were playing with a pair who couldn't add up, we'd have asked for a scorer.'

Incensed by the alleged charge of cheating, Denis replied, 'if I'd known we were playing with someone who took so many shots to reach a green, we'd have requested a longer-life battery for the buggy.'

Denis accused the lady captain of playing out of turn and asked her to play the shot again. The lady captain accused Denis' partner of deliberately standing too close to her as she took her shot and glaringly demanded that he, 'get the hell out of my line of sight'.

He promptly added that if in fact he was standing in her

line of sight, her chances of hitting the ball on the green were about as remote as her chances were of 'being selected to play on the Solheim Cup team.'

Short putts were not conceded by either of the two teams, requests for relief were equally ignored and hints that the ball had, on one occasion, been teed up ahead of the blocks were also dismissed with the suggestion that a speedy appointment be made at Specsavers.

During the course of these pieces of golfing warfare, the only person who noticeably stayed out of these exchanges was the lady vice captain. She seemed more concerned with the state of her personal appearance and her golfing attire than with trading these rather infantile altercations. Her constant recourse to a mirror, comb and, occasionally, even her make-up, suggested that for her, the match was hardly the cause for the outright hostility and venom that was being displayed by the other combatants.

Her remarks to both Denis and his partner seemed to have a rather more mischievous intent to them. Her request, for instance, to Denis that she'd, 'quite like the feel of using his long broom-handled putter' was accompanied by a gentle and quite disturbing stroking of his upper arm. It wasn't altogether surprising, therefore, that Denis went on to four putt that particular green from no more than 15 feet. She looked rather demurely at Denis' partner and enquired, 'whether standing with his legs so far apart made him too stiff as he swung' and 'if the very strong right hand grip that you use causes you to pull it.' Denis was pointedly asked whether he, 'preferred the feel of leather to the more synthetic material in his glove hand.'

The quality and accuracy of the answers they gave were rather lost in both their desperate attempts to interpret the lady's motives for such questions and for any signs of a desire on her part to get a serious reply, as opposed to what they suspected was a not overtly discrete means of inflicting the maximum amount of embarrassment on them

At the end of the game, Denis and his partner, much to their relief, managed a two and one victory. The lady captain vehemently shrugged off an extremely reluctant attempt on the part of both men to deliver the 'traditional peck on the cheek' that followed these encounters, striding off muttering something about, 'damn insolent apologies for golfers'. The lady vice captain did, however, oblige both of them with something rather more substantial than a passing brush of lips on cheek, which was clearly observed by everyone in the clubhouse bar and by the end of the week was being exaggeratedly reported in terms of, 'a full frontal snog'.

Planning for captain's day seemed to start almost as early as the qualifying rounds for football's World Cup. Denis had produced a hit-list of members and officials, or 'mugs' and 'puppets' as someone labelled them, who he was targeting for some particular job during the day. When word got around the seniors' section, for instance, that he was on the warpath for volunteers to look after car parking arrangements, the volume of laughter in the bar, was said to have rattled the collection of fine malt whiskies.

'If he thinks I'm standing around for five bloody hours in that car park trying to get some of these maniacs to park their cars in neat rows, he's got a screw loose,' said one member, 'how many people is he expecting anyway?'

'I hear he wants four or five people to act as spotters on the 4th, 9th, 13th and 17th,' said another defiant dissident, 'well I'm not standing around waiting to be hit by his drives or be asked to go scrambling about in the bushes for lost balls.'

'Ah you'll be quite safe on the fairway with Denis' drives, he never goes anywhere near those; you'd be in more danger supervising the car park,' said a member who'd had the misfortune to draw the captain in a knock out competition.

'My god, he'll want all the fairways roped off and marshals controlling the crowds next; what does he think this is, the sodding Open Championship,' suggested the seniors' captain.

When Richardson got wind of Denis' hit-list, he knew it

wouldn't be long before he got a visit. He wondered whether he could get rid of 'Shanks' for a week by offering him in the captain's raffle to some poor unsuspecting member as a 'slave'. The chances were, he thought, that they'd bring the daft bugger back after a couple of days asking for their money back.

'Morning, Mark, can we have a word about captain's day? I'm going to need some prizes and wondered could you do me a good deal.'

Denis' idea of a 'good deal', in Richardson's experience, usually meant something for nothing. Well he didn't see why he had to subsidise the cheapskate, whose only known purchase in the pro shop in the last three months had been a packet of wooden tees and a pitch repairer, and he'd had the cheek to bring the tees back after a week, claiming they were, 'breaking too easily'. On the other hand, Richardson did see an opportunity to offload some old stuff that had been hanging around in the shop for months, ordered without his permission by that fruitcake, 'Shanks'.

'Well Denis, how about this 'Stingray' driver as a start?' Various members had tried this latest offering from some unknown manufacturer and returned it saying it was absolutely useless. In truth, he'd had to agree, because he'd got the same lousy results with it.

'Oh great,' said Denis who fortunately failed to recognise that, although the thing had been taped up, it still bore some evidence of some members' erratic thrashings. 'What else have you got?'

'Well, there's six of these golf tops you can have,' said Richardson.

'Excellent,' replied the captain, not realising that these were surplus tops that Richardson had ordered for the club's annual golfing pilgrimage to Spain two years ago and that they'd been paid for by a local sponsor so, in fact, had cost Richardson nothing.

'What about something for the winner of the ladies' prize?' inquired Denis.

'Ah, got just the thing. We've just had these new hats

delivered and I think they're going to be very popular with the ladies.'

In fact the hats had all the appeal and fashion style of a Second World War pilot's helmet and Richardson had only managed to get rid of one.

'We can put in a couple of these ladies' sweaters as well if you like,' offered Richardson who was aware that the original ridiculously low price tag was due to the fact that after one wash, they had the reputation for shrinking to the size of a baby's nappy.

With a couple of boxes of cheap golf balls and a pair of shoes that had been worn once and had been returned because they'd reduced the wearer to a hobbling cripple, Denis left believing that these prizes would be talked about as 'the best ever' provided by a captain.

His next port of call was the head chef to make sure that everything was 'hunky dory' on the food front. The title, 'head chef', as Harold preferred to be called was, in truth, a bit daft, since the club only had one, other than a couple of 'casual choppers' as some members had labelled Harold's hangers-on. Denis didn't want a recurrence of what had happened two years ago when the evening buffet had run out before half the people had been fed, necessitating a dash to a local, late opening supermarket for extra supplies of sausage rolls, pork pies and scotch eggs by half a dozen of the lady members dressed in their very expensive evening dresses. The complaints about that fiasco had rolled on for months afterwards.

'Now, Harold, is everything sorted on the food and drinks front for captain's day?' asked Denis.

'Not to my knowledge it's not,' replied Harold Watson, self-appointed irritant to all and sundry.

Denis knew from of old that Harold could be an awkward bastard if he so chose, but this was taking his particular brand of obstinacy to a new and very irritating level.

'Well, you'd better get on with it then hadn't you?' replied Denis.

'I will when someone actually gets round to telling me what they want and how much I can spend; I'm a chef, not a damn mind reader, you know,' replied Harold.

Yes, and a flaming awkward specimen of that notoriously difficult species at that, thought Denis.

'Well, I want a barbecue running from lunchtime through the afternoon and then a buffet starting at 7.00 and finishing at 8.30, just before the presentations and disco start,OK?'

'No can do,' replied Harold, deciding to up the obstinacy stakes a notch or three higher.

'Why the hell not?' shouted Denis, wondering when this infuriating sod's contract was up for renewal. 'It's not that big an ask, is it?'

'First off, can't get the staff for the barbecue and I don't cook outside anyway ...and then the buffet's not worth it for me 'cos the chairman of finance has capped the figure on costs for this 'do' already'.

'Oh, he has, has he? We'll see about that,' said a very twitchy and irate captain and stormed out shouting, 'I'll be back, get some sample menus for the buffet to me first thing in the morning - £7 and £10 a head.'

Denis' next victim-in-waiting was the head green keeper, Bert Harvey, who, when it came to bloody-mindedness, particularly when faced with this particular 'pompous twerp', could captain an English team.

'Bert, I just want to go through some arrangements for captain's day with you, OK?' enquired Denis.

'No sorry, Mr. Captain, got to sort out a problem with the drainage across the 8th, members have complained that the water's up over their shoes.'

'Well can't you do it later or send someone else to do it?' suggested an exasperated Denis, irritated at the very thought that anything could rank above his particular demands.

'Nope, got to see to it myself and anyway, every one else is busy; we've no time to be standing around jawing like some others I could mention,' and with that walked out and left Denis waving his bit of paper with the suggested tee and pin positions like a little boy presenting his home work to a busy headmaster who just couldn't be bothered to accept it.

Denis began to wonder why the hell he'd taken the trouble to make notes of all these arrangements for different people; in fact he was seriously wondering whether anyone would actually notice if he cancelled the whole damn event.

He decided to retreat to his office and make some telephone calls about the hire of the bouncy castle he'd planned and the bungee jumping machine that someone had told him about. He also needed to make sure that his friend at the local BMW garage was going to sponsor a hole-in-one competition in return for being given space in the car park to display four of their current models. He'd actually been asked by the garage and had, in fact, promised a prime space alongside the first tee, but that obstructive bastard, the chairman of greens had kicked up a hell of a fuss about the damage to the turf. He also didn't want some old 'codger' inadvertently putting a ball through the windscreen of a brand new, top-of-the range, £63 000, 7 Series. He'd also remembered that he wanted a press photographer there, secretly hoping that no local dignitary 'popped his clogs' or someone chose to burn down a local factory on that particular day.

He was still trying to find a band that would play on the terrace through the afternoon but most of those he'd contacted, when told it was an outside 'do' in early May, suddenly found they'd got a previous booking that they couldn't cancel.

His route to the office took him past the office of Anderson, the chairman of house, so he thought he'd just risk asking about arrangements for the evening.

'Ah, Brian, just thought I'd check on arrangements for captain's evening, no problems I'm sure?'

'Ah, yes, Denis old man, glad you looked in,' replied the chairman of house.

The phrase 'old man' and Brian's face signified to Denis in some sort of hidden code that everything was not OK.

'Actually, got the health and safety and environmental health 'wallahs' in the week before your 'do'; don't think there'll be any problem, but you never know, do you?' muttered Brian, not, in Denis' opinion, without a slight mischievous glint in his eye.

I bloody well do know, thought Denis, why did they choose this particular time to visit; is this some kind of conspiracy to make this event go arse up?

'But we've never had a problem before, have we, Brian?' pleaded Denis.

'Not that I can remember, it's just that there's a 'new boy' in town and I gather from one or two of my pals in the catering trade that he's on the war path and out to make a name for himself in high places.'

Well if he wants a name in high places, thought Denis, why doesn't he bugger off to Snowdon and run the 'caff 'on the summit instead of making our lives a sodding misery.

'Just let me know how things go as soon as possible, will you, Brian, me old mate, I don't think I can take any more problems on,' and with that, headed for the bar and an early tincture or two.

If he thought his plans for captain's day were going to be difficult to 'pull through the loop', a phrase that that marketing 'nerd', Julian had been using constantly of late to describe his own attempts at making certain 'marketing' arrangements for the day, then keeping the other initiatives on course wasn't exactly going to be a stroll in the park.

He'd managed to get his idea for the plaques of past captains located on the first nine tees with the help of his pal Parkinson who had come up with the necessary spondulicks, though he hadn't quite bargained on having to accept the rather nauseating advertising tag of, 'if you've the drains, we've the brains', which Parkinson had insisted on having on each plaque in return for his largesse. No doubt this latest pearl of marketing jingoism had been the product of hours of contemplation on the part of yet another one of these communication catastrophes that seemed to be springing up everywhere, including the golf club.

As for the other ideas, they had staggered along rather like Denis' own progress around the golf course on occasions. He had taken what turned out to be completely crap advice from the executive committee and organised a competition to name the holes on the course. The entry had been pathetic, amounting to six, one of which was his own and another, his vice captain's. Of the others, there wasn't a single name that he felt he could use. Some bore no resemblance to the particular hole, the area immediately around it, the surrounding views or, for that matter, anything remotely to do with golf. Others were rather crude and in some cases, downright offensive suggestions that could have landed their authors in court. Others were vaguely humorous, but only if you were 'in on the joke', otherwise they were meaningless. There was no way, for instance, that he could allow the 4th hole to bear the title, 'Carole's cleavage', in spite of the phrase being a very apt description of the contours of that particular fairway as well as those of a previous lady captain. Neither was he going to use 'Brewer's Drop' for the very steep par three 15th hole. He could well imagine the modifications that would be made to that title on various club publications, particularly with the current secretary's penchant for not proof reading with sufficient accuracy.

Ultimately, therefore, the hole-naming project was put on ice, until either a reliable person could be found who would undertake to name the lot or a small group of people took the job on.

His flagpole project was a success, in spite of the veiled threats from certain quarters as to what he might, on occasions, find hanging from it.

'There's a line of washing missing from the lady vice captain's garden; she'd like the small bits back and the bobbies suspect it's someone from the golf club,' reported a usually reliable source of gossip.

Equally, he'd found some support for his signposting, largely he suspected because the contract to make and put up the signs had found its way into the hands of the chairman of finance's cousin.

The newsletter had been a complete flop, almost entirely due to the fact that he'd hardly received any newsworthy material. Had it appeared at all, he would almost single-handedly have had to write and edit it himself. One or two submissions had been received, but the standard and style of the English and the appalling punctuation had meant that they were unusable in their presented form. The standard of the photographs that he'd requested, suggested that they'd been taken using a rather badly damaged Brownie 127 camera and a film that had long passed its sell-by-date.

The captain's notice board had made an appearance, but in addition to his own offerings, one or two undesirable additions had appeared from members who fancied themselves as the next scriptwriters for future episodes of 'One Foot in the Grave' or 'Only Fools and Horses.'

One particularly scurrilous piece had purported to be an account of his match with the lady captain and her partner, complete with a number of suggestive, double-entendres related to his and his partner's 'close encounters' with the lady vice captain; the captain's failure 'to get it up' in the requisite 'strokes' on the 5th hole was partly down to the lady vice, 'busting two of her best crackers' to within five feet of the pin. The notice board remained, but was now contained within a locked glass case to which only the captain had a key.

He'd abandoned the 'captain's clinic' after one attempt, when he'd turned up to find a queue of about 30 of the club's practical jokers waiting for him outside his office with complaints ranging from the poor quality toilet paper in the Gents' loo through to the excessive number of wobbly chairs in the bar and, by far the worst, the appointment, in their opinion, of quite the ugliest looking female member of the bar staff that they'd ever seen in their lives. As to their suggestions for improvements, he'd had to call the whole thing to a halt, otherwise it would have been light before he left for home.

He'd been told very politely by Brown, the chairman of finance to drop his idea of the 'captain's call'.

'Do you realise how much the bar takings have dropped on a Sunday lunch time since the introduction of this idea of yours?' demanded Brown irately. 'The departure from the car park of some of our members, following their usual Sunday morning round, resembles what happens on the starting grid of a Formula One Grand Prix when all the red lights go out'.

On first reflection, he felt he hadn't quite made the impact on the club's affairs in those first few months as he'd initially hoped, but he comforted himself with the thought that there was still a long way to go and there were loads more ideas that he'd got up his sleeve. When one or two of the committee members heard this prediction, a number were heard to say that they thought there was another, rather more personal location, that he might consider storing those ideas and that if he was unwilling to oblige, there'd be a number of willing volunteers for the job.

Exactly two months before captain's day, he had a scheduled meeting with the committee to go over his plans for the day. It was not intended to be an opportunity for discussion, simply a chance to make sure that these 'monoliths' didn't screw things up for him at the last minute. So, it was with a great deal of optimism and enthusiasm that he sailed into that meeting with the purpose of motivating these 'reluctant retainers' to get behind him and make it a success.

'Right ladies and gentlemen, apologies for absence?' asked Denis.

'The secretary's just phoned in to say that his new BMW has rather unexpectedly failed to start this morning and he's got to wait for the AA to collect it; doesn't expect to be here for at least two and a half hours,' said Barnes' mate Anderson.

Denis' personal experience of the local BMW agency was that they were 'on the case' the moment anything went wrong, so was very suspicious of Barnes' excuse for not making the meeting. Denis made a mental note to check with his contact at the garage next time they met. If Barnes was 'swinging the led', he'd have his arse as a target for the captain's chipping competition.

Sod it, thought the club chairman, why didn't I think of something like that to avoid having to sit through another two hours of self-promotional claptrap from Denis?

'I just want to bring you up to speed on the arrangements for captain's day and ask for your help with one or two outstanding problems I have.'

Like the fact that you've failed to get a single volunteer for car parking and ball spotting, for instance, muttered Watson, the chairman of greens.

'I have had some wonderful prizes donated by our professional, Mark; please can I have that minuted?'

Do you also wanted it noted that most of it, from what I've heard, thought the assistant secretary, is second-hand 'tat' that he couldn't shift?

'I've got the barbecue set up for the afternoon and the buffet for the evening, in spite of what I felt were some quite unnecessary financial constraints imposed by the chairman of finance on the event.'

'Just trying to ensure we balance the books and don't have to increase the members fees to pay for these sorts of jollies, Mr Captain,' said Brown.

Denis glared at the chairman of finance. 'I hardly think that captain's day at the club deserves to be described as a 'jolly'.

'I've not been able to secure a band for the afternoon, but the local primary school have offered the services of their little orchestra to play for an hour.'

'What the hell do we want with a band, Mr Captain?' inquired Watson, the chairman of greens. 'This is a golf competition, not a brass band festival.'

'Captain's day is more than a just a day for the golfers, it should cater for members of their families who would like to join us.'

The chairman of greens could just see hordes of kids running about shouting and screaming, Walkmans blaring, flags being used for spear throwing competitions and challenges being made to see who could build the biggest sandcastle in the bunkers. Worse was to follow.

'I've personally paid for the hire of a bouncy castle, but there are one or two problems with the bungee jumping machine, I believe.'

There was a stunned silence around the room before the chairman of house broke the silence.

'Did we hear you correctly, Mr Captain; did you say that you'd hired a bouncy castle and trying to get a bungee jump erected?'

'Yes, is there a problem with that?' asked the captain.

'Well I personally, and I am, of course, only speaking for myself,' said the chairman of house, 'think that it sounds as though you're planning to turn the club into a fairground for the day. Might we expect to hear your plans for some elephant rides and a tightrope walker over the 18th green before the end of this meeting?'

The meeting dissolved into uncontrolled gales of laughter, much to the annoyance of the captain. 'I am simply trying to do something a little different this year and make it a day that everyone will remember.'

'Judging by what we've heard so far, Mr Captain, I'm sure we're all of the opinion that you'll certainly achieve that,' replied the chairman of finance, sarcastically.

Denis pressed on regardless with what he hoped would be more acceptable news. 'I have managed to persuade the local BMW garage to sponsor a hole-in-one competition; naturally the prize won't be a car.'

'Thank god for that,' exclaimed the lady captain, 'it would appear that they are a tad unreliable.'

'In return, I've allowed them space to exhibit four of their new cars,' said Denis deliberately choosing to ignore that latest irrelevant contribution from 'Brunhilde.'

'I hope you've checked up on the insurance for that,' muttered the chairman of finance.

Denis added item 36 to his 'Things to do' list.

'Finally,' said Denis, though no-one believed that he actually meant it, 'there'll be the usual competition for the longest drive for gentlemen and ladies, nearest the pin at the 9th for ladies and the 14th for men and nearest the pin with the second shots at the 4th and the 11th '.

'Ah,' said Watson, the chairman of greens, 'I was wondering when we were going to hear the long-awaited news that actually related to playing the game of golf.'

Denis wondered whether he could instigate a captain's prize for the best suggestion on how to remove unwanted and undesirable members of the club's executive committee.

'Well I think that's everything covered, thank you for your support,' he rather pointedly added. 'Oh, I forgot, would anyone be willing to help in the car park and with ball spotting?'

But the speed of every single member of the committee's exit from the room rivalled that of the departure of audiences from Welsh cinemas in those days when they played the English national anthem as the film credits were rolled.

As for the event itself, well it didn't rain, Denis' team came last but one in the competition, everyone grumbled to him because it took nearly five and a half hours to play 18 holes, the holes were cut in impossible positions, the ladies' tees hadn't been cut and the disco was too loud.

The bouncy castle raised the princely sum of £12, the bungee jump had to be cancelled on health and safety grounds and the motorised buggy of one of the 'octogenarian hackers' ran out of control at the side of the 18th green and ploughed into the centre of the BMW hospitality tent, capsizing the entire food and drinks table.

The food at the buffet didn't run out, but three waitresses, hired especially for the evening did, when the unwanted attentions of a few of the more inebriated men, simply got too much for their bottoms. The chairman, somehow or other, managed to lose his shoes and socks, the lady vice captain went unaccountably missing for over an hour, then returned in what was quite noticeably not quite the same immaculately turned out fashion in which she arrived.

Oh, and someone tripped up the lady captain on the dance floor, propelling her at a rate of knots into the disco, fusing the system and bringing the entire proceedings to an embarrassing halt for 15 minutes. Witnesses willing to identify the culprit were very much in short supply. In all, pretty well par for the course for captain's day.

CHAPTER 4

THE LADY CAPTAIN'S TALE or 'I'm the lady captain, I don't have air shots.'

In that hilarious 80's West End stage play based on the famous 'Dear Bill' letters that Dennis Thatcher reputedly wrote to a golfing mate, the actor who played the part of Dennis Thatcher had the line, 'none of you will have had the misfortune to have had your life totally buggered up by having your wife become Prime Minister.' That line could quite easily be lifted out of that now famous political arena and dropped quite comfortably into that of the world of golf and applied to those unfortunate spouses whose lives have been equally buggered up by their wives becoming the lady captain of a golf club.

That is not to say, of course, that the aforementioned lady's absence from her dearly beloved's side is due to the fact that she's fled the domestic nest to chair a war cabinet because some South American 'Johnny-come lately' has invaded a partially inhabited, but largely un-heard of stick of rock off the coast of South America and laid claim to its sovereignty.

On the other hand, reports from lady captains to their naturally very attentive and sympathetic partners, following the club's monthly executive committee meeting or even, dare one say it, their own lady members' committee meeting, provide ample evidence that war-like skirmishing resulting in minor casualties accompanied by declarations of defiant resistance in the face of ferocious hostility, are not an entirely unfamiliar part of even that organisation's proceedings.

Furthermore, the complete absence from the wardrobe of their long-suffering soul mate of any clean and immaculately ironed shirts, underpants, socks, handkerchiefs and other essential items of clothing, together with a totally depleted fridge, is not because their 'good lady' is away stemming off the attempts by some insurrectionist Trotskyite union leader to undermine the entire economy of the country and bring the government to its knees.

On the other hand, heated discussions at the club's annual general meeting on the parlous state of its financial affairs due to the totally inept allocation of budgets for ill-conceived, hair-brained course development projects and the scandalously high expenses paid to club officials on fact-finding 'jollies' to some of the more well-publicised and lavishly equipped hotel and golf complexes in the United Kingdom, have been known to split the ranks of its more militant members and require all the diplomatic arbitration skills of an ACAS representative.

The non-appearance of the nightly gin and tonic, that delicious home-cooked meal and the perfect bottle of Chateauneuf, following an extremely hard day at the office, is not due to the fact that the 'love of one's life' has just boarded a flight to some god-forsaken part of the world to 'chew the fat' with a group of power-crazed, incense-wielding fruitcakes wearing funny clothes. Nor is it because she's besotted with an ageing B-rated American movie star who wants her to play political 'cowboys and Indians' with him.

On the other hand, inter-club rivalry for positions of power and glory in such matters as whose signature should go on a letter to the local council for permission to build an on-course toilet solely for use by the ladies, or whether the lady captain is entitled to a named parking space, have been known to have reached the legislative limits for a UN peace keeping force's obligatory intervention.

The cancellation of that long-awaited and thoroughly deserved long week-end break is not because one's 'better half' has been recalled to her office to defend some irresponsible male colleague who has been photographed, minus his trousers, receiving the amorous attentions of a scantily-clad model to some of the more sensitive parts of his anatomy. Nor is it to scotch rumours that some of her so-called loyal colleagues are 'back at the ranch' plotting some form of coup behind her back in the hope of hastening her departure from office.

On the other hand, the age-old propensity of golfers of both sexcs to get involved in their club's unofficial 'sexual scrambles' or 'fumbling foursomes' has often been the subject of the 19th hole agenda. One club official and senior member of the executive, for instance, when he was inadvertently discovered by his playing partners to have concealed a bra and pair of knickers in his locker rather than having them discovered in the glove compartment of his car, mischievously classified it as, 'Matters hardly Arising' or 'None of Any Other Buggers' Business.' Correspondingly, one notoriously amorous member of the ladies' section of a club was graphically once described by her fellow lady golfers as having a,'36 handicap from tee to green but scratch from back seat to bedroom.'

As for 'clubhouse coups', the lady captain is no more immune from rumour, gossip, innuendo, backstabbing and threats of a vote of no confidence than her parliamentary counterparts. Failure to produce adequate or accurate minutes of ladies' committee meetings, failure to ensure that the soap, towels and other toiletries were of a sufficiently high quality in their changing room, inappropriate capitulation to the men's section over the number of tee times available on ladies' day and car-boot-sale rejects offered as prizes on lady captain's day, have all constituted grounds for her removal from office.

Clearly, the post of lady captain should contain the same labelling as a packet of 20 cigarettes, warning of a danger to the health and life expectancy of the holder, while at the same time, posing an obvious danger to those who are their nearest and dearest in the form of 'passive captaincy contamination'.

Help in the execution of this demanding role of lady captain has quite evidently been extensively researched and subsequently put to good use by some of the post holders, based on the most unlikely historical female role models. In certain clubs, for instance, it is quite clear that the current holder of the post is fully acquainted with those belligerently defiant tactics that the Roman army in first century Britain found so difficult to deal with when confronted with the chariot-driving Boudicca.

The horse-drawn chariot may have been replaced by a top-of-the-range Skoda, but its erratic progress through the club car park bears all the resemblance of those skilfully reproduced images of that manic heroine leading the woad-clad hordes of eastern Britain into battle. In similarly belligerent vein, the vehicle's final resting place across three other parking spaces is a clear testament to the occupant's uncompromising, non-capitulation approach to any form of ill-advised resistance or authority.

This imposing, warrior-like figure, resplendent in an attire that visually offers nothing that might compromise her position of power by inadvertently revealing any obvious physical female attributes, can be seen striding majestically through the clubhouse defying challenges from any quarter, whether male or female, but most likely the former, with whom, in fact, she appears to be on a permanent war footing.

The mere appearance of the lady in the clubhouse has been known to curtail the telling of doubtful jokes, silenced those waves of raucous laughter from members who wrongly believed they were there to enjoy themselves, broken up groups of scheming dissidents and malcontents and sent the kitchen and bar staff scurrying around like a horde of worker bees.

For this lady, taking on the captaincy is not simply a matter of agreeing to organise and run the playing of the game on behalf of a group of ladies; that she would regard as mere child's play and well below her skill threshold. Fulfilling the role of lady captain, in her view, is more about the battling of wills and personalities between herself and anyone in the club who dares to challenge her right to be right. To be seen, for instance, to be accepting, or for that matter, even acknowledging the fact that the ladies' section is required to recognise, let alone accept, decisions made by a committee comprised largely of men, and thoroughly incompetent and ineffectual ones at that, is completely anathema to her.

For her to discover that the standard of the on-course or off-course provision for the ladies varies by the slightest degree from that of the men, is sufficient reason for an all-out attack on those perpetrators of such gross inequalities. Badly mown, or, as is so often the case, not mown-at-all, ladies' tees, ladies' tee boxes tossed casually into the semi-rough and left there by inconsiderate green staff, the ladies' on-course toilet inadequately maintained, a failure to inform her of a committee decision to reduce tee times for ladies' competitions and the refusal to provide extra catering staff for 'open days', are just a few of the many 'battle grounds' which demand her unequivocal and uncompromising resistance.

Those misguided souls, such as a club secretary, who believe themselves to be equal to the task of opposing this imperious figure, risk a verbal battering of humiliating proportions for their sheer audacity, 'how dare you refuse to close the tee 40 minutes before the ladies' club championship starts; what right do you have to tell me it's none of my business when people can or can't play, you insolent little man; don't ever forget you're only an employee of this club and I'm the lady captain.'

Paradoxically, those who do manage to find it within their limited supply of conciliatory capabilities to accommodate the 'iron lady's' point of view, without offering any form of resistance, are frequently dismissed as 'spineless, ineffectual nonentities'; 'I shall inform the secretary that it's his job to sort out car parking arrangements for the visitors, even if he has to stand there all day by himself; he'll jolly well do as he's told like last time, the pathetic little twerp.'

Her severest treatment and harshest forms of retribution are, of course, like her famous historical role model, reserved for those from within her own ranks that dare oppose her or fail to attain the high standards set and expected of them by their leader.

Ladies who dare to object to standing for five hours in freezing cold temperatures as ball spotters for the ladies' county championship are told in no uncertain terms, 'you should regard it as an honour and a privilege that I've chosen you to do this important job; surely you can visit your dying aunt at another time.' Incompetent post holders are left in no doubt as to the nature and extent of their inadequacies, 'you were asked to take accurate minutes of the ladies' committee meeting and you present us with a report that looks as though it was written by a dyslexic six-year-old; if you can't do better than this I'll just have to find someone who can.' Those members whose ideas don't happen to coincide with hers are left in no doubt about the paucity of their intellectual thought processes, 'some people who, for the moment, shall remain nameless have, so I am led to believe, suggested that it would, in their words, 'be a nice idea if we were to arrange a social match with the men's seniors' section; personally I'm not remotely interested in such 'nice ideas' and I've absolutely no intention, as lady captain, of arranging such a ridiculous event and what's more, I'm truly amazed that it should have crossed the minds of any serious lady golfers in this club that it would be worth cluttering up our valuable competition diary with such a trivial business.'

Success in the role for this lady captain is measured in terms of winning, occasionally, it must be admitted, in the actual playing of the game, but more often than not in those off-course skirmishes that feature so prominently in the mini-politics of the average golf club. Nor is it satisfactory to the lady in question to have merely won the day; as with her famous historical counterpart, the winning must be publicly witnessed and the humiliation of the vanquished clearly demonstrated.

'You will write and personally sign a letter of apology to the full executive committee, a copy of which should be sent to the ladies' committee, which I personally will ensure is displayed on the club notice board, admitting that it was you who placed those posters throughout the clubhouse, but in particular on our own committee room door, advertising the personal services of our resident masseuse, 'to any gentleman who cares to make a strictly confidential appointment.'

For other golf clubs, it must be said, 'the winds of change' have swept like a Florida hurricane through those previously male-dominated hallowed portals. The figure of the lady captain is now an altogether different one from that portrayed earlier. With the inevitable arrival of much more liberal and open policies in matters relating to membership, playing rights and privileges and, of course, equality of fees, the nature of the 'battle ground' has changed and with it, the nature of the person occupying the role.

That hitherto male-orientated bastion of golf club affairs, the executive committee, to which a lady captain, if it was deemed necessary for such an appointment to be made, was previously invited to attend only on a 'need to listen' basis. In recent times, golf's own 'Berlin Wall' has very definitely been breached. Its membership and posts of responsibility, and certainly for the position of lady captain, are now without question, open to lady members.

Gone are the days in these particular clubs when members of the men's section would have 'thrown a complete wobbly', even at the sight of a lady on the golf course, even though 'that damned woman' intruder was over half a mile away and these 'guardians of the fairways' were well ensconced in the clubhouse bar on their fourth G&T.

No longer is one likely to hear the alleged response made by an official of one famous club when challenged about its policy towards lady golfers and the principles of equal opportunities that, 'lady golfers are free to play this course, for instance, at any time they wish after 2.00 pm between January and April.'

Of equally 'plus four-splitting' proportions is the fact that the lady captain will not now conform to the stereotypical caricature that her male counterparts would, in the past, have painted of her. Contrary to popular rumour and innuendo, she will probably not have raced hot foot to the committee meeting after first finishing off a jam preserving session, pickling onions, putting the finishing touches to a knitted bedspread or even cooking tea for her other half.

It's more likely that she may well have come straight from a company's business meeting, maybe even her own, in which decisions on such things as market forecasts, sales projections, budget allocations and personnel recruitment were high on her own personal agenda of responsibilities. Other 'new age' lady captains may, quite likely, have just jetted in from some European capital after fronting an international business conference on behalf of a major multi-national conglomerate.

Swapping such a high profile management arena then, for a golf club committee meeting, probably dominated by a group of 'ill-informed old dodderers' who 'couldn't run a lukewarm bath and make an effective decision if their balls were on fire,' would have about the same effect on this 'new arrival' as a cold shower in January.

Very likely attired in the latest fashion designer suit, with just enough thigh and cleavage showing to get the 'old boys' on a heart-thumping, adrenalin run and equipped with brief case, mobile phone, laptop and palm top organiser, the lady captain is quite likely to find herself faced with a discussion on the golf club's strategic business plan with a group of paisley jumpers, cords and hush puppies, equipped only with a badly chewed biro and the back of an old lottery ticket.

The ignominy for the old male guard of being quizzed about the accuracy of their cash flow projections for the club, the questionable wisdom of certain unstable investments and their totally inappropriate procedures for allocating work contracts, has been known to drive some of them to such desperate measures as agreeing to accompany their wives to late night shopping trips or taking the mother-in law to bingo.

To add insult to injury, this latest addition to the club's management ranks has probably actually read the Royal and Ancient's Handbook on the Rules of Golf from cover to cover and equally annoyingly, understood them. This is quite likely to be in stark contrast to most of the committee, with perhaps the exception of the handicap secretary, who couldn't distinguish between a lateral water hazard and a rabbit scrape.

To suffer the indignity of ever so politely but firmly, being informed by, of all people, the lady captain that contrary to their ruling to one member that he could quite legitimately remove grass cuttings from a bunker when they were lying next to his ball, that in fact this was a two shot penalty, was stretching their level of tolerance for the club's equal opportunities policy to the very limit.

'I've been playing this damn game for 30 years,' said one member, when challenged about taking relief from an unplayable lie, 'and I've never needed to look up the rules.'

'That's why you've probably broken every bloody rule in the book,' was the prompt reply; 'your interpretation of the term, 'taking relief' is limited to having a pee in the bushes.'

Committee members whose previous experience of working with the lady captain had been restricted to discussing the flower arrangements and the table layouts for the club's Christmas dinner, or seeking her advice on a suitable colour scheme for the changing rooms, now find themselves having to learn a whole new vocabulary.

With the new female incumbent representing the ladies' section on the full executive committee, blatantly chauvinistic phrases from the assembled males such as 'a few of us men have decided that...' or 'one or two of the more experienced male members want to...'or 'we believe we're right in thinking...' and the one which really threatened to rock the foundations, 'based on our long experience, we know that...' have now been consigned to that other notoriously undemocratic decision-making arena, namely the men's bar, which itself is under threat of extinction from the 'new enlightened order.'

A member of one distinguished golf club who, in committee, happened to use the phrase, 'in recognition of the services of a long-standing senior male member' to justify some outrageous demand for particular dispensation over the use of buggies in the winter when they were banned for everyone else, was bluntly told by a new female arrival to its ranks that, 'only two solutions to your problem are possible, sir, resignation or amputation'.

Words like 'consultation', 'dialogue', 'consensus' and 'co-operation', have suddenly begun to pepper committee discussions and sent some of its long-standing members rushing home to consult a rather dust-covered dictionary or thesaurus for the precise nature of their previous failings in these matters. Committees have suddenly found themselves being encouraged to have more 'empathy' with their members' needs, to 'engage with their agenda' and to be more 'bottom up rather than top down' in their thinking. A number of sotto voce oaths have been overheard from some quarters about what they'd like to do with this particular owner's 'top' and 'bottom', but intentions have never ever quite become a reality.

Alarm and despondency have also increased dramatically among the 'old school' of committee members with the corresponding discovery that this new breed of lady captain could actually speak eruditely in public, frequently without recourse to a fist-full of dog-eared cards covered in indecipherable scribbles.

Making a complete bollocks of speaking at the public functions of a golf club has largely been the undisputed and unchallenged territory of the male members of its committee. In the past, the few contributions that have been made by the ladies at these prestigious events have been restricted to appealing for support for the raffle, providing a vote of thanks to the flower arranger and waitresses, and enquiring as to who among the assembled gathering had lost their free bus pass.

The new breed of lady captain, however, has suddenly introduced golf clubs to a figure which, for all the world, appears to have come straight from the successful defence of a serial killer at the Old Bailey. No longer are long-suffering audiences subjected to the incoherent mumblings and stumblings of a nervous and ill-prepared, yet verbally incontinent 'rambling raconteur'. Nor are they subjected to those badly timed, slightly dubious and unintelligible in-house jokes, nor the bum-achingly detailed description of the speaker's unsuccessful round of golf.

What they are treated to is an almost flawless, supremely confident and erudite presentation that would have rivalled Montgomery's rallying call to the troops at El Alamein. Gone are the halting, stuttering, hesitantly embarrassing monosyllabic performances of previous male speakers, to be replaced by a clearly articulated, well- structured and thoughtful demonstration of just how to speak in a most professional way to a live audience.

Nor is the art of communication among these new 'divas' of golf club management limited to just the spoken word. Much to the absolute bewilderment of many of their male colleagues, many of whom had never actually witnessed a lady writing, nor for that matter reading anything more intellectually challenging from them than a shopping list or 'jobs to be done' list, they found themselves working alongside someone who actually knew how to string words together coherently and, what's more, punctuate and spell them correctly.

Requests for letters to be written to various local council departments about issues of health and safety, environmental health, planning permission, applications for funding from government and private bodies and for sponsorship support from local companies for club events have, in many cases, resulted in the appearance of a superbly worded, well argued and clearly presented document from the pen, or rather the word processor, of the lady captain.

When job applications, contracts of employment and terms and conditions of service were required, they were on the table at the very next meeting, courtesy of the aforementioned lady. Suddenly, overnight, golf clubs appeared to have acquired, a financier, lawyer, management consultant and politician, combining the writing skills of a leader writer at The Telegraph and the debating skills of a front bench parliamentary spokes-woman on law and order.

Most of the male officials of golf clubs where the lady captain has embraced her managerial responsibilities with all the skill, tenacity and drive of an international, jet-setting business woman hell-bent on world market domination, have accepted these developments with a resigned fortitude and got on with the job of being just a plain, 'committee member'.

What, however, still sticks in the throats of many male golfers as the least desirable development in this lengthy catalogue of female accomplishments, is the fact that, above all, they can also play 'a damned good game of golf.' In the past, the on-course exploits of lady golfers, including the lady captain have been sufficient to keep an after dinner speaker in jokes for hours without danger of repetition.

Now, however, it is the male species that is often required to don the mantle of golf's 'ugly duckling' when it comes to on-course performance. It is quite possible to find a lady captain playing off a handicap in the low teens or even single figures and the absolute look of disbelief on the faces of those male golfers when they discover that they're in receipt of shots from a lady golfer, should be compulsorily captured for golf club records.

Paradoxically, with this dramatic change in the nature and, in some cases, status, of the lady captain in a golf club, has come a change in the source of her opposition. Previously, the exclusive source of criticism and opposition to her and her position was the male membership, who exploited the flaws and foibles of the unfortunate occupant of the post like a cartoon caricaturist of a daily tabloid.

Now, however, the most likely source of criticism of her, and the murky origins of those 'back stabbing' antics, is her own ladies' section. With her increased profile in the club's management and the corresponding higher expectations placed on her, any failings or falterings on her part are now much more likely to be the subject of discussion among her female counterparts and so-called colleagues. Had Shakespeare been alive today, he might well have set the 'plottings' of Lady Macbeth, not in that famous castle of Dunsinane, but in the far more dangerous corridors and committee rooms of a British golf club.

Filling the post of lady captain at 'Swankers' had, for many years now, proved just about as easy as it would to get the Royal and Ancient to agree to play The Open on a 'pay and play' municipal golf course. Unlike the situation in other clubs where lady members were almost literally 'fighting' each other to get the nomination, at 'Swankers', when nominations were due, all kinds of little known illnesses were mysteriously contracted by possible candidates, all requiring at least six months convalescence. Other lady members cited the rules of some obscure society of which they were members, such as the famous 'Twats' – 'Torquay Women Against Tantric Sex' – as a reason for their disqualification from holding another similar post of responsibility.

There were a variety of reasons for this situation. At the head of the list was probably no lady's wish to subject herself to the regular monthly torment, aggravation and harassment of having to work with the club's male-dominated executive committee. One lady member who had been seconded to help out, graphically described her experience as, 'menstruation, golf club style.'

Coupled with this was the fact that most lady members

freely admitted to having an intense dislike for Barnes, the secretary, with whom, as lady captain, they'd be required to work quite closely. While quite prepared to cope with levels of administrative incompetence that would put most town councils to shame, such as failing to proof read the ladies' section of the club diary for simple, but very embarrassing errors, they were certainly not prepared to countenance his excessively chauvinistic behaviour. As one lady member pointed out, 'his two main reasons for supporting ladies' membership of the executive committee were apparently that, 'we need someone who can take minutes without interrupting and make the tea and sandwiches.'

On one occasion, he prided himself on having, as he thought, complimented an ex-lady captain with the words, 'well you're a woman, you'll know about things like colours and patterns and what goes with what.' The idea that lady members of the committee and the lady captain, in particular, were capable of organising anything for the club other than 'food, flowers and florals' had completely escaped him.

The other overwhelming reason for the absence of volunteers from among the ladies for the post of captain was the notorious sexual antics of the club's chairman, Neil Tomlinson. His reputation as, 'a bit of a ladies man' was well reported throughout the ranks of all members. The frequency with which urgent meetings with previous lady captains had been called had quickly given rise to suspicions among the ladies as to his real intentions. Matters such as the size of the lettering on the ladies changing room doors, the positioning of an outside light on their entrance and the size of the wash hand basin in the on-course toilet, were hardly of a priority to require the lady captain to make a 30 mile round trip to the club at 8.00 pm on a winter's evening. The offer to meet half way in a local pub and discuss the matters over a drink was treated with equal disquiet by the unwilling recipient of these tactics.

Previous lady captains who had mistakenly strayed into these apparently innocent encounters had soon found themselves the object of some explicit advances which required all the balletic footwork of a prima ballerina to ensure they retained their dignity and composure, not to mention significant items of their clothing. As one lady captain explained in confidence to a friend, 'having to listen to chat-up lines that would have embarrassed a 14-year old school boy, tolerate the presence of someone who sat so close that you couldn't move for fear of getting entangled in some unexplainable clinch, while at the same time having to look into the face of someone who you feel is mentally undressing you, is not why I volunteered to be lady captain.'

In a well-authenticated, but secret email that was circulated to lady members of the executive committee and prospective lady captains, one past captain wrote, 'in the unfortunate event of having to meet with the club's chairman without the close attendance of another female colleague, I strongly advise that, if possible, it be held in the most public of places in the clubhouse, where any attempt at what might be termed, 'schoolboy gropings' on the part of our honourable chairman could be clearly observed. Failing this, I strongly advise that for your meeting you wear nothing with a low cut neck line, anything that is shorter than ankle length in height or tightly fitting to the figure – you have been warned.'

A final deterrent to those ladies who felt inclined to offer themselves as a 'sacrificial lamb to the golfing slaughter' at 'Swankers' was, in fact, the ladies' section itself. The rapid transformation in the attitudes and behaviour of some of the lady members once the individual had stepped over that golfing 'de-militarised zone', which separated lady member from lady captain, was truly astonishing.

Those warm hearted, generous, forgiving souls who previously would have walked through fire to preserve the good name and reputation of this lady have, following her successful appointment, undergone a chameleon-like transformation. No longer is she the epitome of common sense, level-headedness and sound judgement, but the very obvious reincarnation of incompetence, stupidity and indecision. Overnight, she had suddenly transformed into an arrogant, pig-headed, obstinate individual riding for a fall of astronomical proportions. 'I was only saying to a friend of mine the other day, I don't know what possessed her to think she'd make a good captain; I knew from the very start when I heard she'd been nominated that she'd be no good in the job,' said a so-called friend and golfing partner of one lady captain at the club, only a matter of weeks into her captaincy. Needless to say, these were the very same two members who, believing that supporting the lady's application might earn them some future favours, had been quite outspoken in their support of her nomination.

As the lady captain in question confessed, 'I soon found you can't win when you become lady captain; my attempts at trying to run the ladies' section more efficiently became, 'domineering interference', my suggestions for getting more people involved in how it was run were interpreted as, 'dithering indecision' and my ideas for changing some of the out-dated ways of working were actually dubbed, 'arrogant nonsense.''

When Brenda Maddox, or as many members, particularly the men, insisted on secretly calling her, 'Brunhilde', after Wagner's belligerent heroine, accepted the reins of office, there was an immediate outcry of, 'how the hell did she come to get the job?' and 'what in god's name have we let ourselves in for?'

'Simple answer,' said the out-going lady captain, 'when I was looking for a vice, none of you were interested, so you've got what you jolly well deserve: Brenda.'

Brenda, quite unashamedly, had spent a lifetime reaching previously uncharted levels of arrogance, self-assuredness and bloody-mindedness that would have been the envy of most global politicians. In most members' opinion, she had graduated with honours in every single area. Now she was, at last, in a position to apply these qualities to the task of lady captain and woe-betide anyone from any section of the club who had the audacity to take on the role of front or back bench opposition.

Most members of the ladies' committee approached the first meeting with 'Brunhilde' at the helm with a mixture of dread and despair at what might be the outcome. They were not disappointed, as they endured an opening 45 minutes comprising a series of changes to established practice and procedure, all prefaced with the phrase, 'I want', rather like a badly behaved child in a toy shop. For those members frantically engaged in counting the number of occasions the phrase was used for the 'book' that had been opened at the start of the meeting, they noted seven in the first ten minutes, when it was temporarily replaced by, 'I've decided'.

'Ladies, I want a much better turn out on ladies' day than last year, which on most occasions, was frankly a disgrace. I have no desire to be hauled in front of the executive committee to be informed by those 'dinosaurs' that entries on ladies' day have fallen so low that we no longer warrant being given the existing allocation of tee times. I want no excuses about colds or coughs, headaches or any imaginary 'womens' problems'. I want everyone signed in at least 15 minutes before the first tee time.'

'I want everyone playing in all the competitions this year; last year your attendance at these was nothing short of pathetic. If you all think I'm going to spend my precious time organising these competitions just for a carload of members, you're very much mistaken.'

The lady competition secretary, Cynthia Roberts, suddenly had two stark images flash in front of her; one of an on-going battle of wills over various arrangements and procedures and the second, a letter of resignation to take effect immediately.

'Now ladies, I've decided that we need to smarten up our appearance at matches against other clubs. Members have been turning out in all kinds of hideously mismatched outfits that frankly make us look like a staff outing from a charity shop. I've decided that every one should dress in matching coloured sweater and trousers from now on. I've personally chosen the colours and orders should be placed with the outfitters immediately by all those who wish to be considered for the two ladies' teams.'

'She'll be lucky to get enough people for one team, never mind two,' whispered one member at the back, 'if she goes on cataloguing demands like some trade union shop steward.'

'She's got a bloody cheek asking us to smarten up,' said someone, 'she turns up regularly in what looks like leftovers from a jumble sale.'

'If she thinks I'm forking out nearly £75 to turn out in those colours, she's off her rocker, they make us look like the bloody 'Tele Tubbies.'

'Ladies, I've decided that this year we'll have none of those quite pointless competitions like last year, such as going out with just three clubs and a putter, for instance, or playing from the first tee to the fourth green across the course; it's all rather futile and demeaning and doesn't give a good image of the ladies' section.'

'Finally, ladies, I come to the matter of attendance at committee meetings. I understand from my predecessor that during last year, attendance by some members was quite unsatisfactory and my own observations bore that out. Often the reasons offered for non-attendance were completely unacceptable. I realise that children can suddenly be ill, but you've husbands or relations who can surely look after them for a couple of hours. This year, I expect nothing less than 100 per cent attendance at our committee meetings. I'm afraid that if anyone fails to attend on a regular basis, I shall have no hesitation in asking them to resign from the committee.'

'Bloody hell,' exclaimed one member, 'you get treated better than this working in McDonalds and you get paid and all.'

'We'll have to produce a sodding doctor's note next, if we don't show up,' complained another.

'I thought I belonged to a golf club, not a training camp for hostage-taking terrorists learning how to phrase a ransom demand note,' moaned yet another disillusioned member.

Committee members were firmly told at the close of the meeting that, from now on, there would be no item on the agenda called, 'any other business', with the explanation, 'it gives far too many people the opportunity to raise the most insignificant and trivial of matters that are of no interest to the rest of us; if you want something put on the agenda, put it in writing to me and I shall consider it for inclusion.'

The lady members left the meeting feeling like a bunch of naughty schoolgirls who'd just been reprimanded by the headmistress for contravening school rules by wearing the wrong coloured knickers.

Sorting out the ladies' committee at the club had been Brenda's first priority as lady captain. She'd seen how most of them behaved the previous year when she'd been vice. She had lost count of the hours she'd wasted in meetings listening to their inconsequential drivel and their pathetic attempts at making any decision more significant than whether to have toasted teacakes or sandwiches at the end of their meetings. In her opinion, most of them were a total irrelevance that she could have managed perfectly well without, but the ladies' constitution stated that there had to be a ladies' committee, so she was determined to knock some shape into this group of dithering nonentities. They were either going to pull their weight on the committee or she'd make their life hell for the year.

She realised that it wasn't going to be that easy a task. She had Doreen Matthews, for instance, the committee's secretary whose job it was, amongst other things, to take notes and produce the minutes of their meetings. Doreen was rather deaf and so had to have things repeated, often more than once, which inevitably slowed everything down and irritated everyone immensely.

'Did I hear you say, lady captain, that there was a mouse loose in the ladies' loo?' asked Doreen, at one of the first meetings after she'd been appointed secretary.

'No, Doreen, I said there was no excuse for ladies loosing their shoes when there are perfectly good lockers available.'

Inevitably, she also missed or misunderstood quite important items completely, which caused a real stink at the next meeting when members complained about the absence from the minutes of key decisions.

'I distinctly remember us deciding that we would plan well in advance to have our ladies' 'away day' on the first Tuesday in June, so that if anyone couldn't make it they would have time to make their apologies. Now where the hell is that in the minutes?' enquired one irate member.

'You were explaining to us that you were going to be away in the first week of June, so you were making your apologies for not attending now,' shouted Doreen in her defence.

'No I was not, you stupid woman; if we're going to spend half of each meeting, lady captain, having to go over mistakes and omissions from the last meeting, we're never going to get any business done; do we, perhaps, have sufficient funds to purchase a hearing aid for our secretary?'

'Why do we have to purchase a heated tray?' enquired Doreen of the lady captain, to the utter despair of the rest of the members.

Brenda had also inherited another problem, the lady handicap secretary, Glenys. She, like all the others with a specific job to do, had volunteered, not really knowing what the hell was involved and with none of the requisite skills for doing the job in the first place. Glenys had struggled with the ladies' handicapping system from the very start, desperately trying to remember all the categories of the different handicaps and what handicaps they actually represented. The idea of Standard Scratch, CSS, nett and gross differentials, or aggregated competitions, were also a bit of a mystery to her and her chances of working out what constituted the buffer zone, represented a big zero.

Slowly, however, light had begun to dawn. Then along came the computerised system of establishing and recording handicaps, with terms like, 'Handicap Maintenance Operations' and rules prohibiting the software from, 'providing any facilities for the manual override of a calculated Competition Scratch score,' or 'provide any formula for clause 19 adjustments other than as provided in clause 19.8.' It soon became obvious that Glenys had about as much chance of mastering the intricacies of the handicap system as Victoria Beckham had of taking the 'Mastermind' trophy.

Brenda had in mind to approach her friend and next door neighbour, Audrey Martin, to do the job, but realised she'd have to tread carefully so as not to be accused of giving 'jobs to her girls'.

Brenda's one other hope of retaining her sanity amidst this blistering array of bunglers was her friend Celia, who Brenda had wanted as her vice captain. Celia was a 5ft 2in, 14 stone 'smoking battleship' who, when primed correctly and discharged in the appropriate direction, could instil fear into the very toughest opponents, be they male or female. This would have been Brenda's idea of a 'dream team', though to the rest of the club, without exception, it had all the makings of the very best casting that Hammer Films could have created.

Unfortunately for Brenda, Celia was heavily involved in that exclusively female 'Jam and Jerusalem' group, the Women's Institute. Celia had recently accepted the position of lady president and felt that she could not fulfil both roles. Most people who'd had dealings, whether good or bad, with Celia believed she was quite capable of taking on both roles, while simultaneously chairing the United Nations General Assembly, reorganising NATO and running the local pub.

Celia had, in fact, witnessed at first hand, the problems experienced by some of her friends in trying to lead the 'un-lead-able' members of the golf club's ladies' section while, at the same time, deal with those insufferable cretins from the men's section whose fossilised arses had occupied the chairs of power for so long, they could have applied for listing by The National Trust. She had decided that the WI represented an alternative challenge, where nothing more serious than a lousy, lack-lustre rendering of Parry's 'Jerusalem' by a group of discordant, tone-deaf female choristers would require her attention.

Consequently, Brenda had inherited another problem in the form of Jeanette Tyler, her vice captain. To describe them as 'chalk and cheese' would be a substantial understatement; it was almost inconceivable to think of a single situation or issue over which these two would find themselves in agreement. For Brenda, matters were either black or white, whether they were to do with golf or life in general. There was a definite right way and a wrong way to do things; people either did what they were told or had to be told they were wrong.

With Jeanette, matters were never just black or white; there were lots of shades of grey in her life. Right and wrong was just a matter of one person's opinion at one particular moment in time. Telling someone they were wrong was, in her opinion, an open invitation to them to carry on behaving that way just for the hell of it.

Brenda, even as lady captain, felt no burning obligation to seek popularity among the club's members. She had a job to do and if people didn't like her or the way she did things, that was their problem. Jeanette, on the other hand, liked to be liked and had set out to be a popular vice captain with everyone, including, much to Brenda's annoyance, a considerable number of the men with whom she got on extremely well.

This particular side of Jeanette's character had raised a number of eyebrows in the club and Brenda had been quick to pick up on comments like, 'you need to keep an eye on your husband when she's around' or 'she's got a few notches on her driver, from what I hear.' In truth, these kinds of remarks were just evidence of certain lady members' jealousy, because it had to be conceded that Jeanette was an extremely attractive lady who was quite capable of exploiting her looks and her personality to the very best advantage.

Brenda had witnessed Jeanette's so-called 'sexploits', most recently in their match with the men's captain and vice captain. Dressed in the most provocative pair of slacks and a golfing top that left very little to the imagination, she had, in Brenda's opinion, proceeded to flounce around the course using just about every trick in the book to put the two unfortunate males well and truly off their game. To anyone other than Brenda, of course, this would have been dismissed as nothing more than a joke to see these two grown men stumbling around the course, eyes out like organ stops, practically foaming at the mouth, complete with foolish ear-to-ear grins, responding to her every little suggestive remark and fawning over her every sudden movement, particularly those which involved bending from the waist. To Brenda, of course, it was a thoroughly disgusting example of feminine wiles that had no place on the golf course.

Some days after the match, Brenda, in typical bullish style, tackled Jeanette about her behaviour on the course and what she thought she was up to.

'I've really no idea what you mean, Brenda, when you ask, 'what did I think I was up to out there? It was just a harmless game of golf and a bit of fun, but I thought we were still out there trying our damnedest to beat the pants off those two arrogant old buffers.'

'A bit of fun indeed,' said Brenda, 'you had those two characters behaving like two love-crazed teenagers and as for their pants, there seemed to be so much going on inside them, had we been out there another half hour, I think they would have had to beat them themselves to put out the fire.'

'You're not seriously suggesting that I was deliberately trying to get those two old codgers steamed up, are you? You, my dear, may be well passed your sexual sell-by date and your 'bonking bar code' may have expired, but mine certainly has not; but I can assure you that those two are definitely not on my shopping list.'

'I think that is precisely what I'm saying, Jeanette,' replied Brenda, 'you seem to forget that this a golf club, not a Hollywood film set.'

'While you're around Brenda, no-one would ever confuse this place with a Hollywood film set; though they might be forgiven for thinking they'd stumbled into a Dominican nunnery for all the signs of contact with the real world you manage to give off,' replied Jeanette, caustically.

'I think I'd prefer them thinking that than have them believe that they'd joined some infamous night club and revue bar,' replied Brenda.

'Pity that,' said Jeanette, 'I think I'd rather enjoy seeing you getting your old tweed kit off and doing a session on the shiny pole for our male members,' and for once left Brenda speechless and open mouthed at the sheer audacity of the woman.

Both women knew that there were going to be many more such 'encounters' over the year and wondered just how many tactics they would have to employ to keep the other at bay.

Brenda had decided that the other absolutely essential change necessary in the ladies' section was the immediate removal of her competitions secretary who'd been a complete and utter disaster from the very first moment she'd taken on the job. How in god's name this completely scatter-brained, totally disorganised woman came to get the job in the first place was a complete mystery to most people, since it was a well-known fact that she frequently had trouble finding her way from home to the golf club on occasions, let alone organise its competitions programme. And as for remembering and appearing at pre-arranged dates and times for appointments, she was just about as reliable as a one-fingered watch.

Cynthia Roberts had been responsible, as far back as people could remember, for virtually every single cock-up to do with the club's own competitions and matches with other clubs. Quite how she'd lasted this long in the job was only explained by the fact that volunteers to replace her were notable by their absence, they being only too well aware of the complete shambles they'd be required to sort out. They were, however, quite willing to volunteer some unsolicited advice as to what Brenda should do about the woman's complete ineptitude and demands were being made weekly for news of how soon her removal would be announced.

The lady captain also had a sizeable collection of letters from other golf clubs detailing organisational blunders for which Cynthia had been solely responsible. Most intimated in fairly direct terms that if this situation was allowed to continue, it was very unlikely that the fixture with 'Swankers' would be renewed. Brenda had finally decided that she'd have to take this job on herself, bite the bullet and break the news to Cynthia.

'Cynthia, I've come to the conclusion that the very demanding job of competitions' secretary is beginning to prove quite difficult for you, would you agree?' began Brenda. 'I really think now would be a good time for you to pass the responsibility on to someone else.'

'But nobody else knows how to do the job properly, Brenda,' replied Cynthia.

Well, that's damn rich coming from someone who's had the job for umpteen years without actually knowing what the hell they were doing, thought Brenda.

'But we do seem to be having a lot of problems lately with our own club competitions and the arrangements for some of our matches with other clubs have been absolutely farcical; members are getting a little annoyed,' said Brenda.

'No-one's complained to me, I can't think what they've got to get annoyed about,' replied Cynthia.

No-one's complained to you, you stupid woman, because they think it would be a complete waste of breath trying to explain the finer points of organising any event to someone who is intellectually challenged producing a monthly shopping list, thought Brenda.

'Well, Cynthia, just in the last four months, you've managed to organise one ladies' competition on the very same day as the course was made available for 80 of the county's boys to practice, sent one competition out on the course with score cards which just happened to be two years out of date, quite amazingly managed to put up 18 starting times with members' names for two competitions, which had actually been cancelled because of a lack of entries and bizarrely insisted on a ladies' pairs competition being played as a Texas Scramble; how the hell did you work that one out?'

'It's not easy sometimes, keeping track of which competition is which, you know,' admitted Cynthia.

In your case, it's not easy keeping track of which day it is, never mind which competition it is, thought Brenda.

'Cynthia, why did you advertise a mixed foursomes competition and then put the starting times up with teams of four ladies, with not a single man's name on the list?' enquired Brenda patiently.

'Well, one or two ladies said they didn't want to play a mixed competition, so I decided to change it,' admitted Cynthia.

'Yes, but wouldn't it have been a good idea to have warned the 14 men who signed up and subsequently turned up, that they were not actually required?'

'Well, I just thought they'd might like to play among themselves anyway,' explained Cynthia.

What they would liked to have done, had you remembered to turn up, thought Brenda, was string you up from the club's flag pole for being such a complete pillock.

'You know we've had a lot of letters from other clubs complaining about the foul-ups with the arrangements for the matches,' added Brenda.

'No-one's written to me complaining,' remarked Cynthia.

No they wouldn't would they, thought Brenda, because they're not sure that you've graduated to reading and comprehending joined up writing yet.

'Well, I admit there have been one or two small problems,' said Cynthia.

'Cynthia, you sent 24 ladies on a 70 mile round trip only for them to discover, on their arrival at the course, that their opponents had made the same journey to us, they actually passed one another on the motorway, it was a home match.'

'Well they played the match here in the end, when they got back,' rejoined Cynthia.

'Yes, they finished in the pitch dark, absolutely exhausted, someone then had to drive ten miles to get the keys to the locked changing rooms and by the time everyone had changed, the steward and the chef had gone home because you didn't warn them that they were late starting and so would need to stay later; so someone had to go to Tesco to get some sandwiches for them to eat on the coach going home; they've indicated they don't want a return match, by the way.'

'Well, we'll just have to find a replacement fixture,' said Cynthia.

Yes, thought Brenda, but with our growing reputation for organising cock-ups, we'll need visas to get there.

'Oh and two other clubs have informed us that they're not interested in any further fixtures,' added Brenda, 'one, because they had 18 ladies waiting to play the match and we, apparently, turned up with ten.'

'That wasn't my fault, the others didn't show up because it was raining,' exclaimed Cynthia.

'It's your flaming responsibility to make sure everyone shows up, Cynthia,' shouted Brenda, 'whether it's raining, snowing or there's been a bloody earthquake; that's the most pathetic excuse you've produced so far. Oh and by the way, just for the record, it wasn't bloody raining where the match was to be played. The other club said they were not interested in playing us again if we can't turn out a better team,' explained Brenda, 'how did you select that team?'

'Well, I chose the first 12 who put their names down, it seemed the fairest way to do it,' explained Cynthia.

'Yes, but it just so happened that none of them had a handicap of less than 30, so we lost all 12 matches before any of them managed to get to the 13th hole, you silly woman; two of our teams actually lost ten and eight; didn't it occur to you to check the handicaps before selecting the team?'

'Well, if you can find someone who you think can do this job better, they're welcome to it,' replied Cynthia, 'that's all the gratitude I get for all my hard work.'

Most of the children in our local primary school could do a

better job than you, thought Brenda, and they probably haven't even been near a golf club.

'I've decided to do the job myself,' explained Brenda, 'that way I'll be sure that our competitions programme will not be the butt of all the clubhouse jokers who claim we couldn't organise a piss-up in a brewery. It will also ensure that we'll have a set of fixtures which doesn't require using the local branch of Thomas Cook to organise our travel itinerary.'

Organising any event at a golf club can be a nightmarish experience; sod's law decrees that if any one thing can possibly go wrong, probably just about everything will. Lady captain's day at 'Swankers', however, seemed to defy that particular law; just about everything had gone right for Brenda, including the weather, the course, in spite of a last minute attempt by that pig-headed, bad-mannered head green keeper to kibosh things by scarifying seven greens; the competition arrangements, now well and truly out of Cynthia's hands; the catering, though there were the usual complaints about inadequate portions from the more gluttonous members of the ladies' section and finally, the presentation of the awards to the winners.

Brenda chose to ignore the few whispers about the, 'cheapskate, car-boot-sale prizes' that were on offer but pointedly thanked, 'those more generous-minded and well-intentioned members of the ladies' section who took the trouble and time to find raffle prizes for her.' Brenda was delighted to see that her comment successfully hit its intended mean-spirited, vindictive targets, as evidenced by the glares on their faces and the exaggerated squirming of bottoms on seats as she resumed her own seat.

The expected 'verbal skirmish' with Jeanette had not really materialised, though Brenda had fully expected some form of 'onslaught' for putting her vice captain out at the end of the field with two 36 handicappers who just managed to scrape into double figures between them as a Stableford score. What was noticed almost by everyone, however, was Jeanette's sudden disappearance and subsequent reappearance from the chairman's office after an unaccountably long time, allegedly there to re-arrange the seating plan for her company's corporate golfing day. The predictable 'gossip machines' among the lady members were heard to impute that 'judging by the time she spent in there with him, she'd re-arranged a good deal more than just her seating plan.'

Brenda's other big day was her planned 'away day', when her intention was to take 30 lady members to another golf course for a round of golf, dinner and an overnight stay at its adjoining hotel. No other lady captain at 'Swankers' had ever organised an 'away day' on this scale before, but this was thoroughly in keeping with Brenda's style and how she wanted her captaincy to be remembered. There had been no problem restricting the party to 30 because the remaining 'cheapskates' in the ladies' section had ruled themselves out when they discovered they had to pay for the round of golf themselves, while Brenda personally picked up the tab for the travel, accommodation and meal. As one of the 30 in the group said, 'I think some of them expected to get £20 spending money as well.'

It is an undeniable fact that golfers travel all over the world on holidays that they've planned themselves, putting up with all kinds of crap arrangements and organisational disasters, generally without expressing a murmur of complaint or questioning a single detail of the itinerary. Get them in a party from their own golf club, however, on a trip lasting as little as 48 hours, organised by some poor unsuspecting tirelessly patient volunteer and they become the 'golfers from hell'.

Brenda soon realised that her 'away day' was not going to be as plain sailing as she'd hoped, as the comments, delivered personally to her or whispered just sufficiently loudly for her to hear, began to flow.

'Why do we have to travel that far, I would have preferred to have gone somewhere nearer?'

'Why do we have to stay overnight, I would have preferred to have come back the same day?'

'Why do we all have to go on the coach, I would prefer to travel in my own car?'

It was not Brenda's style or intention to dignify all these pathetic questions with individual answers or explanations; she was not of a mind to be apologetic about what she'd planned for these ungrateful 'whingers'. Her standard reply, either direct or via someone else was, 'this is the trip I've organised, if you don't like the arrangements, don't come.'

Secretly, she'd chosen the golf course and hotel because she'd got a very good deal on the daily rates through a personal friend of hers and they were all travelling by coach together because she didn't want some of the stupid old bats getting lost and finishing up anywhere between Hull and Holyhead. She also wanted them all there at the same time; some of the ladies were known to drive at speeds which in a previous era would have warranted a red flag preceding their stately progress.

Once the party of 30 had reconciled itself to the fact that the trip was non-negotiable, they then settled for bombarding Brenda with the usual idiotic and mindless queries about the trip that would have left an observer assuming that Brenda had found a hitherto unknown golfing location, requiring a three day trek into the Amazonian rainforest.

'Does the hotel cater for people on special diets?'

It's a four star hotel, what do you think?

'Can I have a single room, I don't like sharing?'

No, the deal is based on two people sharing; surely you can manage without your vibrator for one night, thought Brenda,

'Does the hotel have non-smoking rooms and a non-smoking policy in the restaurant?'

If it doesn't we'll make up a bed for you in the bus, thought Brenda,

'Has it got a lift?'

'Has it got drying facilities?'

The questions went on relentlessly from people who regularly boasted in the golf club of having travelled the globe, staying in top hotels without, apparently, a care in the world, yet who suddenly became paranoid at the thought of spending one night, just 80 miles from home, in the company of 30 other lady golfers.

Just when she thought that they'd all exhausted the 'who can make the most outrageous request' game, Brenda received the usual last minute imbecilic demands.

'Can the coach pick me up at home, I can't get my husband to bring me in?'

No, it would require us making a 30 mile detour and if I do it for you...'

'Could I possibly bring the dog, I've got no-one I can leave him with?'

No, you bloody can't, the hotel has a no pets policy and it also has a no 'fruitcakes' policy, thought Brenda, so god knows how it's going to cope with you.

Came the day and Brenda reckoned she'd covered just about every possible detail. Every detail, of course, except the fact that some people turned up with quantities of luggage that would have taxed the carrying capacity of two Nepalese sherpas and was certainly going to tax the patience of the driver who was required to manhandle these 'wardrobes' around.

'We're only going for one night, Margaret,' said Brenda.

'I know, but I thought it better to be on the safe side with clothes.'

You could have kitted out the entire group with what you've brought, thought Brenda.

'Can I sit near the front, I get sick sitting anywhere else?' requested Shirley.

'You can sit on the driver's knee if it prevents you from throwing up all over someone,' said Brenda, who was by now getting somewhat irritated by all this nonsense.

'I can't sit over a wheel,' said Audrey, 'can you ask Maureen if she'll swap with me?'

Yes and then I'll come with you to the toilet to make sure you don't wet your pants, thought Brenda.

'I hope I don't have to sit by Vera,' said Angela, 'she just never stops talking.'

'Can I make a quick phone call home; I've left my five-iron in the boot of the car?' pleaded Cynthia.

'There's no time, Cynthia and anyway this is a friendly game of golf, not a qualifier for the British Ladies Open', replied Brenda.

Eventually, the journey got underway, with the coach driver by now wishing he'd volunteered to take the local rugby team to its away fixture. It wasn't long, however, before Brenda was receiving requests for the radio to be turned down,

'It's giving me a bit of a headache', said Thelma.

Not as much as you lot are giving me, thought Brenda.

'I'll need you to ask the driver to stop for me to go to the toilet soon,' requested Pam.

'But we've been travelling less than an hour,' replied Brenda.

'Well, you should have ordered a bus with a toilet then,' replied Pam.

I would have been better off ordering you some incontinence pants, thought Brenda, but said, 'I think one with a padded cell would have been more appropriate for some of you.'

'I hope we're stopping for a coffee soon,' demanded Jeanette, 'some of us want a fag as well.'

Brenda knew that the promise of a two-hour shopping and meal break could be a potential mistake, but had decided to risk it. Inevitably, there were those who were late back, causing a further rescheduling of the arrangements with the hotel.

'We got lost and couldn't remember where the coach was,' said Margaret, who'd just been half way round Australia on a two months holiday.

'We had to wait ages in the queue to the toilets,' explained Pam.

'We lost track of time, didn't we Cynthia?' said Audrey.

I'm surprised you didn't lose track of one another, thought Brenda, knowing Cynthia's ability to be anywhere other than where she was supposed to be.

Their arrival at the hotel and the subsequent evening meal passed relatively uneventfully, though there were one or two complaints like, 'my room's got a funny smell' and 'my water's too slow'. The latter brought a range of somewhat unhelpful, wine-induced suggestions from the group over dinner as to what the unfortunate lady should do about her personal hygiene problems. The complaint from one member that, 'I haven't got enough drawers', brought the loud and somewhat inebriated reply that she should have washed a few more before she left home.

The 18-hole medal competition was arranged for the following morning and Brenda had stressed to everyone the need to be on time on the first tee. It was a vain hope. A number had to be paged in their rooms, some had to skip breakfast and not an insignificant number had to run to the first tee fighting to get into various items of clothing. Brenda was not best pleased at the sight of her vice captain hurriedly requesting the professional to tie her shoe laces while she attempted to wriggle an extremely tight-fitting golf sweater over an equally tight-fitting pair of slacks and rather suggestively promising him that, 'I'll be in later to see what you've got in your trousers section that would fit me.'

Brenda steadfastly refused all requests for changes to partners, 'she had far too much to drink last night, you know, and is in no fit state to play'; 'she was up half the night apparently chatting up that sales rep, I doubt whether she knows how to hold a club.' She also insisted that the competition was over 18 holes, in spite of requests to count only 14 holes, 'I'm feeling a bit tired after all the travelling, I don't think I can do more than 14 holes.' She also resisted attempts by some to get her to change the format to Stableford, 'we're fed up with medals all the time, we want a change.'

By the time she got the last pairings on the first tee, in fact, the game in which she was also playing, she was hardly in a fit state to get the ball to stay on the tee, let alone find the fairway with a half decent opening drive. Most of the pairings got around without any serious incidents occurring, though there were a few unscheduled stops half way around for headache pills and lengthy toilet stops.

Sitting in the clubhouse later, most looked as though they'd spent a day training with the SAS rather than playing golf, though there was a general consensus that it had been a 'good do' and a vote of thanks was made to Brenda for her 'sterling efforts' on their behalf.

The coach was just about to leave for the return journey when someone pointed out that the lady vice captain was missing. It was suggested that someone should try the professional's shop in view of her parting shot to the gentleman after his assistance at the first tee. A correct prediction as it turned out, when Brenda entered the professional's inner office to find Jeanette hastily squeezing herself back into the pair of slacks she'd played in and rearranging the golf top so that its front was actually in the correct position.

'Oh hello, Brenda, come to see what he's got to offer you, have you?' said Jeanette mischievously, 'I'm well satisfied with what he managed to pull out for me.'

'The coach is leaving now,' said Brenda, 'we assume that you are coming back with us tonight, unless that is, this gentleman's allowed you to use his phone to ring your husband to say that you're staying another night.'

Brenda reflected on the journey home that one 'away day' in her captaincy year could well have been one too many.

Golf clubs' annual general meetings have a long-standing reputation in some quarters for opening up and fuelling sectional divisions and tribal loyalties of an intensity that would certainly rival those more politically or religiously motivated skirmishes that daily occur in some corner of the modern world. Just like their political or religious counterparts, some golf club AGMs give every appearance of being the 'graveyards' of common sense, rational thought and logical reasoning to become the 'greenhouse' for unchecked, uncontrolled emotional outbursts and the spawning grounds for extremist attitudes more usually associated with the left-wing elements of known global terrorist organisations.

In truth, it must be admitted, however, that some golf clubs have successfully managed to avoid these bloodletting encounters by acting swiftly to remove all vestiges of what might be considered as democratic processes. In these instances, the term 'meeting' is something of a misnomer, more appropriately being replaced, perhaps by the word 'rally', comprising as they do of a mixture of exhortations for the continued unquestioning and unswerving loyalty to the leadership and unreserved acceptance of the unrivalled quality and wisdom of its decisions. The only major difference between the 'golfing' event and its more militaristic or political equivalent, is that the former is often completed in such record-breaking time that any among the 'faithful' or, dare one say it, the 'unfaithful' that arrive unduly late will probably be greeted with the news of the date of next year's meeting.

Brenda, as lady captain, was not particularly looking forward to the club's AGM this year, though it must be said, it would never be an event that would find its way into her top 20 of all-time most pleasurable experiences. As was so often the case in the past, the 'battleground' this year was not any particular aspect of the game itself or indeed the golf course, but the arrangements and facilities available to members within the clubhouse. Paradoxically, these matters often seemed to generate more disquiet and disgruntlement among members than anything related to the playing of the game.

The 'hot issue' this year, therefore, was not the fact that some of the greens resembled the local football ground's goalmouth, or that some of the fairways were not considered sufficiently wide enough for a four-ball to walk side by side, or that one needed to play off single figures to even reach some of the fairways. Nor was the emotional temperature to be raised to boiling point over the irresponsible massacre of the environment around the third tee. What was going to rock the golfing foundations of the club this year was the proposal that the practice of designating some areas of the clubhouse for sole use by either the men or the women should be discontinued.

Tomlinson, the chairman, had been the main signatory behind the proposal, seconded, surprise, surprise by none other than the lady vice captain, Jeanette. Strangely for 'Swankers', this would be a debate that would not, as in the past, polarise into a verbal punch up between the men and the women members. Both sections were to be equally affected by the proposal and so the battle lines were being drawn up across the sexual divide. The ladies would lose their combined committee room and lounge and the men would lose their 'men only' bar and lounge area. The areas which would naturally not be affected by the proposal were the men's and ladies' changing rooms, though as one male member was heard to forecast even on this arrangement, 'if the lady vice captain has her way, in the next two years us lads'll probably find ourselves having to rummage through a pile of bras and pants for our lost socks and trousers.' A lady member, overhearing the remark was heard to say, 'in the case of the lady vice captain, I think you'll have to get in the queue if there's any rummaging through pants to be done.'

Once the main business of the AGM had been concluded with the reading of the various over-exaggerated, meaningless annual reports from the respective post holders, followed by confirmation of the appointment of the poor unsuspecting sods who were taking over various roles in the following year, the members prepared to 'lock horns' on the proposal. The chairman chose to open with a defence of the proposal.

'We've always prided ourselves here in the club with facing up to the need to change some of the old ways we've done things; as officials of the club, we can't just lie back and pretend that we're on top of every new idea and suggestion for keeping our members happy.'

Someone at the rear of the meeting was mischievously heard to whisper, 'the lady vice captain is apparently very happy with a member in both those particular positions,' causing some of those sitting nearby to reach for handkerchiefs to staunch impending gales of laughter.

The chairman pressed on, only faintly aware of the fact that something he'd said had been capable of being misconstrued by the more 'gutter orientated' minds of those present.

'We need to recognise the need to treat everyone equally and not perpetuate outdated divisions among our members; the existence of separate rooms for men and women in the clubhouse is a case in point; some of us believe that it's time to pull down those outdated walls of segregation between the sexes that have existed here for so long.'

The same anonymous heckler was heard to mutter, 'I warned you didn't I, we're going to be sharing the bogs with the women from now on, just like they do in France.'

The chairman began to sense that there was a mood of hilarity in the room that was threatening to reduce the discussion to the level of a Whitehall farce, so elected to sit down with the concluding phrase, 'as officials, we wish it to be known that we intend to hold on firmly to the belief in all members' rights to have equal access to every facility within the club.'

As he resumed his seat, there were further outbursts of laughter following the muted reference from the same sector of the room, to the fact that, 'we've some club officials only too eager to hold on firmly to certain members' tights.'

Brenda was determined to challenge this over-pompous pontificating rhetoric of the chairman with some more down-to-earth propositions. It was also going to be one of her last opportunities to better her vice captain in the latter's unstinting attempts to turn the club into a cross between a French brothel, a Swedish massage parlour and a Turkish harem.

'Mr President,' said Brenda, 'I've never heard such unmitigated rubbish and downright hypocrisy from the chairman, purporting, as he is, to be the champion of human rights and equal opportunities in the golf club. Is it not nearer the truth, Mr Chairman to admit that you have in fact already commissioned and propose to pay an architect and close friend of yours to come up with a totally new design for the interior of the clubhouse, based around the aforementioned changes to the use of the rooms. You then have a plan to contract the job of restructuring the whole interior of the clubhouse to a builder and friend of yours who has promised to 'do you a good deal', no doubt one which includes use of his apartment adjoining the golf course in Mijas in southern Spain.'

The deafening silence around the room was in sharp contrast to the mutterings and murmurings that had accompanied the chairman's opening remarks, but Brenda had one more missile to fire before sitting down.

'Is it not also the case that the person who seconded your proposal, namely the lady vice captain, is also a director on the board of the company to whom you plan to award the contract to rebuild?'

The reverberating shock waves could not have been more intense if The Sun newspaper had revealed that the Pope had been discovered to have an illegitimate love child with one of the Vatican's secretaries. The chairman was quickly on his feet to cries of 'shame' and 'answer'.

'Mr President, this is an outrageous slur on my work for this club, not to mention my reputation in the local community,' shouted the chairman.

'Which reputation would you be talking about then?' shouted one of the members, 'there's a few to choose from, but one or two you probably wouldn't want us talking about here.'

'Tell us that the story's not true, then', requested Denis and Brenda in unison.

'Mr President, it is true that an idea has been put forward to re-design the interior of the clubhouse, but I must stress that it is only a plan and nothing has been decided,' replied the chairman.

'It's gone far enough for you to get the views and approval of the town planners,' said Brenda, 'does the rest of the committee know about this?'

How the hell does this women know all this, thought the chairman and then remembered that her husband was a close drinking buddy of one of the town councillors.

'I simply needed to know what possible opposition in the form of such things as building regulations there might be to the plan, er... I mean the idea,' pleaded the chairman.

'It might have been a good idea to have discovered what opposition there was to the idea from the golf club members first, don't you think?' asked the lady captain.

There were loud cheers for her remark, even from sections of the club's membership who would have stoutly denied applauding anything linked with her name other than her resignation. It was, in fact, calls for the chairman's resignation that now began to be heard from various quarters of the room. At that point, the lady vice captain got to her feet and attempted some kind of defence of the chairman.

'Mr President, it's a great shame that someone who has been such a loyal supporter of the club both in terms of money, time and unstinting hard work, should be criticised in this way for simply seeking to improve the quality of what this club has to offer its members.'

'We all know what special offer the chairman was giving you,' shouted someone from the back of the room, who was promptly asked by the President to curtail such offensive remarks or leave.

The lady vice captain concluded: 'Regrettably, in the light of these accusations and in view of some of the unpleasantness and downright vindictiveness of some of the members here tonight over what seems to me to be a relatively trivial affair, I now feel that I have no desire to take up the post of lady captain and furthermore will resign my membership of the club forthwith.'

More stunned silence followed, later to be replaced with mutterings about 'guilty conscience' and 'just desserts'.

In order to avoid further disruptive developments, revelations and recriminations, the president decided that, in his position as acting chairman, he would bring the meeting to a close, but with the pacifying suggestion that an extra-ordinary meeting be called, in due course, to thoroughly investigate these matters and secure some answers. He requested the lady vice captain, albeit unsuccessfully, to re-consider her decision to resign.

Brenda, as she left the meeting and reflected on her year as captain, wondered whether president of the WI wouldn't have been an easier option, but concluded that a proposal to replace 'Jerusalem' with 'You'll never walk alone' might have resulted in the same disastrous consequences for that much revered and well-loved institution.

CHAPTER 5

The Head Green Keeper's Tale or 'It's a deal; I promise not sell dodgy cars if you leave the greens to me.'

When, as it claims in the book of Genesis, God set about that rather low-level skills task of creating man in his own image following the much more demanding business of creating such significantly vital things as the earth, the sea and the firmament, he presumably must have included in his DIY, or as those more familiar with things religious would call it 'The Do It Yahweh' self-assembly catalogue, the category of golf course head green keeper.

What is not quite certain, however, is which particular god-like blue-print he was actually working from on that sixth day, prior to taking a bit of a break from the creating business and deciding to have 'a few holes' on the seventh.

In fact, two quite different blue-prints appear to have been in existence at the time of the creation, which most probably led to some quite heated arguments in the bar of the 'heavenly clubhouse', particularly after 18 holes of stroke play where the pins appeared to have been set in positions more suited to that much more devilishly difficult, satanically-designed adjoining course.

One rather rare image from the heavenly filing system that some golfers claim to have seen hanging around their course, is of a kindly, caring, benevolent and beneficent figure whose sole concern is the total wellbeing and happiness of all those mortals who fall within his tender loving and caring control. It reveals a figure that takes pleasure and satisfaction from seeing the happy, smiling faces that are the result of having sampled the sheer brilliance and ingenuity of his creation. No greater reward could there be for this kind and generous 'servant' than hearing the intention of these delighted 'souls' to return to a course that produced such pleasant and lasting memories.

Their subsequent conversation at the 19th hole is of generously wide fairways, gentle rough, even paced greens and pin positions that were fairly located away from those nasty, horrible bunkers. Their praise for the hard working and tirelessly unselfish genius behind the set up and maintenance of the golf course would probably have made this figure worthy of golf's equivalent of the Nobel Peace Prize for clubhouse harmony and contentment.

Other golfers, however, claim that an all-together different file was opened by the Creator on that fateful sixth day, which produced a spiteful, revengeful and extremely vindictive figure whose sole aim appears to be the humiliating downfall of all those mortals who would aspire to golfing fame and glory. His pleasure and satisfaction is gained from the sight of grown men and women, heads in hands, fists tightly clenched, openly weeping and claiming that they've just been through the most outrageously difficult and demanding and, consequently the most miserable, golfing experience in their lives.

Their conversation is more likely to centre on the fact that they'd missed 12 of the 18 pencil-thin fairways, had to extricate themselves from ankle high rough, had been in ten green-side bunkers trying to get at impossible pin positions and had three putted seven greens because their pace was rather akin to the effect of rolling a ball along the bonnet of a car.

Effigies of the creator of this 'golfing nightmare' were subsequently being constructed from any old, discarded golfing gear found in the boots of members' cars and were either being burnt in a secret ceremony behind the starter's hut or taken home to be used as pin cushions.

Of course, as with all relationships, whether simply between fellow human beings or between human beings and the particular god 'that goes with them', feelings and loyalties can change quite suddenly and dramatically. Such is the case between golfers and head green keeper. Their particularly fickle love–hate relationship can outstrip even the most passionate of romantic encounters that a Mills and Boon novel can offer its readers.

The fact of the matter is that the memories and the loyalties, particularly of club golfers, are as short as some of the putts they missed on those treacherously paced greens to pin positions that owe more to a mountaineering manual than a golf course handbook. That head green keeper upon whom the members, in their almost religious fervour, were previously heaping all the praise and glory for a superbly presented and maintained golf course, has, three weeks later, suddenly become a golfing devil incarnate.

As for those highly professional skills that he so clearly possessed a month ago, most members are now demanding that even his grass cutting responsibilities should only be undertaken under the close supervision of those much more knowledgeable members of the greens' committee.

Similarly, where there had been complete and absolute trust in the head green keeper's decisions on the timing of such tasks as hollow-tining, scarifying and top dressing, now those very same members are firmly of the opinion that it is the job of all green keepers simply to follow the instructions with which they have been provided. They are not paid to show initiative or display dangerous tendencies towards self-determination and leadership.

The patently flawed logic of these members is based on the tenuous principles that, firstly, it is 'our golf course', secondly, 'they are our paid employees', thirdly, 'we have a democratically appointed, well qualified committee' and fourthly 'they should do what they're bloody well told, when they're told.'

When, of course, it comes to ascertaining the thoughts and opinions of the head green keeper on those democratically appointed and so-called highly qualified committee members to whom he owes his job, his future and, in their opinion, his very life, it is probably advisable, for the sake of one's ear drums, to stand at quite a discrete distance from the speaker and not be overly sensitive to some of the quaint Anglo Saxon terms and phrases employed.

In yet another futile encounter with the leader of this so-called democratic committee, namely the chairman of greens, who has probably just come hot-foot from the day job delivering king-size bollockings to poor sods who have exceeded their overdraft limit, the head green keeper is subjected to yet another set of misguided and wholly inappropriate demands. This is from someone whose knowledge of the finer qualities of turf and its maintenance does not extend beyond the fact that it is generally green in colour and grows 'green side up'.

Furthermore, his understanding of the timing of particular jobs relating to its care and development would appear to be based more on a version of Old Moores Almanac than on the collective wisdom of the Professional Green Keepers Association. Attempts to explain the finer points of what each of the very expensive pieces of machinery have been bought to do, are rather like trying to take a five-year-old through the intricacies of space shuttle technology.

Worse still, of course, is the arrival of a deputation or, heaven forbid, the entire complement of the club's greens' committee, comprised of a motley collection of second-hand car salesmen, estate agents, insurance salesmen and accountants, whose combined knowledge of golf course management would not fill half a side of a holiday postcard.

Armed with some totally inappropriate information that they've gleaned from a magazine article they've clearly not understood, but felt sure sounded good or from some other equally badly-informed, but thoroughly convincing fellow 'know-all', these 'gullible gougers' proceed to lecture the poor beleaguered head green keeper on the finer points of turf management.

Throw into this information quagmire, the additional and inevitably conflicting contributions from the club's professional, captain, chairman and any members, particularly those who've failed to break a hundred in the monthly medal, whose paths happen to cross those of the head green keeper, when he ill advisedly strayed near the clubhouse at the weekend, and it's hardly surprising to learn that his BT 'Family and Friends' telephone list now includes the Samaritans.

One frequent battle ground between the head green keeper and other club officials, including the professional, is the decision as to whether the course, at certain times of the year, is suitable for play. The desire on the part of some club officials to keep the green fees rolling in, to capture a few buyers of water proofs, umbrellas and bag covers and to boost flagging sales at the bar, at a notoriously quiet time of the year, is a very difficult argument to resist.

The head green keeper, in these circumstances, will be only too well aware of the verbal mauling he'll get when the resulting damage to tees, greens and fairways comes to the attention of the chairman of greens and his committee.

Other questionably helpful suggestions on re-shaping fairways and greens, realigning bunkers or re-siting tees is usually met with a genuine offer not to interfere with running the shop, preparing the club accounts or writing the Annual Report if they promise to stay out of, 'my bloody green keeper's office'.

A most bizarre contradiction can, however, be frequently observed at some clubs' Annual General Meeting. All the aforementioned 'stone-throwers', who have consistently blamed the head green keeper and his team for practically every single problem associated with the course, can be found applauding the reading of the section of the Annual Report, complimenting the green staff on 'yet another outstanding year of hard work and dedication which has resulted in such an excellent course'.

Many of the current crop of head green keepers, of course, have an impressive array of professional qualifications, which are essential for fulfilling the many roles and responsibilities that the modern job demands.

High on the list of essential qualifications is obviously a degree in agronomy. This will allow the head green keeper to deal with that endless stream of stupid bloody questions from members as to why the grass is not growing like it did last year, or why the grass is growing faster than three years ago, or why the grass is growing in some places but not others, why the greens are too fast or why the greens are too slow, why the grass in the rough is so high and, of course, all green keepers' favourite question, why the grass on the ladies' tees is always longer than on the men's tees. This degree will also help them to provide answers to other equally inane questions such as, why the greens were top-dressed one and a half days earlier this year than last and why the fairways were apparently hollow-tined to a level two inches lower than two years ago.

A qualification in meteorology is also an essential requirement. Equipped with such all-important information, the head green keeper will be able to respond to such mind-bendingly difficult queries as 'why is the course so dry?' or 'why is it so wet?' and, if it's raining, 'when it will stop?' and if it's not raining, 'is it likely that it will?' Green keepers will also be able to deal with those perennial questions from golfers, 'do you know where the weather's coming from?', 'is it going to change?' and 'how long do you think this is going to last?'

They will also be able to answer all those tiresome complaints such as those from members who'd regularly claimed that during the winter, certain fairways resembled the Somme, yet when short drainage ditches had been dug across the fairways to alleviate the problem, wrote letters of complaint to the chairman of greens about disruption to their play.

No self-respecting green keeper should, of course, be without a qualification in engineering technology. Armed with the combined knowledge and skills of a top European car designer, the very latest insights into American and Russian space technology and topped up with a liberal sprinkling of the most revolutionary features of Formula One Grand Prix racing cars, the head green keeper is ready for anything the committee throw at him.

Intellectually demanding questions like, 'will that new machine cut the grass better?', 'will that new mower cut the greens more smoothly than the last one?', 'will you be able to cut the rough lower with this new one?' and, of course, the inevitable question or, more often, the statement made after the arrival of some even more expensive equipment, 'of course, you'll be able to save time and do the job faster now, won't you?'

Estate and environmental management is also another vital component of a head green keeper's curriculum vitae. Such knowledge will ensure that he is able to withstand those apparently justifiable complaints from those interfering environmental do-gooders in the club that he has, in their words, 'been indiscriminately hacking away and destroying the delicate and precious areas of the course that are home to rare and beautiful species of flora and fauna'.

Hopefully, it will also equip him to deal with the complaints from that self-same group, when it so happens that their errant drives happen to land in that very area, which remarkably, is no longer an area of outstanding natural beauty, but 'a bloody eyesore of scrub and rubbish that any self-respecting green keeper would have cleared away years ago'.

Personnel management is, of course, a must-have for all head green keepers. Without this essential qualification, how will he be able to manage that group of 'layabouts' that go under the name of green staff? How will he be able to respond to those members who do not regard driving around on tractors and lawn mowers, strolling around carrying rakes, shovels, scythes and other such gardening paraphernalia, as a proper job? How will he be able to refute the charge from members that his highly skilled team of agronomists are rarely to be found actually working on the course, but more often to be found drinking tea and reading the newspaper in some remote corner of the green keeper's shed?

How will he respond to those regularly heard accusations of mismanagement that, 'he couldn't organise a piss-up in a brewery', 'that he couldn't start a fire in a match factory, 'that once he thought he was indecisive, but now he's not sure' and 'why is every Friday celebrated by his staff as POETS (Piss Off Early Tomorrow's Saturday) day?'

A working knowledge of behavioural psychology is also now highly regarded as an essential pre-requisite of being a good head green keeper. Specialist options of particular relevance would include, deviance and conflict management in order to be able to deal with the various types of egotistical, maniacal fruitcakes who present themselves as experts in the field of golf course management. A proven ability to be able to fasten up those smartly fashioned white coats with the buttons at the back and designer straps is also desirable when dealing with the greens' committee.

Conflict management theory provides the modern day head green keeper with a range of strategies, including methods of actually avoiding members on the course such as, hiding behind strategically located trees and bushes, investigating a malfunction in the suspension of the tractor at the precise moment the chairman of greens appears and inventing reasons for having to be somewhere else in a matter of minutes, when members with life-threatening intentions appear on the horizon. It also equips them with essential life-saving skills to curb those unexpected pugilistic tendencies of some members when confronting their opponents with the correct score on a hole.

Last but by no means least, a head green keeper's literacy and communication skills has to be of the highest order to be able to cope with those unintelligible and indecipherable messages received from the various members of the 'lunatic management fringe' and, of course, to be able to think on their feet when some crackpot suggestion for re-configuring the entire layout of the course is proposed.

Some brave souls amongst the fraternity of head green keepers, in the misguided belief that they can actually help members understand what they're doing on the golf course, have had the idea of producing their own newsletter. The contents of these publications offer a variety of advice on care of the course as this set of sarcastic extracts illustrate:

'Golfers should avoid slamming clubs into the tees, fairways and greens following a poor shot; that's what their partners and opponents are there for.'

'Golfers should not pull trolleys or drive buggies across greens; they've probably already exceeded their allotted level of damage in getting from tee to green.'

'Golfers should always replace divots and repair pitch marks; the only exceptions are those golfers who haven't enough golfing skills to produce either of these effects.'

'Golfers should rake bunkers immediately after leaving them using the rakes provided; golfers will be able to recognise these particular areas of the course by the discarded fag ends, used matches, broken rakes, footprints and trolley wheels to be found therein'.

Green keepers have also used these types of publications for setting out their annual plans for maintaining and developing the course. These declarations are usually met with a healthy level of scepticism by most members, mainly due to the fact that these 'paragons of patience' are still waiting to see the targets from three years ago realised. Other more cynical readers have been heard to enquire as to when the head green keeper was actually out on the course formulating his plans or, more caustically, as to whose decision it was to actually pay him to spend his time writing.

The one qualification that head green keepers do not need and which, if it appeared on their CV, would send some selection committees spiralling into a panic, is that of 'golfer'.

The worst news that any club member could hear about the appointment of a new head green keeper is that, 'he plays off a handicap of four'. They then know that, in two years time, they'll have a golf course where about 75 per cent of the fairways are barely visible, let alone reachable from the tee, are just about sufficiently wide enough for two golf buggies to pass, the rough resembles an African game reserve and one will need a mountaineering certificate to get in and out of the bunkers.

This news is often accompanied by messages from the more vindictive 'well wishers' at his previous club who gleefully report on its loss of members, either to other clubs which do not require one to have a scratch handicap to get around or, more seriously, actual fatalities either from exhaustion, dis-orientation or malnutrition. The reported 300 per cent increase in golf ball sales, coupled with the sudden arrival of a large consignment of ball retrievers for use in the numerous lakes and ponds that suddenly appeared and an enormous jump in the sales of lob wedges in order to extricate one self from the crater-like bunkers that were added, was also included in the 'best wishes' that they received.

One of the remaining healthy and energetic members of the seniors' section from his previous club reported that many of the seniors could now not get out of the bunkers that he had created. 'Surely, the new lob wedges have helped', it was suggested.

'Oh, we can get the ball out, no trouble, it's getting ourselves out after we've played the shot that's the problem,' said the arthritic hacker.

Contrary to some widely held views of golf club members, there are some head green keepers who are reputedly quite happy for golfers to play 'their golf course' and would not wish to be associated with those of their colleagues who view golfers as a 'necessary irritation from which their course should be protected at all costs'. This latter group of self-styled 'guardians of the greens' are regularly prone to sudden and unpredictable urges to create temporary tees, greens and areas of the fairways and so, inexplicably, take out of commission pristine areas of the course.

Even those areas of the golf course on to which they deign to allow golfers to venture can frequently be the subject of close and lengthy inspections, followed by painstaking surgeon-like activity. Play will often be severely delayed while some blemish, almost hidden to the human eye, is analysed and finally disposed of.

This cleverly camouflaged penchant for irritating and infuriating golfers is, in fact, the subject of a very closely guarded secret document, known only to head green keepers, the contents of which provide detailed guidance on how to ensure that their Machiavellian objectives are achieved.

The following extracts are reproduced from the document in question:

> 'Wait unseen behind any large natural obstacle until a group of golfers is seen approaching a green before emerging to begin a lengthy cut of the green and its surrounds and extensive repair work on the bunkers.'
>
> 'If you arrive at a green where play is already in progress, ensure that all machinery is A) left running at high revs rather than on idle, B) is located closest to the golfer with a difficult bunker shot or C) is placed directly behind the player with the longest and most difficult putt.'
>
> 'Sweeping greens of early morning dew in the winter should only be done after the first four medal groups have gone through, but are not out of sight.'
>
> 'Rake only those green-side bunkers that players have visited as they are leaving the green.'
>
> 'Watch for those golfers who are just about to play their second shots from the fairway to the green before removing the flag stick.'

'Watch for those golfers who have just driven into the rough on a particular hole before commencing cutting that particular area and ensure that cuttings are adequately covering the ball. Alternatively, wait until the golfer has given up his search for the ball before commencing the cut.'

'Move tee boxes back ten yards as players are leaving the previous green. Alternatively, wait until all players have played their tee shots before moving the tee positions forward.'

'Moving a pin from a difficult position behind a bunker on a green should only be done after a group of golfers have completed the hole and are walking to the next tee.'

'Marking ground under repair should only be done after successive golfers have been seen to miss-hit, miss-time or even completely miss a shot from that particular area.'

'Cutting the fairway of a hole with a blind drive should only commence after golfers have driven off, thus ensuring that balls are either A) buried, B) picked up or C) shredded.'

Other sections in this document offer specific techniques for annoying the seniors, such as the indiscriminate banning of buggies on the second nine holes, 'we always do it on the third Monday in November', for irritating the ladies, such as re-siting all their tee boxes in the semi rough, 'it's time we made some extensive improvements to your teeing area' and finally, for creating mayhem among visitors by removing all the marker posts on the blind holes prior to commencing cutting the fairways, 'can I suggest you buy a course planner in the pro shop, sir.'

Head green keepers can, therefore, be to some people a professional colleague, a professional advisor, a hard-working, conscientious employee, a loyal and thoroughly trustworthy servant, a friend and playing partner and a dedicated guardian of golfing standards for the benefit of all those who love playing the game of golf.

At the same time, they can be complete bastards whose concern for the course itself overrides any thoughts of members' needs, enjoyment or satisfaction. Their loyalty and dedication is targeted, not at those thoroughly ungrateful beneficiaries of their hard work who actually play the game, but solely and exclusively at the visible manifestations of their under-valued labour, namely, 18 tees, 18 fairways and 18 greens and job satisfaction is measured on that infamous, 'tears and tantrums' scale of self-inflicted golfing disasters.

Bert Harvey had been at 'Swankers' Golf Club for almost six years during which time he and his team had improved the quality of the course from a level of mediocrity that had seen members leaving in coach loads, to a standard that at least allowed the current members to admit to where they actually played golf.

This success had largely been achieved in spite of a succession of a largely ignorant and incompetent club officials vainly trying to fulfil their role as chairman of greens and their equally intellectually challenged colleagues who had agreed to join him on the committee in the faint hope that six brains would be better than one. Bert had frequently been heard to say that, in his opinion, as far as maintaining a golf course was concerned, this latest crop of 'power peddlers' would have been hard pressed to rustle up half a brain between them.

Bert remembered with some amusement the interview he'd had for the post of head green keeper. Over the years, he'd had some strange interviews at golf clubs, but the one at 'Swankers' really did outstrip all the rest by a considerable margin.

Evans, the past chairman of greens had been joined by three other members of the committee for the task of interviewing Bert for the post. From the very start, it was quite obvious that they'd not really prepared themselves for the interview, had not discussed or decided what sort of person they were looking for, nor what the job really entailed beyond a very basic idea that it involved looking after 18 tees, fairways and greens. Bert had the distinct impression that the three in particular had been asked to turn up because they happened to be free and 'just play it by ear'.

Watson sort of set the tone for the interview with the question, 'if you got the job, where do you think you'd live?' Bert had, at first, thought it was some sort of trick question to try to catch him out, but quickly realised that Watson was serious and so Bert remembered talking about initially renting and then later buying a property.

He was then asked, 'do you have any hobbies, when you're not looking after a golf course?' Bert decided that they were trying to help him relax before throwing the really serious stuff about golf course management and his plans for 'Swankers' at him.

Not so, the next question was, 'does your wife work?' followed by 'what do you think of the green keeper's shed?' followed by 'is this the first time you been to this area?' By this time, Bert was firmly of the opinion that they'd already decided to appoint someone else and that they were going through the motions of an interview simply out of politeness.

The randomness of their questions was completely unnerving him, particularly as he'd come prepared with detailed plans and ideas for developing the course. He struggled on with answers to questions like, 'have you travelled abroad and seen the golf courses there?' and 'do you watch much golf on television?'

Suddenly out of the blue, one member of the panel started bombarding him with questions like, 'what would you recommend as the ideal cutting height for the turf on the tees?', 'what species of turf grass are best suited to greens in this part of the country?' and 'what in your opinion is the most appropriate rate of water application per unit of time?' Bert, based on the previous 30 minutes of questions, couldn't quite work out whether this guy was actually being serious, taking the piss or whether this was another strategy for throwing him completely off his guard.

He had, however, noticed the faces of the other members of the panel as the questions were being asked and the general impression he got was that neither the questioner nor the rest of the panel had the faintest idea what the questions actually meant or what would be an appropriate answer. It was obvious that the questioner had somehow managed to get hold of a book on golf course management, extracted a few pieces of information and thought he'd try to impress the interviewee and give the appearance of being knowledgeable in front of his colleagues.

Bert responded with what he considered to be quite appropriate answers but soon detected, by the glazed look on the face of the questioner, that the replies were making about as much sense to him as an article on thermo-nuclear dynamics would to a ten-year-old.

After that, the questions reverted to requests for information about his car, his choice of food and whether his parents had encouraged him to become a head green keeper.

At the end of the hour, he'd absolutely no idea whether he stood a chance of getting the job or what they'd thought of him as a potential employee. In truth, he wasn't absolutely convinced, based on that experience, that he wanted the job even if they offered it to him. They hadn't even given him the opportunity to ask questions and the paper he'd prepared on plans for the course never left his briefcase. It came as something of a shock to him four days later, therefore, to receive a letter offering him the job and even more bizarrely, complimenting him on his performance at the interview.

It never ceased to amaze Bert how these particular people actually had the nerve to allow themselves to be appointed to these positions, knowing as they did very little about how a golf course was designed, constructed and maintained. As one of his team pointed out however, 'when did you ever hear of ignorance being a problem in holding office in a golf club?'

It was something of an irony that the two or three people at the club who had some insight of how a golf course should be maintained, resolutely refused to get involved.

'Can you imagine me having to sit and listen to the complete bollocks that they talk about golf course management, coming as they do straight from flogging second-hand bangers, dodgy insurance policies and run-down semis,' offered one of the more vociferous members by way of explanation for his non-involvement.

What Bert also found astonishing was the unswerving confidence and belief that these people had in their knowledge of the subject and that what they were saying was absolutely incontrovertible.

'I can't believe what I'm hearing from some of them on occasions', admitted Bert to one friend, 'they talk absolute non-stop crap, on a subject they know damn-all about, but with such authority that they have everyone hanging on their every word; they're absolutely astonished if anyone suggests that they might just be wrong'.

If being subjected to this semi-official and formally authorized 'golfing garbage' was not bad enough, Bert, of course, was also regularly bombarded by the unofficial ear-bending from those members who felt it was their bounden duty, as one or two expressed it, 'to put him straight on one or two things about looking after the course'. Rarely was it possible to anticipate what pearls of wisdom these characters were going to dispense. Nevertheless, their undiminished sense of the value of their personal research meant that they were quite prepared to walk half way across the course to give Bert the benefit of yet another learned article from some obscure magazine, written by some equally unknown and unqualified pen-pushing 'grass-bagger'.

All this is not to say that Bert was averse to hearing about and trying out new ideas. He regularly talked to other head green keepers and to Richardson, the professional who, at least, had the benefit of seeing what was going well, or not so well, elsewhere and who had enough knowledge of the subject to sort out the truth from the tripe.

He had even attended various seminars arranged by his Association to update his own studies and qualifications. Most recently he'd signed up for a seminar on 'Managing Golf Course Personnel'. He'd hoped it might give him some ideas on how to deal with all the various 'fruitcakes' he had to endure during the week.

The seminar had covered topics such as, 'motivating your staff'. He was told that, 'employees work best when they know what is expected of them'. In his experience, employees worked best when they're told that if they don't 'pull their finger out, they're for the chop'. He was also told that staff are more motivated if they are 'regularly complimented and told how much their work is appreciated'. As far as he was aware, attempts at paying someone a compliment were generally misinterpreted as an attempt to get them to do some other shitty job that no-one else would do.

'Delegate responsibility for decision-making if you really want to motivate your staff', was what he was encouraged to do. When he'd tried to put this into practice, he was firmly told, 'I'm not bloody paid to do your job as well as mine, matey'. 'Improve staff morale by giving them a job description', he was advised. Job descriptions, as far as he was concerned, only provided those bolshie sods with ammunition for refusing to do jobs that were not specifically listed, 'where the 'ell does it say that I have to do that, sunshine?'

'Ensure that your staff are fully trained in the tasks which are expected of them if you want maximum motivation', was another management sound bite. Yes, thought Bert and then wait for two things to happen, either a demand for more money, 'well, I got these 'ere qualifications now, ain't I' or 'I gone and got this other job when I told them I had these 'ere qualifications, din, I'.

'Employee morale and motivation depends on them having a job in which they can take a pride in their accomplishments' was another management commandment. As far as Bert was aware, 'having a job that didn't require thinking, didn't require strenuous effort and didn't require more than ten minutes physical activity in every hour' were the major criteria as far as employees he'd encountered were concerned.

All this so-called professional advice made those tedious monthly encounters with the committee, those unscheduled on-course blasts from the members and his weekly 'run-in' with his 'team', as he was told to describe it, even more difficult to bear.

Reflecting on a typical week, he sometimes wondered how he actually managed to get what he regarded as 'proper' work completed, given the meetings, briefings, informal chats, correspondence and reports that required his attention.

A typical week started with a meeting with his staff of six assistants to plan out the work priorities. He had inherited three of his current staff from his predecessor and the other three had been his own, more recent appointments. This was, on occasions, the cause of a few problems, particularly from two of the team who'd been there the longest.

'Right, Fred, why the hell didn't you finish that work on the bunkers around the 9th, 11th and 12th on Friday? I could have got my bloody granny to do it quicker than you!'

'Cos, first, I was dragged off to sort out a problem with one of the mowers that wasn't working properly, that's why and secondly, your sodding granny was nowhere to be seen,' said Fred, aggressively.

'Who asked you to do that?' enquired Bert. 'It wasn't me!'

'It were Martin; I thought you said when he got the job that he knew all there was to know about machines, we didn't realise you meant knitting machines'.

'I just asked you for your opinion, you awkward old bugger, it took all of ten minutes,' said Martin, 'you make it sound as if you were there all day, that's bloody typical of you to make a mountain out of a mole hill'.

'Well, you certainly couldn't get the damn thing to work

properly anyway, so somebody had to spend time sorting it out,' argued Fred.

'Look, I want that work around those bunkers finished today, OK, Fred?' demanded Bert in an attempt to stop this verbal punch up getting out of hand.

'Chairman of greens been giving you a hard time again has he?' enquired Fred, mischievously. 'No more new toys from Uncle Simon for little Bert if he doesn't do what he's told.'

'No, he hasn't. Now let's get on,' said Bert, refusing to rise to Fred's taunts about his relationship with Simon Watson, chairman of greens.

'We need to cut all fairways and greens over the next two days.'

'You won't if your mechanical genius there can't get the mower working properly,' interjected Fred again.

'I will give Martin a hand with that,' offered Bert, 'you just concern yourself with the work around the bunkers.'

'The other job this week is cleaning up the ditches on the 2nd, 4th and 7th' said Bert, 'I want you on that Colin, it's a couple of days work.'

Colin was the other long-standing assistant green keeper who had expected to get the job of head green keeper when the previous one left. His failure to get it and the fact that he'd failed to get two others for which he'd applied didn't exactly make him the most motivated member of the team. Bert's request that he tackle the job of cleaning the ditches produced a predictable response.

'How come I get given all the dirty bloody jobs to do, I would have thought it was a job for one of the juniors,' argued Colin, staring pointedly at Mark, the kid who'd joined on a job creation scheme. 'Anyway, I ain't here tomorrow, I'm going to a funeral.'

The number of dead acquaintances of Colin's was reaching alarming proportions in Bert's opinion and he made a mental note to have a word with the chairman of greens about Colin's attendance record.

'Mark is here as a trainee and so will work under the

supervision of Tom on the work that needs doing around the tees,' said Bert.

There was no way he was putting a young trainee with Colin, he'd have even more funerals to contend with within the month.

'Since when has Tom been elevated to the role of a supervisor?' inquired Colin, 'I didn't realize that that post had become available.'

'You know damn well Colin that there is no post of supervisor, I was just using the term to explain that he has to have help and guidance.'

'Well, I'll give him plenty of advice on cleaning ditches,' said Colin, 'if that's what you want.'

He'll get more than advice on cleaning ditches if I leave him with you, thought Bert.

'Now on Wednesday,' said Bert, 'I've got a rep coming to talk to me about a new machine for irrigating the greens, I'll be with him most of the morning.'

'More expensive crap that doesn't work properly,' said Fred, 'you'd better check up if Martin's got a nice little picture of it in his book or we'll be pushing that around the course when it breaks down.'

'Take your bucket and spade and piss off to the sand, Fred,' shouted Martin, 'everybody's tired of your bleeding Luddite attitude towards technology.'

'At least I can make my bucket and spade work, not like some people,' rejoined Fred.

'Have you got any particularly important jobs to do this week, Bert?' inquired Colin rather pointedly, 'I just need to know where I can find you if I get stuck with a problem clearing out the ditches.'

'Thank you for your concern, Colin. I will be working on preparing the ground for the new tee at the 3rd and the extension to the green at the 17th if you really need to find me. That is, of course, during daylight hours. On Tuesday evening I have a meeting with the chairman of greens and on Thursday night I have a full greens' committee meeting, OK?'

Perhaps, thought Bert, that sort of attitude is why you're still here making my life hell instead of playing at being an awkward bastard at some other golf club.

'Right, if there's nothing else, let's get started on this week's jobs,' said Bert.

'Before you go,' said Fred, 'can I have a word with you about my annual holidays?'

'No, just write the bloody dates down on a piece of paper and leave it in the office,' snapped Bert, 'you can manage to get that done by next week, can you Fred?'

Bert pondered, as he left for the 3rd tee, where he'd missed the tuition from his Association on conflict and anger management and whether the professional manual he regularly consulted had a section on techniques for beating up staff without it showing.

One of the perils of working on the course at the most popular playing times, apart that is, from being hit by stray golf balls, being shouted at for actually working within 150 yards of someone's play or daring to take a piece of machinery within 500 yards of a four-ball, is being ambushed by a group of members and lectured on some particular development on the course. Those occasions when such a group came over to pass a compliment on the state of the course were about as rare as the sighting of Hailey's Comet. More often than not it was to inquire as to whether he and his team, with the assistance of the greens' committee, had taken leave of their senses and decided on the wholesale destruction of some feature of the course or, alternatively, to abandon all the cherished principles of golf course management.

It was hardly a surprise, therefore, that after only 15 minutes work on the 3rd tee, that he heard the approaching advance of four lady members clearly on a mission to give him the benefit of their opinion on what he was doing, whether he wanted it or not.

There had been a long-standing problem with this tee because of the very poor quality of the grass. Being a par three, it suffered more than others from members taking divots, in the case of some of the club's more notorious hackers, deep enough, in fact, to bury a small animal. The grass on the tee did not recover very quickly and so there was the inevitable batch of complaints about the tee resembling, 'the local football club's goal mouth'. The solution was relatively simple, remove two or three of the largest trees, thin some of the branches of the others and take out some of the shrubs and bushes, all of which together were the main culprits responsible for the poor quality grass on the tee, preventing as they did adequate sunlight getting through.

A simple and inexpensive solution, that is, until some of the environmental 'anoraks' in the club heard of the plans. Judging by the uproar and flow of correspondence to the chairman of greens and the verbal protests to Bert, one could have been forgiven for thinking that the entire ecosystem within a hundred miles was under threat. Any day, Bert was expecting to find a Greenham Common-type encampment pitched on the tee, complete with tents, sleeping bags, portable stoves and banners demanding his immediate incarceration for crimes against the wildlife.

One of the more dangerous forms of 'wildlife' were on their way just at that moment to berate him yet again for this 'mindless act of barbarity' and to demand an explanation for what they described as, 'a typical piece of management insanity'.

'We're not going to let you do this, you know,' said Belinda Macklin, the leader of this particular mini-charge, 'we're going to fight that crackpot committees' decision to chop down those lovely trees and clear all the flowering bushes, you're just a load of ageing, irresponsible hooligans, that's what you all are.'

'Absolutely, well said, Belinda,' chorused the other three rebels.

In actual fact, there wasn't anything particularly lovely about the three trees in question. They were extremely poor specimens of ash that did nothing to enhance the overall quality of the environment and were, in fact, contributing significantly to some of its problems. As for the bushes, they hadn't flowered in years.

'Look, ladies, it's a really very simple and straight forward choice,' said Bert.

'Don't you adopt that patronising turn of phrase with us,' said Edith, 'we recognise when we're being talked down to and fobbed off with someone's convenient excuses; it's an unnecessary piece of vandalism, that what it is, it'll spoil the whole appearance of the place.'

'Those trees and some of the shrubs are spoiling other things, including the quality of the grass on the tee and the surrounding area,' explained Bert, 'we wouldn't chop them down without a good reason.'

'Don't be so silly, man, of course they're not, what a preposterous claim. Trees can't spoil the grass, it's just an excuse so that you don't have to look after them any more,' shouted Belinda.

'Belinda, I'm afraid…'

'It's Mrs Macklin to you, young man,' interjected the offended lady.

'Very well, Mrs Macklin, but I'm afraid to say that you're wrong about those trees, they are the cause of the problem,' replied Bert.

'My husband said that the fault was with the grass that had been sown, not the trees,' said, Daphne, another of this insufferable set. 'He said he'd read about another type of grass seed that would grow better and quicker here.'

What your husband knows about turf, thought Bert, wouldn't cover a torn postage stamp. 'It's a matter of whether we want high quality grass or continue with these bald, muddy patches for ever,' explained Bert, 'it wouldn't matter what grass we used.'

By this time, the four had had to let two other sets of players through and there was a men's four-ball just arriving on the 2nd green, fully expecting to walk on to the 3rd tee to continue their game.

'Those shrubs and bushes are very colourful in the summer, you know, and we should keep them in order to save the wild life that we have,' said Edna.

'I don't remember the wildlife getting much of a look in when we had to cut down some small trees and bushes to make room for the ladies' toilet,' replied Bert and then wished he hadn't opened his mouth.

'Don't be so impertinent, young man,' shouted Edna, 'the ladies' toilet was much more important to us than fiddling about with a tee that the ladies are not even allowed to use.'

'We can quite easily plant some other bushes and shrubs somewhere else where they'll do no harm,' offered Bert, in a final attempt to get rid of the four.

'You've promised that before and it never happened. You just stuck a few plant pots in front of the clubhouse, which hardly constitutes a re-planting programme, does it?' said Belinda.

'Are you ladies going to get a bloody move on or can we come through?' enquired a member of the men's four-ball.

'There's no need to use that sort of language with us, you're not in the men's bar now, you know,' said Daphne, 'we've said all we're going to say for now to this pathetic apology for a green keeper, we're carrying on.'

'Oh my God,' said one of the men, 'I'd better ring the wife and tell her I'll be home for breakfast'.

Bert suddenly realised it was lunch time and that he'd hardly got any work done on the tee thanks to that misguided set of 'environmental do-gooders'. He wandered back to the shed to find Colin already well into a lunch pack that would have been sufficient for four people and Fred, seemingly, fast asleep under a copy of The Sun. There was a note from Simon Watson, chairman of greens asking to meet him the following afternoon on the 2nd green, before their meeting in the evening. Bert could see yet another three hours disappearing without much serious work getting done, resulting in some further sarcastic comments from these two malcontents.

Bert had spent most of Tuesday morning trying to think of the reason why the chairman of greens would want to meet him on the 2nd green. As far as he was aware, there were no problems with that green, nor were there any plans to make any changes to it.

The chairman of greens arrived carrying a box that he proceeded to open in a rather excited fashion in front of Bert.

'I went over to the States on holiday last month and while I was there I found this on sale, it's one of those Stintmeter things that you see them using on the tele to test the speed of the greens. I saw Ken Brown, the golf commentator, using one at Augusta.'

'I think you'll find they're called a Stimpmeter,' explained Bert as diplomatically as he could.

'Yeh, well anyway, whatever it's called, I brought one back so that we can try it out on our greens,' muttered the chairman, looking rather put out at being corrected on his mispronunciation.

'What the hell for?' thought Bert, 'it's not as though we've been put on the Open Championship rota, we can't even get the county to play its matches here.'

He decided that it was yet another one of those vain attempts by the chairman of greens to try to impress his committee and give the impression that he actually knew what he was talking about.

'OK, Simon,' said Bert, 'go ahead and test it out,' knowing full well that the chairman would not have the first clue as to how to use it, but at the same time, would not want to look a complete prat in front of Bert.

The chairman got past the first test of getting it out of the box and started on the task of trying to understand the instructions on the nine-step procedure for using it.

'Right, now on the box, it says you need 'three golf balls, three tees, a data sheet and a 12-15 foot measuring tape,' explained the chairman, pulling two very badly damaged Top

Flites from his pocket, 'have you got any old paper in your overalls, I can write on, Bert?'

'I think we'd better use three balls in slightly better condition than those,' said Bert, 'they look as though Colin has taken aim at them with the gang mower.'

The chairman of greens was getting slightly annoyed at Bert's attitude, particularly as these balls had been among the better specimens in his golf bag.

'Right, let's get on and try this out, it should give us some very useful information.'

Yes, thought Bert it'll be very useful if you know what the hell you're doing and can understand what it's telling you.

As Bert suspected, Simon Watson really had no idea how this piece of equipment worked, nor of the significance of the information it was designed to give him. By Step four, the look of puzzlement was changing to one of frustration and by Step six of the instructions, there was every chance that the Stimpmeter would soon be dispatched into the nearby bushes.

'You need to use the Su and Sd algebraic formula provided to work out the speed of the greens,' goaded Bert, knowing full-well that Watson would have problems even pronouncing the word let alone employing it to make the calculation.

'The sodding thing doesn't seem to be working properly,' complained Watson, about a piece of equipment that simply comprised a 36 inch aluminium bar with a V-shaped groove and a milled ball-release notch 30 inches from one end.

'Are you holding it at the correct angle?' enquired Bert, in a final attempt to be helpful.

'I don't understand what the sodding correct angle should be,' replied Watson, 'why don't you have a go, you're the head green keeper; in the meantime, just give the damn greens the same cut as last week, will you?' as he headed back to the clubhouse.

Bert suspected that the Stimpmeter had probably made its one and only appearance on the course, though no doubt, the report to the committee later that week would describe the trials of a very valuable piece of equipment which had provided an extensive amount of useful data on the quality and pace of the greens. Bert awaited the fall-out when Watson presented the chairman of finance with the bill.

Bert's experience of attending the monthly meeting of the full greens' committee was rather similar to being on jury duty. You never quite knew whether you were going to be required, you could sit around for hours without actually being called upon to do anything. Just occasionally, you could be dismissed as surplus to requirements and, of course, most of the time you couldn't understand what the hell was going on or what they were talking about anyway.

The meetings were generally a complete shambles because the agenda, that is, if the chairman had bothered to produce one, was frequently ignored as members got on to their personal 'soap boxes' and hijacked the proceedings for their own particular golfing 'crusade'. The chairman's ability to control these proceedings was non-existent and consequently whole areas of what was quite important business were never reached or if they were, were hurriedly discussed and dismissed or left to the next meeting. Rarely were formal votes taken on any decision, the chairman apparently telepathically being able to 'take the mood of the meeting'.

Bert had no high expectations of this month's meeting, though he hoped that the scheduled item on the need to start work on the cultivation of the greens would not be lost. He wanted a chance to respond to some of the all-too predictable ill-informed crap that some of the members and individuals on the committee had been dispensing around the bar about what should to be done immediately by their 'half-brained' green keeper.

'Gentlemen, any apologies for absence?' enquired Watson.

'Sam can't be here, he's had to take his wife to the vet.'

There followed an unnecessarily lengthy explanation of

this statement in which a family pet also featured, thus removing the danger of a rumour spreading that Sam's wife was receiving treatment from a 'heavy animal' specialist.

'Matters arising, Mr Secretary?' requested Watson.

There followed the usual trivial reporting of the repair to the ball cleaner on the 6th tee, the repainting of four fairway marker posts, progress on the purchase of pin indicators for the flag sticks and the re-siting of a ground under repair sign. Various inconsequential questions were posed, such as a query about the paint used on the marker posts, which lengthened this already mind-deadening section of the agenda even further. Finally, it was time to turn to the main agenda items.

'We've got to make a final decision on the changes to the 3rd tee, involving the removal of the trees and shrubs,' explained Watson, 'I've been getting some irate comments from some members about our so-called act of vandalism.'

'Oh for God's sake,' said Thompson, one of those members who had little time for, as he put it, 'all this bloody environmental conservation bullshit', 'just let's get on with it and chop the damn things down and if they don't like it, they can sod off somewhere else.'

'Perhaps you'd like to phrase a letter to the members in those tones,' suggested Watson.

'I damn well will if you like, we've been discussing this for six months now and we're still nowhere nearer a decision, I think you should get off your arse and get on with it, Mr Chairman,' shouted Thompson.

'Yes, thank you for that very helpful suggestion,' said Watson, who dearly hoped that Thompson would be replaced at the next AGM by someone who had more to offer by way of advice than the removal of one's arse from whatever seat of responsibility one currently occupied.

'Well I think we've got to explore other alternatives,' said Williams, who was someone who would happily go on exploring options for every action if it actually removed the need for him to make a decision.

'I think we've exhausted the alternatives, Mr Chairman,'

said Bert, 'this is now a good time of the year to do the work on that tee.'

'Here, here,' voiced Thompson, 'let's stop fannying about and get on with it.'

'We could, of course, move the tee,' said Andrews, one of Williams' buddies.

'We bloody well couldn't,' said Brown, the chairman of finance, who sat on this committee for the sole purpose of stopping such ludicrous suggestions being passed, 'do you realise how much that would cost?'

'Perhaps you could report back to the next meeting with the exact costs of that proposal and then we can take a final decision,' said Watson, playing his usual non-committal 'card'.

'Oh sodding hell, yet more time wasting tactics; hasn't anyone got the balls to make a decision on this committee,' interjected Thompson.

'It sounds to me,' said Watson 'that most of your decisions, Eric, are influenced by those particular parts of your anatomy; they certainly crop up frequently in the expression of your ideas.'

There was a mild rumble of laughter around the room accompanied by Thompson's look of absolute hostility towards Watson.

'I take it that we're all agreed then, our chairman of finance will cost the proposal to move the tee and report to the next meeting.'

Yes, thought Bert, and in the meantime I'm going to carry on being the object of further verbal attacks from that lunatic fringe of 'wildlife wankers'.

Thompson, meanwhile, was mentally composing his letter to the chairman of the club, proposing a vote of no confidence in the chairman of greens.

The meeting then developed into another series of hostile skirmishes about changing the shape of one of the greens, building three new bunkers and allowing the rough to grow in on two of the fairways. Naturally, no actual decisions were taken, but numerous reports were commissioned that would have kept an army of parliamentary researchers busy for six months.

'Well, gentlemen, that seems to conclude the business of the meeting. I think it's been another constructive session with progress on a number of issues,' said Watson.

'Perhaps, you could just quickly remind us all of what particular progress we've made,' Mr Chairman, enquired Thompson sarcastically.

'You'll be able to read it all in the minutes, Eric,' replied Watson, 'I assume you do actually read the minutes do you?'

'Mr Chairman, I had hoped that we might discuss the plans for the cultivation work on the greens,' said Bert, rather aware of the fact that members were edging towards the door and the bar.

'Ah yes, Bert,' said Watson. 'Gentlemen, perhaps we could just have five minutes on this before we close.'

Looks of dismay and frustration covered the faces of the committee at the thought of a further bout of indecisive ramblings.

'Perhaps you could just quickly take us through your plans, Bert,' said Watson

'Why don't you just bloody well get on with the work, then we'll know what your plans are won't we?' interrupted Thompson.

Bert chose to ignore the prat and press on. 'We are proposing to start hollow tining all the greens next week because the weather forecast is good and the greens will recover quicker.'

'But the seniors have got a match next week, you can't expect visitors to play on hollow-tined greens,' said Williams, 'it's embarrassing for us as well.'

'Sod the seniors,' exclaimed Thompson, 'if you need to do it, Bert, get on with it.'

'Yes, so that there'll be no disruption to your bloody corporate golfing day next month, I suppose,' rejoined Williams.

'Got nothing to do with that,' said Thompson, 'work's got to be done for the good of the course.'

'Can you explain, Bert, just what is involved in hollow-tining and how it differs from slicing?' asked Watson.

What the hell difference would it make me explaining, thought Bert, you wouldn't understand and judging by the faces of the committee, they would not appreciate it if they subsequently found the bar closed when they left the meeting.

'I'll let you have a note with a description of what the differences are,' said Bert, diplomatically.

'Well, I think it's too early to be doing this,' said Andrews.

'Since when have you been an expert on turf cultivation, Andrews,' said Thompson, 'you couldn't grow a bloody window box, just leave it to someone who knows what they're talking about.'

'Well, not knowing anything about a subject doesn't seem to have ever held you back from having an opinion, Eric,' said Watson.

'Gentlemen, we've got to make a start right away on this hollow-tining in order to improve the quality of the grass and avoid the problems that come from compacting,' explained Bert.

'Who said our greens are compacted?' asked Williams. 'That's the first I've heard of it; why have we not been informed before now?'

'Don't get your knickers in a twist, Williams,' said Watson, 'all greens suffer from compaction because of the amount of use, it's natural.'

'It doesn't sound natural to me,' shouted Williams.

'Sex is not natural to you, Williams,' said Thompson, 'but we've got to have it.'

'Gentlemen, we've got to bring this to a close,' explained Watson.

'First sensible thing you've said all night,' said Thompson.

Watson pressed on in spite of the interruption. 'I propose we let Bert get on with the hollow tining immediately if he believes it's the right time to do it.'

Everyone recoiled in amazement, including Thompson and Bert, both of whom in particular, suddenly realised that they'd been present at the precise moment when the chairman of greens had actually taken a decision.

It's the accepted lot of all head green keepers to have their time and energies constantly disrupted by reps from manufacturers of golf course maintenance equipment trying to flog them the latest gizmo that they claim will, 'save time, money, energy' and if you believe everything they say about it in the brochure, even their marriage. What, of course, they don't say it will save the poor beleaguered head green keeper from, is the interrogation from the head of the finance committee, hell-bent on not spending another penny on something that is claimed will make this work-shy group of malingerers lives even easier. Neither, of course, will it save him from the observations of those allegedly well-informed members who claim that, 'the damn thing hasn't made one iota of difference; we might as well have spent the money on a new green keeper.'

For some head green keepers, there's even the need to overcome the Luddite mentality of some of his apparently highly motivated and dedicated staff. 'I've never seen such a useless piece of crap in all my life; what in hell's name did you go wasting your money on that for, we could have had better seats in the shed with the money you spent on that.'

At 'Swankers', Bert was fighting all of these attitudes and more from the mixed bunch of uncooperative incompetents with which he was saddled, typified by Watson, the chair of the greens' committee.

'Ah, Bert, what you doing reading brochures when you should be out on the course getting those fairways cut?' said Watson on one occasion.

Bert detected a hint of surprise in Watson' tone that he could even read, let alone understand the complicated data provided in the brochure. He felt like saying, 'I'm really only looking at the pictures Mr Watson', then realised that this piece of humour could easily have been misconstrued.

What Bert chose to do was blind Watson with some extremely technical details from the brochure that he knew the latter would not have the first clue about.

'Well,' said Bert, 'we urgently need some work doing on aerating the greens and fighting the compaction, so I'm looking into adding some slit tiners, hollow corers, solid tiners and disc slitters to our range of equipment.'

Judging by the expression on Watson' face, Bert might as well have been speaking to him in a dialect of Gujerati, but Watson was not one for revealing his ignorance too easily.

'I'm not sure we need both the tiners, Bert,' said Watson, 'one will do the job well enough.'

It was obvious to Bert that Watson had no real basis for this claim other than to avoid having to ask for more money from that cheapskate Brown, the head of the finance committee.

'Our consultant agronomist, in his report to the executive, said that we needed both, but, of course, if you think you know otherwise I'll arrange for you to explain your reasons to them,' said Bert.

Bert thought that Watson was going to have a heart attack judging by the colour of his face after being challenged in this way.

'That won't be necessary, Bert, the executive can make their mind up based on the report, I wouldn't want to influence their decision,' said Watson.

They wouldn't take any bloody notice of what you said anyway thought Bert. You're only in the job because no other stupid sod volunteered to do it.

'Perhaps I could borrow that brochure, Bert, to read up about the relative merits of these different pieces of equipment,' said Watson.

'Certainly, be delighted to lend it to you, Mr Watson, I'm sure you'll find the pictures and the diagrams very helpful,' said Bert pointedly and smiling as Watson stormed off, clearly annoyed by the inference that he wouldn't have a clue as to what the words in the brochure actually meant.

If dealing with the retards in the club wasn't bad enough, it fell to Bert to have to cope with the motley collection of sales reps that pitched up at the club virtually every month eager to off-load some new fangled piece of machinery with jargon that would have baffled the combined talents of every professor of engineering in the country. Coping with the comments from these 'smart alec salesmen', as Bert often branded them, demanding to know how he'd personally managed to survive in the business for the last 30 years without the invaluable help that his equipment offered, was also a test of Bert's tact, diplomacy and patience.

The group varied from the 'know-alls' to the 'know-nothings', though when it actually came down to it, they were really one and the same, the 'know-alls' evidently knowing nothing and the 'know-nothings' pretending to know everything. Their sales techniques also varied in style and quality from the pushy, 'you'd be crazy to turn down this offer' types to the nervous hesitant, 'I'll have to ask my boss for an answer to that' type every time they got a question more difficult than what day it was.

Bert's style with the pushy types was to be as infuriatingly non-committal as possible, giving nothing, offering nothing, while at the same time still holding a barrage of questions up his sleeve designed to aggravate them even further, just when they believed they were making a break through on the sale. With the hesitant types, Bert would put his interrogative technique into overdrive, firing one question after another, always with the full knowledge of what the correct answer should be and prepared to take the 'twitcher' on if any part of an answer was less than 100 per cent accurate.

His meeting on this particular day was with one of the pushy set who had repeatedly come back to try to press Bert into buying some new aerating equipment and, seemingly, either had endless patience or a very large expense account to justify returning so many times.

'Bert, my old mate, how the devil are you, today, busy as ever I bet, still giving them hell on the exec, I'm sure!' was the opener.

Bert hated this 'old mates' approach; he would rather have volunteered to take part in a bungee jump off the Clifton suspension bridge than share five minutes in the company of this pompous prick.

'Got a closure on the machine deal, then? I'm sure you'll want this in the bag for the autumn work on the greens,' said the rep.

'Well, I'm still thinking about it, I'm still not sure it's going to do exactly what I want,' said Bert adopting his non-committal approach in spades.

'But Bert, my old son, this is the best piece of machinery on the market, they don't come any better than this and you'll not get a better offer than the one I put on the table.'

'Well, we're putting next year's budget together at the moment and deciding on our priorities for equipment, so I've got to wait for the nod as you know.'

'Well, the offer's not on the table for ever you know, Bert, but, of course, I'm prepared to hold it for you just that little bit longer as a valued customer.'

Valued customer, my arse, thought Bert, I've never bought anything from you before, you prat.

'I can arrange a demonstration up here, you know,' said 'pushy', 'if that would oil the jolly old wheels of the decision makers.'

'Well that's very kind of you, I'll get back to you when I've put that offer to them, they'd need to be free to see it working as well, of course, and I can't commit to a date without consulting them.'

'Well, can we say this time next month, then?' said 'pushy', 'put it in the diary provisionally, eh, to be confirmed later.'

You can put what the hell you like in your damn diary, thought Bert, but I'm not committing to anything just yet.

'Now, are you coming to see us at the NEC next month on our stand, Bert? Spot of free booze and lots of nosh, you know; come and see my boss and have a word about your requirements; won't do any harm to press the flesh you know.'

Oh shit, thought Bert, the only flesh I think I'd really like to press would be your arse in propelling you out of here as fast as possible.

'I'll have to see about that when we get nearer the time,' said Bert perpetuating the non-committal approach as long as he dared, 'we're going to be very busy around that time.'

'All work and no play, you know Bert, you know what they say,' said 'pushy'.

Well, thought Bert, the work bit could never be applied to you, sunshine.

'I'm afraid I've got to go now to clear some ditches out at the far end of the course, so if you'll excuse me,' said Bert, hurriedly thinking of just any excuse to get rid of this tiresome oik.

'I'll give you a call on the old dog and bone next week, see if there's any progress with the executive dinosaurs, what?' said 'pushy'.

You can try, thought Bert, but you'll get the same flaming answer as you got today, that is if I decide to even answer your call.

As he watched 'pushy' wander off down the drive in his black BMW, he wondered whether salesmen and chairmen of greens' committees were put on this planet to deliberately make his life hell. Then he also remembered Colin and Fred, two of his ground staff and half the rest of the greens' committee along with that raging sex maniac of a chairman of the club and came to the conclusion that the good Lord must have been on some kind of overtime bonus when it came to creating people who were guaranteed to drive him to levels of complete desperation and despair.

CHAPTER 6

THE SENIORS' CAPTAIN'S TALE or 'It's generally a case of the un-lead-able resisting the ungrateful against the unbearable.'

It's 8.00 on a crisp, bright Spring Monday morning in the car park at 'Swankers', though, in truth, it could be at just about any golf course in the country. Four stalwarts of the club's seniors' section are just about to arrive, having yet again successfully escaped the clutches of their respective spouses, vainly standing in the doorway waving the weekly chores list at them, to play their regular friendly four-ball. The four have kept this appointment for the last 15 years or more, setting out from the first tee in conditions that, over the year, vary from the sub-tropical to the sub-arctic and returning three and half hours later either resembling four long lost 'extras' from a re-make of Lawrence of Arabia or four ice-clad 'drivers' whose frozen huskies have themselves finally succumbed to the sub-zero temperatures.

Non-appearance by any one of the four over the course of those years could be counted on the fingers of one hand and in those instances where apologies had to be urgently dispatched, it was probably a close call between either ringing the golf club or the local undertaker with an order. Moreover, all four have been known to struggle out from sick beds, much to the absolute amazement of their partners, whose earlier request for help with the monthly shopping had to be regrettably declined, suffering from a variety of illnesses, which had they been contracted while in full-time employment, would have required at least two weeks 'on the sick'. The merest hint or suggestion by a family member or friend that their presence would be much appreciated elsewhere or that their 'condition' required some form of domestic confinement, would be met with a mixture of responses ranging from incredulity and disbelief to outright hostility.

Attempts by fellow golfers, occasionally, to dissuade them from going out in conditions better suited to the successful running of a down hill slalom at the Winter Olympics, are usually dismissed with utter disdain and the accusation of coming from a 'load of wimps'.

Even Richardson, the professional's attempts, such as threatening to close the course, have met with little acceptance, 'guys, it's bloody freezing out there, some parts of the fairways are under water, the greens are very soggy so we'd have to use ten temporaries and you'd be on mats on 12 holes, you can't seriously want to go out and play.'

'Right we'll get off straight away then, I hear the forecast's not good for later in the morning,' replied one of the four.

Given the enormous differences between the four in personality, behaviour and general attitudes, coupled with the fact that, during the course of every round of golf, each of them will be the object of some form of personal, but good-natured abuse, ridicule and humiliation from one or more of the others, it might surprise an outsider that the relationship has lasted this long, but of such stuff are golfers, particularly senior golfers, made. Woe-betide, for instance, any member of the senior section who, within earshot of any one of the four, dared to criticise the playing or the off-course behaviour of one of the other three. A resolutely stout defence of the injured partner, followed by the demand for a grovelling apology would usually be the very least that the offending speaker could expect.

Reg is always the first of the four to arrive, mainly because it takes him three times as long as everyone else to locate and assemble the various items of golfing equipment and clothing he carries with him. On arrival, he opens the capacious boot of his battered, scratched and patched 1989 Rover 820 that has over 160 000 miles on the clock and which he resolutely claims, 'has hardly given me a moments trouble since the day I bought it new.' His wife, of course, would tell a different tale of breakdowns, tow-ins, side of the road 'sit-ins', rescues and garage bills that would cover the walls of an average sized lounge.

He extracts his trusty set of Peter Thompson clubs that he's had for almost as long as the Rover along with his one concession to modern golf, his battery-powered trolley from among the rest of the personal and domestic paraphernalia that seems to permanently reside in the boot. Reg also retrieves from its depths an extra large clothes bag containing his plus fours, his co-ordinated coloured socks and Gabicci sweater. Despite the fact that there's hardly a cloud in the sky, he also retrieves an umbrella, a bag cover and various other items of wet weather gear and heads off for the changing rooms to change into his Dryjoy golf shoes.

Close behind him is Tom, desperately trying to ease clubs, trolley, shoes and clothes bag from the rear of his 12-year-old top of the range Mini Metro Kensington. Unlike Reg's Rover, Tom's Metro does look exactly like it did on the day he bought it; its bodywork would need to be scrutinised with Jodrell Bank's finest microscopic equipment to unearth the slightest of blemishes to body or paintwork. The interior bears no visible signs that any human or animal form has ever come into contact with the car's simulated leather upholstery. His six-year-old set of Taylormade golf clubs are in the same pristine condition as the Metro as is the Power Kaddy trolley that looks for all the world as though its just arrived from the manufacturer. Sporting some new, smartly pressed cords, he too heads off to the changing rooms.

Out of a cavernous Toyota Landcruiser, climbs Martin who has recently purchased this 'wardrobe on wheels', as Reg has nicknamed it, because it's reputedly large enough to carry all

his and his wife's golf clubs, their trolleys and their respective, colour coordinated Samsonite luggage, transport two large dogs, pull the horse box and tow the boat.

'Probably all at the same bloody time', said Tom on the first occasion that Martin appeared in it and managed to park it diagonally across almost three spaces in the club car park.

'Haven't quite got the hang of the size of this damn thing yet', he admitted.

His latest set of personally-fitted Ping clubs is hauled out of one of the far corners of the boot to be fitted to the golf buggy that he recently purchased on the Internet from what Martin characteristically claimed was, 'the most technically advanced golf manufacturing company in Sweden'.

'It's probably the only bloody golf manufacturing company in Sweden,' suggested Tom, rather sarcastically.

Martin heads off to the buggy park to locate his new 'toy' and then heads for the changing rooms.

Finally and rather late by the standards of the other three, all of four minutes in fact, and in a flurry of dust and locked wheels, there's Brian who emerges after a bit of a struggle from his BMW MZ sports coupe. Brian only lives half a mile from the golf club and in the time it takes him to get the car out of the garage, check it for any offending dust or mud acquired since he last used it, peer under the bonnet to give the neighbours the impression that he actually knows how what's there actually works, he could have made the journey on foot. Walking anywhere other than on a golf course, however, is not Brian's style. Brian's clubs and trolley, of course, have to reside permanently in his locker because with a pair of golf shoes and a toothbrush, the boot of the MZ is full.

'Bloody Schumacher's just arrived,' said Martin as he joined the others walking to the first tee, 'he'll catch us up as soon as he's parked his helmet and changed out of his fireproof racing overalls.'

Just four senior golfers who might be found in almost permanent residence at any golf club in the UK throughout the year, come rain or shine. Yet, together they represent that motley collection of 'happy hackers' called the 'seniors' section.' The only other relevant piece of information on this particular four is that Tom Darby, for his sins, is captain of the seniors' section at 'Swankers' Golf Club.

Just four senior golfers from one particular golf club they may be, but between them they happen to represent the four major categories of senior golfers that, week-in week-out, pit their ever decreasing physical and, for some, mental capabilities against the apparently ever-increasing difficulties of their local golf course. That is perhaps, with the significant exception of the 19th hole where their capabilities will not have waned to anything like the same degree as those used to circumnavigate the previous18.

Reg, for instance, represents that endangered group of 'traditionalist' golfers for whom almost everything about golf today is in a state of steep decline. Nothing that has been developed in the last ten or fifteen years can, in his view, match the quality of what was produced in the mid-50s and early 60s, when, according to Reg, 'the game was played properly with the proper looking equipment.'

On the first tee, Reg eyes up, with a look of utter disdain, the 'jumbo-headed' Ping driver that Martin has just acquired, describing it as a, 'brick on a stick that should have been be banned for reducing courses to pitch and putt tracks.'

'But Reg,' says Martin, 'I'm 40 odd yards past you off the tee.'

'Yeh', says Reg, 'but I'm in the middle of the fairway and you're in ankle-high rough behind a line of 50 foot high oaks that are blocking your shot to the green.'

Martin represents the 'egotist' clan of golfers, so-called because all his utterances, particularly those relating to golf, start with the pronouns 'I' or 'my' and move remorselessly on to 'me' and 'my'. His clubs, he will claim, are the 'best on the market', the golf balls he uses are 'second to none' and the new putter he's just acquired is 'out of this world.' And so the list goes on to include waterproofs, shoes, gloves and most recently, even tee pegs.

'It's like listening to a bloody advert on the Golf Channel when you're with him', says Tom, 'basically it's a matter of what he hasn't got is not worth having'.

Martin was a past captain of a golf club so his brand of egotism also extends to expecting everything to be currently done according to the way he once did it. 'Now when I was captain, I would never have allowed social golf in the middle of a monthly medal, I just wouldn't have stood for it'. 'When I was captain, I insisted that the tee was closed one hour before a match against another club, I don't know what this captain is thinking about; it wouldn't have been tolerated in my day.' Unbeknown to Martin, Brian had once opened a book with the other two on how many times Martin would use the word 'I' in a round. By the time they got to the 10th tee they had to give up the unequal struggle of counting and Reg won with an estimated 53 hits.

Two-thirds of the way down the first fairway, Brian checks with the others that they're still playing winter rules, picks up his ball and cleans it before playing his shot to the green.

'Two shot penalty,' says Tom.

'What the hell for?' asks Brian.

'You didn't mark your ball before lifting it,' replied Tom.

'It's a bloody friendly game of golf or at least that's what I thought,' said Brian.

'Bad habit,' said Tom, 'always advisable to get in the habit of playing to the rules, just in case.'

'Just in case of what?' asks Brian tetchily, 'that I get my card to play on the European Seniors Tour.'

Tom is of the 'perfectionist' persuasion as far as golf is concerned. Golf has to be played strictly according to the rules, whether it's the club championship or a friendly knock-about.

Martin also receives a 'yellow card' for walking ahead of Tom to his ball and getting in the latter's line of sight for his shot to the green.

'It was you who shanked the bloody shot, you can't blame me for that,' said Martin.

'Yeh, but you should stay behind the player, it's proper etiquette.'

'Etiquette, my arse', said Brian who was firmly of the 'nonconformist' school of golfers and not renowned for his adherence either to R & A rules or the finer points of golf etiquette, 'if I'm ready to play, I'll sodding well get on with it; I'm not standing around freezing my nuts off waiting to take my turn while simultaneously being treated to yet another rendition of Rule 675b, subsection 402, para 94, about when and where on the course I should blow my nose or scratch my arse.'

It would, perhaps, be quite remarkable to a non-golfer that these four completely contrasting characters ever completed a round of golf together, let alone continued to play in each other's company week after week; yet to those who play the game and particularly those who play among the senior ranks, it is a perfectly natural phenomenon and one that could be found in practically any Monday morning four-ball.

The group eventually reach the first green. Brian takes out his own particular latest golfing acquisition, a broom-handled putter.

'Oh bloody hell', remarked Reg, 'will you look at that contraption; you haven't joined the ranks of the 'twitchers' as well have you and actually bought one of those washing line props? Why can't people play with things that look like putters, not some thing you could use to sweep the chimney!'

'Ah, give it up Reg,' said Brian, 'if you had your way we'd all still be playing with gutta percha balls and hickory shafted clubs; anyway if it's good enough for the likes of Langer and Torrance, it's good enough for me, you wouldn't have the balls to call Torrance a 'twitcher'.

'Well, you never saw the likes of Nicklaus and Player having to resort to those sorts of monstrosities,' replied Reg.

Martin is standing over his putt and looks about to hit it.

'Hang on a minute, Martin', says Tom, 'it's Reg to putt first, you're going out of turn.'

'Well why the hell doesn't he get on with it instead of

treating us all to another of his golfing history lessons, I'm giving up the will to live here.'

As luck would have it, of course, after driving off from the very next tee, Martin's three partners are roped in to search for his new Japanese-designed tee peg that is claimed will provide him with an extra 20 yards.

'Hell fire,' said Reg sarcastically, 'I must get some of those new tees, that one's gone further than your drive, Martin.'

'I'll look for your ball for the statutory five minutes,' said Tom, 'but I'm buggered if I'll spend five minutes looking for some over-priced Japanese plastic crap.'

The game proceeded for the remaining 17 holes with the same extraordinary blend of banter and sarcasm being given and taken by all four players. Tom called another penalty on Martin who'd accidentally driven over Reg's ball with his buggy when he'd gone on ahead of them to try to locate it in the deep rough.

'That's the last sodding time I'm helping anyone find their ball if that's what I finish up with.'

Brian, never a person to conceal his forthright views, twice insisted that Tom, who had something of a reputation among the seniors for dodgy counting, had miscalculated his shots to particular holes, though the way Brian phrased his remark was a little less ambiguous.

Martin had a dig at Reg about failing, on no less than four occasions, to get out of a green-side bunker at the first attempt and pointedly remarked, 'of course, if like the rest of us, you'd had the latest lob-wedge, you'd have no problem with those shots'.

Brian's claim that since he'd bought one of the latest 'rescue clubs' that he'd had no problems getting good distance from the rough, promptly sparked a comment from Tom and Reg that, 'perhaps you should have bought an entire set of them.'

Martin continued to regale the group with endless suggestions of how he would, if he'd still been captain, ask for certain greens to be re-shaped, bunkers to be moved and hazards to be re-aligned.

'Ever thought of going into golf course design,' said Brian pointedly, 'somewhere like Tibet'.

At the end of the game, Martin and Brian, as partners on this occasion, had to part with the princely sum of £1.50, having lost the first nine, the second nine and the match.

'Well, that's your petrol money for the Metro sorted for the week, Tom,' said Martin, 'set the table up when you get in, we'll have a game of snooker over a few tinctures and we'll play you for double or quits.'

Once the four had exhausted their personal bank of on-course sarcasm, banter and ridicule on each other, they naturally turned their attention to the officials and management team of the club, who were inevitably not immune from the 'verbal Exocets' that these four were capable of delivering.

'I hear that the chairman has made a complete 'horlicks' of this business of changing the use of the men's and women's rooms in the clubhouse,' said Reg.

'Well, I find that hardly surprising with this current lot, not the sort of thing that would have happened in my day, though' said Martin on hearing of further tales of bungling incompetence, 'he couldn't find his arse in the dark, the prat.'

'No, but I gather there's a certain female member of the management who's been helping him out recently,' said Brian whose personal collection of club rumour and gossip would have probably kept most tabloid newspaper headlines in copy for a month.

'From what I've heard, she's been helping him in as well,' said Martin.

'Now come on you two', said Tom, 'you can't go believing everything you hear in the men's bar.'

'Men's bar be buggered', said Brian, 'this is straight from the ladies themselves, you can't get a more reliable source than that.'

'That's not what you said when some of the ladies reported

you for having a pee by the side of the 17th tee,' said Tom, 'you called them a load of shortsighted old gossips.'

'Well, there can't be much wrong with their eyesight if they managed to locate Brian's tackle from the other side of the course,' said Martin.

'Have you heard that our honourable secretary has made a complete shambles of the club diary for next year?' said Tom, 'why can't this club get people who can do things properly first time!'

'Well, what do you expect appointing an ex-policeman as secretary!' said Brian who was famously known for his 'anti-plod' attitudes. 'He can barely read, let alone write.'

'That view would be nothing to do with the fact that you've now got nine endorsement points for speeding on your licence, would it?' enquired Reg.

'Nothing whatsoever old boy,' said Brian, 'I've always been of the opinion that being intellectually retarded is a key requirement for recruitment to the high ranking office of PC Plod.'

'Well, it's caused a hell of a stir amongst the ladies and their committee, who've accused him of being incompetent and a male chauvinist,' said Reg.

'Blimey,' said Martin, 'Barnacles'll have a job spelling 'chauvinist' on the charge sheet, let alone understanding what it means.'

'You going to the captain's dinner this year, Reg,' asked Brian.

'Not on your life,' said Reg, 'it was absolutely disgraceful, the behaviour last time, people shouting, drinking too much, throwing things and generally acting like over-grown schoolboys, I don't know what the place is coming to.'

'Sounds like a good night,' said Martin, 'I'm sorry I missed that.'

'I hope you've ticked the list of matches you're available to play in this year,' said Tom, 'as Seniors' captain, I need as big a pool as possible to pick from.'

'Ah, I've decided that I'm not going to play in many of

them this year,' said Martin, 'I think the overall standard of the players who put themselves up for this is getting worse. If I was captain I certainly wouldn't select some of the hackers that have put their name on the list, they'd never get a game in my team.'

'Well said,' interrupted Brian, 'oh by the way Martin, you did a net 98 today.'

'Right fellows, I'm off for some lunch, everyone OK for Wednesday, same time, I assume?' said Brian.

The rest nodded and headed for the changing rooms and the car park, desperately trying to remember whether today was their wives' WI day, thus allowing them the opportunity for a few uninterrupted chore-free 'zeds' through the afternoon.

The only one of the four who was not heading straight home was Tom. He had a meeting with the seniors' captain of a nearby club to try to patch up some differences over their annual fixture, after their threat to cancel it following various incidents that occurred in the previous year. He was not exactly looking forward to the encounter, largely because he'd secretly had to admit that it had been some of the more bloody-minded, arrogant and down right ruder seniors from 'Swankers' that had been largely responsible for creating the problems in the first place.

'Ah Basil, nice to see you, come in and have a drink before we get down to business,' said Tom in the hope that a couple of glasses of wine or a scotch or two might help to mellow the proceedings a little.

'Thank you Tom, I'll have a diet coke,' said Basil.

That'll go a long way to oiling the wheels of reconciliation, thought Tom as he headed for the bar; I've got a feeling that this is going to be even harder than I expected.

'Right now Basil' said Tom on his return from the bar, 'I think we're both agreed that we don't want to lose the fixture between our two clubs, we've always had a very amicable relationship until recently.'

He was hoping that this conciliatory approach would set the tone of the discussion and bring it to a speedy conclusion.

'Well, you might think so Tom, but our seniors think the fixture with Swancliffe has been going down the pan for some time and quite frankly they've instructed me to find an alternative club. They've no desire to replay the farce of last year, or the year before, or for that matter put up with the antics of some of your bad-mannered, unsporting members.'

'Well I'm sure that there was no intention on the part of any of our members to be deliberately rude or un-sporting,' lied Tom, knowing only too well that at least three of those who'd played in the last match were quite capable of raising the bar of bad-manners to Olympic standards.

'Well, after the match, at least six of my members came up to me to complain about some of the things that had been said to them or gone on during the game,' said Basil.

'It was all probably meant as a joke, they weren't meant to be taken seriously, we do have one or two jokers amongst our crowd,' admitted Tom.

'We can all take a joke, but there's jokes and rudeness,' replied Basil, 'and most of it was the latter in our opinion. After three holes, for instance, one of your players turned to one of our team and said, 'you've done awfully well to be playing off a 24 handicap with a swing like that.' Our guy went to pieces after that and hardly finished a hole.'

'He might just have been trying to give him a bit of encouragement,' offered Tom.

'Are you kidding? Apparently the bastard had a grin from ear to ear and was nudging his partner in the ribs as he said it!' replied Basil. 'Two others said that half way around their opponents had, within earshot, sarcastically said, 'well I suppose the exercise has done us a bit of good if nothing else' and another of your pairings rather pointedly said to our pair, 'I suppose you find it tough when you have to play a good golf course like this.' I agree that the fixture is after all only a bit of fun, but for one of your team to turn to our pair who'd lost rather heavily and say, 'well I don't suppose you found that much fun, did you?' is hardly in the spirit of the game.'

'Yes, I take your point,' admitted Tom, 'I'm afraid we have got one or two members with a reputation for speaking bluntly.'

'One doesn't mind people speaking bluntly, it's when it's downright rude and personal that people get annoyed,' replied Basil. 'The antics of some of your team we also thought were pretty questionable; the old trick, for instance, of one of your team regularly going to stand in the eye line of our player as he played his shot. One of our members said, 'every time I went to play my shot, I could see one of our opponents out of the corner of my eye, I could practically touch him with the end of my club.'

'Perhaps he was doing it so that he could spot the line of the ball through the air,' offered Tom.

'Oh yeh, sure,' said Basil, 'I might accept that if he was hitting a driver into the sun, but not over a 25 yard wedge shot or a 10 foot putt. One or two of our members also eventually spotted one of the oldest tricks in the book of having the wrong head covers on the irons and making a point of casually throwing them on the ground before the shot was played. They told me, 'they must have thought we were a right couple of Noddys to fall for that one.' One of our players thought that the offer of some sweets by one of your members was very generous until he discovered that they were coated in such a sticky substance that he could hardly prise the club off his glove.'

'Well as I said Basil, we do have a few jokers in the club and they do like their bit of fun,' said Tom.

'Yeh, well I'm afraid that their liking for 'a bit of fun' as you put it, along, may I say, with one or two other things has reached a point where none of us wish to come back for another dose.'

'I'm sure that most of our senior members will be very sad to hear that, Basil,' said Tom, 'I can assure you that I'll do everything to ensure there's no repeat of that sort of behaviour.'

'It's not just the antics of a few of your members, either,' said Basil, 'we had that farce where we turned up with 14 pairs and you had ten, so there was no match for eight of our players. Then there was the previous year at our club; hardly any of your lot turned up because they'd been told the match was off because the weather was too bad. The bloody sun was shining at our place and most of our players had turned up in shorts.'

'Yeh, I believe that that was just a misunderstanding over the weather forecast,' admitted Tom, 'there was apparently a mix-up over which particular day it referred to.'

'Sodding hell,' said Basil, 'you'd only have had to look out the window to have seen it was semi-bloody tropical on that day, hardly a cloud in the sky, even the damn Met Office could have got that one right.'

'Yes, well I'm sure that lightening won't strike twice, Basil,' joked Tom, 'as far as slip-ups like that are concerned.'

'We've had more flaming 'slip-ups' as you call them, with this damn club than an old age pensioners day trip to an ice rink,' said Basil. 'As one of our members said at the meeting the other day, 'if we want to be involved in a farce with a load of jokers like them again, we'll give Billy Smarts' circus a ring and see if the clowns can have a day off.'

'The seniors' section takes its golf very seriously and that includes the matches with other clubs,' replied Tom, defensively, 'none of them would like to be thought of as treating these games as just a joke. I hope you can persuade your members to keep the fixture going.'

'Personally, I'm not sure I want to be the one to try to persuade them. A repetition of last year's fiasco and they'd put me on a free transfer to the local council allotments committee. I'll have to see what I can do. I'll give you a call with our decision.'

Basil departed and left Tom wondering whether putting himself up for the captaincy of the seniors and having to endure this kind of torture and aggravation had really been worth it after all. Which one of those buggers in the seniors' section, thought Tom, had told him that being captain would be a 'walk in park', it's more like a walk over bloody red hot coals, if they really want to know. He remembered then that it had been Martin and Brian, the sods, who'd badgered him into standing, saying, 'it'll be a piece of cake, no problem to you at all, you'll really enjoy it, we're all such a friendly, co-operative bunch of lads.' I'll give that lot 'friendly' and 'co-operative' thought Tom as he drove home, wondering whether the dog had managed to cross its legs long enough to avoid flooding the kitchen again.

Trying to captain this so-called 'set of harmless, inoffensive old buffers', as someone had, in his opinion, inaccurately described the seniors to him, was about as difficult as trying to compete in the 'One man and his dog' sheep dog trials with a three-legged, half blind poodle.

Whoever said that, 'with age comes the wisdom and understanding of just how much you don't know,' had obviously never captained the seniors' section of a golf club. He would be hard pressed, he reckoned, to find any subject from anaesthetics to Zoroastrianism on which this lot would admit to even a modicum of ignorance. When it came to golf, Tom would have defied anyone to come up with a subject that the average Monday morning four-ball of 'grumpy gougers' wouldn't have an expert on.

Only just recently he'd overheard a heated argument among four senior members about why the greens seemed to be developing areas of moss. He listened to one self-styled expert claim, 'well, I could have told you this was going to happen months ago when they started using that new mower; its completely the wrong type for our greens.'

'Don't be such a prat, Frank,' said Harold, 'moss isn't caused by using the wrong kind of mower, it's something to do with cutting the grass too closely.'

'Well exactly my point,' said Frank, 'that new mower is cutting them too closely.'

‘They can adjust the height of the blades on these new fangled machines, you know, you stupid old sod,’ said Dennis sarcastically.

‘Ah well, that particular model doesn’t have enough settings on it,’ replied Frank in his defence.

‘Frank, the damn thing cost nearly five grand, it’s got more settings on it than a barometer, you pillock.’

‘Well, when I worked for the local council, it was common knowledge that those types of mowers caused problems,’ argued Frank.

‘Frank, when you worked for the council, the mowers hadn’t even got engines and anyway, you worked in the rates department, so what the hell would you know about mowers?’ replied Sid.

Tom finally moved on, after having listened to further idiotic utterances from Frank about intrinsic failures in modern mower design; utterances that were apparently based on something his uncle had once told him, whose only claim to ‘the knowledge’, it eventually transpired, arose from his discussion with a farmer to whom he’d once delivered milk.

On that particular day, Tom’s playing partners had been a group of retirees, comprising bank manager, personnel manager and head teacher. Before going to the bar for his round, he’d made the mistake of admitting that he was not sure how to deal with the complaint he’d received from the ladies’ section about Brian’s own personal interpretation of the rule about ‘taking relief’.

Charles, the retired head teacher had no doubts, ‘suspend the blighter for a month, you can’t have members going around exposing themselves to the ladies like that,’ he offered.

‘Don’t be such a pompous prick, Charles,’ said Huw, ‘the guy just wanted a pee, he wasn’t found starkers draped across the lady captain’s Skoda posing for the centre fold of Marie Claire magazine.’

‘Not the point at all, we need standards to be upheld and our captain should make an example of him, to send a message to everyone else,’ replied Charles.

'Have we got an epidemic of 'flashers' then?' asked Robert, 'perhaps we should put it to good use and have a seniors' male model calendar made.'

'I think this is just symptomatic of the decline in the standard of behaviour which every one seems happy to tolerate these days,' argued Charles, 'the captain should put his foot down on behaviour like this.'

'Be careful where you tread in future, Tom, it could be mighty painful for someone,' jibed Huw.

'Charles, this is 'Swankers', you're talking about, not the 18-30 Club on holiday in Benidorm,' said Huw; 'anyone listening to you would think we've joined a strip club, not a golf club.'

'I don't suppose you were ever caught dropping your trousers in front of the 5th Form girls when you were at school, then Charles?' said Robert.

'I actually went to an all boys' school,' said Charles, 'our trousers remained firmly around our waists at all times.'

'It must have been the only one of its kind in the country, then,' remarked Huw pointedly.

Tom reflected that the prat who'd claimed that age brought wisdom and understanding probably also maintained that it brought tolerance and humility, another palpable nonsense if you spent even a day in the company of some senior golfers, and as for patience... oh yes?

'Tom, I need an urgent word with you about Fred and Derek and those two other 'golfing tortoises' they play with, I forget their names,' said Ralph, 'we were stuck behind them all the way round yesterday, took us nearly four hours, it's not damn good enough, they need to be told to get a move on or get off the course.'

Tom had often wondered why some golfers seem to lose the power of frank speaking on the golf course, only to find it again when they return to the clubhouse and are within three metres of the captain.

'Did you approach them on the course and ask them if you could go through?' enquired Tom.

'It should have been sodding obvious we wanted to come through, we were waiting on every shot, they were just oblivious to everyone else on the course,' said Ralph.

'But if you didn't actually say anything to them, then its unlikely they'd speed up or let you through, you have to let them know,' replied Tom. 'If you didn't want to say anything to them on the course, why didn't you speak to them when you got in?'

'Hell, Tom, I think it's your job as seniors' captain to tell these people that slow play is not acceptable,' remarked Ralph.

Yeh, and I suppose it's also my flaming job to help them locate their damn glasses and car keys when they lose them and ring their wives to say they'll be home late 'cos they're pissed, thought Tom.

'Well actually Ralph, considering the poor conditions and that all four were walking, three and three quarter hours was not bad and I suppose you were using your buggy.'

'Ah, so I'm wasting my time am I, asking for your help to stamp out slow play?' said Ralph angrily. 'I sometimes wonder what the hell we have a seniors' captain for in this club except to keep the balance of male and female official photographs on the clubhouse wall.'

'OK,' said Tom, 'I'll have a word with them about slow play and point out that they held you up all the way round yesterday.'

'Well, it was certainly for most of the back nine anyway,' conceded Ralph, 'and if you're talking to them about slow play in general, I don't think there's any need to mention my name exactly, do you, best to leave me out of it.'

'Oh I disagree entirely,' said Tom, 'there's never any point in talking in vague terms about these issues; as seniors' captain, I'm firmly of the opinion that you need to be precise about the exact nature of the complaint and who is making it.'

As Ralph strode off to locate his fellow complainants, Tom reflected on yet another of those senior golfers who was very happy to have others fight their battles on their behalf, but were never prepared to actually put their head above the parapet, when the flak started flying.

Captaining the seniors' section, in his opinion, involved trying to lead the downright 'un-lead-able,' manage the patently 'unmanageable' and support the blatantly 'unsupportable'. The job, in actual fact, probably required the combined skills and acumen, not to mention the cunning, of a Churchill, a Montgomery and a Mussolini.

Some of these past 'captains of industry and commerce', that is, of course, if one was gullible enough to fall for the exaggerated rhetoric they used to describe the dizzy heights to which they claimed their careers had climbed, now considered themselves above being told to do anything, particularly if they'd had nothing to do with suggesting the idea in the first place.

'What's all this nonsense about having to change out of the golfing clothes we've worn on the course before coming into the clubhouse; downright cheek, if you ask me,' said Arthur, whose claim to have been a finance and investment consultant was vigorously disputed by those sceptics who said he'd never really risen above selling dodgy insurance policies 'on the knocker'.

"It's to stop scruffy, mud-splattered buggers like you covering the furniture and carpets in bits of the course that should have been left outside or in the changing rooms,' said Terry Alport, who wouldn't have dreamt of walking into the clubhouse without having first showered and changed out of the slightly grass-covered plus fours and bark-stained jumper, regardless of the fact that he was then three pints behind everyone else.

'Well, it's a flaming liberty,' said Arthur, 'telling me what I should and shouldn't wear and me paying for the privilege of being told an' all.'

'Just like being at home, eh, Arthur,' said Graham Swift, who was known to be working through a DIY list at home that would have kept the television's 'Changing Rooms' team busy for two years, 'you just put them straight, that you're not prepared to be told how to behave.'

'I will, Gray, 'cos people like me who've been used to dressing with the best, don't need telling by the likes of them how to dress properly,' said Arthur, 'when I was a financial consultant, it was second nature to me to always be smartly dressed and you never lose that ever, do you, Gray?'

'That's true Arthur,' admitted Graham, 'your dress sense has often left the rest of us lost for words.'

'Exactly right Gray,' said Arthur, 'and here's these officious so-and-so's trying to tell me what to wear and what not to wear; who the hell do they think they are?'

'Well, for starters, Arthur, they're the committee and they've been appointed to run the club and uphold some standards of things like dress,' said Terry, having now caught up with the drinks rounds, but wondering where the hell his order for large 'fries' had got to.

'Committee be buggered,' said Arthur, 'I don't want those up-starts telling me what I should and shouldn't be doing.'

'Well, perhaps you should have turned up at the AGM and voted,' said Graham, 'or better still, put up for the committee yourself.'

'Ah stuff that for a game of soldiers, Gray,' said Arthur, 'I'm not going back to wasting my time with all that nonsense; I had enough of all that management crap when I was in business as a financial consultant.'

'Yeh, I know what you mean,' said Graham, who was beginning to wonder just how much winding up this thick-skinned bugger could take. 'There's only so much you can take from those management trainers about how to keep those buggers from slamming the door in your face or what to do when they let the dog loose.'

'Yeh, well anyway,' said Arthur slightly unsure of what Graham was referring to, 'I'm going to carry on coming in dressed as I've always done and if they don't like it they can lump it.'

'Good for you, Arthur,' said Terry, having fought off near

starvation with the 'fries' and a club sandwich, 'I'm sure they wouldn't have the nerve to throw Tiger Woods out if he came in here with cords covered in mud, socks that appeared to be still leaking sand and a sweater that looked like a reject from the local Oxfam shop.'

'Your right there, 'Tell', there's no excuse for turning up looking like a tramp, is there?' said Arthur innocently.

Tom hoped that this latest act of belligerence on the part of one of the senior members would be taken up by the chairman of house and not be left yet again at his door to resolve. He wasn't particularly optimistic about this happening in this instance, mainly because the person in question was himself notorious for regularly appearing in the clubhouse dressed in apparent readiness for the lead in a new series of Wurzel Gummidge.

The seniors' annual match against the ladies' section of the club carried a reputation for having produced some quite controversial and bruising encounters in the past, quite literally epitomised by the occasion two years earlier when, in a quite unprecedented moment of unrestrained fury, the lady captain had taken a swing at her opposite number for allegedly calling two of her team, 'a pair of deviously dishonest cheats', as a result of various tactics they were reputed to have employed in their match.

The slightly bruised and shaken recipient of this attack claimed that what in fact he'd said at that precise moment, was that he'd recently played in a corporate golf day with someone with, 'a flair for serious business deals', but that in the noise and commotion of the clubhouse at that particular moment, the lady captain had completely misheard and misinterpreted the phrase. There were, however, a number of members, particularly amongst the men's section who regarded this as a very clever piece of 'semantic jiggery pokery' on the captain's part to extricate himself from a potentially embarrassing situation. One outcome of all this, however, was that the fixture was dropped from the calendar and would have remained so had not Tom received a letter from the vice captain of the ladies' section requesting that the fixture be reinstated.

The present lady captain, 'Brunhilde' Maddox, when canvassed for her support for its reinstatement, had clearly indicated her total opposition to the match in totally unambiguous terms. 'I have no desire to spend four hours in the company of either some harmless, but boring old cretin hell bent on poring out his entire life story over 18 holes or some misogynistic-minded anthropoid incapable of expressing anything more stimulating than the unrivalled merits of his latest Cobra driver or Ping putter.'

'We can take that as a 'no' then, can we?' said Tom's vice captain on hearing this outburst, 'I can't say that I'm overcome with grief at the news that 'Brunhilde' will not be joining us; it saves me the trouble of having to find some excuse not to play, had I been unfortunate enough to have been paired with that cantankerous old bat.'

There'd been no mad rush to sign the availability list for the fixture when it appeared on the seniors' notice board, though the anonymous comment that did appear requesting additional health insurance and immunity from prosecution for physical violence, rather summed up the mood of many in the men's section when it was first posted. Others had approached Tom requesting some form of incentive for offering themselves up for this form of 'ritual slaughter'.

'I want a cast-iron guarantee that I get to play in all the away matches for the rest of the season, if I agree to play,' said one reluctant participant.

'This has got to be worth a round of drinks for a month on the captain,' bartered another press-ganged member.

'Only if I get to play with 'Big Jugs', as Jeanette, the lady vice captain, had been christened by David Macklin.

He was one of the 'sex and sanatogen set', as a small group of senior members had been appropriately labelled by the ladies after a particularly raunchy mixed foursomes match in which he'd been involved.

'I'd be quite happy to offer her some suggestions on how to be more front-on and square at the top', offered David.

Macklin's coaching tips, whether to the ladies or gentlemen, were infamous and had been known to set some peoples' golf swing back years, paralysing them into indecision and uncertainty and causing gridlock on the course from the delay as the poor unfortunate pupil struggled with a '12-point' pre-shot routine before actually addressing the ball.

Tom had to use all his skills of negotiation and persuasion, combined with the occasionally explicit piece of bribery and corruption to get a team of 16 to turn up on the appointed day.

It was reliably reported that the lady vice captain had experienced the same degree of difficulty in raising a team as Tom had. Excuses for non-availability ranged from burying deceased, but previously unheard of, relatives; an excuse viewed with a great deal of suspicion as the game was still three weeks away, to needing to be home for the delivery of a new kitchen; an excuse viewed with equal scepticism given that the lady in question was reliably known to have steadfastly refused to countenance the merest hint of a suggestion by 'hubby' that some form of domestic improvement might be a welcome addition to the household.

Other members of the ladies' section had insisted on certain codes of behaviour being upheld by the opposition.

'If there's any of that swearing, rude remarks or obscene gestures like the other time, I'm coming straight off,' said one of the less liberal-minded lady members.

'I'm not standing for any of those club-throwing tantrums, I'm straight back to the clubhouse,' replied another.

'I'm not going to be drawn into playing for money, paying for the drinks, paying for the meals or any other of that kind of silly nonsense,' insisted yet another.

Selecting the pairings was allegedly done on the basis of 'first names out of the hat', but no-one really believed that this method had been employed since the risk of some misfit pairings occurring was too great. Both Tom and Jeanette had been warned by various members of their teams that if they were drawn against certain opponents, they'd immediately go AWOL.

Making the draw then, had been about as complicated for the two acting captains as that made for football's World Cup, endeavouring, as did their sporting counterparts in FIFA, to keep known combatants apart. Even having, in their humble opinion, exercised their diplomatic and arbitration skills to the very full, both acting captains were, on the day, confronted with the inevitable chorus of bad tempered resentment at having been drawn against a particular individual or pair with whom, in normal circumstances, they would have refused to even share the same room, let alone each others close company. All kinds of bizarre and totally erroneous excuses were paraded.

'Did you know he once told me off in front of everyone for taking his seat?' complained one lady, 'I can't stand the bad-tempered old fool anywhere near me.'

'She plonked herself down in my bloody seat while I was at the bar without a 'by your leave' or an 'I'm ever so sorry' and sat there as bold as brass ignoring me,' said the old boy, 'the pompous old bat; I'm stuck with her for the next four sodding hours.'

'Do you know, she drove straight out in front of me in the club car park the other week, if I hadn't have braked sharpish, we'd have had a right smack; not fit to be behind the bleeding wheel,' said Brian.

'I'm playing against that lunatic with that sports thingy; thinks he's Michael Schumacher he does, nearly had us both in the wall, he did,' complained the lady in question.

Tom and Jeanette were on the first tee to send everyone off with a few, extremely carefully chosen words of encouragement and good humour, most of which rebounded on them like a ferociously hit tennis ball.

'Have a good game everyone and don't forget it's only a bit of fun after all,' said Jeanette, 'we don't want any casualties.'

'We're never going to be sufficiently close to one another,

thank god, to suffer casualties, judging by those opening drives from the ladies,' shouted one of Tom's team.

Tom glared at Martin and indicated that his predilection for hand-to-hand combat should be reserved for his weekends away with the Sealed Knot.

'We want no unfair tactics or questionable gamesmanship,' said Tom, as David Macklin left the tee, 'everything must be fair and above board.'

'You should have told 'Big Jugs' that before she turned up in those white skin-tight pants and that top,' said Macklin, 'talk about casualties; with a pair of 'Toby's' like those, she'll have someone's eye out, she will.'

The matches proceeded with, on the whole, remarkably few incidents of any serious nature, though there were numerous examples of minor skirmishing between some of the pairings. Notably, the four-ball in which Martin featured, was punctuated by a series of attempts on the part of both pairs to upset each other's frame of mind and consequently their game.

On the 4th tee, one of the lady members remonstrated loudly to Martin as he roared past her in his buggy.

'Would you mind awfully if we actually took our drives before you start charging off down the fairway in that contraption of yours, I'd be terribly upset if we put a ball through your buggy.'

Later, on the green, Martin, turning to the same lady, said, 'could you possibly move over to your right, you are casting quite a large shadow over my line.'

There were further examples of sniping on the 7th, when Martin duffed a chip to the green at the same time as one of the ladies called across to her partner for help with club selection.

'I hope the poor standard of my game isn't interfering with your conversation ladies,' said Martin angrily.

'Absolutely not,' was the reply, 'you seem quite capable of making a mess of it without any outside assistance from us.'

The tee shot of one of the ladies on the short par three 11th was accompanied by rather a loud uncontrolled fart from Martin causing the lady in question to drive her ball into the nearby bushes.

'If the state of your bowels is such that you can't predict their undesirable intervention in our game, perhaps you'd be kind enough to at least stand at a distance down wind of us for the remaining holes,' suggested one of his opponents.

Coming up the 16th hole, the men were 'dormy' on their opponents, only requiring a half to win. Both men were on the green, Martin in three shots, his partner in two. The approach shot of one lady ended up in the pond in front of the green, putting her out of the hole. Martin and his partner approached the ladies with the intention of offering to shake hands, believing the game was theirs. Her partner was also in some trouble, at least 60 yards from the green behind a sizeable tree, having already played four shots.

The men were firmly told, 'will you two stand out of my way at once, if I hole this with my shot, you'll jolly well have to get down in two for a half.'

'Well my partner's on the green for two, ten feet from the pin and we only need a half anyway, you stupid apology for a golfer,' said Martin in a half strangulated frustrated shout.

The outcome was somewhat inevitable; the lady's ball hit the tree and ricocheted into the pond. Both women immediately stormed off towards the clubhouse leaving Martin and his partner to proffer each other their own form of congratulations.

The mood and manner in which Brian and his partner's game with their opponents progressed was hardly better. Brian was quite severely told off for playing out of turn on no less than three occasions, his partner was categorically refused relief from clear evidence of animal burrowing activity and on three occasions they were asked to hole out putts from no more than 18 inches.

'If I have to mark that putt,' complained Brian, 'my marker will fall in the bloody hole.'

In response, Brian claimed that one of the ladies contacted

the sand with her club in a bunker and called a penalty that was vigorously disputed, leading to the necessity to record two scores for the hole prior to querying the penalty back in the clubhouse. Three times his partner questioned their opponent's score and was categorically told to mind his own business, adding, 'if you're calling us cheats, then we'll end the game right now.' Brian and his partner were seriously tempted to take their opponents up on the offer and head back to the bar. These acrimonious exchanges continued until the very last hole, where much to Brian and his partner's embarrassment, the ladies made a net birdie and won the match.

'We're not conceding the damn match until we get a decision on that penalty shot in the bunker,' claimed Brian, dreading the thought of the 'stick' he'd get from his mates when news got out of his loss.

'You're just very bad sports who can't stand the thought of being beaten by the ladies,' said one of his opponents, as they headed off to consult Richardson, the professional.

Much to Brian's annoyance the professional turned out to be no bloody help to him either because he just said that if, in these circumstances, the player allegedly responsible for the penalty did not call a penalty on themselves, it was one person's word against another. As a result, the win for the ladies stood and Brian marched off to face the music.

By comparison, Tom's match with the lady handicap secretary and her partner was nothing but sweetness and light. They chatted and joked their way round the course, encouraging one another's good shots, commiserating over the bad ones and conceding what appeared to be outrageously long putts.

Two of Tom's team on an adjoining green, overhearing all the friendly banter and conceded putts were heard to remark, 'Christ, old Tom must be on a promise the way he's getting on with the lady handicap secretary.'

The meal and presentation that followed the match could hardly have been described as the height of 'entente cordiale'. Two of the ladies left without staying for either event, claiming they had no desire to spend a further hour in the company of their opponents. Three of the men's teams, including that of Martin's and Brian's, refused to sit with their opponents at the meal and pointedly bought their own drinks. Two other pairings actually sat together, but sat in stony silence throughout the proceedings, saying 'it was like this all the way round, so it was hardly likely to change when we got in was it!'

Tom and Jeanette put a brave face on the presentation. The match was narrowly won by the men, but strangely there was little in the way of celebration, even from that quarter, rather the feeling seemed to be one of relief that it was all over and there'd been no injuries, at least that is, of a physical nature. No-one was prepared to admit to scars of any other kind.

Both acting captains concluded the encounter with the highly optimistic suggestion that perhaps a return match could be arranged. The pace at which everyone departed, following this truly amazing suggestion, might have suggested to a casual observer that the building was on fire.

In his desire as seniors' captain to create something of an identity for the seniors' section and provide it with more than just a few games of golf with neighbouring clubs and the occasional in-house match, Tom had proposed a few ideas for additional club activities, for which he'd canvassed the member's support. In a spirit of openness, he'd also invited them to offer their own suggestions. His short, but carefully worded questionnaire, therefore, asked them for their opinion and more importantly, their level of support for such things as, a four day golfing trip to Scotland, an organised trip to one of the seniors' Euro Tour events, a visit to a golf club manufacturer and an evening with a well-known professional golfer as a visiting speaker. He'd also asked them if they were interested in him organising such things as a deal with the professional for a series of lessons.

Tom's over-riding sense of optimism, coupled with his

refreshingly positive attitude and approach when it came to introducing any new ideas that might, in his judgement, be of benefit to his fellow golfers, did rather tend to cloud his judgement on basic human nature and, in particular, its unqualified acceptance and support for any new ideas or suggestions.

In vain he waited for the eagerly anticipated stream of returned questionnaires containing those carefully considered and precisely worded responses of members to his ideas and plans, along with some imaginatively phrased suggestions of their own for his consideration. Tom's optimism that he would get a good response from the seniors' section was, in part, based on the proud claims made regularly at the bar that for a good part of their working life, many of his fellow golfers had been extensively engaged in producing lengthy business reports and analyses requiring well-reasoned and logical responses to the most complicated of enquiries. 'Hardly a day went by without me getting some request from the powers that be that I put pen to paper and write them a tightly-worded, convincingly argued case for some course of action or other that would give them an edge on our competitors,' was a typical response from these closet pen-pushers.

He had also been somewhat encouraged in his optimism by the almost daily announcements by numerous members of the seniors' section of their dispatch of some venomously written letter of complaint or reproach to some 'thoroughly incompetent and inefficient set of prats' that had failed to provide this patient and long-suffering member with satisfactory goods or services. 'When they get that letter, they won't know what's hit them, I gave it them straight, no 'namby-pamby' phrases like, 'would you mind' or 'if it is at all possible', I laid it on the line in no uncertain terms.'

After two weeks, he'd received just four responses, two of those from close friends who'd been cajoled with the help of a number of single malts, to fill them in over dinner at his house one night.

There was, of course, a plentiful stream of excuses from

members attempting to explain their non-return, most of them on a par with the pathetic attempts of an errant teenager to justify to a gullible teacher, the non-appearance of a piece of homework.

'I've done it, but I can't remember where I've put it,' was a fairly typical standard response.

'I gave it to the wife to hand in and she's lost it, apparently,' was typical of those who attempted to switch the blame for their failure to someone else.

There was even an attempt on the part of some to conceal their forgetfulness or disinterest with a veneer of conscientiousness, 'I filled it in, but when I read it again I wasn't satisfied with what I'd put.' The only missing excuse from among this welter of deceit and deception was that well-known classic, 'the dog eat it when I wasn't looking.'

The only group of non-responders who had the decency to give an honest reason for the failure to return the questionnaire were those who simply told him that, as far as they were concerned, they didn't really care what he did, 'no offence Tom, but frankly, I just want a game of golf, I'm not really interested in any of your attempts to bring this rag bag collection of misfits together,' was the most explicitly worded answer that he'd received.

By one means or another, he finally managed to extract 14 responses from this pen-shy set of malingerers. At least, thought Tom, I've got something on which I can base my plans. What he was presented with, however, would probably not have been acceptable to even the most sympathetic of tutors to a group of learners enjoying the privileges of residence at 'her majesty's pleasure.'

Responses ranged from the unintelligible through the indecipherable to the unworkable and, in a very few cases, to the unprintable. One or more of the 14 respondents had, either misread, misunderstood or misinterpreted virtually every question he'd posed. His suggestion of a four day golfing trip produced the following pieces of tangential thinking,' I've never liked the Scots, thcy think they know it all,' and 'it's alright if you drink whisky, but their beer's crap.' This was hardly the rational basis for foregoing a four-day golfing trip to the St Andrews area. Tom's idea for a trip to a seniors' Euro Tour event, produced two more blisteringly arcane pieces of logic, 'you never see as much as you do on the tele' and 'those places charge the earth for sandwiches.'

The space on the questionnaire reserved for members' suggestions remained almost universally blank, except that is, for two responses, one of which Tom suspected had come from Brian and the other from Macklin. One proposal was for what was euphemistically called 'a gentlemen's evening', which the writer was able to 'fully recommend' as a 'very good do'. Tom had visions of certain over-enthusiastic members of the seniors' section finishing on stage with only marginally more clothes on than the so-called 'female entertainers'. The other suggestion, for a 'gambler's night', while on the face of it, quite a reasonable one would, he felt sure, stir up some problems for him in certain quarters, particularly among the less liberal-minded, sanctimonious members of the house committee for whom 50p on The National would dispatch the misguided punter to the 'eternal flames'.

In a desperate attempt to salvage something from this thoroughly demoralising and depressing exercise, Tom seized on the fact that half a dozen members had expressed some, though by no means overwhelming, interest in his idea for lessons from Richardson. Ignoring the contemptuous remarks he'd received to this suggestion from others, 'I'm not going to pay money to have that sarcastic bastard take the piss out of my golf swing', and 'if I ever feel that I need help, I'll go to someone who can teach me, not just shout obscenities at me,' Tom decided to arrange a meeting with the pro to set up the arrangements.

'Shanks', the assistant professional, was looking after the shop when Tom walked in and hurriedly tried to conceal a lavishly illustrated 'girlie magazine' under the counter.

‘Checking out some new swing tips?’ said Tom pointedly to the red-faced assistant.

‘You bet, there’s an absolutely cracking pair of ti...’ said ‘Shanks’ and then stopped suddenly as he realised just what the seniors’ captain had actually said to him, ‘ah, yeh, er, swing tips, yes, just keeping abreast of some new techniques, Mr Young,’ before realising the slightly unfortunate phrasing of his reply. ‘Have you come to buy something, Mr Young?’ enquired ‘Shanks’ rather sheepishly. ‘We’ve just had some new golf shoes in that might interest you.’

‘Thank you ‘Shanks’, but you may remember that I won a prize in the club raffle last month and your boss finally flogged me a pair of Etonics that he’d been trying to get rid of for months, that is after you’d tried to palm me off with some new fangled practice driving net,’ said Tom.

‘Shanks’ wondered whether his time really would be better spent reading one of those ‘Duffers’ guides on selling rather than dribbling over the latest centre spread, near-naked pin up.

‘I need to speak to Mark about some lessons for the seniors,’ explained Tom patiently, ‘when will he be back?’

‘Well he’s not here at the moment,’ replied ‘Shanks’.

Well that’s pretty damn obvious you prat, thought Tom, otherwise I wouldn’t be wasting my breath talking to a plonker like you.

‘Have you got an appointment in the diary, Mr Young?’ asked ‘Shanks’, desperately trying to give the impression of at least knowing some of the right words to use when put in a position of even minor responsibility.

‘Bloody hell, ‘Shanks’, I want a quick chat with the pro, not an audience with the sodding Pope,’ explained Tom, ‘I just popped in on the off chance he’d be here.’

‘Well, I don’t know how long he’ll be really, he went a while ago,’ added ‘Shanks’, with yet another devastatingly shrewd example of his logical thought processes.

‘With that level of knowledge, ‘Shanks’ you’re wasted here, you should be working for British Rail,’ said Tom.

At that precise moment, Richardson walked into the shop, much to the relief of Tom who, had he been required to continue in conversation with this idiot of an assistant for much longer, would probably have removed one of Ping's latest jumbo drivers from the display stand and employed it in an unprecedented act of physical violence.

'Right, Mark, now I've got six seniors interested in having a set of lessons and I was wondering whether you'd be interested in doing some sort of deal, say for a set of eight lessons.'

Richardson's initial reaction was to jump out of the pro shop window. The thought of spending even one hour trying to instil the fundamentals of the golf swing into some of those old 'codgers', most of whom appeared to have neither the ability nor the inclination to improve on their current level of staggering incompetence, was about as attractive as agreeing to take part in Big Brother and finding that the lady captain and 'Shanks' were to be his main companions for two months.

'Well, Tom, I'm sure that I can get 'Shanks' to book some time with them in the next few weeks, he'd only be too delighted I'm sure,' offered Richardson, in the faint hope that the seniors' captain would go along with his ideal compromise.

'Ah no, Mark, that's not what I had in mind at all, having 'Shanks' giving golf lessons is a about as attractive an idea as a bargain weekend break in Baghdad, either you do it or we forget about it,' replied Tom.

Richardson would have been very happy to forget about it, but suddenly remembered that some of these senior golfers had the 'ear' of the club's executive committee and if he was going to get any support for his plan to employ a female assistant professional and eventually get rid of that prat 'Shanks', it might be an idea to get some of these 'old boys' on-side. He'd been working on this idea for some time, particularly among those in the male ranks who he knew would be in favour of substituting 'Shanks' for a bit of glamour and sex appeal. He'd been given plenty of unsolicited advice by these members on what to look for in a new female assistant, none of which had anything to do with her ability as a golfer. 'Sod her 'greens in regulation', her 'fairways hit' or 'sand save' statistics,' said one lecherous character, 'what's the carry across the cleavage, that's the sort of statistics that'll get us in the shop!' So, if it succeeded in getting some of these tight-fisted buggers to part with their cash instead of swanning off to those 'flash gits' at American Discount, then he'd happily break the news to 'Shanks' that his P45 was in the post.

'OK, Tom, let's see if we can work something out; I suppose I'll have some time, particularly if this plan of mine to have a female teaching assistant works out,' said Richardson.

'Ah, um, well er... on second thoughts, perhaps we could just wait awhile until she arrives and see if she's prepared to help us, if you really are busy Mark; I don't think the six senior members would mind waiting,' offered Tom.

Got you, thought Richardson, you lecherous old so-and-so, you fell for it hook, line and sinker, I bet some of those old buggers would wait forever at the thought of getting into some sort of close clinch with a Michelle Pfeiffer look-alike. Richardson could see the bookings for golf lessons soaring and the sales of all sorts of clothing gear rocketing as these 'helpless hackers' shamefacedly tried to force their 38-inch waists into 32-inch slim-fit golf slacks.

'Well, if you're absolutely sure Tom, I wouldn't want the senior members to feel I'd let them down by not doing the lessons myself,' lied Richardson.

'No, no, I'm sure that'd been fine with them,' replied Tom, 'I'm sure that the seniors will look forward to this new addition to your staff and give her all their support when she arrives.'

'Well, it's still got to be approved by the executive committee, you know, Tom,' admitted Richardson, 'before it's a definite.'

His trump card was, of course, the club's chairman, who he'd first approached with the idea. The gentleman in question couldn't have been more enthusiastic if he'd just been informed that he'd been nominated to be the next chairman of the Royal and Ancient. Ever since Richardson had floated the idea to him, the 'old letch' had been pestering him with ideas for drawing up a short list and suggestions for an interview panel, naturally with his own name at the top of the list.

'Oh, I'm sure there'll be a great deal of support for your idea, not least from among the ladies' section,' replied Tom.

Strangely enough, that's exactly where Richardson most expected some opposition, particularly from the likes of the lady captain, 'Brunhilde' who would view it as a further attempt on his part to swell the ranks of the Richardson's golfing 'harem' and encourage some of the male members to even more outrageous examples of lascivious behaviour.

'Of course, you do realise, Tom, that the lessons will be a little more expensive than they would have been if I'd have had 'Shanks' take them because, unlike him, the new female assistant will be a fully qualified PGA teacher,' pointed out Richardson.

He knew this lot well and was aware that they would be fully expecting some cheap deal, otherwise they'd be threatening to head off to that 'plonker' running the nearby golf range. He also knew that many of these old boys were certainly not short of a bob or two as witnessed by the flash cars that appeared every couple of years, the nicely bronzed ridges and wrinkles from the three holidays a year and wives with enough expensive metals draped around themselves to knacker the navigation system on a jumbo jet. He frequently over-heard some boring old fart at the bar bemoaning the fact that his shares in some multi-national had taken a bit of tumble which probably meant he was down to his last £100 000 or someone's pension fund had gone a bit pear-shaped and was wondering how he was going to survive on just 40 grand a year. There was no way he was going to give these cheap-skates the satisfaction of going around crowing about how they'd, 'beaten a damn good bargain out of him,' which was another frequently heard load of old 'tosh' from some offensive little twerp who, in retirement, made a hobby of making every salesperson's life hell until he'd got the satisfaction of having extracted £1 off the price tag of some piece of trivia.

'Oh, that's perfectly OK, Mark,' said Tom, 'I'm sure that the seniors will be able to raid a few more pennies from the piggy bank to pay for the lessons with your new assistant.'

Richardson thought he'd like to be a fly on the wall in one or two households when ''er in doors' discovered the weekly budget being plundered for the prize of a 30 minutes close encounter with his new female assistant.

'Will the lessons be on a group basis or will we get individual tuition for particular problems?' enquired Tom.

Richardson had this image of some of these 'old boys' now pitching up with a catalogue of requests to improve various problems with their game that they would never in a million years have admitted to, simply in order to extend the number of lessons they'd need with this 'vision of golfing loveliness'.

'Well, of course, it will depend on how many my new assistant feels she'll be able to handle at any one time, Tom,' replied Richardson.

Knowing the behaviour of some of your lot, he thought, she'd be well advised to opt for the group class rather than run the risk of having 'handling' problems of an altogether unwelcome kind. He made a mental note to bone up on his health and safety manual, particularly the section dealing with emergencies, such as heart resuscitation.

'Some of our members will probably prefer to have what one might call 'the personal touch' when it comes to teaching, rather than just be one of a group,' explained Tom.

I'm sure they would, thought Richardson, but the last thing I want is a resignation on my hands after three months, because of the antics of some disreputable old 'hackers'.

As Tom left the professional's shop, he thought that perhaps he'd just stumbled on an idea that would jolt some of the more indolent members of the seniors' section into taking a more active part in their club, beyond just turning up for their weekly four-ball. He went back into the clubhouse to put a notice on the seniors' board with details of these proposed lessons with Richardson's new assistant. Three days later, on his next visit to the club, he discovered that the group of six had suddenly grown to 14, all requesting their names be considered for the golf lessons. His arrival at the bar was the cue for a barrage of questions requiring extensive details of the forthcoming addition to the professional staff.

As he might have predicted, the list now contained names of seniors who, had it been suggested to them earlier that they might benefit from a few golf lessons, the person offering the advice might well have been running the risk of being hospitalised and taking only liquids. Now, members were falling over themselves to detail the obvious flaws in their swings with comments such as, 'course I should have had lessons years ago, but I couldn't find the right teacher' or 'I can't remember when I was playing so badly as I am now, I can't wait to have someone sort me out.'

As Tom received the unexpectedly generous accolades of his fellow golfers for having come up with such 'a fantastic idea', 'it's only a set of golf lessons after all, fellas,' said Tom, he recalled the paucity of responses both to his original ideas and to his request for others and wondered whether he'd ever be able to repeat this turn-around in the level of support with another eye-catcher; perhaps the 'gentlemen's evening' might be worth a try after all.

CHAPTER 7

THE STEWARD'S TALE or 'Lies, damn lies and what you tell the wife when she rings.'

If Sir Arthur Conan Doyle had let his famous deer-stalker clad detective loose in an average British golf club, charged with the task of uncovering evidence of the status and standing of the employee known as the club steward, his stay would barely have taken him beyond mid-morning coffee. A 15 minute walk from the car park, through the grounds and into the clubhouse would have provided Holmes with all the vital clues as to whether the person in question enjoyed the unqualified support and backing of the club, as an essentially invaluable member of its professional staff, or conversely whether the individual was no more than a low status, pint-pulling 'lackey'.

First stop, the car park and the allocated parking spaces for 'the great and the good' of the club: namely, the president, the white lines of whose space usually look as new and unmarked as the day they were painted; the chairman, evidence of slightly more use here, but painstaking scrutiny is still required to prove consistently regular usage; the captain, generally plentiful evidence of use here, including an extensive quantity of cigarette butts and discarded bar tabs; the lady captain, supporting evidence here would include small shards of glass where an impact with other vehicles has occurred at some time; the treasurer and the secretary and, in some even more status conscious organizations, spaces for its committee members.

But is there somewhere among this highly prized and bitterly fought-over privilege, a space for the club's steward?

Well, the answer in some instances is 'yes', which indicates to our shrewd detective, one of two possible conclusions. Either the individual does genuinely enjoy, along with the aforementioned, the status of professional staff member or, alternatively, the club doesn't want to run the risk of the steward not being able to park sufficiently close to the clubhouse, with the resulting unacceptable delay in the opening of the bar and near-riot conditions breaking out in the men's changing rooms.

Of course, a marked, but nevertheless, empty car parking space won't tell us the full story about where exactly the steward stands in the club's golfing hierarchy. More tangible proof will be required by our sleuth in the form of some type of vehicle. It's extremely unlikely, of course, that the club will have allocated a highly-prized parking spot simply for its steward to park his battered 12-year-old Ford Escort estate car alongside the galaxy of BMWs, Mercedes and Jaguars. Such a vehicle would certainly not make it on to the front or even back row of this 'starting grid'; rather it would probably be consigned to the gravel strip behind the green keeper's tractor shed. At the very least, one might expect to find an Audi, Volvo or possibly a second-hand Range Rover, indicating at least some semblance of motoring respectability. Something more exotic such as a Porsche or Aston Martin residing in this space should not immediately be interpreted as proof of an over-generous salary or incentive scheme on the part of the club, rather that the gentleman in question is probably engaged in some out-of-hours 'scam' involving either, illicit booze running, redistributing 'dodgy' cars, flogging holiday property in Bulgaria or maybe even all three.

In pursuit of further evidence as to the status of the club's steward, our detective will need to look for other status symbols in the form, for instance, of signposting, possibly to an office; something which would certainly constitute proof of a reasonable level of standing in its professional ranks. Many clubs display photographs of the 'great and the good' in their reception area, which will naturally include club president and chairman, both sporting a sun tan that could not have been acquired in England in January, when the club's photographs are normally taken, but more likely to be the result of their regular three months in the Bahamas or some other such exotic location. Spaces will also be allocated to the current men's captain and, in the more enlightened clubs, even to the lady captain, though in some clubs, this latter space has been the subject of heated debate over whether such a ground-breaking move wouldn't open the flood gates for photographs of other members of the ladies' section to adorn the club house walls.

Should our super sleuth be lucky enough to also find a picture of the club's steward among this glittering array of non-descript talent, then it would be further evidence of a reasonable level of status for this gentleman in the organisation. Either that or the employee in question had somehow or other been instrumental in finding someone who would do the framed photographs for next to nothing, or at least in return for having his membership application fast-tracked through the selection committee. In recognition of the steward's efforts in this direction, the club had seen fit to include his 'mug-shot' on the reception area wall.

Clubs that provide their steward with a smart uniform, even possibly a bow-tie and maybe a name badge and accompanying photograph, are also sending out signals that they place great value on the contribution that this individual makes to the smooth running of the club. This, of course, will all be in sharp contrast to other occupants of this post, who will be found performing their duties in over-sized tracksuit bottoms, trainers and a Manchester United T-shirt, only partially covering a not-so-discrete tattoo expressing their undying love for someone called Tanya.

More subtly, our investigator will need to look for other evidence in the form of such things as the staffing levels provided by the club in support of its steward. Where he's been blessed with the approval of the ruling 'godfathers'- naturally, it's unlikely to be 'godmothers'- our detective will find that he's being helped by a dutiful group of smart, polite and highly efficient staff, providing him with prompt and unquestioning support and ready to meet the club members' every conceivable need. Where, of course, such blessings have not been bestowed, our sleuth will observe our hard-pressed, over-worked steward attempting single-handedly to fulfil a range of tasks from serving drinks, clearing tables, taking orders, emptying ash trays, washing glasses and clearing quantities of debris from spaces vacated by members who, in their own homes, would probably be refused permission to even open a box of chocolates if it threatened the pristine condition of Axminster's finest shag-pile.

Interspersed with such duties would be the need to keep a watchful eye on a very small group of belligerent, unco-operative, work-shy malingerers who were allegedly there to work alongside him, but who in truth, no self-respecting employment agency would even consider allowing through their doors.

If our super sleuth could delve further for evidence, of course, he may wish to establish the existence of a written contract and the full terms and conditions of employment, including a detailed description of duties. Such documentation would also clearly set out such things as, hours of work, remuneration, holidays and accommodation entitlements and, as such, indicate the level of professionalism among the management team of the club.

By contrast, the less fortunate stewards will be working in clubs where such documentation is either non-existent or so loosely worded and ambiguous as to permit any power-crazed member of the executive committee, at the slightest whim, to demand immediate compliance with the most outrageous demands or change just about every part of their duties without the slightest recourse to negotiation or improved remuneration.

The poor beleaguered steward, studying the poster on his kitchen wall, which announces that, 'the lack of forward planning on my boss's part should not be the cause of a heart attack on my part', wonders why news of the arrival of a party of 50 golfers from Ireland, for three days, has only just filtered through to him with 24-hours to spare. Even worse, some club officials have been known to ride roughshod over clauses dealing with termination of contract and dismiss employees with all the sensitivity and discretion of a South American drugs baron dispensing with the services of an incompetent 'pusher'. Of course, these are the self-same club officials and 'captains of industry' who, in committee, either claim to have one of the best local employment and industrial relations records of any of their neighbouring companies or, in their past, were the champions of workplace rights and equal opportunities for all workers.

At 'Swankers', the office and tenure of the post of steward had all the stability, safety and security of a three-wheeled Reliant Robin being driven flat out on a skidpan. The club had employed and summarily dismissed more stewards and, for that matter, others of its service staff than there were unrepaired pitch marks on the first green following the visit of the national 'Grave Diggers' Golfing Society. The basic problem as always with the employment of any of its staff was the total inability of the executive committee to decide precisely what type of person, qualifications and experience they were looking for in the post of steward. Their ill-defined ramblings and inadequate pontificating conclusions on such things as the need for reliability, honesty, hard work and conscientiousness, as though someone had been audacious enough to suggest appointing an unemployed burglar and car thief with an eight year prison sentence for fraud and embezzlement, left the selection committee rather short on what might be termed, quality criteria. The whole process was further hampered by the failure of the committee's self appointed pen pusher to word a half-decent advertisement capable of attracting anyone with the requisite stewarding skills beyond the level of casual temping at a 'Little Chef'. Naturally, this then rather hampered the short-listing and selection process from the considerable number of no-hopers who applied for the post and subsequently also turned the job of interviewing into a complete and utter farce.

The reasons for the dismissal of previous stewards had been

wide ranging, not surprisingly among them being the abject failure of one person in question to look after and manage the bar properly. The eventual dismissal of this particular employee was not surprising, when it was subsequently discovered by a club member that his experience in such work was limited to part-time bar work in a famous chain of British high street pubs.

'Didn't anyone think of checking or questioning him about his claim to have been assistant manager?' inquired a justifiably mystified member of the club.

'This lot are gullible enough to have believed him if he'd said he'd been the bar manager at London's Savoy,' said one of the more cynical members.

'Nah, with their limited knowledge of top international hotels and restaurants they'd have probably rejected him on the grounds that he needed more experience with a better class of clientele,' said one of the more widely travelled members.

Over-friendliness with members, particularly the ladies, was the reason for the dramatic departure of yet another steward. There was only room at 'Swankers' for one officially registered 'groper' and the chairman tolerated no challengers to that particular position.

'Apparently, our chairman told him in no uncertain terms that as chairman he had a duty to protect members, particularly lady members, from the unwelcome attentions of those staff who attempted to take advantage of their position,' claimed one reliable source of club gossip.

'Judging by what I've heard, our esteemed chairman knows more about 'advantageous positions' than the Kama Sutra,' said another observer of club members' social and sexual gymnastics.

Conversely, stewards were dismissed for being rude and officious to members, particularly those that happened to be related in some way to a member of the club's executive committee, and on one occasion for allegedly getting their fingers trapped in the till.

'If being rude and officious to members was a sackable offence,' suggested one regular at the bar, 'then we'd have been able to appoint an entirely new executive committee by now.'

'As for getting fingers trapped in the till,' said one senior golfer, 'I think it's more a question of some members of the exec getting caught with their entire anatomy trapped in someone else's well-lined pocket.'

On just one occasion the committee seemed to excel itself in making what was clearly an outstanding appointment, electing to employ a person with all the requisite knowledge, skills and experience for the job and with a charming manner and personality to boot. All the members breathed a sigh of relief at the thought that, at last, the club seemed to have secured the services of a professionally competent and socially acceptable employee, as opposed to the untrained, unqualified 'Rottweilers' that had previously been making their lives hell. Of course, as some gloom and doom dispensers predicted, 'it'll never last.' Competent, efficient and professional he may have been, but being constantly subjected to the sudden and often outrageously rude and bad-mannered demands of certain members of the executive committee stretched the tolerance levels of even this rare breed of professional employee. The result; he was gone within three months to a neighbouring golf club where staff were reputedly treated as fellow members of the human race, not as asylum-seeking galley slaves on the run from an oriental despot.

The current holder of the post of steward at 'Swankers' had been there two months following the abrupt 'walk out' of the previous occupant of the post after a major and very public bust-up with the chairman when he'd refused point blank to serve a few of the latter's business cronies after official closing time. On failing to get the expected and thoroughly deserved support from the spineless, too-faced, ineffectual chairman of the house committee, after simply upholding the club's rules on bar closing hours, which the latter had himself insisted on being rigorously applied, the beleaguered steward decided to up-sticks and inform the executive in no uncertain terms what they could do with their job.

It was widely rumoured that the new, young steward, Guy, already sporting the additional label of 'the gorilla' after the famous screen partner of Clint Eastwood in the film, 'Any Which Way But Loose' was, in some distant way, related to the chairman. The 'gorilla' label had stuck principally because of the severely limited range of communication skills that Guy seemed to have mastered for dealing with customers, comprising as they did of incoherent grunts and monosyllabic mutterings. No one was absolutely sure whether the paternity link with the chairman was true, or just another piece of malicious gossip, alleging that Guy was the 'product' of one of the chairman's notorious extra-curricular entanglements with a local lady. There was no doubt that both got on very well, judging by their very visible exchanges in the clubhouse; something of a record for the chairman in his relations with stewards and providing the only visible evidence for members that the new appointee actually possessed any of the requisite charm and good manners to fulfil this important role. On the face of it, it still looked to most members as yet another disastrously incompetent appointment.

'Yeh, what'd you want?' This sudden and unexpected barking of a demand from behind the bar rather caught the golfer eager to quench his and his partner's and his opponents' thirst unawares, given that he was currently reclining into his sixth minute of solitary bar stool meditation, having given up all hope of actually being served before the calling of last orders. He had chosen to position himself in what he considered to be a strategically direct line of sight with Guy in the vain hope that this would ensure relatively prompt attention, coupled with the fact that, at that precise moment, the sole demand on this idle sod's time and attention involved checking the condition of his hair in the bar mirror. He half hoped that the sight of a waved £20 note might also be a bit of a give-away as to the reason for his prolonged occupation of the bar. Clearly, however, the severely limited peripheral vision which Guy enjoyed and, for that matter, apparently cultivated, prevented any immediate and direct contact, whether of a visual or physical nature, with a customer until the precise moment before the customer erupted in a blaze of anger and frustration and the very reasonable suggestion that he might consider 'getting off his fat arse and providing some bloody long-awaited service.'

The 'Yeh, what'd you want', greeting had further caught the long-suffering golfer on the hop since he'd rather been expecting the usual, 'Good afternoon sir, nice to see you, had a good round; now what can I get you to drink?'

'Oh, ah, yes, I'd like two lagers, one gin and tonic and a pint of bitter, please.'

'Bitter's off till tomorrow, doing the pipes,' came the 'gorilla's' curt reply.

Quite what 'doing the pipes' actually meant and why it couldn't have been done out of bar opening times was not a subject on which the club member felt he wanted to further test Guy's limited powers of communication. He was not actually convinced that Guy, in spite of being the current holder of the post of steward, was actually capable of providing either an intelligent or for that matter intelligible explanation.

'Pints or halves, d'you want?' Clearly the club's daily rate of remuneration for the exchange of pleasantries and grammatically correct sentences had plummeted since the departure of the last occupant of the post.

'Sorry, pardon, what did you say?'

'Of lager'

'Ah, sorry, yes,' answered the baffled member, desperately trying to decipher these rapid-fire verbal exchanges, 'pints, please.'

'Ice and lemon?'

This, the golfer, now beginning to get the hang of this restricted language code, took to refer to the gin that seemingly he'd ordered in a previous life.

'Ice and no lemon,' he replied, suddenly aware that he too was beginning to be afflicted by the same language impairment.

This quick-fire staccato exchange seemed suddenly to drain both the physical and mental capacities of Guy as he disappeared for all of five minutes into the recesses of the bar, presumably to re-charge what little was left of the 'customer service, short-life batteries' with which he'd clearly been fitted. The half-filled ice bucket that he carried on his return to the bar was further testament to his steadfast working principle of delivering just the bare minimum to customers, whether it be service, sentences, sense or servility.

'Eight thirty.'

Eliminating the possibility of this being an incorrect time-check, but rather a demand for money, the member offered up a £20 note.

'Got anyfink less?' came the reply.

'Sorry, I'm afraid not.'

'Your pals got the right money, have they?'

'No, as a matter of fact I've checked already,' said the golfer, now getting rather irritated with this continuous interrogation from behind the bar.

'S'pose I'll have to go find some change then, back in a sec.'

'Back in a sec' seemed a very optimistic forecast based on the time taken to complete the process so far. By the time this exchange was complete, there'd be no time to actually consume the drinks, thought the golfer.

'Just had a riveting verbal exchange with our latest Neolithic 'grunter' behind the bar,' said the golfer, finally returning with the drinks to his morning four-ball, 'seems we've got another graduate from the 'Cave Dwellers Language and Interpersonal Skills Academy' on board, lads.'

'We could've played another nine holes in the time it's taken you to get here with those drinks,' said one of the four, 'we'd better get another round in, the bar shuts in two hours time.'

'Doesn't seem to know much about running a bar,' said another of the four, 'I asked him for a spritzer for my wife the other day and he asked me if I wanted tomato or pineapple juice, would you believe? Where do they get these people from?'

'Comes highly recommended apparently,' said one of the four.

'Who by, the KGB?'

'Ah, no, our esteemed chairman found him so I'm told,' said one of the four.

'Where would that be then, bouncing the local yobs out of the town's night club or more likely, knowing Tomlinson, escorting female strip-o-grams around the more expensive residences in the town?'

'Judging by my latest encounter at the bar, he's trying to fine tune his talents in here, then,' said the aggrieved golfer, vainly hoping that the change for his £20 note might soon appear. In fact, just at that precise moment, Guy appeared and tossed £11.30 on the table, a proportion of which rolled across the table and onto the floor.

'Got no tens,' was offered by Guy as a form of explanation before disappearing back to the bar.

'Got no manners, either by the sound of things,' replied the golfer, hopefully just within earshot of this offensive sod, as he struggled to retrieve the wayward coins from under the feet of three fellow golfers at the next table.

'Are you going to eat?' inquired one of the golfers of his fellow golfers.

'What's the chances of getting a menu out of Stalin's nephew, d'you reckon?' said one of the three.

'Zilch, I expect, but I'll give it a try.'

'May I have today's menu, please, we'd like to order something to eat?'

'Same one as yesterday, mate,' said Guy as he tossed it across the bar.

Mate, thought the golfer, where the hell did that form of greeting come in the training manual of professional stewards? This was the language of a bloody building site, not a respectable golf club.

'Well since I wasn't here yesterday, I wouldn't actually be

aware of that fact, would I?' said the golfer in a vain attempt to get back at this cheeky up-start, 'and as for your reference to me as 'mate', I only ever respond to this term of endearment from people who have succeeded in mastering two basic skills, smiling and speaking recognisable English, neither of which you have appeared to have learnt. Forget the menu, we'll go and eat somewhere where they understand what it means to provide a service.'

'Suit yerself, I ain't bothered either way.'

'That's precisely what we are doing and as for 'being bothered', that plainly doesn't even register on your daily checklist of duties to members.'

If only the job of a golf club steward was limited simply to the business of looking after the bar and the cellar and ensuring that the former was well stocked and the latter was all 'spit and spotlessly clean', then for most of these characters it would truly be a 'life of Riley'. Admittedly, the peace and tranquillity of life behind the bar might occasionally be disturbed by having to administer a bollocking to some untrained 'oik' who had just upset a tray of gin and tonics over five imperious lady members, because he'd wrongly assumed that one hand was sufficient for that task and the other could be more usefully employed pinching the bottom of one of the more well-endowed waitresses. Or to instruct another 'computer illiterate' that the techniques employed in operating the controls of Game Boy 2 were rather different to those required for using the computerised bar till.

In reality, as most golf club stewards will only too readily admit, these, what one might term, 'bar tending' and 'staff bending' tasks only form a very small part of their daily round of chores. The simple reason for this is that golf clubs are, in actual fact, the second home of a motley collection of quite badly behaved, deceitful, incompetent, mischievous and untrustworthy individuals and the responsibility for curbing and controlling the worst excesses of these behaviours often falls on the broad shoulders of the club's steward.

The previous occupant of the post at 'Swankers' had left a discrete, but extremely informative note for his successor detailing some of the tasks that he would undoubtedly be required to fulfil but which he'd singularly fail to find in any job description with which he would presented.

The note carried the heading 'Golf Club Steward: The only mug behind the bar should be the one you fill!'

'You will need to be extremely competent in the following areas:
'Invention'- you will be required to invent all kinds of versions of the truth and moreover deliver them in a most plausible tone and manner, principally to cover up various misdemeanours by members and officials of the club that they do not wish to be made public. The following examples will illustrate the point.

Explaining to the wives of missing or late husbands that they are:

- *Having to play extra holes because their competition was level after 18 holes.*
- *Helping to look after a fellow golfer who's been taken seriously ill on the course.*
- *Having to stay behind because the competition started late and they've won a prize.*
- *Having to help resolve a serious dispute over a rules infringement in their game.*

The above four excuses have proved, over the years, to be the ones which seemed to be the most successful in diverting attention from the real reason for the golfer's absence, namely:

- *He was too drunk to drive home and had to be sobered up before getting a lift.*
- *He left with one of the lady members over two hours ago.*

- *He got into an argument and was having stitches for the cuts in the local A & E.*
- *He threw his bag with the car keys into the lake on the 10th hole after taking 14 shots.*

The following four excuses have not proved successful and have, in fact, resulted in the steward incurring greater displeasure and, in one case, physical abuse, than the original perpetrator of the lie:

- *He left a message saying he'd gone early to buy flowers and chocolates for his wife.*
- *He left a message saying he'd gone early to buy flowers for his mother-in law.*
- *He had contracted food poisoning at the club and was receiving treatment.*
- *He had offered to take two old ladies to visit their dying friend in hospital.*

Telephone manner is, of course, all important in relaying such a litany of deceit, but stewards should note the following points in dealing with inquiries on the telephone:

- *Provide only one excuse per 'offender'; offering more than one is dangerous because at some future date you might be required to recall precisely which excuse was used with whom and, on a busy day, you may well find yourself providing as many as five different excuses for five different 'clients'.*
- *Under no circumstances try to embroider the one excuse; adding detail which may later drop the 'offender' in a worse mess, will not be appreciated.*
- *Always have a plausible excuse for hanging up; telling the irate spouse that the captain has just been shot for not getting a round in, for instance, would not sound plausible.*
- *Avoid answering all direct questions for further information such as, 'what time did he leave?', 'how long ago did he leave?', 'did he leave alone?', 'in*

which direction did he leave?' and the one that usually provides the greatest scope for perjury, 'had he had much to drink?'

In some extreme cases, you will have to deal with these inquiries face-to face, delivered by an irate spouse, possibly capable of inflicting grievous bodily harm on a person or persons providing implausible information or being economical with the truth. In these instances the steward should note the following:

- *Check the club's Industrial Injury Policy; treatment and convalescent charges can be extortionate.*
- *Always have to-hand some clearly visible evidence of an existing injury or impairment; your local joke shop will, for instance, provide you with a fake plaster cast that can be hurriedly attached. Even the most venomous, irate, handbag-wielding spouse will flinch at the possibility of inflicting further injury on an already indisposed target. Do not under any circumstances, however, over do this approach; golf club stewards with white sticks are very rare.*
- *Make sure that there is another member of the bar staff, preferably a junior, with you when this encounter erupts. Their memory of what took place may be suspect, but they can be effectively used as a barricade.*
- *Do not make any placatory offers, 'can I get you a drink?', 'would you like to sit down?', 'would you like me to see if I can contact him?' or 'would you like a word with one of his friends?' The offer of a drink will simply act as a reminder that this is the probable reason for her other half's 'no-show.' Sitting down will reduce her feeling of holding the upper hand in the matter and the 'offender's' mates will not thank you for dragging them into this mess and possibly incurring the wrath of their own wives for aiding and abetting the miscreant by 'perpetuating the porkies'.*

'Arbitration'- you will be required to help resolve all manner of disputes which take place on a regular basis in every golf club bar and, in some cases, even outside it in places like the Gents' toilet, the changing rooms and the car park. The following constitute the most frequent causes of disputes among members upon which the beleaguered steward may well be expected to arbitrate:

- *Arbitrating in disputes between golfers as to who bought the last round and whose 'shout' it is now. In some extreme cases of memory loss among the 'short arms-deep pockets brigade', it has been known for stewards to be expected to recall circumstances that may have occurred as far back as three weeks. If memory loss or absence is not accepted by the group as a sufficient reason for you not helping to resolve the dispute, always select the miserable bastard who never invites you to have a drink or invites you to 'keep the change'; that way at least you do have the satisfaction of seeing him having to part with money.*
- *Acting as a witness to the fact that golfing debts either have or haven't been settled. The key determinant in getting involved in such disputes is the sum of money at stake. It is rarely worth your while getting 'stuck in' for a debt less than £10 because your personal 'return' on the help offered will probably be non-existent.*

  Over that figure, your decision should again be based on the previous track record of the alleged debtor in recompensing your efforts. Some stewards operate a sliding scale of support based on the sum involved, ranging from, 'he may have paid', 'I'm fairly certain he paid' to 'I personally saw him put the money on the table'.
- *Resolving disputes at the bar as to whose turn it is to get served. This is such a frequent dispute that trying to apply any hard and fast rules is difficult, though*

the criteria used should always be to choose in favour of the person least likely to 'bend your ear' about your decision. As a rule of the thumb, find in favour of the person who has drunk the least, the more frequent visitor to the bar can be politely reminded that the first casualty of excessive drinking is memory loss.

From time to time, you'll also be invited to get involved in other disputes, generally the result of a very lengthy occupation of the bar by the disputants. The subject of these disputes will vary widely and include such subjects as, who the chairman is currently having it off with, who is the worse cheat in the club, who will be next to be expelled from the club, which member's wife is most likely to 'oblige' and who was the worst captain the club has ever had? Generally, it matters little whose side you take in such disputes because within the space of the next half an hour, they'll have probably forgotten your name, never mind whose side you took in an argument they'll deny they ever had.

Finally, there are what some of us term the 'Dogsbody Duties'. These are all the thankless tasks that various senior officials of the club will try to drop on you simply because you happen to be in the wrong place at the right time. The chairman would like his car cleaned, the captain's wife is stuck at the hairdresser's and he's out on the course, the lady captain's dog needs to be walked while she's playing bridge and the secretary needs someone to pick up all the new club diaries from the printers, otherwise the club will have to pay the carriage.

Refusing to comply with such requests on the very obvious grounds that, 'it's not in my contract to do that,' will simply produce a look of absolute amazement on the face of the individual that you would even consider citing the contents of a legal document when all that was being asked was that you clean the chairman's car or fetch the captain's wife from the hairdresser. Someone would think, on hearing your response, that you'd been asked to go out and clean the on-course toilets – it's not beyond the bounds of possibility, by the way, that even that request could also come along eventually – or even paint the ladies' changing rooms.

Assessing the fall-out from such a refusal is not rocket science. It's unlikely to do your cause a great deal of good when salary negotiations, bonus agreements and even renewal of contract discussions take place in committee. You can almost hear the evidence against you being amassed, 'do you know, he actually refused to walk my dog just around the car park while I finished off a rubber, I know what I'd tell him about his suggestion for an increase in his percentage on the drinks' and 'it cost my wife £13 to get a taxi home from the hairdresser just because that obstinate sod refused to help me out and he's got the bloody nerve to ask for another three year contract' and 'he's got the damn cheek to ask for another £1000 a year and he wouldn't even clean my car.'

While dismissal on the grounds of not cleaning the chairman's car is unlikely to get very far in an industrial tribunal, there are other rather less obvious ways in which your life will be made hell as a result of your stand apart, that is, from salary increases and bonuses being deferred or simply rejected. Your allotted parking space will suddenly get given to the chef's assistant or deputy head green keeper, your photograph in the reception area will be replaced with one of the recipient of the club's new monthly award, 'For the most helpful and obliging member of staff,' the first recipient being a part-time member of the cleaning staff and your title of steward will probably mysteriously get dropped in all the club's memos to plain 'barman'.

Paradoxically, you'll probably earn the undying respect of most members of the club for your stand, who've been desperately waiting for someone to demonstrate that, contrary to a widely held belief, it is possible to be in possession of both a back bone and spine and still get appointed to a post by the club's executive. Whether this will be any consolation when you learn that, in future, all decisions relating to the running of the bar will become the sole responsibility of the club's secretary, whose knowledge of that side of the business rests solely on having once organised a chief constable's leaving party that finished early because he forgot to apply for a bar extension, is uncertain.'

Guy's first major challenge at 'Swankers' was to look after all the bar arrangements for the club's annual past men's and ladies' captains' dinner, to which were also invited all the respective husbands or wives along with the current captains and their partners from eight other local clubs. Apart from the captain's day event, this was probably the most prestigious event in the club's calendar. In spite of the most unexpected reassurances about Guy's competence from the chairman who could barely be relied upon even to recognise members of the club's staff, let alone remember having been involved in their appointment, both Denis, as the men's captain and Brenda, the ladies' captain decided that it might be prudent to discuss the bar arrangements with the new arrival.

'Now Guy, we've got the past captains' dinner in three weeks time, so we thought we'd just run through a few details with you. We're sure you've heard it all before and know the ropes but we thought it would be better to be safe than sorry, we don't want any cock-ups with this lot,' explained Denis.

'We've received 46 replies to our invitation, so the arrangements shouldn't really be much of a problem,' explained Brenda, somewhat optimistically in Denis' opinion.

'Will they all be drinking?' inquired Guy of the captain.

What sort of damn stupid question is that, thought Denis, wondering just how much this chap really knew about running a bar.

'Well nobody's written to me to tell me they've signed the pledge, so I think we can safely assume that some form of drink will be consumed by everyone, can't we?'

'I meant, will everyone be wanting alcoholic drinks?' explained Guy.

Oh Christ, thought Denis, this is not looking very promising when you're getting such half-arsed questions from a so-called professional.

'I don't bloody know, Guy, do I, whether everyone will be wanting alcohol or not, we'd rather assumed that you'd know how to cater for these different kinds of things.'

'If we get a serious run on tomato juices, do you think you'll be able to manage, Guy?' said the lady captain rather sarcastically, 'we wouldn't want angry scenes at the bar with last year's lady captain fighting with the wife of one of our guests over who gets the last bottle, would we?'

The lady captain's brand of sarcasm didn't seem to penetrate Guy's thought processes, merely serving to fuel yet another disturbing inquiry.

'I wonder whether I should order more Lea and Perrins, then,' remarked Guy, 'if that's the case?'

'Hell's teeth, Guy, Brenda's taking the piss, you daft sod, we couldn't care less if you've got a whole cellar full of bloody Worcestershire sauce, we're here to talk about making sure that there's a good supply of quality wines,' exclaimed the captain.

'We want pre-meal drinks ready to be served to our guests as they come in,' explained Brenda, deciding that it was safer to stick to straight forward statements of fact rather than deliver caustic asides, 'a selection of sherry, wine and fruit juices would be fine.'

'Would you like me to mix a punch as an appetizer?' inquired Guy.

'No, we would not,' said Denis, 'we don't want everybody completely rat-arsed on some weird concoction that looks like it's been drained from a local pond before they even get to the table.'

'Will you be wanting mainly sweet or dry sherry?' asked Guy.

'Would it be asking too much of you to ask you to decide things like this, on the basis that after all, you're are the steward and we're just your customers?

'You'll be asking us how many bottles to order, next,' replied Brenda.

Oh bugger, thought Denis, don't start feeding the prat questions, he's producing enough of his own.

'Now, I assume that you'll have enough staff on duty that night, I don't want people getting their sweet before the wine arrives,' explained the captain.

'But, they'll probably want a wine with their sweet, won't they?' said Guy, looking slightly puzzled.

'I meant the wine with the main course, you barm pot,' said the captain, 'you know, the red and white stuff that you tend to have with meat and fish.'

'Well, I'll be on the bar with Sandra and I think I'll have Norman and Wendy serving drinks at the tables,' explained Guy.

'If Norman's that fruitcake who tried to persuade me last week that Piat D'or was an acceptable replacement for a Gevry Chambertain, then you can put him on serving bloody ice creams and as for Wendy, it'll be time for the brandy and liqueurs before she gets the orders from the first table sorted,' said Denis, 'haven't you got someone who at least looks as if they've served in a restaurant rather than two that look as though they're more used to selling choc ices in the pictures?'

'I'll see what I can do Mr. Captain, but on what we can pay them, there's not many people interested in working on a Saturday night,' explained Guy.

'Well what I've seen of the lot we've got, I wouldn't damn well pay them to work any night,' said Denis.

'Right, well I hope that you'll have it all under control on the night,' said the lady captain forcefully, 'because if it's not, I personally will be making the chairman's life hell for the rest of my year, do I make myself clear, young man?'

Denis was about to say that she'd been making everyone's

life in the club hell ever since she'd become lady captain, so why the chairman of all people should be excused a 'Brunhilde bashing' was beyond him.

'I'll do my very best to see that everything goes absolutely like clock work,' said Guy, desperately trying to get these two belligerent bullies out from under his feet.

Three weeks later, the evening of the past captains' dinner duly arrived along with 46 guests, most of whom turned up resplendent in quite bizarre and largely out-dated fashions that gave them the appearance of preparing to re-enact some kind of Victorian melodrama.

They were greeted by Denis and Brenda and two extremely nervous waitresses who looked as though they might drop the trays carrying the choice of wine, sherry and fruit juices at any minute, judging by the cacophony of clinking glasses every time they offered them up to a new arrival.

'Just put the blasted glasses down on the table, will you,' said Denis, 'and let people help themselves; standing by you two is like being accompanied by a junior school percussion band with opening night nerves.'

At least Guy had managed to find a half decent sherry. Bets were being taken in some quarters in the club that they'd be treated to some diabolical cooking sherry that was left over from a recently disgusting concoction that he'd claimed was a trifle. Denis was relieved that he'd continued to resist Guy's offer to produce one of his famous 'Jekyll and Hyde' steaming punches that could have quite easily transformed the evening into a grotesque conglomeration of wild and uncontrollable behaviour.

Things seemed to be going quite smoothly in the early stages of the meal, even with Norman attempting to give everyone he served a masterclass in fine wine consumption and Wendy making an attempt on the Guinness Book of Records entry for the longest wait from order to delivery.

The first sign of problems arrived with the red wine and its sampling by one of the guests from a neighbouring club, who claimed to 'know a thing or two about good wines'.

'This red is not at room temperature, it's stone cold,' he shouted across the table, 'I'm not accepting this, take it away and bring us another at the right temperature.'

The wisest course of action for Norman in these circumstances would have been to offer a quiet apology and go in search of a red that was at the right temperature. Instead, he chose the 'bullshit' option and tried to argue with the guest that, 'I think you'll find sir, that some French wines are in fact better drunk when they are slightly chilled,' backing up his claim with the, 'many French people, I have found, prefer their red like this.'

The strategy that Norman adopted was flawed on a number of counts. Arguing the toss with a guest and lecturing him on French wine consumption was definitely a recipe for the 'grand order of the boot'. Making out the guest to be an ill-informed 'swiller' in front of his fellow diners was also likely to result in the need for him to renew his membership of the local employment offices. Finally, his claim to have first hand experience of this French preference was known by most people in the club to be a downright lie because he'd never been closer to France than Great Yarmouth.

Worse was to follow, however, in that Norman opted for the second flawed strategy of offering a solution that would have had the average wine connoisseur impaling the unfortunate waiter on his bottle opener.

'I'll just warm it up for you then, sir, under the lights of the carvery; back in a tick,' offered Norman.

'Have you any idea just how long that will take you fool?' said the diner, 'we'll be on the sweet course by the time it's at the right temperature; has no-one ever told you that a red should be opened at least one hour before being drunk,' explained the guest.

'That would have been a bit difficult, sir, it only got here from the off-licence 20 minutes ago,' said Norman, much to the absolute astonishment of the guest.

'Just go and get another bottle, would you? Preferably one from which I'm not likely to get frost bite when pouring from it.'

The, by-now, almost inevitable occurrence from an adjoining table served by 'Wandering Wendy' was the arrival of a bottle of Muscadet that appeared to have been attacked by a blowtorch for several minutes.

'This white's not chilled,' said the lady deputed to taste it on behalf of every one else, 'it's not been stored at the right temperature for drinking.'

'What d'you expect me to do about it then, dear?' was not quite the response expected of a professionally trained restaurant waitress, nor for that matter, what the lady guest was eager to hear.

'I expect you to find me a bottle of Muscadet that is correctly chilled and ready to drink immediately,' replied the previous year's lady captain.

'Might take a while,' explained Wendy, 'I think most of them are still in the boot of Guy's car, we ain't had time to unload them yet, rushed off our feet we've been.'

'Get the steward here immediately, I want to speak to him,' demanded the lady golfer.

Wendy shuffled off to deliver the bad news to Guy that he was wanted at last year's lady captain's table.

'What does the old bat want?' asked Guy of his waitress.

'Somefing about wanting cold wine, I think,' explained Wendy.

'The word is 'chilled', Wendy; what did you tell her?' demanded Guy irritably.

'Nufink really, just that most of it's still in the boot of your car, so she'd better be prepared for a bit of a wait,' admitted Wendy.

'Oh my god, you stupid sod, what the hell did you want to go and say that for?' said Guy. 'We'll all be in the shit now if this gets around, you daft mare.'

'I won't be in anyfing,' said Wendy, 'cos I'm buggering orf. Nobody's calling me a daft mare to my face.'

'If you leave now,' said Guy, 'it won't be just your face that'll be the target of my attention, I'm warning you.'

'Threatening me with physical harm now, are you, well that's very nice. We'll have to see what your nice friend the chairman has to say about you using threatening language on me. Bye!'

Guy headed off to try to appease the past lady captain with the offer of another white wine that he just happened to find in the chill cabinet.

'But this is a Grave,' complained the lady, 'I specifically asked for a dry white, you clown; oh just go away and leave it, we'll drink it with our sweet, if we're still here by the time that course arrives.'

Meantime Norman was heading back to the table he was serving with another bottle of red wine that he'd unexpectedly found in the back of the kitchen.

'There we are sir, I think you'll find that's much more to your liking, it's at a most suitable temperature for drinking.'

Norman had hardly made it back to the sanctuary of the bar when a further outburst exploded from the table he'd just left.

'This stuff looks like fizzy bloody pop,' was the cry, 'come back here at once and take it away.'

Norman returned, wondering just how he was going to deal with this person who was threatening to turn his evening into an unmitigated disaster.

'Right sir, am I right in thinking that we're still unhappy with my latest offering from our extensive wine cellar?' inquired Norman.

'Too bloody right we're not happy, I asked for a red wine, not something that looks like cherry-flavoured Alka-Seltzer,' complained the irate drinker.

'What exactly appears to be the problem, sir?' asked Norman, 'that is one of our best South African Pinotage.'

'Have you looked at the glass, it's bloody fizzing around the edges you twerp, are you in the habit of serving bubbly red wine?' said the drinker, 'what the hell are you going to serve us next?'

'It would appear that we do have a tiny bit of a problem with the wine tonight,' suggested Norman.

'Wrong, waiter, we don't have a problem; you have a problem because you and that bone-head steward are going to be collecting your P45s unless you turn this shambles around smartish.'

'I'll do my very best, sir,' said Norman, wondering whether the job of wine waiter was quite the 'push over' job he'd been told it was by Guy.

He also thought it was very noticeable that Guy was nowhere to be seen during the course of these altercations.

The current men's and ladies' captains were not faring any better on their table, having to suffer further examples of incompetence by 'Wandering Wendy's' replacement. The girl, who clearly had never been inducted into the more subtle differences between wines, like the fact that red and rosé are not the same, pitched up with two bottles of rosé instead of the two Shiraz and tried to blame it on the poor light behind the bar.

'Well, it's near enough in' it,' was also not quite what the captains had hoped to hear as a statement of contrition on the part of this latest addition to the ranks of Guy's collection of incompetents.

The evening turned out to be nothing short of a disaster as far as the provision and serving of drinks were concerned, with virtually every table with their occupants at some point waving their hands in the air as though attempting to wave down some imaginary passing taxi, but really trying to sort out yet another 'balls up' on the wine front. Wine was served that was corked, red wine was poured into white wine glasses, glasses were presented with traces of the previous wine still attached, wine arrived for the main course well after it had been eaten and in a few cases, never actually appeared at all. Both captains left the club that evening determined to storm the chairman's office as soon as was practical and attempt the immediate removal of the club's incompetent steward and, if possible, a fair number of his team.

Someone once compared the role of the golf club steward with that of a Roman Catholic priest. While there's no actual record of a steward ever having to administer the last rites to a golfer who had decided to end it all after having taken 130 shots in the monthly medal, there is plenty of evidence of stewards fulfilling 'confessional' duties as they are patiently required to listen, from the sanctuary of the bar, to an outpouring of golfing misdemeanours committed by the regular group of 'wayward' transgressors of the club's rules and golfing etiquette.

'Every time he goes in the rough, you know, we have to follow him in; I've never known balls hit into such desperate areas finishing in such fantastic lies,' said one irate golfer of a member of their four-ball. 'What would you do in our position, steward?' would be the next question.

'Do you know that bugger can't count beyond six; he putts out, claiming to have played five shots and to my certain knowledge I've seen him hit it seven times,' explained an exasperated golfer over the bar. 'How can we get this sod to count properly, steward?'

'You should see him replacing his ball after marking it, it's often four or five inches ahead of his marker and if we say anything to him he gets really arsey and says we're calling him a cheat, would you believe it, steward?'

'I've lost count of the times that fellow has flung a club after playing a bad shot, he gets more distance with some clubs than he does with the ball.'

'What would you do with someone who regularly stomps all over your line on the green, leaving it looking like a mini crater on the moon. I'm sure you wouldn't have it would you?'

And so the catalogue of misdemeanours is paraded to the ever-patient and hopefully attendant steward, who is naturally expected to lend a sympathetic ear and offer condolences to the equivalent of the golfing 'bereaved' on such examples of outrageous golfing behaviour on the part of these miserable specimens of the golfing 'congregation'.

No-one actually expects the steward to provide golfing 'absolution' for these 'sinful souls', there's no golfing equivalent of the ten hail-Marys but woe-betide any steward who fails to display the appropriate amount of righteous indignation at these golfing atrocities to the injured party.

When the ever-patient and tolerant golf club steward is not having to listen to the 'golfing sins' of these 'hell-bound hackers', he's probably having to put up with a steady stream of constant whinging and complaining about some aspect of a form of recreation and relaxation that is supposedly a source of pleasure and enjoyment to the participants. Someone once claimed that in the course of a week, they'd counted 86 different complaints and moans from across the bar, leaving the puzzled employee wondering just exactly why they subjected themselves week after week to this mental as well as physical torment.

The week in question began, as might be expected, around the bar at 'Swankers' with the usual Monday lunch time tirade of pent-up anger, complaints and frustration aimed at almost every official and employee of the club and into which the steward was dragged like an unwilling correspondent in a court, to testify to some outrageous acts of sexual infidelity on the part of half the membership.

'Fred, I told you the other month didn't I, that I was going to buy what that conniving sweet-talking twerp of a pro, Richardson assured me was the last word in golf club technology? Some crap about a bigger sweet spot, a load of old bollocks about an intelligent weight system, forged titanium face and some bum-aching twaddle about a deeper centre of gravity and a high launch angle. Well I'm telling you, believe it or not, that sod, McPherson, with a set of 15-year-old clubs that he claimed to have bought in Woolworths is knocking the bloody ball 40 yards past me off the tee,' moaned one golfer who'd just lost 12 balls in 18 holes, 'you don't wanna buy a set of nearly new clubs for a 150 quid, do you, mate?'

Guy, who had never even considered taking up what he considered to be a crack-pot sport anyway and at whom this offer was aimed, wisely chose to decline what appeared to be a very magnanimous gesture, knowing full well that the golfer in question would be back the next week loudly demanding to know what could have possessed him to part with such a 'fantastic set of clubs for a song' and strongly recommending that everyone should heed the very sound professional advice and judgement of the pro before choosing clubs or being tempted to accept some knock-down offer from one of the 'discount desperados'.

'McPherson, did you say Tom? Don't talk to me about that so-and-so, he's an absolute bandit; four sodding times in two weeks I've had to shell out to that bastard. It's about flaming time that his handicap got cut; hitting it miles off the tee he is, chips and putts like God and claims he's off 21; like hell he is, it ain't right is it? I blame our handicap secretary, useless bugger, for letting these sods get away with handing in all those no-returns; big mate of Dickson, isn't he, steward, wouldn't want his handicap reduced now the pairs competition's just started, would he; what do, you say?'

'Ah, don't mention the damn pairs competition to me Sid; played our first round the other week. Do you know, we were out there five and a quarter hours? I began to wonder whether we'd get back before they shut the bar. I've never seen such slow play from the pair we played with, ought to be banned they did. You know the two I'm talking about, steward, don't you, right pair of old whingers aren't they? But nothing ever gets done about slow play in this club, does it because the captain's so damn slow! That's why they play medals over two days, so he can finish his round.'

'That reminds me Sid, is the club captain in charge of team selection this year or is it that prat of a competition secretary? Whoever it is has definitely got it in for me. Three times now, I've put me name down and keep getting put as reserve. I blame the captain; wants all his old cronies in the team he does, doesn't give the likes of us a look-in, 'cos we're not in the Lodge, are we old son? Don't suppose you get a look in either, steward, do you; you being a mere paid employee and all that?'

'Talking about paid employees, Jim, what do you reckon on the latest antics of our esteemed head green keeper? Right clown he's turning out to be; reckon we could have done better giving the job to your old woman; she knows a thing or to about where the grass is greener; only joking, honest, mate, didn't mean anything, like. Apparently, he's only going to close six holes for three weeks again 'cos he claims they're too wet to play; what does he know about looking after greens, bit a water won't do them any harm? He's an idle sod he is; I reckon he's just making excuses for not getting the drainage right the first time.'

And so the complaining goes on, with rarely the expectation that the listener behind the bar will actually respond or provide some valuable insight into why things are the way they are. Any attempt at providing a reply, in fact, would probably be regarded as an impertinence on the part of the listener whose sole job it is to take this verbal barrage of moaning in their stride without, in any way, halting the flow of alcoholic sustenance.

If close affiliation with the priesthood, with its near saint-like qualities and virtues, as well as its skills of mediation and conciliation, is an important pre-requisite for fulfilling that part of the role of golf club steward that involves dealing with the members, then full-blown membership of the 'Magic Circle' is another essential requirement for dealing with members of the club's executive committee. The ability to mind-read, practise sleight of hand, juggle, pull rabbits out of hats and generally perpetuate the illusion that nothing is really quite as it appears, are daily demands from the 'power and glory' brigade that occupy the inner sanctum of the club's offices. The only difference between the professional magician and his amateur counterpart behind the bar is that the former can perform his art under the watchful and admiring gaze of an appreciative audience, whereas the latter has to exercise the same skills without the 'audience' even being aware of his presence, let alone his capabilities.

An unexpected visitation from the secretary or, if the crisis has really hit the buffers, the club's chairman usually indicates that some super-human act of prestidigitation is required on the part of the steward. Such a situation was a frequent occurrence at 'Swankers'.

'Ah, steward, how are things today?', was the opener that usually indicated two things; firstly that Barnes, the club secretary, had forgotten the steward's name, not perhaps surprising in view of the fact that Guy was the fourth arrival in so many months and secondly that the inquiry about how 'things' were, was a foretaste that 'things' were undoubtedly about to go pear-shaped within the day.

'I'm sure I mentioned it to you before, but I thought I'd just remind you that we've got a party of 50 visitors arriving from abroad tomorrow and we agreed that we'd put on a welcome evening for them, a few drinks, a light buffet, you know, nothing too grand. I'm sure you've got it all in hand already,' said Barnes rather sheepishly.

Of course, true to form for the executive committee of the club, this was the first time Guy had heard of the event. Consequently, two options immediately presented themselves to the frustrated employee: explode into a raging tirade of expletives on the subject of the lack of communication between an incompetent bunch of prats in management and its hard-pressed staff, resulting in the kind of monumental cock-ups which they were now facing or calmly and coolly reassure Barnes that, as he predicted, everything was 'in hand' although it would, in fact, require all the staff to be running around like headless chickens for the next ten hours. The other obvious option, that of denying all knowledge of the event and of any previous communication with the secretary on the matter, naturally wasn't an option at all, since this would simply be seen as a totally unwarranted attempt to apportion blame to one of the club's senior management staff and as everyone knew, that was doing the un-do-able.

Other options, of course, might occur to employees placed in a similarly unenviable position, but physical violence on the perpetrator of this oversight is probably not to be recommended if continuing employment is required and simply 'downing tools' and walking out in these circumstances is rather akin to cutting off one's nose to spite one's face.

The fact of the matter was that the steward at 'Swankers' yet again found himself between a 'rock and a hard place'. Resorting to some well-chosen home truths about the secretary's inability to hold down a job with any greater responsibility, than giving away free ice creams in a heatwave, would probably have ultimately resulted in him having to cast around for work of that very nature himself. To opt for the conciliatory approach would be a sure-fire guarantee that there would be a further re-occurrence of this memory lapse in the not-too-distant future.

Producing rabbits from hats, birds from coat sleeves or making scantily-clad females disappear from wardrobes therefore, would, to a golf club steward, be relative child's-play by comparison with what they are frequently asked to produce by the club's management. The comparison between the professional magician and the steward is further flawed, however, in that the former is able to surround himself with the very latest and most expensive technological gizmos and apparatus, not to mention disturbingly attractive and well-endowed female staff in order to create that genuine sense of awe and admiration in his audience. The under-resourced steward is probably struggling to manage with equipment that should long ago have been consigned to an industrial archaeological museum and with staff with all the visual appeal of a badly assembled chamber of horrors exhibit.

While the enraptured audience is left in absolutely no doubt that the magician, who is preparing to make two caged lions disappear before their very eyes, is in total control of every aspect of his art and would brook no form of questioning or interference with his performance, the golf club steward struggles, generally in vain, to perpetuate that particular illusion.

'I've had a friend of mine approach me,' began the chairman of the house committee on one occasion in one of his rare conversations with the steward, other, that is, than to make his usual demand for instant service at the bar ahead of everyone else, 'asking if we could find eight weeks temporary employment for his son while he's home from university; I said we were usually short staffed through the summer and that it'd probably be fine; no problem is there?'

Even if there was a problem, like the fact that the son in question was known locally to be a complete delinquent, with about as much sense of responsibility as a hardened terrorist, even Guy was shrewd enough to know that he had no real option other than to go along with the request, knowing full well that he was taking on a complete liability that would probably make his job twice as a hard rather than easier.

'Fine, I'm sure we'll be able to find him something to do,' offered Guy, fully accepting, of course, that it would be his arse on the line in front of the committee, when this near-criminal youth dropped his first clanger by managing to transform the normally immaculate clubhouse lounge into something resembling the average university student union bar in the early hours of a Sunday morning.

And, if that was not enough of a burden to bear, hard on the heels of the club's chairman of house, the chairman of the finance committee arrived with another 'irresistible' offer.

'I've just had this brochure from a company offering to supply all our wines and spirits at very competitive prices, certainly cheaper than where we're getting them at the moment. I thought you'd be interested in taking a look to see how much we could save; I'll leave it with you, but do let me know how you get on, won't you?'

Guy, though not the brightest of souls, was all too well aware of the sub text of this offer, which was basically that an old drinking mate of the chairman of finance just happened to have set up in business retailing what was known to be fairly sub-standard booze, at knock-down prices, from a disreputable distributor known to have had a number of run-ins with just about every law enforcement agency north of Dover. He was looking to exert a bit of pressure on his friends to put some business his way by taking some of this third-rate 'sludge' off his hands. Top of his hit list just happened to be his old mate at the golf club.

'Well, you know what our discerning members are like when it comes to decent wine, they won't be fobbed off with any old 'plonk'; one or two of them pride themselves on knowing a thing or two about good wines', explained Guy in a desperate attempt to avoid becoming the predictable target of some member's angry accusation that he'd taken to decanting 'coloured rain water'.

He also recalled the debacle of the past captains' evening with that fruitcake, Harold, dispensing unadulterated crap about the wines he was serving.

'Oh, I understand entirely, but I'm sure that if there were savings to be made, your efforts would be much appreciated and would not go unnoticed by the finance committee of the club,' argued its 'wheeler dealer' of a chairman.

And, of course, thought Guy, they'd certainly not appreciate losing the promised offer of the free crate of wine that would be delivered to their door on receipt of the club's 'esteemed' order.

'Well, I'll certainly study the brochure carefully when I'm next placing an order and see how the prices and quality of the wines compare,' he said, knowing damn well that he was bound to get a second visit in the very near future, if news of a sizeable order was not relayed back to this particular officer of the club at his next boozy encounter with his old drinking pal.

And so the requests went on:

'Could we borrow some glasses for my daughter's 21st birthday party next week?' asked the captain.

'You don't happen to have any of that cheap Canadian stuff left that I could buy off you, do you?' asked the professional.

'Would you mind moving your holiday week on three weeks, we've got rather an important dinner scheduled for that particular week?' requested the lady captain.

Someone once said that the main prerequisites for a successful golf club steward were short-sightedness, so that turning a blind eye to all the under-handed 'goings-on' of members and officials came that much easier; deafness, so that the verbal abuse and outrageous demands could be ignored with impunity and colour blindness, so that 'puce with anger', 'green with envy' and 'red with guilt' would never even register.

Guy's eventual departure from 'Swankers', after only six months, was something of an inevitability, given the volume of dissatisfaction from just about every quarter of the club. Not even the chairman could 'hold the line' on his continued employment at the club, given the catalogue of rudeness, inefficiency and incompetence he'd managed to demonstrate over the six months he'd occupied the post. He'd successfully managed to loose his entire staff who, over that period, had summarily walked out on him following various humiliations to which they'd been subjected. He'd angered virtually every supplier with wrong orders, forgotten deliveries and missed payments. Almost every member could cite some incident of rudeness, lack of cooperation or downright stubbornness on his part, with the ensuing embarrassment and humiliation among guests.

'Guy, it's unfortunately true that this club has had a succession of incompetent stewards over the last four years who, for one reason or another, we've had to get rid of, but I have to say that you've scaled the heights of incompetence with an ease that would leave every one of them way behind', was the chairman of house's opening remark. 'Your time at this club could only be described as an absolute bloody disaster of cataclysmic proportions; I don't really know where to begin, but I'm damn sure I know how to end this nonsense.'

'I take it that you're not happy with me, then,' said Guy.

'Describing us as, 'not happy', would, I imagine, be an

understatement of similar proportions to the Prime Minister's reaction to finding that No.10 had been advertised as a superior 'bed and breakfast' on Late Rooms.com.' explained the chairman of house.

'Well, no-one's complained to me about anything,' replied Guy in his defence.

'That's easily explained,' said the chairman of house, 'by the fact that no-one here believes you have the basic intellectual capacity to recognize a complaint when it's actually made and also by the fact that, were you able, by some means or other, to actually comprehend what was being said, you wouldn't have the gumption to put it right.'

'Not all the problems were down to me, you know,' complained Guy, 'the staff were crap and half the time I never knew what was happening.'

'The staff may, I agree, not have been of the calibre likely to be head hunted for a vacancy at London's Savoy Hotel, but at least we had managed to retain their limited services, that is until you arrived with your 'boot camp' style of management. As for not knowing, 'what was happening', as you so eloquently put it, our early attempts at ensuring you were fully informed had about as much effect on the eventual quality of service as it would if it we'd have supplied you with the information in Braille.'

'Well I'm not exactly happy with the way I've been treated by the members here, you know, treat you like dirt, some of them do, just like a skivvy,' countered Guy.

'And just exactly how did you deal with those situations, Guy? Did you come to me and report their behaviour and ask me to speak to them and get an apology? No, what did you do? You simply matched their rude behaviour with your own specialist brand of abuse, so the end result was a slanging match; well done, very professional,' explained the chairman of house.

'Well, there was no way I'd ever get an apology out of the likes of them, was there?' said Guy.

'Possibly not, but I might have got one for you, if you'd

had the nous to talk to me first, what the hell do you think I'm here for?' shouted the chairman.

'I don't bloody know what you're here for, if you really want to know the truth,' said Guy.

'Well let me give you your first, and for that matter, your last word of explanation on one of my roles in this club. It's to ensure that you're out of here by the end of the week before any more damage is done; you'll be paid up to the end of the month. I do hope that satisfies your need to be, as you put it, 'fully informed on what is going on. Goodbye.'

The chairman of house felt sure that out there somewhere was an intelligent, polite, efficient, reliable and thoroughly hard-working soul just waiting for the opportunity to demonstrate his multi-talented approach to the job of being a golf club steward. But, there again, would he want to give up the day job at the Savoy to come to 'Swankers'? On reflection, he thought; probably not.

CHAPTER 8

THE CHAIRMAN'S TALE or 'Whose bloody stupid idea was it to consult the members?'

If one were to ask a sample group of members of an average British golf club to explain how their current chairman came to be appointed to the post or perhaps more importantly, for what purpose, many would probably struggle to find an adequate answer. In fact, in some cases, they might even ask the questioner to remind them of exactly who the chairman of their club was or worse still, confess to not knowing that such a post existed.

Most golfers know, of course, that the club's president is an honorary position, offered to some local or famous dignitary for that best of logical reasons, 'well, we have to have one, don't we?' or that even shrewder piece of rationality, 'well, we've always had one, haven't we?' It's probably wiser if the questioner doesn't, for the sake of their health, pursue the matter further with questions as to why the club 'has to have one' or why the club 'has always had one?'

As for the post of chairman of the club, the best that some members will manage is that the person in question is a long standing, perhaps even founder, member of the club and was appointed to this post purely and simply for his, and it is, by the way, almost invariably a 'he', loyalty and devotion to the club over many years. The reverse side of this somewhat 'generous-minded' coin is that, over the course of the many years with the club, the gentleman has held a number of other posts, made a complete mess of all of them and so finally, has been 'pushed upstairs' to the post of chairman where it is considered he can't do quite as much damage.

This damage limitation strategy works very well, of course, in those cases where the executive committee is populated by a group of highly intelligent, shrewd and efficient administrators, capable of controlling any dangerous tendency on the part of the new post holder to believe that he is in charge. Unfortunately, the terms 'intelligent', 'shrewdness' and 'efficiency' are not always synonymous with golf club executive committees, as many members will only be too keen to point out, that is if they can actually speak through the gales of laughter induced by the initial description. In those committees, therefore, where the frontiers of intelligence and efficiency are still very much a distant blur on the horizon, the arrival of yet another 'bungler' now, however, armed with the title 'chairman', spells even greater disasters for the poor beleaguered occupants of the clubhouse.

Other members struggling with the question as to why their current chairman was seen as fit to be appointed to the post may point to notable golfing achievements, probably at both club and county level, possibly even at national level. It was felt that in recognition of his outstanding performances on the golf course and the consequent honours bestowed on the club, here was an ideal person to be given the very highest management and administrative responsibilities anyone could possibly have at the club. Again, of course, the judgement may be sound. This 'giant of the fairways' may also have the administrative skills, together with the personality, to coordinate this bunch of often unruly, disorganised and incompetent 'flounderers'.

On the other hand, how the mere fact that this gentleman played off a handicap of two, won every club and county championship going, played in national championships and once qualified as an amateur to play in The Open, qualifies him to chair the club's executive committee and oversee the organisation of all the club's business is not actually clear. He may well be off a two handicap on the course, but substantially 'over par' when it comes to matters of finance, staff contracts and building maintenance.

A few other members faced with this question of how their

chairman came to have this honour bestowed upon him, might cite the fact of his overwhelming popularity with the majority of club members. The basis of their argument is that the most important criteria for selection to chairman is someone who is well liked by the majority of members; in other words, someone whose effigy is not the subject of a monthly ritual burning ceremony behind the green keeper's hut, someone who does at least acknowledge their existence as fellow-occupants of the same planet and finally someone who, in the club car park, can distinguish a member of the club from the local window cleaner.

In the case of this argument, the occupant's ability to attract large quantities of sponsorship deals to the club, to manoeuvre bids and proposals through the 'local political minefield' or entice little known celebrities to come and hack their way around the course, get paralytic in the hospitality tents and insult the members for the remainder of the evening, is not what is required. This chairman has to be one of the 'lads', someone who enjoys a drink in their company, though, in truth, there's usually no objection to this particular appointment from the ladies' section either, that is if he's prepared to play the genial, well-mannered host.

The problem for this particular individual is being able to distinguish the social duties of the job from the more 'professional' duties. It is rather hard for a person in this position to have to discipline a fellow member with a severe warning for rather publicly using the course as a public urinal in front of a ladies' four-ball, when only 12 hours earlier, he was in the very same person's company, cavorting down the first fairway, arm in arm with a 'strip-o-gram' at midnight, minus his trousers, following a particularly heavy session 'on the sauce'.

In one last desperate attempt to find a plausible justification for the appointment of their club's chairman, there will be those few faithful 'camp' followers that have allowed themselves to be convinced he possesses that essential set of management and business skills that are needed to steer the club to greater and more impressive heights. They would point, in all probability, to his successes in his own particular field of business and, equally importantly to his acknowledged standing and influence in the local 'corridors of power', where not only a sprinkling of business acumen, but liberal helpings of guile and 'street cred' are essential. Equally, he would also appear to these 'converts' to have the necessary personal leadership skills to control the more extreme members of the lunatic fringe that would have the club engage in all kinds of bizarre and potentially damaging and dangerous schemes.

Some golf clubs have managed very successfully to unearth such characters, some with all the experience and insights from years of working in the field of international business and finance, others with the experience of navigating the 'minefield' of the legal or local government arenas. Many will have had responsibility for large teams of staff and consequently such things as employment contracts, terms and conditions of work and statutory rights will be relatively child's play. The challenge for a chairman drawn from this group, who either out of a misguided sense of loyalty to their club, or just sheer stupidity, has decided to help inject some of his rich and valuable experience into golf's equivalent of 'Jurassic Park', namely the executive committee, is to 'up-skill' a set of local retards for whom managing their weekly 'pocket money' is well nigh impossible and who fight shy of the responsibility of being left to look after an incontinent pet. The inevitable result of this clash between the managerial 'high rollers' and the intellectual 'low tiders' is that the club's affairs often sinks into a trough of unsatisfactory compromises that leaves everyone frustrated or the 'high rollers' in desperation, 'shipping out' to pastures new, like the local bridge club where, low and behold, they find exactly the same problems and, in the worse case scenario, the same bloody retards.

The alternative, of course, is that far from welcoming the addition of an international business 'guru' or financial wizard, with extensive knowledge of the world's major money markets to the ranks of the executive as its chairman, the club has, in fact, acquired the services of the local pet shop owner, whose business skills are limited to sourcing suppliers of cheap dog food, flogging sub-standard goldfish, advertising second-hand rabbit hutches and whose grasp of basic finances just about extends to being able to add up a customer's bill without the aid of a calculator, but not the addition of the vat. Pillar of the local community, stalwart of the club for umpteen years, correct political affiliations and generally 'all-round good egg', he maybe, but when it comes to pulling into line a group of wilfully uncooperative and sometimes downright obstinate, pig-headed individuals, the 'all-round good egg' has about as much chance of success as he has of getting the franchise for dog food at 'Buck House'.

Where such circumstances as these exist, instead of the executive committee functioning with all the impressive power, control and handling of a highly tuned, high performance grand prix racing car, it stutters hesitatingly and unsteadily along like a poorly serviced and badly loaded milk float. The main reason being, that all its plans and proposals are inevitably the subject of the hijacking antics of particular individuals on the committee whose only chance of success at getting their own pet schemes through is based on having a louder voice, a larger wallet and an even bigger ego than any of their fellow members. Without any checks or controls from the 'chair', the executive committee becomes 'open house' for all kinds of ill-conceived, crackpot schemes, the sole purpose of which are to further the already bloated, over inflated reputations of their proposers.

So, for the ordinary golf club member, being subject to the whims and wishes of a chairman and his 'control freak' executive committee, is rather like being on board a holiday cruise ship, where, in one case, the captain has decided to throw the published itinerary overboard and sail off to wherever the hell he likes for however long he likes, stopping and starting wherever he likes and if the passengers don't like it, they can damn well leave, either 'over the side' or at the first 'port of call.' Those who choose to stay 'on board' are, in due course, informed of where, 'they're being taken' and assured that 'they will definitely enjoy the experience' and that in fact it will be 'a far better and more beneficial destination than the one they'd originally wanted to visit.' Those belligerent souls who take a firm stand and decide to leave the particular 'cruise' are firmly told that it was probably their fault for choosing to take this 'cruise in the first place' and that 'the 'cruise' will proceed much more smoothly and happily without them on board.

In the other scenario, the 'captain' has the published itinerary of the 'cruise', but doesn't know how the hell to get to where he's supposed to be going and the crew are not disposed to assist him in reaching his destination. 'Passengers' are, therefore, informed that 'arrivals, departures and destinations' on this trip will all be subject to unforeseen delays, changes and alterations, but that they should rest assured that everything will work out well in the end. Those 'passengers' who have a mind to complain are reminded that they should be grateful that the 'captain' is, 'doing his very best for them and should just relax and put their trust in his judgement.' Those who feel inclined to 'jump ship' at the first opportunity are labelled as 'ungrateful sods' who are never satisfied, even when people are working their butt off on their behalf.

In the final analogy, control of the 'cruise' is determined not by a rather weak and ineffectual 'captain', but by the particular crew member who just happens to be 'in charge' on the day and so the long suffering 'passengers' find that a decision to 'head off' in one direction, has, on the following day, been rescinded by another member of the crew who, 'didn't fancy going there again, 'cos, I didn't like it when I was there before, so we're going somewhere else instead.' 'Passengers' who complain to a 'senior officer' about the crap organisation and administration of the 'cruise' are told that, 'its nothing to do with me, I've no idea where we're going either.' 'Passengers' also find on this particular 'cruise' that loyalty among the 'crew' members is not exactly in plentiful supply, 'well, what do you expect with that prat in charge?' or 'he couldn't make a decision if his life depended on it.'

The one consolation for those passengers on a real holiday cruise, of course, is that at least at the end of it, they can walk away in the sure knowledge that they will never again be subjected to the whims and foibles of either the captain of the ship or its unpredictable crew. Neither will they have to suffer the tediously boring life stories and personal family tragedies that they've had to contend with from their fellow passengers.

For golfers, 'adrift' on their own personal 'cruise from hell', the nightmare at the hands of some idiosyncratic 'captain' or club chairman and his 'mutinous crew' can go on year after year with seemingly no end, until some 'deus ex machina' event occurs to effect the departure of the former and the removal of the latter. In the case of a departing chairman, reasons can vary from the simple ones of exhaustion, other more pressing priorities and sadly, enforced departure to those 'heavenly links', to the more complicated reasons of incompetence, mal-practice or just occasionally gross misconduct, the latter often involving a member of the opposite sex and some remote corner of the golf course or clubhouse.

'Swankers' had its own particularly idiosyncratic chairman in the form of Neil Tomlinson, a local accountant by profession and out and out 'bon viveur' when it came to engaging in the social side of life, whether at the golf club, the local Conservative club or the corridors of power in the local council. Like so many of his predecessors, Tomlinson was not a particularly good golfer, neither was he particularly interested in improving his game. In fact, his playing visits were something of a rarity. Nevertheless, by one means or another, Tomlinson had, over the years, managed to inveigle his way into the life of the club, via membership of various committees, generous support in the form of cash and by 'pressing the right flesh' in terms of gaining support for his onwards-and-upwards progression to eventual chairman.

His motives for wanting the job had never been clear to those simple souls among the members who naively assumed that accepting this honour had something to do with the love of the game and the club, but there again, very few could truly admit to really knowing him. Most knew him only by reputation, something that enjoyed almost as many colours as the rainbow. To most people, it seemed as though he just simply enjoyed being at the centre of any form of 'power game' and sphere of influence where he could play out his personal ambitions. This was, in fact, very close to the truth, because what the golf club actually offered Tomlinson, as its chairman, was a means of playing in the 'premier league' of local influence and power, which was Tomlinson's sole reason for taking on the job. The fact that he knew very little about how golf clubs should be run, was to him, of little concern. He was too busy steering his own personal agenda, using the golf club as the vehicle by which he'd ultimately reach his destination.

His strategy was a simple two-way process. Anything the club wanted, whether it be an extension to the hours the bar could open, to planning permission to extend the clubhouse, put floodlights on the driving range, build a new swimming pool and squash courts or a supplier for wines and spirits for the bar, Tomlinson had a contact who provided him with all the necessary information and advice to get it through the executive committee and more importantly, when it mattered, through local planning bye-laws and regulations. At the stage where the plan was to become a reality, Tomlinson drew on another set of contacts that could provide, with a little help from the chairman, competitively attractive tenders for the job that would go through the executive committees approval process like a knife through butter.

In return for this guaranteed source of revenue that Tomlinson regularly provided for those people who subsequently were to become his close friends and business associates, various benefits found their way into Tomlinson's wallet, house or his ever-expanding sphere of influence. Expensive holidays in various parts of the world, breaks at luxury hotels, meals at expensive restaurants, corporate days at the races or other major sporting events, evenings at the theatre or at a concert, invitations to celebrity gala dinners and so on, all fell into his waiting arms. But above all, and something of far more importance to Tomlinson than all these casual extravaganzas, it provided more rungs on the real 'political ladder' to the real corridors of political power and with it, the chance to jettison those other tiresome intermediary channels, like golf club chairman, for a more self-fulfilling alternative.

His rise to the position of chairman had been fairly meteoric, having made it to that position in four years from first becoming a member of the executive, so his appointment was certainly not on the basis of his long-standing membership of either the club or its committees. Neither could it be claimed that he'd made any really outstanding contributions to the club, apart from one or two well-timed financial donations or achieved any great accolades in the game itself. As for his popularity with the members, this was very much restricted to a few carefully chosen 'cronies' who played in the same 'power league' as Tomlinson and, of course, a number of female members of the club who had succumbed to his charms, personality and over-active sex drive.

Those members of the club, particularly those from among the executive committee, that had openly aided and abetted Tomlinson's rapid progress towards the post of club chairman, knew exactly what could be achieved with him at the helm. A few even managed to concede that it might actually benefit the club. Some of the more astute members of the executive were aware of Tomlinson's own personal agenda and motives for taking on the job, but were happy to go along with his schemes if some of the 'fall-out' ended up in their 'back yard'. Unlike Tomlinson, most were not looking for progress up the greasy political pole, but were more than satisfied to be the recipients of more immediate sources of pleasure such as 'freebie' lunches, corporate days on the golf course, at the races or the odd case of quality wines and the occasional use of a luxury villa in Spain.

Those less astute members of the club's executive simply saw all the apparently wonderful cost savings and attractive developments that Tomlinson was helping the club to make and were content to bask in what they assumed was the memberships' admiration for their tireless efforts on their behalf. The fact that a number of the members were only too well aware of the reasons and motives behind all the apparent largesse from Tomlinson, only served to confirm in their minds that there were certain members of the executive who were not fit to be in charge of a kindergarten tea party.

There was, however, another side to Tomlinson's character and personality than that of political manipulator and 'ring master' of the 'movers and shakers' of the local government and business community and one which at times threatened to undermine his relentless, all-consuming drive to greater and greater positions of power. Tomlinson had an overwhelming and apparently all-consuming drive to pursue and impose his amorous attentions on any young and attractive female that happened to cross his path. In truth, he was not averse to trying his hand with any female he met and took a fancy to. If youth and physical attractiveness were no longer critical or realistic criteria for his seductive techniques, mere availability seemed to suffice. His reputation for 'skirt-chasing' was well documented, both among the female members of the local business community and, more recently, in the golf club, where his over-attentive and solicitous approaches to various females had been the subject of many whispered exchanges in the ladies' lounge and even the subject of a secret email from a past lady captain.

Coupled with this passion for pursuing anything in a skirt, preferably one which barely covered the essentials of the female figure, was also his love of the 'good life' which frequently manifested itself in riotous parties and dinner evenings where alcohol and, if rumours were to be believed, other stimulants were freely consumed in quite large quantities. These were occasionally held at the Tomlinson residence, where his wife would act as hostess to a variety of the 'great and the good' from both her own business and that of her husband's. At other times, these social events would be held at local hotels, where it was reliably reported by the staff that apart from the bar and dining requirements, bedrooms were rented by the hour and guests regularly left with a different partner from the one with whom they'd arrived.

'Swankers' had also been the venue for various riotous evenings in which Tomlinson had played a central part, including his own chairman's dinner and the captain's annual ball. Witnesses to both these events testified to Tomlinson's wildly exuberant 'joie de vivre' and, at the captain's ball in particular, to his relentless, but seemingly unsuccessful pursuit, of various lady members into the darker recesses of the clubhouse.

Thus, Tomlinson's reputation as a 'work hard, play hard' figure had been scurrilously supplemented by the phrase, 'stay hard' by certain of the more mischievous members of the club, particularly those who had either witnessed or had reported to them his strenuous efforts to retain the title of 'club Casanova'.

One of Tomlinson's closest allies on the executive committee at 'Swankers' was Don Thompson, a local photographer and camera shop owner, who also had contacts in printing and publishing; hence the secret destination for much of 'Swankers'' print jobs and the possible source of the cock-up or conspiracy, depending on one's point of view, over the ladies' section of the club diary. Thompson was known to detest Barnes, the club secretary, as a pompous, incompetent prat, hence the rumour of a conspiracy rather than a cock-up over the incorrect diary entries.

Both Tomlinson and Thompson had unofficially been talking about a possible major re-design of the entire clubhouse, which would allow its expansion to take on bigger and better regional functions, such as weddings, banquets, conferences and business seminars and exhibitions. The added attraction of a golf course and other leisure facilities meant that there was potentially a sizeable market for such events, not to mention the personal benefits that would accrue from such developments for both their particular businesses. Naturally, none of these discussions included any other members of the executive committee and certainly none of the other club members, because of the possible repercussions when the implications for this re-development were discovered in terms of the loss of certain facilities for both the men and the women. The two men had arranged an unofficial meeting with an architect who could advise them on their plans.

'Now, Peter, let's begin,' said Tomlinson, 'by establishing that the subject of this meeting is just between ourselves. If what we're proposing gets out to club members, the shit will definitely hit the fan.'

'What we propose,' said Thompson, 'is to put up an absolute cast iron plan to a few carefully chosen members of the executive who can be relied on to go along with us, but not bright enough to ask too many searching questions, detailing all its benefits to the club and hope to get it through on the nod, without having to go through the rigmarole of a full executive meeting and worst still, having to consult the members, where we wouldn't stand a cat's chance in hell of getting it passed.'

'Some of those buggers who are not on the executive,' said Tomlinson, 'but who are a lot sharper than that set of morons, would see through our plans straightaway and move heaven and hell to kibosh it.'

'There's a lot of bucks to be made here, what with the various professional services that would naturally be required to support a permanent business conference and banqueting facility, but naturally most of it would not, as a few members would be damn quick to realise, be wending its way into their pockets, but ours and yours and, of course, a few other select business people.

'What these eagle-eyed members would quickly suss out,' said Thompson, 'is that a few of their prime facilities would be for the chop and then we'd have one hell of a fight on our hands. The fact is that this place is a potential money-making machine going to waste. It's rarely ever filled by golf club events because half the bloody membership is either too idle or too mean to support what few events are laid on for them. Even when the club is used, it's only for very short spells and on most evenings the place is empty after about 6.00 pm.

'So, Peter, what we want you to do is take a look at the place, bearing in mind it's still got to function as a golf club and come up with a plan for adapting the current layout and extending it to cater for a complete new business opportunity.'

'The thing is,' said Tomlinson, 'when you do go to the club, don't for Christ sake, make it look obvious what you're up to, like taking notes, making drawings or wielding a damn tape measure, else some bugger's bound to smell a rat. And don't get tempted into answering any bloody nosey parkers' questions. If anybody does ask you what you're doing, say that you're a professional golfer inquiring about facilities for an event; that should shut them up. Oh and by the way, if you do happen to bump into us when you go, crack on you don't know us, OK?'

The following week, both men met with a friend of theirs who knew the local planning laws and regulations inside out, to check out where the problems for such a development might come and more importantly, whose palms they might have to 'cross with silver' to get things passed with the minimum of delay. The meeting was held in a local pub and Tomlinson repeated his request for the utmost secrecy.

'Neville, we've got this plan to re-develop major parts of the clubhouse at the golf club so that we can expand its business potential,' said Tomlinson, 'but we don't want to go too far down the road without knowing if we're going to hit the buffers on planning permission.'

'Do your plans include any extension to the current building?' asked Scott.

'Well, they might; actually they almost certainly would,' said Thompson, 'how much of a problem would that be, then?'

'Well, you'll probably get some opposition from certain people in the council and then, of course, the local residents might have something to say about it,' he explained.

'Oh shit', said Thompson, 'do we have to tell the locals what the plans are, that could banjax the whole sodding plan?'

'Well, if it's a major development, yeh, you do, otherwise some sod's bound to blow the whistle on you for flouting regulations.'

'Well, tell us how major it has to be before we have to go public,' asked Tomlinson.

'I need to see exactly what you're proposing before I can give you a clear answer on that,' said Scott.

'How about your lot, Neville, can we expect any bloody obstacles from the council on this?' inquired Thompson. 'We don't want the plan to get bogged down in all that damn red tape that seems to flood out of the council offices every time someone wants to put up a bird table in their garden.'

'I'll do my best to get it through all that, but we'll need to be careful when we present it, and to whom, and in what sort of detail,' said Scott, 'I'll need to check when certain people who might kick up a fuss are on holiday and have a quiet word with those who we can expect to support the application.'

'Do we need to offer any inducements to anyone to get in behind this application? We're not averse to offering the odd night or two in a nice hotel, you know,' offered Tomlinson.

'Well, I wouldn't mind a weekend at the Savoy, if you're offering, Neil,' said Scott.

'You cheeky bugger, Scott,' said Thompson; 'you can have my caravan at Clacton for the weekend, if you want.'

'Big deal,' said Scott, 'you two buggers really know how to push the boat out when it comes to coming across with the 'sweeteners', don't you? Any vacancies for an assistant secretary at your club, I've got a friend of a friend in planning whose wife's looking for a part-time job?'

'I'll see what I can do,' offered Tomlinson, thinking that they could do with getting help for that incompetent secretary, Barnes, preferably someone who could manage to highlight his inefficiency to an even greater degree than the executive committee, 'get her to give me a ring or better still ask her to come and see me at the club.'

Thompson looked knowingly at the chairman, wondering whether this was going to prove to be yet another of the chairman's appointments to the non-existent post of, 'chairman's playmate'.

A week after this meeting, the draft plans for the full re-development of the clubhouse arrived for Tomlinson at the club, thankfully to be opened up when no-one else was around to witness the detailed drawings that tumbled on to his desk. He was immediately impressed by what he saw but was also aware of the implications that these plans would have on facilities for the membership. He rang Thompson with the news.

'Don, got the plans for the clubhouse development, they look absolutely fantastic, just what I was looking for, but it's going to need some stealthy footwork to get this lot through without the members first getting wind of it, because if they do, we could both finish up in intensive care at the local hospital.'

He went on to explain the changes to the ladies' lounge area, to their office and committee room and to a portion of their changing rooms. He also outlined the changes needed to the men's bar area and to a part of the snooker room.

'Bloody hell,' said Thompson, 'do you think it would be better if we could put it out to contract and have it accidentally burnt down, so that we could start again?'

'Don't even joke about a thing like that,' said Tomlinson, 'there's already a few notable instances of where ancient clubhouses have suddenly and inexplicably gone up in smoke. I don't want us to join that particular file, thank you.'

'Well, what's the next stage, Neil?' inquired Thompson.

'I've already got a meeting planned, if you want to join me, with a local builder friend of mine whose offered to give me a very competitive tender on the rebuilding,' said Tomlinson.

'What about any building regs, though?' asked Thompson.

'Ah sod those for now, we'll let Scott sort those out, that's why we're letting him have your caravan in Clacton.'

‘I haven’t got a bloody caravan, and if I had, I wouldn’t site it in that god-forsaken hole, Clacton; I only told him that to keep him on-side.’

‘Even by my standards of generosity, I thought that offering him a bloody caravan in Clacton was a little on the tight side,’ joked Tomlinson.

‘Well, you can fund the bugger at the Savoy if you want, but don’t ask me to chip in with a contribution. I’ll see you at the meeting with the builder; same pub, same time, I assume?’

Later that day, Tomlinson’s phone at the club rang and a lady by the name of Denise Ratcliffe introduced herself. Tomlinson vainly tried to remember any lady he’d recently met by that name, possibly at some party or dinner and to whom he either owed an apology for some indiscretion or for simply forgetting to show up at their next scheduled rendezvous. It was only after the mention of the post of assistant secretary that he remembered the request by Scott on behalf of a friend’s wife for any vacancy for secretarial work at the golf club.

‘Ah, yes, Denise, I understand you’re looking for part-time work as a secretary and I do remember suggesting that you ring me at the club. Can you pop over sometime and give me an idea of your previous experience of office work and what kind of commitment in terms of time you were looking for?’ said Tomlinson.

‘Yes, I appreciate that you could give me some details on the telephone, but I’m not very good at taking notes and talking into the phone and I would very much prefer getting the details from you face-to-face; would 5.00 on Wednesday afternoon be convenient? Good, see you on Wednesday then.’

Tomlinson decided that come hell or high water, he was somehow going to get Denise Ratcliffe on the staff at the club the moment she walked into his office, though to be honest, he wasn’t exactly sure just where she could fit into the administration team or what skills she had to offer the club. At this stage, he wasn't even sure there was a vacancy for any staff whatsoever. Frankly, he couldn't have cared a damn if she'd proceeded to tell him she couldn't type, work a photocopier and went completely to pieces trying to answer the telephone. He was much more interested in her physical attributes which were very clearly on display the moment she walked in and sat opposite him in his office.

It took all his self-control to stop himself continuously staring down the front of the low cut blouse she was wearing which, coupled with the bra she had on, was affording him an extremely generous view of her two beautifully proportioned breasts. He was also aware that the tight, figure-hugging skirt she'd chosen to wear for the interview was also short enough to reveal a quite exquisite set of legs which from time to time she chose to cross and uncross, seemingly it appeared to Tomlinson, to ensure that, not only his personal self-control but also his professional hold on the interview and its direction were absolutely minimal from the word go. Tomlinson couldn't believe that someone would deliberately choose to dress so provocatively as this for an interview and not be sending out other messages than her shorthand and typing speeds.

He somehow managed to make the interview last over an hour; he'd never, in the past interviewed anyone for more than 30 minutes.

'Can you be flexible over the hours you work, Denise, because there are times in the club calendar when we're quite busy here and it may be necessary to work late into the evening?' inquired Tomlinson, hoping to introduce his own personal agenda into the contract at an early stage.

'Oh, that's not a problem, I would be quite happy to put in extra hours if it would help you out,' replied Denise.

'It may be necessary to attend meetings away from the club occasionally,' said Tomlinson, 'I assume you'd have no problem travelling with me to such events.'

'Not at all,' said Denise, 'I'd quite like the idea of getting out of the office and travelling to other places.'

'Occasionally, we do have to entertain guests and take them

out for meals, could you help out in that direction?' inquired the chairman.

'Certainly, I'd be delighted to act as hostess to your guests at any such function, even if it meant staying overnight somewhere, it wouldn't be an inconvenience.'

Tomlinson thought the answers he was getting were sounding better and better by the minute and also seemed to detect a knowing expression on Denise's face, which told him that she was not exactly unaware of what was implicitly being proposed by these seemingly business-like questions.

Tomlinson asked further questions about her tastes in food, wine, music and local restaurants, none of which had any relevance to the nonexistent post at the club, but satisfied Tomlinson that she, rather like him, enjoyed the good life and was, as he was so often described, 'up for it'. There was one other question he was dying to ask and eventually got around to finding the right wording for it.

'How would your husband feel about you working at the golf club, Denise?' inquired Tomlinson tentatively.

'Oh, he'd be delighted, I think,' said Denise, 'running his own company keeps him very busy, often into the evenings and weekends, so he'd like me to get involved in something that kept me occupied when he was not around.'

'Right, well that's fine,' said Tomlinson, 'could you start next week, Denise?'

'Well, I could, but can you tell me exactly what I'd be doing and with whom I'd be working?' she asked.

Not a hope thought Tomlinson, at least that is, nothing I'm prepared to go into detail about at the minute, as he still desperately tried to stop his eyes wandering to that cleavage which was tormenting him more and more, the longer the interview went on.

'I'm working on the exact job specification at this precise moment,' lied Tomlinson, 'perhaps you'd like to join me for a spot of dinner and we could go through some of the details and see if they are to your liking, at least that is if you've not got any other pressing engagement.'

'That's very kind of you, thank you, yes I'd be delighted,' said Denise.

Further informal conversation carried out in a carefully selected quiet and secluded corner of a somewhat off-the-beaten-track restaurant, revealed that there were no children she had to rush home to look after, that she had her own sports car and that she was seriously thinking about taking up golf. The way in which Tomlinson had strategically positioned himself beside her in the restaurant meant that what was also further revealed throughout their discussion was Denise's quite exquisitely shaped thighs as the tight fitting dress struggled unsuccessfully to contain these two other stunningly attractive features.

At the end of the evening, Tomlinson somewhat surprisingly found himself managing to restrain a desperately strong urge to invite her back to his place where he would certainly have very quickly tried releasing the physical and emotional tension he'd been experiencing from the first moment she'd walked into his office, but equally, he thought, he was damn sure he'd also take a shot at releasing the tension that Denise's skirt, blouse and bra were very evidently experiencing trying to contain that quite phenomenal figure. Instead, after a somewhat restrained arm on her shoulder as she walked to his car and a formal handshake, he went home to ponder just exactly where he was going to get Denise employed at the club and how he was going to get it past the executive committee.

Although Tomlinson rarely had time to play much golf and, in truth, took very little interest in the game apart from a few social rounds with friends, he had got himself and 'Swankers' involved in a golf exchange arrangement with an American club in Pennsylvania. On a holiday and business trip to the States, where he was negotiating a deal on some real estate, he casually mentioned to his host that he was chairman of a golf club in England. He'd immediately been introduced, via his host, to his opposite number at the local golf club, where he was invited to play and later extremely lavishly wined and dined. During the course of the evening, the chairman of the club had casually mentioned the idea of an exchange with 'Swankers' and Tomlinson must have expressed some interest in the idea because three weeks later, an email from the American club arrived with the proposed arrangements for a visit to England.

Tomlinson, by this time, could not recall any details of such a conversation. In fact, he would probably have been hard pressed to recall them the following morning, given the amount of wine he'd consumed and the late night session that had followed with the wife of one of the business men who just happened to be away on that night. But he now felt obliged to try to finalise the arrangements, particularly as his American business associate and his wife were part of a 24-strong party wanting to spend a week in and around the Midlands and playing golf at 'Swankers'. Tomlinson had no desire to waste his precious time getting involved in such arrangements, which he guessed would simply produce a mountain of problems in terms of setting them up, but saw no way out of agreeing to do it, particularly as the letter from the American club said that, 'they were delighted with the enthusiasm which Mr. Tomlinson had shown towards the idea.' And then, he remembered the 'delicious Denise' for whom he'd promised a job at the club. So, under the pretext of getting an assistant for that prat Barnes, the club secretary, he'd pass all the organisational details over to her, which would get him off the hook with the Americans, but, more importantly, provide him with the perfect excuse for getting better acquainted with that gorgeous figure of hers.

When Denise showed up for work the next week, Tomlinson introduced her to Barnes, who didn't seem to have the first clue as to what he could give her to do, so was relieved when the chairman outlined the American exchange trip as her first responsibility. Barnes was slightly puzzled by the fact that, in spite of the fact he'd been told that she'd been appointed to work with him, Tomlinson had cleared part of the desk in his own office and set up a spare computer for this woman to work there. So, when he didn't see sight or sound of her for the next four days, he began to wonder whether she'd decided to leave or whether Tomlinson, perhaps, had got rid of her. It was only when he casually walked into Tomlinson's office one morning and interrupted the two of them obviously in a very amorous clinch which, though it had broken up immediately on his entry, still revealed even to Barnes' inexperienced eye the mouth-watering location where Tomlinson's attention, not to mention his hands, had spent the last few minutes, that the 'penny had dropped' as to the real reason for this appointment.

Six weeks on and with only two weeks before the American party arrived, however, it became quite clear to Tomlinson that neither Denise's intellectual capacity nor her organisational skills came anywhere near close to matching her capacity for handling his sexual demands, nor for that matter, fulfilling her own apparently insatiable sexual appetite. As Tomlinson somewhat crudely expressed it to a very close friend, 'between the legs she's dynamite, between the ears, she's a disaster.' So, in spite of numerous, lengthy meetings between the two of them, in which eventually, 'matters in hand', moved on from the physical to the organisational 'agenda', the trip was far from what one might describe as, 'in the can'.

'OK, Denise, have we got the transport from Birmingham airport sorted out, yet?' inquired Tomlinson.

'Well, I just assumed they'd get the train from Birmingham International; after all, it stops pretty close to where they'll be staying,' replied Denise.

'Denise, darling, just think on a minute; these people will probably have been travelling for over 12 hours; the last bloody thing they want to be told is that they have do the last bit on one of BR's cattle trucks, lugging mini-wardrobes and sets of golf clubs behind them; now be a sweetie and get on to that coach firm and get a quote for collecting them from the airport.'

'The coach firm will probably want to know where they're going, won't they?' inquired Denise.

'Yes, they will,' said Tomlinson, 'and you'll be able to say that it will be bringing them straight from the airport to the golf club, won't you?'

'Yes, but they're not staying here at the golf club are they?' replied Denise.

'No, but you've arranged for all their hosts to collect them from here, haven't you, dear?' replied Tomlinson.

'Oh hell, I knew there was something I had to ask the families; now I remember what it was,' said Denise.

'You mean no-one knows yet that they've all got to be here at 6.00 pm to meet them,' groaned Tomlinson.

'Well, there's no rush, is there? They're not coming for another two weeks,' said Denise.

'Denise, these are very busy people that we're asking to help; we can't just assume that their diaries will be empty at that precise time; now get on the flaming telephone... no, don't write, and tell everybody to be here at 6.00 on that evening.'

'Ah, well, there's another problem; I'm still five hosts short. I'm not sure who else I can ask,' explained Denise.

'For Christ sake, Denise, you've had five weeks to sort this out; what the hell have you been doing?' shouted Tomlinson.

'Well, if you must know, in the few brief moments in this office that you've managed to keep your hands off me and I've managed to keep my clothes on, I've been trying to sort out their travel itinerary while they're here,' replied Denise.

'Right,' said Tomlinson, ignoring the provocative accusation, 'how's that coming along, then?'

'Well, I can't get them any tickets for the plays on at Stratford; there's a Van Morrison concert in Warwick, but I thought the tickets were too expensive so I left it and I didn't think Americans would be interested in Freddie Starr's type of humour, so it's a bit of a blank really,' confessed Denise.

'So, in other words, we've got nothing for them to do other than play golf and nowhere for them to go afterwards, so we're probably going to be stuck with entertaining the buggers ourselves all week,' said Tomlinson.

'Well, there's a flower show in Lichfield and an exhibition of Black Country art in Wolverhampton,' said Denise, 'oh and I've just found out there's a vintage car show in Malvern.'

'Oh, bloody great', said Tomlinson, 'if were lucky enough to be playing host to a group of flower arranging, paintbrush wielding Morgan enthusiasts, we've cracked it.'

'Well, if you can do any better, you damn well try,' shouted Denise.

'That's the whole bloody point,' explained Tomlinson, 'I probably couldn't; that's why I employed you.'

'Let's be honest Neil, we both know you only employed me because you fancied the knickers off me from the moment I walked into your office,' said Denise.

'Well, I haven't heard you complaining about the arrangement,' said Tomlinson.

'Absolutely not, I'm fine with our private arrangement; just don't come all heavy with me when some other plans you dream up for me don't get delivered; I never claimed that I had any experience of this sort of thing and, as I seem to recall, your questions were probing, but certainly not about that particular aspect of my skills and experience.'

'Well the shit's really going to hit the fan if this exchange goes pair shaped and I'm not just talking bloody golf, flower arranging and vintage cars; there's potentially a lot of money at stake, here,' said Tomlinson.

Probably for you, thought Denise, but there's bugger all in it for the rest of us.

'OK', said Denise, 'let me see what I can do on the accommodation front today and then I'll start looking for other things we could do with them.'

'Are we meeting for a drink tonight as usual?' inquired Tomlinson.

'Absolutely not', said Denise, 'clearly I'm going to have my hands full with far more important matters than your over active sexual faculties,' she added, and headed for the car park.

Tomlinson, in the meantime, had to plug some gaps in his plans for the re-development of the clubhouse, in particular the meeting with his builder friend to sort out a schedule

'Right, now Eric, you've had a chance to look at the plans for the re-development of the clubhouse; oh and by the way, you do know this is all hush-hush at the moment don't you, not a word to anyone until I've got everything nailed down, then we can go public with it.'

'Well, there's no problem as far as I can see, it all looks pretty straight forward,' said Eric.

'Good, but let's get down to the cost; you know I've got to get three tenders; well I should, in fact, get more, but I'm going to tell anyone who tries to stick their oar in on that, that the two other builders didn't submit a tender; that should keep the sods quiet,' said Tomlinson.

'You're looking at about a half a mill, Neil for what you want,' said Eric.

'Jesus Christ, Eric, how the hell have you managed to jack it up that high. I thought we were talking less than 200 originally,' exclaimed Tomlinson.

'Well, originally, we were, but now I've seen what your friend the architect's proposing, you're definitely looking at half a mill, maybe even a bit more.'

'I can't do with phrases like, 'even a bit more' and if you want this job, neither can you, Eric. I want it on the button exactly. It's going to be damned hard enough to get the club to agree to 500.'

'Do you think we're going to get this through, Neil?' asked Thompson; his closest ally on the exec. 'It's a big ask and they're not renowned for throwing money away, particularly that tight-fisted sod Brown, the chairman of finance and from memory, particularly not on projects that you've had a hand in.'

'Just leave them to me,' said the chairman, 'I've got a plan for getting them to go along with this that they can't refuse; but Eric, how about the time it'll take?

'About four months, I reckon, by the time everything's been finished.'

'Well, we certainly don't want things half finished do we, you stupid sod,' said Tomlinson, 'nor, I warn you, do I want to hear in four months time that it's going to take another month, or you're into penalty clauses, mate.'

'OK, OK, I hear what you say, but you never know with these sorts of jobs what snags you are going to hit,' said Eric in his defence.

'Two minutes ago, you bugger, you were telling me it was a straightforward job with no problems. Suddenly we've got problems; do you want this job or not? If you do, don't find problems, find answers, preferably quick ones.'

'Are your members happy to put up with some inconvenience for two or three months?' asked Eric, 'because there's going to be a bit of mess and re-arranging to be done.'

'You've obviously never met a golfer, Eric; of course they won't like the inconvenience and the mess, they'll moan and groan and they'll make my life and yours absolute hell for the entire time, I warn you; but they'll just have to lump it, this is going to happen. In particular, if you see a small, fat old bird dressed in tweeds heading towards you, either look for something to protect yourself or run, that'll be the lady captain and no-one messes with her,' said Thompson.

'Christ, I hope there's not too many like that,' said Eric.

'Well, there's our resident fruitcake, the marketing manager, Julian, who'll talk you to death with building theory if you let him, even though he knows bugger all about it and then, there's Barnes, who'll get you locked up if you as much as hint that he's doing something the wrong way,' said Tomlinson.

'When do you want me to start?' asked Eric.

'Well, as soon as I've fiddled the other tenders I get in, checked on any building regs and pushed it through at the club's AGM, you can start, let's say, two months,' said Tomlinson.

'Let's say three, then shall we?' said Eric, 'because I happen to know just how long those things can take; don't count on too easy a ride with the local council.'

One of the other issues that had been rumbling on, particularly since Barnes had taken it upon himself to stir the waters, was the matter of the rumpus at the previous captain's dinner, when one or two members had got a little the worst for wear and things had got a bit out of hand, particularly the bun throwing incident. Barnes had sort of demanded that 'heads should roll' because of this incident, though the chairman had tried to dissuade him from going in too heavy handed. Barnes had insisted on grilling two of the alleged miscreants, though Tomlinson was aware that his own behaviour later that night had been somewhat 'off the wall' and the last thing he wanted was for these two to start 'dishing the dirt' on him. So, he approached the meeting with Barnes with a certain degree of apprehension over what had emerged from the discussion.

'I assume that your little chat with those two members, Basil, resolved the matter over the misbehaviour at the captain's dinner,' inquired Tomlinson.

'Well, er, yes and no, Mr Chairman,' said Barnes, 'neither of them, naturally, would own up to that appalling piece of behaviour and as we might have expected of them, they tried to incriminate one or two others as well.'

'I see,' said Tomlinson, 'did they actually mention anyone by name?'

'Well, not exactly, but they did hint that it was the strip-o-gram incident which might have sparked this nonsense off,' said Barnes.

'But the strip-o-gram happened on another occasion,' said Tomlinson, then immediately wondered whether Barnes would pick up on his knowledge of that particular incident.

'You saw what happened, then, did you, when various members of the club set off down the first fairway with the lady, discarding various items of their own clothing? Someone apparently even ended up in the bunker with her by the first green,' probed Barnes.

'Well, er, yes, I seem to recall one or two of our more boisterous members getting involved in that incident,' said Tomlinson, 'I hope they had the decency to rake the bunker afterwards,' he joked, in an effort to divert Barnes from probing this incident much further.

'They also inquired as to whether you ever managed to recover your trousers, Mr Chairman,' said Barnes rather pointedly, 'and they also apologised for not thinking to offer you a lift home, but were relieved to find out that Mrs Ratcliffe had been able to help you out on that score.'

'I never recovered my trousers, Basil, for the simple reason that the person who took them from the drying room where I'd quickly hung them under the dryer while I went to the toilet, never had the courtesy to return them,' explained Tomlinson.

'Dear, dear,' said Barnes, 'it's very difficult to get wine stains out of trousers, so I believe.'

'I wouldn't know, would I, Basil? Because I never got the chance to take them to the cleaners,' he replied, whilst beginning to wonder where this interrogation was heading next.

'Did you manage to return the shorts, then Mr Chairman, apparently they belonged to one of the seniors who'd inadvertently left them behind?'

'I put them back three days later in exactly the same place I found them, namely the lost property basket, having had them cleaned at my expense,' said Tomlinson, thinking if this sod carries on in this vain, I'll throw him out.

'You seem to have a bit of bad luck, then, with stains on trousers,' said Barnes.

'Basil, the shorts were not stained, I just felt it was courteous that since I'd used them, I should get them washed.'

'Quite so, Mr Chairman, I remember seeing Mrs Ratcliffe coming back to the office with a dry cleaning bag and thought I spotted a pair of shorts in it.'

'It would seem that your police training in observing

everybody's movements and whereabouts has never left you, Basil,' said Tomlinson somewhat irritated by this continued probing of his personal life, 'we seem to have rather wandered off the purpose of this meeting which was for you to tell me what happened in your meeting with Watson and Bellingham; I seem to have spent most of the time recounting my movements and giving explanations for what I was doing; I sincerely hope that your interviewing of the criminal fraternity was not subject to such diversionary tactics as you've just displayed.'

'I think we'd better discuss the agenda for the club's Annual General Meeting, Mr Chairman,' said Barnes, 'I've prepared a draft based on last year's meeting, if that's OK.'

'Just add one more item, would you, Basil?' said Tomlinson, 'under the heading, 'new building developments'.

'Oh, can I ask to what that heading actually refers, Mr Chairman?' inquired Barnes.

'No you bloody well may not, you'll find out on the night; now if that's all I've got quite a lot of things to do with regard to the exchange visit,' said Tomlinson.

'Ah, is Mrs Ratcliffe doing a good job for you on that score, she never seems to be out of your office these days?'

'I'm very satisfied with Mrs Ratcliffe's efforts on my behalf, Basil,' said Tomlinson looking him straight in the eye and thinking to himself, make what you like of that statement, you nosey old shit.

Tomlinson's outings on the golf course were generally restricted to occasions when they had a purpose other than hacking a little white ball around for almost five hours in the company of some boring old farts whose only conversation consisted of details of their latest golfing acquisition and its amazing impact on their game, a blow-by-blow account, almost literally, of their last four rounds or an excruciatingly tedious description of a two weeks' golfing holiday in some horrendous, golf-saturated location in Florida. The club's annual corporate golfing day for local businesses was, however, an event that he never missed, providing, as it did, ample opportunities for that new phrase on the block, 'networking'.

This particular year, he'd invited a group of friends that were closely involved in his scheme for the development of the clubhouse, including Eric the builder's co-director. Eric himself, was a self-confessed golf-hater, preferring to spend his time in complete solitude on the banks of the local rivers doing a spot of fishing and not as he maintained having to socialise with a 'whole load of toffee-nosed, up-your-arse, self-opinionated head cases.' His co-director, Trevor, was a keen golfer and promised to provide a team and more importantly, sponsor a hole and the drinks for the dinner, on the basis that the contract for the development was, 'in the bag'. Tomlinson himself, was in a group consisting of a recently acquired contact who happened to be a venture capitalist by profession, a property developer with contacts in Spain, America and Saudi Arabia amongst many others and the managing director of a corporate entertainments company with what he claimed was a 'hot line' to some of the top celebrities in show business. Tomlinson, quite naturally, was not remotely interested in any of these four as far as their golf ability or the interest of the club itself was concerned. What all four would hopefully offer was limitless opportunities for developing his numerous other burgeoning interests, including property, travel and leisure promotions.

This year's event was, as it turned out on one level, extremely successful as far as Tomlinson was concerned, cementing a number of potentially lucrative business arrangements with both his partners and one or two other guests. It did also, however, throw up one or two unexpected and slightly hairy incidents, which could have seen Tomlinson's reign as club chairman come to a very premature end and in one case might have resulted in a lengthy spell in the local hospital's intensive care unit.

The first of these occurred some three weeks before the

event with the arrival in his office one day, of Jeanette Tyler, the current lady vice captain. His dealings with this lady had, up until that point, been minimal since he had little to do with the ladies' section of the club and would not have been seen dead actually playing golf in the company of a female. He seemed to recall that she'd waded in with a few choice remarks and some quite flowery expletives for a lady when the subject of Barnes' 'balls up' over the club diary had been discussed in the executive committee meeting.

'Neil, I've come to talk about the arrangements for the corporate golf day and the exhibition space available to companies involved in sponsoring the day,' explained the lady vice captain, 'I'm here on behalf of Hutchison's the builders with whom, I believe, you are having some quite close discussions.'

Tomlinson suddenly put two and two together and realised that Eric's co-director, Trevor, was in fact, Jeanette's husband. Tomlinson immediately panicked at the sudden realisation that news of his scheme for the club could very well leak out via this woman to, of all people, that wretched 'Brunhilde' woman, whatever her real name was, the lady captain and then all hell would certainly be let loose.

'Ah, yes, Jeanette, my... er... discussions; just exploratory and very open-ended at the moment of course, nothing very concrete or definite yet, no commitments,' stuttered Tomlinson.

'Oh really, Neil; Trevor seemed to think that they were all just about nailed down and ready to go,' said Jeanette, 'of course, naturally, I've not said a word to anyone in the club myself about this, I just happened to see the plans in our office, you see.'

That stupid sod, Eric, thought Tomlinson; he'd told him not to leave the things lying about and now someone no less than the lady vice captain had had sight of the bloody things.

'Oh, they're just a few rough sketches I've had done by a friend, nothing as grand as plans,' lied the chairman.

'Neil, stop trying so hard to cover up your tracks for this business of the clubhouse development; I know exactly what you're up to and what you've got in mind and I'm on your side; this development makes really good business sense for us all; you mustn't worry about opposition from a few crusty old buggers that are only interested in keeping the place for themselves.'

Tomlinson was, at that moment, caught by surprise on three counts. Firstly, he'd not realised that she was a sufficiently clever enough cookie to have fathomed out exactly what he was up to; secondly he'd not appreciated that she'd be a staunch supporter of his scheme and finally he'd not bargained on her cementing her support for him by coming over, hoisting her skirt well up around her ample thighs, plonking herself on the arm of his chair, putting an arm around his shoulder and running her hand up and down the inside leg of his trousers. Perhaps it would have been time well spent discussing matters with representatives of the ladies' section after all, thought Tomlinson, as the impact of Jeanette's attention began to sweep dramatically through his groin.

'I'm very happy to play along with your game, Neil; in fact, I think the two of us could play very well together,' said Jeanette, not letting up on the massage treatment she was administering to Tomlinson's leg and now much more potentially serious for him, his crotch.

What the hell is this woman's game, thought Tomlinson. She couldn't be trying to influence his decision in favour of her husband's company; that decision was already made in their favour. Perhaps this was some form of bribery for her to keep quiet around the club, but there again, she'd said she was on his side. The way things were developing at that precise moment, he thought, she was on much more than just his 'side', she was practically on top of him and was making it abundantly clear by the way she was steering his hand further and further up her skirt towards the contents of what felt like a very skimpy pair of briefs, where she wanted his ultimate destination to be.

'Come on, Neil, I'd got the distinct impression you'd be up for this, or are the rumours around the club, just that, rumours?' said Jeanette.

'Jeanette, as you're obviously aware, as a result of your expert attention to the more sensitive parts of my anatomy over the last few minutes, 'being up for it', as you so graphically put it, is not a problem; what may be a problem is if the club secretary, his secretary or for that matter any one of a number of ladies playing in your lady captain's day happens to decide to pay me a visit and finds us using the chairman's best mahogany table for uses not actually listed in the manufacturer's brochure; may I suggest that we continue this exploration of our mutual interest at another more convenient time and in a more appropriate location?'

'OK, Neil,' said Jeanette, easing herself off Tomlinson's now totally reclining figure, zipping him up and adjusting her very slightly crumpled skirt and blouse, 'perhaps we'll pick up where we finished at another time? Call me when you've got clearance from 'ground control' at home or when Denise isn't lavishing her charms on your reluctant body.'

Tomlinson couldn't believe it was possible for her to have sussed out what was going on between him and Denise, but realised that Jeanette was either going to prove to be a very powerful ally or a very dangerous opponent of his plans.

Normally, it was not in Tomlinson's nature to refuse such advances, but this had been a potentially dangerous situation. The last thing he wanted was for all his grand plans for opening this venture to be kyboshed because an irate husband and key figure in the building of the development suddenly discovered that his wife was screwing the club's chairman and instigator of the plan. Neither did he want anybody in the club, at that precise moment, suddenly discovering him 'in flagrante' with the lady vice captain and broadcasting the news at the very moment he was about to launch news of his own scheme to the assembled membership. Lastly, there was Denise; if she'd got wind of a 'committee room coupling' between himself and Jeanette, the shit would really have hit the fan and he could see her wreaking her own brand of havoc on top of her natural incompetence on that other important event, namely the American exchange.

On the day of the corporate event, he'd asked Denise to act as hostess to the guests as they arrived, taking details of such things as their food requirements and also giving them information on the competition itself and the arrangements for the dinner afterwards.

'Now, are you clear about all those details you need to give them and what I need you to find out from them?' asked Tomlinson in his office on the morning of the event. 'It's important we give an impression of super efficiency because I've invited some quite influential people and I don't want any cock-ups.'

'I think I've got most of it, but I missed that bit about getting them to give me their email addresses when your hand was roving about following the outline of my bottom,' confessed Denise, 'perhaps you could go over that bit again.'

'Do you mean the emails or your gorgeously shaped bottom?' inquired Tomlinson, attempting to resume his mapping of her quite exquisite contours.

'It's hard for me to keep my mind on this job, Neil, when I'm constantly in danger of finishing up looking like a shop window model for ladies underwear every time I come in to see you.'

'Let's see what special window display you're wearing for me today, then,' said Tomlinson, setting about opening the top buttons on Denise blouse and attempting a quick peek under her skirt.

It was at the very moment he had one hand on another button and was tugging at the zip on her skirt, that there was a knock on the door and in walked Denise's husband.

'Denise, you've got to take my name off the golf team, I've...'

He stopped and took in the scene, clearly trying to make sense of what he saw.

'Brian,' said Tomlinson quick as a flash, 'thank goodness

you're here, Denise just fainted and collapsed on the floor, she's just come round, I was just trying to give her some air, she went very pale; you're not pregnant or anything are you, Denise?' joked Tomlinson.

If Denise's husband wondered whether the latest techniques in first aid required undoing all the buttons on the victim's blouse and unzipping her dress, he didn't pursue the question at that precise moment.

'I'm better now, Brian, I think it must be something I ate last night,' explained Denise, hastily doing up at least a few of the buttons on her blouse and trying in vain to conceal the open zip, 'thank goodness Mr. Tomlinson is trained in first aid.'

'I've been called to an urgent presentation in Scotland and I've got to set off more or less straight away; I'm going to be in Edinburgh for three days; I'm sorry to have to let the team down Mr. Tomlinson, can you get a late replacement?'

'Don't worry about it, Brian, business must come first, the golf must take a back seat in times like these,' said Tomlinson, already beginning to plan his next 72 hours; plans which would undoubtedly involve the lady standing next to him who, thankfully seemed to have completed re-arranging her clothes into a more appropriate condition for the position of secretary to the golf club chairman.

With just two days to go before the Americans arrived, Tomlinson decided he'd better have a meeting with Denise to assess the level of damage limitation he could expect to exercise with the group while they were here.

'OK, Denise, where are we at with the American's visit?' inquired Tomlinson nervously.

'Where are we at?' repeated Denise, 'well, I'll tell you where were at, Neil; for once, you're 'at' sitting behind your desk like a well-behaved boss; I'm 'at' sitting over here like an efficient secretary reading my notes and staying well out of your reach and I'm 'at' keeping my clothes on; how does that suit you?'

'Well, if we must, we must!' said a rather frustrated looking chairman. 'Give me the problems, then.'

'There are none,' explained a rather smug looking Denise.

'You're kidding; the last time I spoke to you, the visit had Titanic 2 written all over it,' said Tomlinson.

'Well, now it doesn't; it just shows you what a bit of self control on both our parts can do when it really matters,' explained Denise. 'I booked a coach to pick up the party at the airport and before you ask, yes, it is big enough to take 24 people and all their luggage and golf clubs; I've arranged a small sherry reception here at the club for approximately 6.30 pm at which you're expected to say a few words; the host families are all fixed and they will be here at 5.45 for me to brief them on arrangements for the week and the party's departure. I have all their telephone numbers, so if there's a problem with a delayed flight, I will call them.'

Tomlinson was about to ask about arrangements for the week, when Denise launched into phase two of her presentation.

'I've arranged two shopping trips for those who are non-golfers, there's a visit to the Cheltenham Theatre for an Alan Ayckbourn play and a trip down the River Severn with a jazz band later in the week. I've arranged for a visit to the Worcester Porcelain factory, Elgar's birthplace, which is nearby and then on to an evening concert in the Malvern Theatre. I've booked all the start times for the golf with that nice Mr Richardson who took me for a coffee and explained how it all would work.'

Tomlinson wondered whether that sex-on-legs machine had tried it on with Denise but didn't like to broach the subject. He'd personally apply the bums-rush to that sod if he ever learnt that he'd been applying his notorious sexual antics on her.

'On their last evening, I've arranged a barbecue at the club, with a few small prizes for everyone and, of course, I've invited all the host families. If it rains, and it's not forecasted, incidentally, I've got a provisional booking with a local pub landlord who is supplying the food for the barbecue in return for us agreeing to take the event there if the weather's bad. The coach is booked for 7.30 the following morning and all the host families have been told that they will need to have their guests here by 7.15 at the latest. I think that covers everything I needed to do since we met last.'

Tomlinson could not believe what he'd just heard, the transformation was unbelievable and it took all his self-control not to rush across to Denise, drag her to the floor and demonstrate his own brand of gratitude to her there and then on the carpet of his office, so overcome with delight was he at the progress she'd made. Instead, for once he exercised a bit of uncharacteristic self-restraint and said, 'darling, that is absolutely fantastic, you've done a tremendous job and I'm absolutely over the moon with those arrangements; now can we go out for a drink tonight and then back to my place?' which was just about at his maximum on the old self-restraint scale when it came to his relationship with Denise.

As to the week's arrangements, they went like clockwork, with not a single glitch on any day. All the visits went down a bomb with the Americans and the host families didn't have a single complaint about their guests or the arrangements. The praise for Denise's hard work was echoed by both hosts and visitors, and the Americans complemented Tomlinson on his highly efficient member of staff and rewarded her with an expensive piece of Worcester porcelain. After the departure of the Americans and later that night, Denise agreed to accept Tomlinson's own request to express his gratitude; an expression that, in fact, lasted well into the small hours and left both quite unsurprisingly completely exhausted.

The final hurdle that Tomlinson had to clear for his plans to re-develop the whole internal layout of the clubhouse was the annual general meeting, that yearly blood-letting event when people who were hardly ever seen around the place could be relied upon to pitch up and sound off about all kinds of apparent irregularities and failures on the part of the club's officials. In the run up to the meeting, he and his pal Don Thompson had been bending the ear of one or two of the more influential members of the executive committee, who, if things started to get difficult, could be relied upon to throw in their support. By the time of the meeting, they were convinced that they had the backing of the majority of the exec's membership, though nothing as official as an actual vote.

Tomlinson had prepared his opening remarks for the proposal with great care and not a bit of artful cunning, presenting the idea as a positive response to the changing values and attitudes towards equality between the sexes. Hopefully, this would be sufficient to cover up the fact that the changes were not just small-scale 'tweakings', to the use of the odd clubhouse room, but, in fact, a major reorganisation of its entire layout and a whole new role for the building from simply a golf clubhouse to a full scale corporate business and conference venue.

In the event, his opening remarks did not go as well as he had hoped, with one or two of the 'yob' elements in the audience using his words to hone their crudely humorous quips. What, of course, he did not anticipate was the outburst from that bloody Maddox woman, who, judging by her inside knowledge of his last three months conversations, had tagged his underpants with a listening device. All that crap about needing to consult the members before doing anything; if he'd had to wait for most of that load of intellectually constipated morons even to take in the details of his proposal, let alone make a decision, he'd have been of pensionable age before getting the development done, even if they'd approved the idea. And anyway, she had a bloody nerve lecturing him on consulting the members; according to his sources, she had a reputation for railroading her pet ideas through the ladies' section like one of those Middle Eastern potentates and woe-betide anyone who tried opposing her. Even that prat, Scott, the captain had waded in with his ten penny worth and he himself, was not above pulling a few stunts to further his own disreputable ends. What the hell was a club flag or badly reproduced carvings of past captains stuck to misshapen bits of discarded granite going to do for the club by comparison with what he had in mind.

The result was that the meeting descended into a bear fight and Jeanette Tyler's intervention on his behalf had made matters worse. Tendering her resignation from the post of lady vice captain was, as far as he was concerned, giving in to the mob instead of standing up to them and defying their sabotaging tactics. What annoyed him even more was that those bastards on the exec who had pledged their support, sat through the entire sodding proceedings like British Museum exhibits, leaving him high and dry facing what felt like a lynch mob.

To crown it all, the president of the club, another of those mummified relics that are brought out and put on display once a year and who simply serve to clog up the proceedings even more, acting in his capacity as chairman of the meeting, had brought the whole damn thing to an end, offering those loud-mouthed yob elements of the membership, the sense of a moral victory. Why the hell he hadn't allowed some sort of discussion to go ahead, giving the chance for others to support the plan to speak, god only knows; though probably rapidly advancing senility, incontinence and arthritis were the three most likely reasons. To make matters worse, the ageing old buffoon had then recommended a committee be set up to investigate the whole matter of the clubhouse development with the possibility of the whole thing being kicked into touch.

It had not been a good night for him, but Tomlinson was not a quitter and he was determined to find a way around this impasse. For the time being, second prize would have to be an extended session drowning his sorrows in some remote pub with Denise, who he'd arranged to meet after the meeting, and the prospect of a gratifyingly lengthy session of unbridled sex.

Unfortunately, this night of total frustration was not quite finished with him. The liberal quantities of wine and whisky that he subsequently consumed certainly had the effect of anaesthetising the more painful memories of the earlier part of the evening. Conversely, however, it served to seriously activate his libido on the journey home with Denise now at the wheel of his Mercedes. In what Tomlinson thought was an amorous move on his part to get Denise 'into the mood' for what was to follow, he'd reached across her as she was driving and attempted to remove her pants and knickers. Had he been just content with her perfectly willing attempts to help him slide both these items over her bottom, down her legs to her ankles, all would probably been well, but as ever, true to form, he wanted to go the whole way and remove them completely. Inevitably, the ensuing tangled mass of Tomlinson's hands and arms and Denise's now severely bunched-up undies around the accelerator and brake pedals of the Mercedes made her control of the car well nigh impossible and on a sharp right hand bend where early braking would definitely have been advisable, she found her right leg movement completely restricted by her best pair of silk knickers and as a consequence, drove the car straight off the road into a ditch at some speed.

It was a testimony to the quality build of Stuggart's best export, that its semi-clothed occupants–because Tomlinson himself had, in fact, also begun to take part in this form of motoring striptease–were unhurt. Some major damage was suffered to Tomlinson's libido and to the more exotic items of Denise's lingerie collection. The disasters of the earlier part of a night that should have ended in them giving each other a passionate and unforgettably erotic 'ride', ended up with them experiencing a distinctly uncomfortable, unromantic and definitely forgettable ride in the back of an AA relay truck.

Three months in the life of a golf club can bring substantial changes to its fortunes as well as to its individual members, both on and off the course. As Eric, the builder predicted, Tomlinson's grand plan for the clubhouse development had not materialised; not because of any heel-dragging tactics on the part of the planners or regulators in the council offices, but simply because of the fall-out from that notorious annual general meeting, orchestrated so ably by 'Brunhilde' Maddox, the lady captain. Tomlinson was, however, prepared to be patient for a little while and await developments.

As he predicted to his close confidant, Don Thompson, those developments eventually materialised, helped naturally by a little assistance from Tomlinson himself. First off, was the departure of the lady captain herself, away at last, thank god, to the relative obscurity of just ordinary club member. A communal sigh of relief was emitted by just about everyone who'd had any contact with her, particularly the ladies who relished the end of her bullying and ear-bashing regime. Male members of the club could now feel free to roam confidently through the clubhouse without the threat of being told to, 'behave oneself and stop acting like a silly schoolboy' or 'either tidy yourself up immediately young man or go and join those tramps in the rugby club.'

Maddox's replacement, now that Jeanette Tyler had moved to pastures new or, as one joker in the club put it, 'to trousers new,' was Don Thompson's wife, Shirley, who had been persuaded to stand by a group of her lady friends, but more importantly and influentially, Tomlinson himself. Shirley Thompson ran her own small, but very successful outside catering company and Tomlinson and Shirley's husband were both quick to point out the benefits that would accrue for her business from the clubhouse development. Not one to turn down an opportunity to turn pleasure into business, Shirley seized the opportunity and walked in unopposed to the post of lady captain. Her presence on the executive, together with her lady vice captain, was already beginning to swing the balance in Tomlinson's favour for another crack at the plan.

Scott, the men's captain also departed along with his hair-brained, megalomaniac ideas, which seemed to revolve around turning the club and course into some kind of open air picture gallery and sculpture park. In his place came his long-time friend Tom Parkinson, the managing director of a drainage and sewage cleaning company. Fortunately for Tomlinson, Parkinson was driven in most of his activities by a sound business brain, unlike Scott, his predecessor, who appeared not to have a brain of any kind. Having to deal with all kinds of shit and unpleasant odours on a daily basis, thought Tomlinson, should stand Parkinson in good stead for being captain at 'Swankers'.

Tomlinson, in an early meeting with Parkinson, recognised a kindred spirit.

'Neil, let's forget about this bloody place as just a golf club, it's not going to earn either of us enough money to get us a week's holiday in Bognor Regis,' said Parkinson, 'we've got to wake this lot up to a business opportunity and together we can do it.'

Coupled with the arrival of these three on the executive, there were also some unexpected changes to its composition. Two members chose to resign when they were apparently 'got at' and, 'had their life made an absolute hell,' for allegedly being part of Tomlinson's behind-the-members-back scheming. The fact that neither of them had given the slightest hint of supporting his scheme made the mystery of where the rumour which fuelled the attack actually came from, but there were one or two very intelligent guesses.

One member of the executive decided that Sotogrande was preferable to Swancliffe as an address, sold up and packed his and his wife's bags and left for warmer and more attractive climes in Spain. One member decided that the 25-year-old attractive brunette at the local estate agent's office was preferable to his 45-year-old singularly unattractive, nagging wife and packed his bags and, as he put it to a friend, 'left the other bag behind,' to shack up with the brunette in Torquay. The departure of yet another member, sadly to that clubhouse in the sky, meant that an almost new-look executive faced Tomlinson when he presented his slightly re-vamped and now even more extensive and elaborate plan for the development of the clubhouse a second time. Within a month, the plan had been passed, the budget, now slightly increased had also been passed and Eric and his mates were being mobilised to make a start.

As for Tomlinson's other 'pursuit', namely Denise Ratcliffe, she, in what might be termed her 'vertical' position as the chairman's part-time secretary was fast growing in confidence and competence and already planning the next exchange with America; her name, along with that of the chairman's, were the first two on the list for Pennsylvania. Her other job was the planning of the next and even bigger corporate day, along with a number of other social and business events, designed to project the chairman's 'star' into an even greater ascending arc. In what might be termed her 'horizontal' position as Tomlinson's regular 'bit on the side', in truth it was more like 'side', 'back' and 'front', she was also performing wonders. And what was remarkably good news was that the chairman's mahogany table was standing up to the strain of over-use surprisingly well, coping as it was regularly with load-bearing levels and constant movements well beyond the manufacturer's recommendations.